MASKED

HANNAH ROSE LEWIS

Blue Rose Publications

CONTENTS

Content Advisory:	VII
Dedication	IX
Author's Note	XI
1	1
2	8
3	15
4	26
5	36
6	43
7	48
8	55
9	65
10	74
11	82
12	87
13	95
14	100

15 107

16 117

17 125

18 132

19 143

20 151

21 162

22 167

23 176

24 190

25 196

26 202

27 207

28 213

29 221

30 236

31 244

32 252

33 258

34 268

35 272

36 281

37	291
38	300
Special Thanks	307
About The Author	309

CONTENT ADVISORY:

This book contains mature themes including strong sexual content, violence and gore, suicide ideation, and fetecide (referenced). Reader discretion is advised.

DEDICATION

I think it's fitting to dedicate my first official book to my first official fan. I dedicate this book to Denya. Denden, Dana Koala, Reader Extraordinaire. Without your encouragement, telling me to hurry up with the next chapter, or our shared love for fiery hearts, I wouldn't be writing dedication pages at all. I'll never forget who my first and greatest fan was through all those beginning years. Thank you for giving me that gift.

AUTHOR'S NOTE

You might've noticed in my bio that I graduated from Brigham Young University—a school known for its Mormon roots. Some people picked up this book expecting it to be written by a "good Mormon girl." If that's you, then you might be disappointed.

I buried that version of me years ago, with no plans to exhume her.

I wrestled with whether to include detailed sex scenes, strong language, and morally gray characters. In the end, I wrote the story I wanted to read; not the one people expected me to. I dabble in themes revolving around purity culture, restricted rules, and patriarchy.

I'm not trying to lose readers, I just need to be true to myself, and honest with those who may feel offended by this. I'm done apologizing for being myself. I'm flawed, sexual, and human, and so are my characters. It makes for better stories. I'm both proud of the school that helped me perfect my craft, and proud of my storytelling ability. If you choose not to support this book, let's part on good terms.

To the rest of you—sinners, skeptics, seekers: Jump in. We're taking the scenic route to hell.

1

The brothel was closed.

The brothel *never* closed. That should have been her clue. A warning that the streets of Althenia had grown too dangerous to walk after dark.

But Audra walked them anyway.

She was staring into death now: a man with unmistakable Althenian-black hair, standing motionless in the shadows. He hadn't moved since she first noticed him. That had been twenty seconds ago. Now, he stood ten feet away, watching her. A black mask concealed his face, sculpted to fit the contours, revealing only his jaw and mouth beneath it.

Last night, three were killed.

In Althenia, missing brothel girls weren't uncommon, but three in one night? That had never happened before. Witnesses whispered of a masked figure spotted at dusk and dawn. Silent. Fleeting.

There one moment.

Gone the next.

Now he was here.

Close.

Hidden in the darkness and nearly invisible, except for his hands. She saw them moving, twiddling fingers like a man warming up before a kill.

Her fingers slipped into the pocket of her skirt, curling around the dagger's hilt. If he lunged, she would strike first.

He watched.

She waited.

Nothing.

Until he said her name.

"Audra..."

It was so soft she might've imagined it. A chill licked up her spine, and sweat pooled in her palms.

A whistling sound to her right startled her. She turned, breath caught in her throat, but saw nothing.

Heart pounding, she looked back toward the masked man.

Gone.

The shadows were empty.

Confused, she squinted into the darkness. Where did he go?

A hand clamped over her mouth. Another seized her waist.

So this was how it ended.

Her screams were muffled before she could even make them. Their strength outnumbered hers, more than she could fight. The other arm of the perpetrator pulled her toward their stout body. The man leaned down and whispered in her ear, "What in the world do you think you're doing out here alone, Audra? Do you have a death wish?"

Ugh. Kolbe.

Audra attempted to jab her elbow into his gut, but he moved before her bone met his stomach. He released her mouth, now confident she wouldn't scream and alert any sleeping townsfolk.

She paused, turning back to the shadows. Still nothing. Had Kolbe been messing with her? No. The mask the man wore was unmistakable.

Audra shook her head, long blond curls escaping her hooded cloak. "Why are you following me?" Audra snapped, still trying to calm her heart from what she thought would be her demise moments earlier. She knew Kolbe as the nephew of her stepfather. He was also the sole heir to Hillsfield, the wealthiest estate owned by the wealthiest lord in all of Althenia. Six years prior, Audra's mother had wed Lord Byron, and now they resided in Hillsfield. The paths of Kolbe and Audra did not cross as often as she would have liked.

"You're behaving like a fool. You should thank me for catching you sneaking out," he said, his voice sounding more like a hiss. "Again, what are you doing out here alone at night? Where are you going?"

Audra analyzed her perpetrator, not having noticed before how much broader his shoulders became while he was away at university for the last year. His bluish-black hair appeared like a void in the shadows, and his deep brown eyes leered into hers, the expression serious. Her annoyance took precedence.

"I'm going to visit Margaret," Audra replied, as if this was something Kolbe would understand, but she predicted he would not understand one bit. Kolbe disapproved of Margaret's recent endeavors with King Henri, who had asked Margaret to join him at court a few months prior. Earlier that afternoon, Audra overheard the servants around Hillsfield gossiping about Margaret's return to her father's home at Mayview. Audra figured that the only way to see her friend would be to sneak out of Hillsfield after Lord Byron went to sleep for the night. Neither Lord Byron nor Kolbe approved of the king's liaisons or the women who agreed to be a part of them. Therefore, neither would approve of her determination to catch up with her old friend. Margaret was her most favored one since meeting at finishing school in their teens.

As Audra had predicted, Kolbe sneered at the mention of Margaret. A small pain jabbed at her heart, knowing it was one more thing about her he disapproved of. Nevertheless, Kolbe's opinion of Margaret would not change Audra's own opinion of her friend.

"Isn't she with King Henri?" Kolbe asked, his tone a mixture of confusion and ridicule.

Her eyebrows contorted into a V. It wasn't his business where Margaret was. "Not according to the servants at Hillsfield," Audra replied, making up her mind about how to proceed. "Well. You won't be able to drag me back to the estate without waking up half the town, so either you can let me go alone, or you can come with me." Audra crossed her arms in front of her, hoping it made her seem more intimidating and determined. While she didn't wish to bring Kolbe along, she suspected that if she wanted to continue, he would have to escort her.

As if considering his options for a moment, Kolbe heaved his shoulders and released a dramatic harrumph, like a horse obeying with disdain. "Alright, we'll go. Even if I managed to drag you back to Hillsfield, you'll just do this again until you get your way. Let's hurry and get it over with."

Many years of learning had taught her how many different ways the world could be untrustworthy and cruel. Kolbe was four years her elder, almost thirty, but the way he treated her always reminded her of the way Audra's mother treated Eva, her seven-year-old sister. What Audra wouldn't give for Kolbe to look at her another way.

Satisfied, she pressed forward again toward Margaret's house, no longer lurking in the shadows, secured with the protection Kolbe had to offer. Not quite finished speaking his mind, he continued, "It isn't safe to be out alone, and they've yet to find the killer on the loose. What was so important it couldn't wait until morning?"

"It isn't your business," Audra said with a mumble. If he ever discovered the real reasons, he'd never look at her again. Some secrets were best left between only the people who harbored them.

Down the market way street, as they walked side by side, Audra kept her eyes peeled. She admired all the shadows cast upon the flowers that were in full bloom, some closed up and waiting for the next day of sun on the windowsills of the street. She wished she could see their colors in the night, vibrant and contrasting against the beige stone walls surrounding them, the bricks all made from the cliffs found by the seas on the northeastern coast of Althenia.

She used to visit the cliffs often when she lived in the countryside with her mother. She missed the wildflowers growing in the long-bladed grass of the fields; she missed the breeze carrying smells from the mossy rivers and the peachy scent wafting from the Whisper Forest. In the city, it smelled of dirt and old, rusted wood. This was nothing like the fresh fields that surrounded her old home.

Audra smiled at the memories of the countryside, contrasting the grim look on Kolbe's face as he walked beside her. She wondered how different her life would be if she'd been able to grow old there in the countryside. She loved a man once. It was the first time she discovered that not all questions have an answer that we may ever learn in our lifetime; it was the greatest injustice life offered.

Brushing away the stinging memory, she returned her thoughts to images of flowers in the shadows as they rounded the bend towards Margaret's home. Mayfield, a home that was once ratted and worn, now appeared adorned in florals and organza ribbons draping from each window. A fresh coat of white paint sealed the gate surrounding her estate, and the roof boasted sleek new thatch.

On the west side of Margaret's home, Audra spotted the candlelight coming from the window of the Margaret's room. Though this was the first time Audra had been caught sneaking out in a while, it was not the first time she'd snuck out to see her friend. Audra motioned to Kolbe, pointing to the room with the lit window.

"That's odd," Audra noted. Where thorny rose bushes once stood beneath Margaret's window, a ladder sat against it. In the past, Audra had to fetch it from the barn herself. Confused, Audra approached the bottom of the ladder leading to the window, no longer needing to avoid the thorns that used to stick out from the dead rose bushes. Now, new, trimmed bushes brought fresh life to the estate. King Henri must have rewarded his riches to Mayview as a token of appreciation for Margaret's contributions to the king.

Attempting to get her friend's attention by calling out Margaret's name in a loud whisper, Audra wondered if Margaret had snuck another friend inside already. With no response, Audra determined to see for herself. She didn't want to risk waking up any of the servants, or worse: Margaret's cruel father, who Audra once overheard telling a nobleman that the moment his wife passed, he'd take Audra to wife. She hoped Lord Byron would turn him away if the day ever came, just as he shooed away every previous suitor who had attempted to seek Audra's affection in the last six years.

She turned her attention to the window where the candlelight dimmed more and more by the second, and adjusted the ladder against the wall a foot more to the right.

Kolbe grunted again in disapproval. "It really does not suit a lady to hike a ladder wearing her dresses."

"Are you suggesting I climb up naked?" Audra asked. She smirked at her joke, finding fun in teasing him. He didn't react, so she rolled her eyes and continued. "I won't be long. Ten minutes at most."

"I'll be here outside if you need me."

She took the wooden planks in her hands and climbed up as she had many times before, holding her skirts to avoid stepping on them. Once, near the top, Audra almost lost her balance on a rung as she staggered up the shaky ladder. Through the years it had been met with worn steps and rusted screws, so she took her time with each step and didn't dare to look into Margaret's window until she steadied herself on one of the larger rungs of the ladder. The instant she looked inside Margaret's room, Audra used one hand to stifle a gasp.

That night, on the floor of Margaret's room, lay Margaret with her arms extended above her head, her eyes open and glazed over. Her throat displayed a long cut as deep as the bone. Margaret's red hair appeared stained with richer oxblood hues, drenching her locks. The thick liquid pooled everywhere around Margaret, dying her white nightgown crimson. The wound bled so fresh that the blood still trickled down her throat. As slow as Audra's climb had been, her descent was much quicker. She stumbled back in horror, losing her balance from the ladder, and careened toward the ground.

2

Audra's eyelids felt groggy and stiff, much like the rest of her body, as she regained consciousness: first in her limbs, then in her mind. Images flashed behind her eyelids as her dreams retreated, dissolving into memory. A man's head in her lap, black hair, teal eyes. Her own sputtered cries rang in her ears, empty promises whispered into the void.

Now, she lay on the cold stone ground, her back searing with pain as though a knife were slicing into her flesh. No longer picturing cradling another's head, now her own was supported by Kolbe's hands. When she opened her eyes, he loomed over her, mirroring the posture she had taken in her dream. Her spine stiffened, aching from the fall, and for a moment, she wasn't sure she could move.

Panic surged through her as the last thing she witnessed before she fainted resurfaced in her mind. Body burning with pain, she realized the fire in her chest wasn't just from the bruises of her fall. Images clicked through her mind. Margaret's pale face. Blood, so much blood. She closed her eyes, trying to shut the thoughts out. In her imagination she heard Margaret's screams, envisioning the horror she must have felt before her neck was slit. Audra tried to sit up, heart racing, but dizziness crashed over her, forcing her head back into Kolbe's hands.

"Whoa, not so fast."

At first, his voice confused her. Everything hurt. Then, as she looked around, it became clear that not much time had passed since her fall.

"Sorry," Kolbe said. "I only managed to keep your head from hitting the cobblestone. Do you think anything is broken?" Concern edged his voice as his eyes roamed over her, assessing the damage.

Audra groaned, her entire body pulsing with pain, stiff and bruised. "How would I know if something's broken?"

Kolbe chuckled, much to her irritation. She was fairly certain that every bone in her body was shattered beyond repair. Her muscles ached, her joints felt raw.

"Trust me," he said, "if you have to ask, nothing is broken."

She grunted, not entirely convinced. She flexed her fingers, testing the limits of her body. Though sore almost everywhere, she didn't think she bled.

Blood. The gruesome image she'd witnessed moments before her fall forced its way back into her mind. She shuddered, struggling to piece together her thoughts. Kolbe didn't know.

"Margaret's dead," she said, her voice dry as she met Kolbe's gaze. "On the floor of her room." A shiver ran through her as her eyes glazed over, thoughts scrambling.

Kolbe froze, his face flushing white. "Dead?" he repeated, as if he hadn't quite heard her. "How do you know she was—" His words trailed off, expression stiffening. His gaze darted toward the window, then flicked around the premises, scanning for unseen threats. The silence felt eerie.

"Her throat was—" Audra's fingers drifted to her neck, recoiling at the memory of so much blood. "And her insides were—" She choked on the words, unable to finish. The scene burned into her mind. Horrible, gruesome, unforgettable. She had witnessed death before, but never like this. The last time she'd watched someone die, there hadn't been any blood at all.

The realization settled over her like a suffocating weight crushing her sore body. "We have to tell her family," she started, her voice rising with urgency, "and—"

"No," Kolbe interrupted, his hands still cradling her head. "Absolutely not. You can't tell anyone."

His voice was firm, his head shaking in a way that left no room for argument. "If you do, you'll be imprisoned. Or worse." He took a steadying breath. "How do you think we'll explain sneaking into Margaret's room in the middle of the night she died? With a ladder from her barn?" His tone grimmed. "We have to leave. Now."

"We can't just leave her like that." The idea of walking away as if she hadn't seen her friend's mutilated body seemed like a betrayal to her friend.

"We can, and we will," Kolbe said. "Someone will find her in the morning." His words were logical, but they made her feel hollow. She couldn't believe it. Margaret was gone. Murdered. Horrifically. Why?

She remembered her encounter with the man in the mask. Was this him? She clenched her jaw to keep herself from crying in front of him, the sheer abruptness of it all making her mind spin.

"Audra," Kolbe snapped, drawing her back. "Focus. For all we know, whoever did this is watching us right now."

A cold chill crawled up her spine. Yes. The blood had been fresh. The ladder had been left against the wall before they'd arrived. The murderer could still be near.

Her gaze flicked toward the treeline of the Whisper Forest. The trees stood stark and lifeless, not yet touched by spring. The silence around them pressed in, thick and heavy as the hairs on the back of her neck stood up. He might be watching them.

Kolbe shifted. Then, without warning, he slid her arm over his shoulder and scooped her up in one fluid motion, as if she weighed nothing.

Startled, her heart jolted. She reminded herself to stay calm. It didn't mean anything, right? He was only helping because she was injured.

That was all.

Kolbe moved swiftly, careful not to jostle her too much as he carried her away from Margaret's estate and toward Hillsfield. She focused on the sound of his beating heart, his heated body warming her. The world around her disappeared as memories of Margaret continued to resurface. Secret. Friendship. Blood.

As they approached the cobblestone streets of town, the quiet rhythm of Kolbe's breathing calmed her. She kept her gaze averted from his face, resisting the temptation to look at him this close for too long. Was he a ghost? Was she dead, too, and that was why he was holding her?

Her mind reeled. Margaret's death was the fourth she had witnessed. The thought made her shudder. It was as if anyone who got close to her was cursed with the promise of inevitable death.

Swallowing, she shoved the memories down as Hillsfield came into view. Would Kolbe put her down before they arrived? It wouldn't surprise her. He had always been careful about their interactions, cautious about appearances. He rarely allowed them to be alone together, citing propriety and her reputation.

This time, he didn't set her down. Still, he never glanced at her.

Even when they reached the estate, he carried her up the steps, through the door, and to her chambers. The passing halls were a blur as she considered the masked man she stumbled on in the alleyway.

Kolbe didn't put her down until she was safe in her bed. She hardly recalled the journey.

Blue silk sheets looked gray in the darkness, matching the rest of the moonlit room. Kolbe, kneeling beside her, broke the silence and spoke in a hushed tone.

"In the rush of things, I forgot to say how sorry I am for your loss."

The simple words broke her.

Tears slipped down her face, hot and silent. Turning her head away, embarrassment mixed with her grief. She hadn't had time to feel Margaret's death until now but once the tears started, they wouldn't stop.

Margaret. Her best friend. Margaret had made her laugh when she'd thought she'd never laugh again. She had reminded Audra what it felt like to hope again.

Now... she was gone.

Audra would never forget the deep red of Margaret's hair. Their unique hair colors, standing out in the sea of black Althenian hair, had drawn them to one another.

Before tonight, the murders seemed like ploys to scare Althenians back into their homes. Unlike the murdered brothel women, *everyone* knew Margaret. Another death added to a string of mysteries would not go unnoticed in the town.

To Audra's surprise, Kolbe stayed at her side, offering his hand. She hesitated, then took it, grasping it like an anchor. For a fleeting moment, she wished she could throw herself into his arms and weep.

Instead, she whispered, "Margaret was the only person who knew everything about me and still called me a friend. Now I have no one."

A fresh wave of tears stole her voice.

Kolbe's fingers tightened around hers, his expression unreadable in the darkness. "I'm your friend."

She let out a short, bitter laugh. "You wouldn't be if you knew everything Margaret knew."

Silence. She wondered if she'd hurt his feelings. What he didn't understand was that there existed secrets so perilous they held the carriers of them captive for the rest of their lives. The burden of bearing one's secrets concealed the most sincere trust between two friends that could exist. In the end, the distinction between friends and foes is whether the secrets are unearthed, or entombed forever.

After several stiff, hushed moments, Kolbe said, "I think I'm aware of more than you realize."

Her breath caught, and her eyes narrowed. How could he know anything? Margaret wouldn't have told a soul. If anyone at Hillsfield uncovered the truth about her past, she'd be ruined forever.

"I mean it," he added, his tone serious. "You can tell me anything."

Audra's heart clenched, wishing she believed him. She rolled her eyes.

"If we're friends, then why do you never look at me?" The question slipped out before she could stop it.

Kolbe's gaze snapped back to hers. He held it for a long moment before replying, "I do look at you. I'm looking at you now."

She huffed. She should know by now she'd never receive a straight answer from him. Gesturing to him, she persisted. "Why are you kneeling so far away? Like you think I'll bite you if you get too close?"

He chuckled. "Would you?" Then, more seriously, he added, "If someone walked in, I wouldn't want them to think this is anything other than what it is. I shouldn't even be here. But... I am here. Because I know you need a friend."

She wasn't sure if he spoke true, but with Margaret gone, maybe she did need someone.

Still, she sighed, turning away. He'd never shown any interest in being her friend before, and she didn't want one who did so out of pity. "I need time to process her death. Alone."

Kolbe nodded like he understood. Once again, his eyes strayed away from hers, as if by habit. Standing up to leave, he faced the door as he paused, not looking back as he said, "If you call for me, I'll come."

Without another word, he left her alone with her thoughts. In haunted darkness, Margaret's image seared into her mind over and over again. So did the face of the masked man. Where sleep beckoned, nightmares answered.

3

Three hundred years ago, Althenia won the most glorious victory the kingdom had ever known. However, the war resulted in the loss of almost every Althenian man except several members of royalty, including the king, who would become known as the King-of-One-Thousand-Wives. The men of the royal family sought to impregnate every widow of child-rearing age and bore over one thousand children. Their lineage of dark, black hair later repopulated what once was lost.

Although Audra realized her blond hair stood out in Althenia, the members of Hillsfield never paid her any heed. Most days, she might as well be invisible. Today, it was different.

The way Lord Byron watched Audra throughout breakfast made it clear he knew something. Though her mother denied ever telling him anything about their past, Audra always felt as if he could see right through her. His judging glances were nothing compared to the cold shoulder he gave her, darting from the room almost as quickly as Kolbe did whenever they were alone.

Her mother, Lady Mystine, often dismissed Lord Byron's behavior, but Audra felt the weight of his condemnation burning into her every move this particular morning.

What did he know about last night? Was it disapproval she sensed? Disapproval that Kolbe had been in her room? Did he know she had left the estate?

Thankfully, Lord Byron diverted his attention to Kolbe's younger sister, Kathleen, who was chatty that morning as usual. Kathleen was the same age as Audra, yet their personalities were years apart. Sometimes, Audra wondered if Kathleen's carefree nature made Kolbe view Audra as just another child. Still, Kathleen was the light of Hillsfield. Always giddy, always optimistic. Despite her flightiness, she made Audra's days tolerable.

Kathleen twirled a lock of her long black hair. "My maid told me they found Margaret Bristwood dead in her room this morning. The scene was quite gruesome."

Audra and Kolbe exchanged fleeting glances across the chestnut dining table. Lord Byron preferred dark decor, covering the gray stone walls with tapestries depicting battles and landscapes. Large stained-glass windows inside a dome on the ceiling gave the room a colorful glow, while the arched windows lining the wall offered additional sunlight and a view of the courtyard.

"How terrible," Kolbe said, feigning surprise. "Wasn't she a friend of yours, Audra?"

Audra was a terrible liar. She pressed her lips together and looked away, avoiding the eyes fixed on her—Kathleen's, Kolbe's, her mother's, Lord Byron's, and Eva's. Lady Mabel, Lord Byron's sister and mother to Kolbe and Kathleen, seemed lost in thought. Mabel's mind had wavered ever since she'd become prone to frequent seizures.

"Yes. I overheard the servants talking about it earlier," Audra said, her voice steady but distant. "I apologize if I seem unwell. I've been quite distraught." Her tear-streaked face was evidence enough.

"I'm so sorry," Kathleen said, offering Audra a sympathetic look. "I remember how close you two were. It's tragic. I can only imagine her mother's grief when she found her."

16

Servants arrived, placing trays of eggs, biscuits, bacon, and fruits on the table. Audra found Hillsfield's food bland and unseasoned but welcomed the distraction as the servants filled their plates. Kathleen continued speaking.

"They found a black mask in her hand. A masquerade one. The ribbons looked like she ripped it off someone. The authorities think it might be the same person responsible for the other murders, based on the way the blood—"

"Kathleen," Mystine interjected, smoothing an ivory ruffle on her periwinkle dress. "Perhaps this discussion is too gruesome for breakfast." Then, turning to Audra, she added, "Dear, please meet me in my room after you take Eva to her lesson."

Audra silently thanked her mother for the interruption. She wasn't sure how much longer she could keep her composure. The image of Margaret's body flashed in her mind. She didn't remember seeing a mask, but her view had been brief.

The conversation shifted to Lord Byron's business dealings, which Audra tuned out. Once she finished eating, she excused herself, taking Eva to meet her tutor. At least Eva's presence would be a welcome diversion.

Eva, with her braided golden hair falling down her back, prattled happily as they walked. At seven, she was almost chattier than Kathleen. She told Audra all about Muse, the old white cat they had brought from the countryside, and how Mystine had allowed the cat to sleep in her room last night to ease her nightmares.

Audra took Eva to the study where Eva attended tutoring five days a week. The room displayed a large kelly green rug, floral tapestries, and bookshelves filled with educational texts. A cluster of chartreuse settees circled a glass coffee table on one side, while a larger table occupied the opposite end, surrounded by books.

Since they were early, Eva chose a book to read aloud. Audra listened, impressed by how much she had learned. After a few pages, Eva set the book down and turned to Audra.

"I know Mother says not to worry about the murders, but it's scary," Eva said, fidgeting with her braid. Her face pasted a frown. "What if the murderer sneaks into my room next?"

Audra's stomach twisted. She had asked herself the same thing.

"My darling, you don't need to worry," Audra assured her. "Lord Byron is the wealthiest man in Althenia. Hillsfield is more guarded than the castle itself. No one can reach you here."

Eva studied her, then her doe-like expression turned to a sheepish grin. "Kathleen says you sneak past the guards sometimes. What if the murderer sneaks past them, too?"

Audra flushed. She thought she had been more discreet. "Kathleen shouldn't have told you that," she said, backtracking. "I haven't snuck out in a long time. The guards always caught me, so I gave up."

Nodding, Eva turned back to her book. Before she resumed reading, the door opened.

Jed, Eva's tutor, entered the room, followed by Eva's handmaiden, who was there to chaperone. Jed had the same brooding presence as Kolbe, with the infamous black Althenian hair. His brown eyes flickered toward Audra the way most men's did... the way she wished Kolbe's would.

Running a hand through his dark hair, Jed looked away, flushing. He smiled at Eva before turning back to Audra. "Miss Audra, it's been a while since you've joined us for lessons." His voice sounded hopeful. "Your mother asked me to tell you she'd like to meet with you in her chambers now. Perhaps you will join us next time?"

Audra had stopped attending Eva's lessons years ago, ever since her mother warned her that spending too much time with Jed would lead to rumors. If she was honest, it was for the best.

"Perhaps next time," Audra said with a polite smile, using the same answer she always gave. She bid farewell to Eva and left to find her mother.

As she walked through Hillsfield's gray stone corridors, she predicted what this meeting was about. It had to be about Margaret. Mystine knew Margaret had been her friend, so Audra expected her mother would offer comfort.

However, when Audra entered her mother's chambers, the mood was far from comforting. Mystine sat on her bed, her expression stiff. "Lock the door," she said.

Audra complied. The room smelled of lavender, its elegant sky-blue wallpaper and rich satin bedding a reflection of her mother's refined taste. The fireplace flickered, casting long shadows across the room.

Mystine patted the spot beside her. "Sit."

Audra obeyed, though unease settled in her chest when Mystine wouldn't meet her eyes.

For moments that felt like an eternity, silence filled the room. When Audra felt as if she'd burst with anticipation, Lady Mystine turned and spoke.

"Kolbe told Lord Byron that you snuck out again last night."

Audra's blood ran cold.

What?

Kolbe had told? The very person who had sworn her to secrecy? *He* had been the one to say they must act as if nothing had happened.

Audra had spent years convincing herself that Kolbe didn't hate her. Now she wondered if he did, in fact, hate her.

Mystine continued. "Because of that, Lord Byron has decided it's time to inform you of your betrothal."

Audra's breath caught in her throat.

Her betrothal?

To whom?

Since when?

For the first time since entering the room, Mystine met her gaze, gauging Audra's reaction.

Again—*her betrothal?*

The first noise that escaped Audra was a dry, humorless laugh. "Oh? You summoned me to announce that Lord Byron wants to hand me off like a prized cow from his field? After milking me dry for six years, congratulations to me, I'm ready for slaughter."

Mystine pressed her lips together, unimpressed by Audra's flippancy. "You've been betrothed for years. Why do you think Lord Byron sent all those suitors away without consideration?" Her voice sharpened. "And what do you mean by that? Lord Byron has not treated you poorly."

Audra pushed to her feet, needing to move, to pace, to gather her thoughts, but her mother wasn't finished.

"It's because of Lord Byron's influence that we secured such a favorable match for you, Audra. You should be grateful." Mystine's tone softened, as though trying to make her daughter understand. "Prince Elijah has returned from university and intends to make good on the arrangement. The castle will host a ball next week to announce your engagement."

Audra felt the air leave her lungs.

"The prince?" she echoed, her heart hammering like a war drum.

She knew little about Prince Elijah, only that he was around her age and had... *a reputation*. Some whispered of him as a flirtatious drunkard, while others described him as a refined scholar, wise beyond his years. Some called him cruel. Which stories were true? She had never bothered to wonder because marrying a prince had never been within the realm of possibility.

Until now.

"Are you mad?" Audra blurted.

"I had no choice," Mystine continued. "With any other suitor, I could refuse. I could insist that you were a prize, or that you deserved better. But the prince—" she shook her head "—we cannot refuse the crown."

Audra's pulse roared in her ears. She paused, trying to choose the perfect next words.

They weren't allowed to talk about it. They weren't supposed to say.

How could she not say?

"But you understand why this can't happen," she whispered.

How could her mother not see the problem?

"There's no guarantee, anyway," Audra grasped for logic. "After the ball, he may not want me—"

Mystine cut her off. "You and I both know why he will." She reached up, grasping a lock of her golden hair and letting it slide through her fingers. The rarest hair color in Althenia. Their hair.

Audra's thoughts raced. What did she recall about the prince? She had seen a sketch of him once, years ago. That was all. The rest was speculation.

Her mother's next words settled like lead in her stomach.

"This has been a match long in the making, and it's time for you to face it."

A thousand thoughts clamored for attention in Audra's mind. Escape. Defiance. Bargaining. But only one argument slipped through her lips.

"If I marry the prince and go to the castle, who will..." Audra hesitated, her voice dropping to a whisper as she checked the room for eavesdroppers. "Who will take care of Eva?"

It was a weak argument, and she knew it, but her mother would understand what Audra was really asking.

The look on Mystine's face sharpened as her eyes darted to Audra, her gaze growing cold. "Eva will stay here with me, of course. Her life will continue as it always has." Then, with a pointed look, she added, "Besides, she told me she knows you've snuck out before. It's best she doesn't follow in your footsteps."

Audra stiffened. A sick feeling coiled in her gut.

"What are you saying?" she demanded, her voice trembling. "I've done everything you told me to. I've obeyed every rule—"

"And in doing so, you've kept Eva safe," Mystine snapped. "She will remain here."

The words struck like a tiger clawing through her skin.

"How can I be without her?" Audra whispered, feeling the walls of her world closing in. Her throat grew sore as she choked back tears.

Mystine replied, "We'll visit."

Audra's hands curled into fists at her sides. Her mother didn't understand.

Anger surged through her, raw and unchecked. "And how do you expect to visit me when the prince has me executed after our wedding night? When he finds out I am not untouched?" Her voice dropped into a harsh whisper, panic bubbling to the surface. "He will kill me, Mother. I'll be hanged for deception or imprisoned for life. You cannot think this ends favorably for me."

Silence. She was doomed, and her mother didn't seem to care about it. Her mother stood, her face red as she shook her head, pacing the floor.

"I have only ever protected you, Audra." Her voice was sharp, her blue eyes ablaze. "I hid us away. I took responsibility for your foolishness. I made excuses for your behavior with Eva. I gave you more time, more freedom than you ever deserved." She paused, inhaling a sharp breath. "Everything we have done for the last eight years was for you. To keep you safe. And all you have ever done is prove how ungrateful you are."

Audra's heart sank as the hurt cut her deep. Her mother had never spoken to her this way before.

Mystine's voice lowered, but the weight of her words did not.

"I see the way you look at Kolbe. At Jed. It was only a matter of time before I would have to spin more lies to protect you." Mystine's lips pressed together, fingers circling against her temples. "This marriage is the only way forward. A match to the prince will give you everything. *His* children will be the ones you can call your own."

The words clawed at Audra's insides.

She hated the guilt that rose inside her. Yes, it was true that Audra's choices had led to Eva. But hadn't her mother chosen this deception as well? Hadn't *she* been the one to construct this life for them?

Memories surfaced, unwanted and sharp. The years spent in hiding. The whispers. The hurried lies.

Her mother had planned this with their old friend, Douglas Freeman, so that the child could be legitimate. They rushed into a marriage, and in exchange, Mystine took care of him through his illness.

Audra's heart tugged at the memories of having to raise her daughter as if she were her sister. Sometimes, she wondered if it would have been a better life to raise Eva alone in the countryside. Their neighbor, Cynthia Lorent, had done it. So had her mother. Why couldn't she?

Throughout Audra's life, people had compared her beauty to her mother's. Of course, this proved unfair. The ravishing type of beauty her mother possessed was the kind that took people's breath away. Nobody could compete with her mother's demure and intoxicating presence. After Audra's father had passed away from the onset of apoplexy, noblemen began doting on her mother, scrambling for her attention despite her lack of familial prestige. Before Lord Byron, Audra's mother had turned down every suitor who approached her. She'd said she would rather starve than settle for another unkind man.

At a young age, Lady Mystine taught her daughter to sew her own dresses, and the two of them kept their old house in the countryside by making ball gowns for the wealthy ladies of Althenia. Audra joined her mother working at their shop in town, then each night they would ride back home. Audra worked all but one day a week back then. She spent her free day with the children from the other farms, but her favorite throughout all the years was Cynthia Lorent's son, Garrick.

Audra and Garrick had been friends since they met by the river while she fetched water from the nearby stream. She was eleven, and he was thirteen. He saved her from two cruel neighbor boys who thought she was a witch or a siren and wanted to drown her. From there, a lifelong friendship also formed between Mystine Dione and Cynthia Lorent, both raising one child, both supporting each other through years of poverty and illnesses.

For years, the four of them spent many evenings and most Sundays together. Garrick and Audra would sneak away to play in the river, while Mystine and Cynthia gossiped and caught up in one of their homes. It was the life Audra knew best until Cynthia fell ill. After that, nothing was ever the same again.

Grounding herself back in the present, Audra blinked. She considered her mother's words, hearing for the first time the very things she had always suspected her mother believed but had never admitted aloud. It wasn't as if Audra had asked to form such strong emotions for the men around her at Hillsfield. She yearned for something she once had. If she could not desire love, then what was she allowed to desire?

Her life would never be her own.

"There cannot be children if the prince kills me," Audra snapped.

Mystine sighed, reaching into her sleeve and pulling out a folded note.

"I visited an old friend. They gave me this."

Audra eyed the paper suspiciously.

"It's a mixture," Mystine explained, tucking it into Audra's dress pocket. "A concoction to make it appear as though you are untouched. You'll apply it every night until the supply is gone."

Audra felt sick.

Her mother continued, undeterred. "You'll also meet with Lady Ann this afternoon for a dress fitting. Take Eva with you and get her fitted as well when she's done with her tutoring for the day. She's outgrowing her dresses."

Mystine reached forward, tilting Audra's chin up to meet her eyes.

"Your life is about to become extraordinary," she said, giving Audra a pointed look.

Audra wished she believed her. With Margaret dead and her betrothal set, fear encompassed her like iron bars.

4

T he carriage rolled to a stop, jolting Audra awake. Her head spun as reality collided with the memories in her dreams. It was the kind of dream she wished was real, the sort that made her want to drift back to sleep just to see him alive again. Any hope of returning to slumber was barred by the reality of what awaited her.

The ball. Not just any ball, though. She was reminded of that as her mother reached across the carriage, handing Audra the remainder of her attire: a mask, sapphire blue and trimmed with white lace to match her gown. Audra clutched the top layer of her skirt, admiring the white, patterned lace resting atop the brilliant blue chiffon beneath. Layers of underskirts made her skirts bulky, and somewhere under all the stacks of fabric, she supposed, were her legs.

Audra took the mask from her mother, who was already wearing one. Lady Mystine sported a black-and-gold mask that complemented her golden dress, which was adorned with black lace at every seam. Next to Lady Mystine sat Lord Byron, while Kathleen sat beside Audra, pointing out every impressive sight she saw through the window. Unlike Hillsfield's gray stone fortress, the palace rose majestically. Its walls boasted of white marble, its towers stretching a hundred feet high. Golden spires crowned each tower, and wide marble steps led to the main entrance, flanked by golden balusters. Against the night sky, the palace appeared to glow.

Audra tied the mask behind her head, securing the ribbon. As usual, Lord Byron refused to look at her, his lovesick eyes too focused on her mother to pay attention to anything else. Imagining the other carriage, Audra pictured Kolbe and his mother sitting in bored silence.

She sensed that the instant her hair came into view, she would stand out like a red stone amid a pile of gray ones. She was certain there would be more than a few curious onlookers eager to judge her beauty in person, craning their necks to get a view. Her vibrant hair offered them an easy target, and the notion made her squirm in her seat.

The line of carriages in front of theirs shortened as men and women stepped onto the palace grounds. As always, the nobles displayed their slick black hair while their ball gowns and hair jewelry were the only means they had to set themselves apart. Some wore lavish dresses dripping with pearls, diamonds, and gemstones. Audra knew none of it would help her blend in, and she wanted nothing more than to hide.

When their carriage finally pulled up to the castle steps, two guards opened the door. One glanced at the other and said in a low voice, "Let him know she's arrived." They gestured for them to exit. Lord Byron's expression grew serious as he turned to check the next carriage, where Kolbe assisted his mother's exit.

Outside, the palace décor proved to be the opposite of Hillsfield's. White palace walls lined with vines creeping up the bottom. Roses, tulips, gardenias, irises—every flower Audra had come to love in her countryside days. In every window, magnanimous floral displays leaped out, with iron vases painted in gleaming gold.

At least there would be no shortage of beauty if this became her new home, Audra mused. Her stomach churned at the idea: another dazzling place that would serve as her prison, the sort of confinement she had grown accustomed to. It wouldn't be like her childhood, playing in the fields and picking flowers from the ground herself.

She shook away the memories of Him. He was gone now, and it had been years since she'd shed her last tear for him.

From the other carriage, Mabel approached first, wearing a conservative navy gown devoid of embellishments. She complimented Kathleen's pale yellow dress, who twirled to display it. Audra realized Kathleen would thrive in this opulent lifestyle. Given Kathleen's previous marriage, Audra suspected that was why she had been chosen to wed the prince instead of Lord Byron's actual family. If given the choice, Kathleen would pick a life of limitless grandeur, whereas all Audra yearned for was autonomy—and someone she loved to enjoy it with.

Kolbe joined them, clad in black. A matching black mask made him look more intense than usual. To Audra's surprise, his eyes locked onto hers, and he appeared unable to look away. Lord Byron offered each of his arms to Mabel and Mystine. Kolbe then escorted both Kathleen and Audra up the palace steps behind them. Every guard seemed to recognize exactly who Audra was, signaling each other with short gestures as she passed.

The palace interior was as impressive as its exterior. White marble walls shone in every corridor, golden sconces lighting the way. Outside the ballroom, a short line of guests waited to be introduced by name. About a dozen people stood ahead of them. Audra's palms perspired, and she was sure her cheeks flushed redder with each step forward.

"Audra," Kolbe said, his voice low enough that Kathleen might overhear, but not Lord Byron. "I meant what I said the other night."

She glanced at him, his gaze aimed straight ahead. Kathleen, on his other side, listened without a word.

"What thing that you said?" Audra asked, unsure of what he meant.

He swallowed. "I'm your friend. As your friend, I offer my help tonight if you need it. All you have to do is ask."

Unsure of his true intentions, Audra wondered if he knew something she did not. She'd already forgiven him in her heart for telling her mother about her sneaking out, convinced it was more out of duty than spite. As she mulled over his words, Lord Byron and her mother entered the ballroom first. Kathleen, Kolbe, and Audra paused while the courtier confirmed their names.

"Save a dance for me," Audra blurted, surprising herself. She turned to Kolbe, watching his reaction.

He answered without missing a beat. "That's the thing... I'll save them all for you if you wish," he said, eyes locking onto hers, the intensity in his eyes revealing his sincerity. Before she could respond, the guards motioned them forward.

"Kolbe Byron of Hillsfield, escorting his sister Kathleen Byron, and Audra Dione," the herald announced. A hush fell over the ballroom. Audra sensed every eye on her as she descended the broad marble steps with Kolbe and Kathleen. She fought the urge to vanish, feeling more like a rare artifact than a human. Her fingers trembled as she grasped Kolbe's arm for stability, facing the same sorts of stares people gave her in the market or from passing carriages.

It was her hair—the brightest in a sea of black. Though her mother shared her hair color, Audra bore the extra weight of a betrothal to Prince Elijah. She suspected Kolbe sensed her tension because his arm stiffened beneath her grip. She scanned the masked faces, but with so many guests, there was no telling which was the prince. Her unseen fiancé might be watching her even now, and the thought made her breath stall.

At the bottom of the stairs, a man in a golden mask and dark hair approached and asked her for a dance. Men had once fawned like this over her mother after her father died. Audra knew that a single refusal or social slip on her part might rouse Lord Byron's disapproval, so she accepted the man's hand. With a final glance at Kolbe, who winked at her, she allowed the stranger to whisk her onto the dance floor. Enormous crystal chandeliers gleamed overhead, their light reflecting off the towering arched windows surrounding them.

"My, you are ravishing," the man said, offering a sly grin. His crooked teeth struck her as unsettling, and something about him felt threatening. "I am Sir Pildrex Morden, Audra. The prince and I were good friends at University. If you're lucky, I'll introduce you to him myself." Her heart sank, and she withheld the urge to glower at him.

Still, her tongue sometimes outran her caution. "What luck that would be, Sir Pildrex," she replied, sarcasm seeping from her lips. "However, since my stepfather is Althenia's wealthiest lord, I imagine he's already handled such arrangements."

The man's grin widened, revealing yellow-tinged teeth. His breath carried a sickening odor as he leaned in. "A saucy lady. Must be the golden hair," he said, wrapping a strand of her hair around his fingers before letting his gaze slide down to her breasts, then back to her eyes. She fidgeted, understanding why Kolbe had offered his help. However, after scanning the room, Kolbe was nowhere to be seen.

"So tell me," Pildrex continued, undeterred, "aren't you a little old to be the prince's bride? I'd assume he'd want someone younger, with more childbearing years left."

Audra pressed her lips together, thinking how reprehensible the prince must be if this was the company he kept.

"Yet here you are, acting as though your words have any effect on my betrothal," she said in a sharp tone. Pildrex released a cruel laugh.

"Your age doesn't bother me," he said. "I like them a bit m ore... experienced. Keep that in mind if you ever grow bored of him." He leaned closer, his rancid breath making her stomach quake. "And trust me, darling, I know experience when I see it. A naïve girl wouldn't have half the tongue you do, or the same skill in licking—"

Before Audra drove her heel into his foot, another man cut in, towering over Pildrex with a more muscular frame. He wore a larger black mask that covered his forehead, nose, and cheeks, and after a glance at Audra, the stranger shifted his attention to Pildrex.

"I believe it's my turn to dance with the future queen," the newcomer said. Sizing him up, Pildrex bowed and scurried off. Though Audra braced herself to be tossed around all night, she was grateful for the rescue.

"That man is slime," the new masked stranger said. "I thought I'd intervene."

"He's a boy," Audra replied, "and I don't hate the interruption." She looked him over, noticing he was tall and broad-shouldered, his mask hiding most of his face... like the masked man in the alleyway. Despite that, he radiated a strange sense of comfort. He pulled her into a waltz, meeting her gaze in a way few ever did. Most avoided her eyes, as if she were a monstrous gorgon. Oftentimes, people stared at her hair or her figure, but this man stared right into her eyes.

"Have we met?" Audra asked, breaking the silence. She couldn't shake the blend of familiarity and strangeness she felt around him.

"Yes," he replied, smirking. "Do you recognize me?"

She squinted, trying to make out his features beneath the mask, to no avail. Her puzzled face must have given away her confusion. He leaned in and whispered, "I believe you saw me in the alleyway the night of Margaret Bristwood's death."

Audra froze, her face flattening as her heart pounded. It was the masked man, the murderer. Hiding in plain sight, camouflaged in a forest of masks. She envisioned him grabbing her and forcing her to cause a scene to escape, but he loosened them instead and paused their dance. "My apologies, I didn't mean to frighten you. You're not in danger, and you weren't that night either. At least, not from me. You... surprised me that night. That was all."

Examining him, she wondered if she believed. She thought she'd witnessed him fleeing the scene of her friend's murder, but the sincerity in his voice made her second guess herself. "What were you doing in the streets, then?" she asked.

He smiled, and though she couldn't see most of his face, something about him captivated her. "I was going to ask you the same thing," he said. "Perhaps we both had our reasons. I'm not the man behind the murders, if that's your true question. I've heard the rumors. Should you feel unsafe at this time, you're free to go. I won't stop you. But... I hope you'll stay."

Her heart fluttered, despite herself. Who was this man? Leering eyes hovered in every direction, noblemen waiting their turn, biding their time. It wasn't proper to cut in the way he'd cut into her dance with Pildrex, but if he hadn't she might have caused a scene. His offer to let her walk away tempted her less than her piqued curiosity desired to know more. She gripped tighter to his hand, signifying she intended to remain. "How do you know Pildrex?"

He responded with a faint smile, his hand on her waist pulling her body closer. "I make it my business to know everyone connected with the prince. The slimier they are, the more interesting they are. You might say I have a knack for unearthing people's secrets."

Audra smirked. "Is that why you came to dance with me? To discover my secrets and see if I'm a threat to the prince?" she teased.

He pulled her even closer, his left hand moving to the small of her back to reel her nearer so he could speak in her ear. "I doubt you're much of a threat to anyone, Audra. But what makes you think I don't already know all your secrets?" His words and the bold way he touched her made her pulse quicken. She recalled her mother's accusation: that she was too prone to catching feelings. Now wasn't the time for intrigue, not with Lord Byron prowling around, the prince somewhere in the crowd, and her future at stake.

"If everyone here knows who I am, I'm not sure why I bothered wearing a mask. You might know my name, like you whispered that night, but you don't know a thing about me," she countered.

His laugh rumbled low in his throat. "I wouldn't be so certain. Don't fear, you aren't in danger, but I might know more than you think."

Audra tilted her head, both wary and fascinated. Who was he to speak with such boldness to the prince's fiancée? She studied him, attempting to place his familiarity.

A soft whistle broke the moment—three short notes. The same whistle she heard the night she saw him. She glanced over her shoulder but found no obvious source. When she turned back to her dance partner, she noticed his gaze appeared distant, a frown crossing his lips. He lifted her hand with a gentle touch as their dance came to a halt.

"I must go, but we'll meet again when the time is right," he said. He locked eyes with her, adding, "Better a brief meeting than none at all. Until next time, Audra." Just as quickly as he'd appeared, he vanished into the crowd.

Audra stood there, reeling from his cryptic departure. Who was that man, and why did he mention seeing her again? Before she constructed theories, another man approached. She excused herself, pleading thirst, and wove past more eager suitors. She spotted her mother near the feasting tables, alongside Lord Byron, Kathleen, the king, and a scantily clad woman draped over the king's arm.

"Your Highness," Lord Byron said as Audra neared. "May I present your future daughter, Audra Dione?" She offered the most polished curtsy she could manage, the one she had rehearsed since finishing school.

"Ah," the king said, smiling at her. Dazed, she couldn't stop thinking about that masked man, wondering if she had been enchanted. Who was he?

"She's as lovely as her mother," the king added. "Just as you described, Lord Byron, and my son will be delighted to meet her. As delighted as I was when I met my beautiful mistress here, Isabelle." Audra realized this woman was the king's newest mistress, replacing Margaret. He had an unquenchable thirst for affairs, and Isabelle would not be his last.

Audra remembered how Lord Byron had once called the king unsentimental in love, though he never dared to voice that opinion in public.

That was the reason Lady Mystine had convinced everyone that Eva was her daughter from a second marriage to a man who died months later. Audra envisioned that if Lord Byron learned the truth about Eva, neither she nor her mother would be permitted on his estate. They'd be on the streets, their reputations in shambles.

Still, Lord Byron's face betrayed no dislike as he spoke with the king. "Where is Prince Elijah?" he asked.

"Oh, *pfft*. He said he had some urgent business. I'm certain he'll return soon," King Henri replied, then beckoned a servant. "Shall we have some wine? I'd like to propose a toast." Servants hurried over with goblets as though anticipating his order. Once everyone was served, King Henri lifted his cup. "To new beginnings!"

They cheered in unison and drank. Audra took a sip and glanced at Isabelle, who grimaced as though tasting something foul. The king continued speaking with Lord Byron, not noticing Isabelle's sudden, violent cough. Within seconds, she vomited onto the floor.

Alarmed, the king spun around. Isabelle's coughing fit intensified, forcing her to her knees. In a horrifying display, her face turned red, then purple. King Henri called for help, onlookers flooded in, and chaos erupted, but it was too late.

In less than a minute, Mistress Isabelle lay dead on the floor.

5

The masquerade screeched to a halt as the bewildered crowd gathered around Isabelle's body, many craning for a closer look. Audra pushed her way out, desperate to run anywhere but there.

This was the fifth death she'd witnessed, and it seemed the most gruesome. Seeing Isabelle's head loll to the side thrust Audra back into a memory she tried so hard to bury: the day her childhood friend, Garrick Lorent, died of poison in her arms. Back then, no one was around to help or explain how it happened.

He'd left her alone in the world, pregnant with the daughter she'd raise alone.

How could she not recall it, having just beheld another poisoning mere steps away? The details blurred in her mind as she remembered that a mask was found in Margaret's hand after her death. Now, the entire ballroom was full of masks, and the death had taken place right beside the king.

Could the murderer be trying to seize the king's attention? Audra wondered as she kept forcing her way through the onlookers toward a side doorway she spotted on the upper floor. Why couldn't she shake the feeling that she was next? Imagining her own body lying cold on the floor, she felt her lungs seize, as though they refused her any more air. So many faces. Any one of them could be the killer. If it wasn't about the king, then maybe it was about her.

Reaching the stairs, heart hammering so hard her vision blurred, she sprinted up. Free of the crush of people converging on Isabelle's body, Audra fought the spinning in her head. Thoughts and memories crashed together.

She escaped into a nearby hallway, ducking behind a large potted plant near the ballroom doors. Collapsing against a white marble wall, she buried her face in her skirts and sobbed. The room spun, even behind her eyelids. Margaret hadn't died of poison, so how did this connect? Could there be more than one murderer? Did safety even exist anymore?

Audra thought of the masked man she'd danced with earlier, the one who claimed to spy for the prince and disappeared at a small whistle. Had she danced with the killer? Did he lie? Though she had no idea who he might be, *he knew her*. If he'd singled her out, was that a sign she'd be next?

Her mind whirled. He'd told her he'd see her again soon, so maybe that was how he discovered so much about her—he'd been following her. She tried to recall the names and faces of the previous victims, wondering how many more were in danger and *why*. Yet, she suspected that if she voiced her suspicions to anyone, they'd dismiss her as paranoid. A person can only witness so much death before they start seeing ghosts.

Just as panic threatened to overwhelm her, she heard a voice near the ballroom doors. "Audra, there you are. I saw you leave the ballroom." Kolbe stood over her, still wearing his simple black mask, his brows knitted in concern. Audra's eyes were red and puffy from weeping, but seeing Kolbe pulled her from that crushing despair.

She rambled in a frantic burst. "I danced with him," she blurted, reliving the moment the masked man had pried her away from Sir Pildrex. "I know it—I danced with the murderer. He's going to kill me next."

Kolbe's brows furrowed even tighter as he crouched in front of her. "What are you talking about? What happened?" he asked, voice tight with urgency. He looked both ways down the corridor, then settled beside her, keeping watch.

"A man I danced with. There was a whistle, and then he said he had to leave, but he said that he'd see me again soon," she managed between gulps of air. "That's how it starts, right? He stalks them, then he kills them. I'm next."

Before Kolbe replied, another voice interjected. "Pardon me," it said from the right. Audra jumped, searching for a route to flee. However, the speaker was no stranger: he wore no mask, and atop his black hair sat a golden jeweled crown. His identity was undeniable.

Blushing, Audra stood and curtsied, while Kolbe bowed. Both fell silent in Prince Elijah's presence—the heir to Althenia, and Audra's supposed future husband.

"Forgive me. I overheard part of your conversation," said the prince, his tone polite. "I'm returning to the ballroom after hearing of Mistress Isabelle's murder. What did you say about a man and a whistle? Could you describe him?"

Audra swallowed. The prince stood taller than Kolbe, with thick brows and broad shoulders—traits rumored to run in the royal family. He smelled of forest air, and his manner was calmer than she'd expected. She wondered if he realized they were meeting for the very first time, or if he even knew of the betrothal. He seemed familiar. Her palms grew clammy, but she forced herself to speak.

"Forgive me, Your Highness, you startled me," she began. "I believe I may have danced with the man responsible for Mistress Isabelle's death."

The prince remained composed, nodding at each of them. "I see. May I learn your names?"

Kolbe answered first, almost interrupting her. "Kolbe Byron and Audra Dione, Your Highness."

Prince Elijah's eyes widened, turning to Audra with a faint smile bordering on a smirk. Offering his hand, he took hers and kissed her fingertips, never breaking eye contact. "I had imagined meeting you differently, Audra," he said. "I've heard tales of your beauty. The stories don't do you justice."

Kolbe cleared his throat. "Your Highness, there's the matter of the murder that needs our attention."

Prince Elijah nodded and released Audra's hand. "Yes, of course. Let's speak in private." He offered an arm for Audra to take, and she glanced at Kolbe, who offered no reaction beyond a subdued stare.

She slid her arm through the prince's. Kolbe trailed behind as they navigated the castle's main corridor to a discreet side exit. Outside, they walked around the castle, hugging the outer walls until they came upon a green carriage half hidden by the trees. Two guards stood outside it, opening the door when they approached. Prince Elijah gestured for Audra to enter first, then followed, with Kolbe last.

Inside, Audra and Kolbe sat facing the prince, whose proximity made her heart flutter with nerves. There was something familiar about him, though she couldn't guess why. Despite the tension, Elijah's smile helped calm her.

"All right, tell me about the man you danced with," he said. "What did he look like?"

Audra took a steadying breath. "He was tall, Althenian, black hair. He wore a large black mask. That describes half the men here tonight. Sorry. Let's see... He cut in while I was dancing with your... uh... *friend*. Pildrex."

Prince Elijah snorted in amusement. "Pildrex. 'Friend' isn't the right word. We benefit each other from time to time," he remarked, a trace of contempt in his voice. "Continue."

Relieved that the prince seemed to dislike Pildrex as much as she did, Audra considered again. She worried she'd sound paranoid, but something about that masked man had felt off. "He said Pildrex was slime. I asked how he knew him, and he replied that it was his job to know the prince's affairs. I assumed he was a royal spy, that he worked for you."

Elijah's expression hardened, making it difficult to read his thoughts. "Go on," he said again.

Audra decided to skip the flirtation. It wasn't the best time to confess how the masked man had caught her attention. Besides, she didn't want Kolbe to hear those details, either. "There was a whistle, and he said he had to go, but he'd see me again soon. Then he disappeared."

The prince folded his arms, eyes narrowed in thought. "You mentioned earlier you believed he planned to kill you. Why?"

Embarrassed, she glanced at Kolbe, who was equally inscrutable, then back at the prince. "I don't know who he is, but he seems to know me. He said as much, and I believed him."

Prince Elijah studied her face for a moment, then relaxed, leaning back against the seat. "You're terrified," he said. "Believe me, you have nothing to fear." He offered a small, reassuring smile. "Do you know what links these murders, why these women were targeted?"

Audra shook her head. The prince continued. "The common factor is that each victim was... unchaste. They were all unwilling to wait until marriage. A man was killed as well before, one of the victim's fiancés, while trying to save her. It appears the killer despises women who, in his view, stray from virtue, and he's taken it upon himself to punish them."

Audra's chest tightened at his words. The masked man had hinted he unearthed her secrets. So maybe he was the murderer after all, and he'd lied to her so she wouldn't run like a mouse being chased by a cat. Did Prince Elijah realize Margaret also hadn't waited until marriage? Of course he did. She was his father's mistress, like Isabelle. Audra forced a polite smile, her insides churning.

"As I said," the prince continued, "you're safe, assuming you haven't broken that rule. Being a woman is not a crime, the danger exists only if you've been with a man prior to your wedding."

Although the prince intended to comfort, his statement filled Audra with dread. She tried to maintain a calm facade.

"You're right. I have nothing to worry about," she said with a forced smile, hoping she sounded convincing. Inside, her fear grew sharper. If the truth of her past ever emerged, she would be next.

Did that mean Eva's life might also be in danger? She prayed that her secret was safe. Only her mother knew... except that once, when she'd told Margaret under the influence of wine. But Margaret would never have betrayed her, right?

A knock sounded on the carriage door. "Your Highness," a guard called from outside, "there's something you need to see." The prince turned back to Audra, his features composed, and lifted her hand in his.

He kissed her knuckles, sending color rushing to her cheeks. "I wish our meeting had been under different circumstances. We will talk again soon. For now, I must attend to this matter with my father's mistress. Goodnight, Audra."

He left in a swirl of expensive fabric, slipping out of the carriage. Alone with Kolbe in the stillness, Audra reeled from her first encounter with her future husband. He was kinder than she'd expected, but her thoughts lingered on Eva. Was her secret safe? Whatever came next, she anticipated it wouldn't be long. She had to find the killer before he found her.

6

A week passed after the gruesome conclusion of the masquerade ball, which ended the festivities in a rush. Audra returned to Hillsfield that same night without any formal announcement of her betrothal, and no indication of what might happen next. Even Lord Byron seemed unsure of the future.

Much of that week Audra spent watching Eva, grateful for the distraction. The child's laughter and innocent play heightened Audra's fear of losing her. Every time Eva's teal eyes met her own, a pang of memory surfaced. While Eva had inherited her mother's blonde hair, her father's teal eyes recalled his haunting memory. Her mother's temperament, mixed with his kindness, was living proof of the man who once existed. No matter how hard Audra tried to forget the day his body went rigid, or those eyes growing cloudy, Eva's existence always brought it back. When he was buried, most of Audra's heart went into the ground with him. She was convinced no one would ever love her like that again.

With her marriage approaching, Audra also realized she might go months at a time without seeing Eva, forced to watch her daughter grow up from afar. Another fear nagged at her: what if she didn't even get that much time? Deep down, Audra believed her life was already doomed.

Night after night, sleep offered no reprieve. She lay wide awake, staring at shifting shadows, scanning for a cloaked intruder, jumping at every faint noise. Others in the estate remained untroubled, but each sound made her pulse race and her hands tremble. A few days earlier, she'd even slipped through the conjoined door into Kathleen's room and slept on the chaise. When Kathleen found her there the next morning, Audra blamed nightmares. Often, she tried to slip out and check on Eva, but guards stood posted at her door, assigned by Lord Byron after her last escape; the one Kolbe had informed him about to provide himself an alibi.

That night, however, would be different. Audra waited, watching for shadows that never showed. She counted the seconds until the guards would change shifts, biding her time. If she ever wanted to rest again, she must act. Otherwise, she'd spend the rest of her short life waiting for death to claim her.

When the sun began to rise over the eastern mountains, Audra knew it was time. The guards stood watch only until daybreak. She needed to move fast in order to slip back before anyone noticed her absence. Swiftly, she hurried her way through the estate's gray corridors and out a ground-floor window.

Clutching her black cloak, she stepped into the chilly morning. Her breath fogged in the cold air as she raced to a spot where she'd dug a small hole beneath the gate—a trick from her childhood days roaming the countryside. Moments later, she was out of sight, heading down the winding streets of Althenia. The rising sun was lost behind the mountains, keeping her in the shadows as she wove through the beige-walled marketplace to her destination: the apothecary. She had often passed by, but never stepped inside. At this hour, the front door would be locked, so she walked through they alleyway to a narrow set of stairs leading down to the cellar. Taking a steadying breath, she banged on the service door.

As predicted, there was no response. She knocked again, louder, hoping not to wake half the town in her desperation. When she lifted her hand for another attempt, the door opened a crack.

"What in all hell is a lady doing here at such an hour?" a gruff voice demanded, betraying the speaker's annoyance.

Audra refused to be deterred. "I'm on urgent business from the palace," she lied. "He needs certain items back at the castle before he wakes. If you'd rather turn me away, I can inform him you aren't willing to help at this hour."

The old man eyed her from head to toe. "Prove it."

Audra shook the bag of coins she carried, a substantial sum saved from her dressmaking days. That convinced him. He opened the door wider, letting her in. She felt a surge of relief that her ruse had worked, though she prayed it wouldn't come back to haunt her.

"What does His Highness need that's so urgent?" he grumbled. The room appeared cramped and dark, with little more than a bed and a small table. He limped along the wall toward a set of stairs leading to the main shop.

"Information about poisons, on behalf of the murder of Mistress Isabelle," Audra said, following him up the steps. They emerged into a large space lined with shelves bearing potions and remedies. Gesturing for her to wait at the counter, he looked her over warily. She turned her back, hiding her face from anyone who might peer in from outside.

The old man raised an eyebrow. "Poisons? Don't you mean Mistress Margaret?"

Audra's stomach dropped at her friend's name, but she forced herself to stay composed. "No, Mistress Isabelle. The king's latest mistress."

"He's got another one?" the man said, shaking his head. "Not my concern, I suppose. What's your name?"

Audra hesitated, then answered, "Elizabeth Point, sir. And you are?"

"I'm no 'sir.' Call me Limney, Miss Point."

She nodded, steering the conversation back on track. "Since you haven't heard, the king's mistress was poisoned last week during the prince's engagement ball. The prince suspects whoever sold the poison may have information. Locals say you're the only apothecary in Althenia who deals with the needs of the crown."

Though Audra's certainty wavered, she kept her voice steady. She had her own life and Eva's to protect. Now was no time to falter.

Limney glanced at her from behind the counter. She noted the rows of dried herbs and spices on the shelves, reminiscent of the shop she'd known from her life before Hillsfield. His brows drew together. "I don't sell poison, miss. I sell herbs, plants, medicines, the like. If someone else knows how to turn them into poison, that's on them, but I don't do that here. Let's get that straight. However..."

He paused, tapping a gnarled finger against the counter. "I do recall a man coming in two weeks ago. Tall, Althenian. He wore a black mask. I thought that strange, but he asked for dried larkspur. Said it was his wife's or mother's favorite. I can't remember the specifics."

Audra's lips thinned. Larkspur was her mother's favorite flower, a plant that grew in Doth and was outlawed in Althenia after it killed some livestock. Her mother's birthday was two weeks ago. Was the masked man someone from Hillsfield? As Audra mulled it over, Limney went on. "I didn't have larkspur, so I offered dried lavender instead. He bought that and left. Didn't seem odd to me at the time."

Larkspur. The masked man. Audra remembered the flower from her father, who had once imported it from Doth to sell in Althenia. After his death, though, no one brought it across the border. She herself had searched in vain for it as a gift for her mother.

Was the killer taunting her? Did the victims see their deaths coming? And was Lord Byron, who valued chastity, behind such crimes? Audra chilled at the thought. Something was amiss.

She couldn't shake the notion that larkspur was a warning meant for her. She had spent years believing no one knew her secret. Now it seemed the killer did, and that threatened both Audra and Eva. That meant one option remained: she *had* to find the masked man before he found her.

Audra gave Limney the bag of coins and thanked him, cautioning that the prince demanded discretion about her visit. He agreed with a brief nod, and as Audra slipped out the way she'd come, she braced herself for whatever might follow.

7

Doth. If the larkspur hadn't come from the apothecary, then someone obtained it elsewhere. Audra felt sure her next clue lay in Doth, where she could learn who was buying the plant... and whether Hillsfield was the only place it was going to. Could Lord Byron be involved? It made no sense. The masked man was too young to be Lord Byron, and besides, Lord Byron kept his hair short. Audra realized what she had to do to get answers.

Stepping out of the apothecary's service door, she detected the sun crouching behind the taller mountain, shadows lingering in the strange morning light. She could borrow a horse from the Hillsfield stables and reach Doth by nightfall. Returning afterward would result in even more guards dogging her every step, but she had no other choice. For Eva's sake, she must find the person selling the larkspur. She *must* find the masked man before he discovered her.

Rounding a corner, she ducked into a back alley to remain unseen.

There he stood. Dressed in black. *That masked man.*

He was, without question, the same man she'd danced with at the masquerade.

He'd found her first. "Soon" hadn't been an exaggeration. How foolish to imagine she could outwit him. Her heart thudded, and her first instinct was to run. Looking around, it was clear he'd trapped her in a dead-end, someplace unfamiliar to her.

"Hello, Audra. Fancy seeing you here," said the masked man, flashing a strange grin. Audra turned, trying to dart past him, but he moved fast. His hand clamped over her mouth before she could scream. It happened so quick she had no time to do anything but struggle. Fear spread through her veins, certain he would cut her open like the other victims, or pour poison down her throat. His grip revealed how strong he was, anticipating her kicks and thrashing limbs as if they'd fought before. His hand muffled every possible attempt to scream.

"I realize you won't believe me, especially since I'm keeping you from screaming, but I will not hurt you," he said through grunted breaths. Audra fought to free an arm, remembering her dagger was strapped to her leg, just out of reach.

"Stop this. I have no reason to harm you. I want to talk," he continued, shifting his arm around her waist as she almost slipped free. Adrenaline spiked in her blood, and she tried again to wriggle an arm loose. If she could reach the dagger, she might stab him. He growled as he tightened his hold on her. "God, woman, you're not making this easy."

Audra twisted just enough to ram her elbow into his stomach. He grunted but didn't relent. "My spies saw you sneak out," he said, his tone still calm. "I followed you to make sure you arrived safely. If I intended to harm you, I already would have."

She paused, willing herself to breathe. He hadn't killed her yet, nor brandished a weapon. Despite her body relaxing, his grip stayed firm.

"Good," he said. "I'm going to let go now, but if you scream, I'll vanish. You have questions, I have answers. If you alert anyone, I'll vanish, and they'll never catch me. Let me remove my hand so we can talk, and I promise you won't be harmed. Decide now, because I'm letting go."

He released her in a quick motion, giving her a push toward the alley's exit. She stumbled on the cobblestones, heart racing. Glancing toward the street, she wondered if she could make a break for it. He stood there, large, though not menacing. His stance suggested he wouldn't pursue her if she fled. Curiosity pulled at her: what was he doing here, if not to kill her? Straightening her clothes, she steadied herself and decided not to run.

The masked man's shoulders eased, as though relieved by her decision to stay. She studied him, searching for any sign that she might know him.

"Do you know who I am?" he asked, his inquiry sounding almost amused. He rubbed his chin, where morning stubble shadowed his jaw.

Audra swallowed hard and tightened her hold on her skirt. "Seconds ago, I assumed you meant to murder me and add me to the string of dead women in Althenia, but now I'm less sure," she admitted, the words tumbling out before she could think. Her eyes narrowed, trying to see past the black mask. With his dark hair and the alley's dimness, it was impossible to identify him.

He nodded, a small smirk tugging at his lips. She discerned a faint lavender scent clinging to him and lingering on her mouth where his hand had covered it. *Lavender.* "If I planned to kill you, that was my chance. It's best if you don't know who I am. Safer for us both."

Audra slumped her shoulders, folding her arms across her chest. She stepped further into the alley's shadow so no passerby would see them. "You said you'd give me answers," she began, noticing that behind his mask, his smile widened.

He leaned a shoulder against the wall, about five feet away, picking at his thumbnail. "First, tell me this: what were you doing at the apothecary this early? Looking for something you don't want anyone to know about?"

She shook her head. "One question for each of mine that you answer," she insisted. "So far, we're at zero. If you weren't planning to kill me, why were you following me?"

He tilted his head. Another smirk lit his face, revealing white teeth. "I said at the ball, it's my job to stay informed about royal affairs. You're betrothed to Prince Elijah, which makes you my concern for the moment."

"So you work for the prince?" Audra pressed. His tongue clicked a small sound of disapproval.

"Your turn to answer," he reminded her. His gaze flicked toward the alley's mouth, where the sky began brightening. "What were you after at the apothecary?"

Audra hesitated. If he wasn't the murderer, then who was he? And why hide behind a mask? She realized she'd have to give him something if she wanted real answers. "I was looking for the poison that killed Isabelle at the ball."

He tipped his head up, as though considering this. "Poison," he repeated, though she couldn't see his full expression. "And what did you discover?"

Audra allowed herself a hint of triumph, suspecting she could keep him off-balance if she doled out information in small doses. "My turn," she said. "Who are you?"

His eyes locked on hers for a heartbeat, then he shook his head, as if he'd already made up his mind. "I told you—the less you know, the better."

Audra rolled her eyes and moved closer, thinking she might get a better look if she closed the distance. He straightened, backing away. "You said we'd trade questions," she pressed. "At least tell me whether you're the one killing these women. Am I a fool to stay here with you?"

He chuckled, his deep voice echoing in the narrow space. "I'm not the murderer. But I *am* dangerous. Whatever it is you're doing, looking for this killer, stop. As the prince's fiancée, it's in your best interest to keep out of the kingdom's darker business. I may not be murdering innocent women, but that doesn't mean I'm not a killer. Understand?" His tone made her shudder.

She peered at him. Oddly, instead of being terrified, she calmed in his presence, like some part of her recognized him. Was that why he'd asked if she knew who he was? "Have we met?" she asked.

"Hmph. You're clever, but all your questions are misdirected," he said, resting his back against the wall and stuffing his hands into his pockets. "Let me help you focus on what matters. My turn again: you learned something at the apothecary. What was it?"

Audra pressed her lips together, bothered. He was getting more out of this conversation than she was. "The apothecary said a man came in two weeks ago asking about larkspur. He wore a black mask," she said, arching a brow as she gestured to his mask, implying she suspected him. "Do you wear this getup all the time?"

"Is that your next question?" he asked, flashing a playful smirk.

"No," she snapped, thinking. "Why were you looking for larkspur, if not to poison Isabelle?"

He shrugged. "Whoever bought the larkspur in that shop wasn't me. It seems we're both hunting the same person. The question is, why are you interested in who bought it?"

"Is that *your* next question?" she quipped, allowing a coy smile to tug at her lips.

He released a rueful grin, then stepped away from the wall, pacing a few feet. Audra clasped her hands, noticing the muscles in his neck and arms. She caught herself picturing a handsome face beneath that mask.

At length, he said, "I think I've figured out your next move. You planned to ride to Doth, where they sell larkspur, presumably alone. I must say, not the wisest plan. It's good that I intercepted you. You won't go. I will."

"How did you—?" Audra started, feeling exposed. How could he have guessed that from so little information?

"I'm ten moves ahead of you, Miss Dione. I've been at this for a long time."

She exhaled a frustrated breath. "Fine, go to Doth, but that won't stop me from following. You might as well take me along."

He frowned, his lips tightening. As dawn brightened the alley, she saw the shape of his mouth more clearly, though the rest of his face remained shrouded. "No. It's not safe. I have the resources and experience to handle myself. You should return to Hillsfield and wait. In exchange, I'll meet you again in one week with what I find, on the condition you remain at Hillsfield."

Audra narrowed her eyes. She didn't understand what he gained from this deal. How could she be sure he'd keep his word and not vanish? She also couldn't rule out the possibility that time might be running out for her.

"What's in it for you?" she challenged.

He sighed. "I'm guessing I can't persuade you to give up your hunt?"

She shook her head, mouth set in a firm line. No. He could not.

"Then let's say it's for my peace of mind. I want you safe," he said. He did? To her surprise, her heart fluttered. Why should the idea that he cared about her safety thrill her? He was a dangerous man, possibly a spy, and *definitely* a problem. What kind of problem, she wasn't sure. *Yet.*

She took a step forward. He edged away. Understanding, she stepped back and sighed. "Fine. Any more questions?" she asked.

Grinning, he nodded. "Yes, one more: why the fascination with Mistress Isabelle's poison?"

She gave him a level stare. Perhaps this question called for an honest answer. "I've been living in fear, thinking I'd be the murderer's next victim. I wanted to outsmart whoever's hunting me. That led me here."

The masked man exhaled, pacing to her right and looking her over. "You suspected it might be me. Well, I won't reveal my name, but trust me on this: I have no intention of harming you, and I've never killed a woman." He glanced at the sky. The shadows were fading. "The prince will visit Hillsfield later this week, so you'd best return soon. Wash up, and ready your nicest gown. You can thank me for that warning some other time. For now, I must go, and you must return to Hillsfield. One week from now, meet me here—*alone*—if you want answers."

With that, he shot her a final look and slipped toward the alley's dead-end, vanishing through a narrow passage she hadn't noticed until now. As quick as he'd appeared, he was gone again, leaving her with a strange longing and a tangled curiosity. Despite all her instincts, part of her wanted to trust him.

But that might be the most dangerous impulse of all.

8

Audra spent the first night waiting in Kathleen's bedroom, surrounded by silver-vine wallpaper and yellow accents in every corner. Sitting at her vanity, Kathleen brushed her long black hair while prattling on about the masquerade and lamenting that she never got a glimpse of Prince Elijah to see if he was handsome. "If he looks anything like his father," she declared, "I'm certain he's as handsome as ever."

Though Audra found it odd that Kathleen fancied a man as old as the king, it wasn't surprising, given Kathleen's flirtatious nature. She fell in love with a new man every hour it seemed.

Audra hadn't told anyone about her meeting with the prince after the murder. As far as she was aware, neither had Kolbe. Instead, he went out of his way to avoid her, leaving any room just as she entered, always finding an excuse to disappear upon her arrival. As usual.

She didn't tell anyone about the masked man, either. Keeping that secret proved difficult, given that he occupied all her thoughts. The week of waiting felt like psychological torture.

Although they were the same age, Audra always felt like an older sister to Kathleen, who often seemed oblivious to reality. Peculiar, though, was the fact that Kathleen had been married once. She seldom mentioned it, except to complain about how cruel her husband was, hitting her whenever she didn't behave as he liked. He racked up serious gambling debts and was murdered in his home for it two years ago.

No one mourned him when he died.

Kathleen, now widowed and penniless, returned to Hillsfield to live under its protection. Upon learning of Kathleen's abuse, Lord Byron promised that her next marriage would be of her choosing.

Kathleen's monologue continued about the hundreds of handsome men she had encountered at the ball and how she'd fallen in love with three of them. Then, she turned to Audra and asked her to braid her hair—a rare request, since Kathleen didn't let anyone touch her hair. Audra welcomed the distraction. Standing behind Kathleen, she ran her fingers through Kathleen's silky black strands, which reminded her of someone else.

"If only you could fall in love one day, Audra," Kathleen said, smiling at her reflection. "Once you fall in love, you become addicted."

Audra smirked at the remark. Kathleen always claimed to be in love with any man who so much as complimented her. Audra doubted Kathleen knew much about real love.

"I have been in love," Audra said after a pause. It was true. She didn't like to think of it, but with so many uncertain changes looming in her life, she decided someone might as well know. Her mother would take Audra's secrets to the grave, but then who else might ever learn the real her? Who knew if she'd get another chance to share?

In the mirror, Audra saw Kathleen arch an eyebrow, her dark eyes waiting for Audra to admit it was a jest.

"He was my childhood friend," Audra continued, braiding Kathleen's hair as she smiled at the memory of her adventures in the woods with the boy who saved her life. Unlike the other boys, he never made fun of her blonde hair. He always said he liked it. "In the countryside, there was a widow who lived on the property next to ours. She had a son two years older than I. His name was Garrick." His name caught in her throat. She couldn't recall the last time she spoke it aloud. "We played in the woods and the river. Our mothers became close friends." Their families had leaned on each other for everything: farming, chores, loss, and grief. Audra's eyes glowed with the recollection.

"After my father died, our mothers grew even closer. Garrick's mother had been ill for years, so my mother often cared for her. That was also when we started the dress shop, which you've heard about. Garrick worked our fields as a boy, and my father paid him. When I witnessed my father's death, Garrick was the one who wiped my tears."

Tying a ribbon around the end of Kathleen's braid, Audra allowed the memories to wash over her. Their home was a place of comfort, something she missed when she remembered her younger days. Kathleen turned to her, eyes wide, lips parted. "You've never mentioned him before," she said, both surprised and curious. "What happened?"

Drawing a breath, Audra looked down at her hands that had once cradled his head as she watched him fall cold and lifeless. "He was killed," she managed, closing her eyes upon the well of tears that threatened to fall. That was the first *murder* she'd ever witnessed.

There were so many moments she wished she could rewind time to bring him back. Ever since, she'd feared she would never be loved that way again. Try as she might, nobody would ever replace him. Men like Kolbe intrigued her, but nothing ever grew from it. Whether or not Elijah realized it, he had a hole to fill that might be bottomless. She wasn't certain she wanted him to. The months she spent mourning were months she never wanted to live through again, and the thought of loving someone again and losing them made her feel like love could kill her.

If the murderer didn't do it first, anyway.

Had it not been for Eva, Audra might have ended her own life back then. He'd left her with a gift before he died: their child, who shared his perfect teal eyes.

Kathleen took Audra's hand, leading her to the bed draped in a yellow satin duvet. Sprawling onto it, Kathleen patted the spot next to her. Audra lay beside her, resting her head on Kathleen's shoulder with a deep sigh. Kathleen offered her condolences, then asked, "Would it help if you told me more about him?"

Audra released a faint smile, letting the memories spill forth. They'd been friends for years, but only one night had they been more. She replayed that night in her mind many times, hoping to make sense of it all.

"I once confessed my feelings to my mother after Garrick and I fought. I made daily trips to town to manage the dress shop. It was a brutal winter, his mother was growing weaker, and each day trudging through the snow in the carriage was misery. I didn't see him outside of supper. My mother and I helped his mother as much as we could, then we would head home to collapse in our own beds. One morning, we found she had passed during the night. Garrick never told us, or we would have come sooner." Kathleen listened, playing with Audra's blonde hair as she paused to sigh.

"Garrick always dreamed of becoming a knight. He'd delayed going off to train because of his mother's condition. Before my father died, he'd given Garrick a sword he'd traded at the market. Garrick practiced every day, swearing he would leave the countryside, compete in tournaments, and see the world."

Audra paused again, recalling Garrick's passion. He had practiced with local boys and tried teaching Audra once, but his sword was too heavy for her. However, with time, she excelled at handling a dagger. He'd gifted one to her after the time he saved her from two neighbor boys who tried to drown her for her blonde hair. She might have become even better with a dagger than he was by the end.

"I fell in love with his voice. His kindness. The way he made me laugh," Audra continued. "I never quite sensed how I felt at first, with him being two years older and calling me his little sister. He insisted he never planned to marry. It seemed like his way of telling me not to get my hopes up. Nothing happened between us until my sixteenth birthday, when he told me I wasn't his true love."

She remembered him almost kissing her at the waterfall that day, pulling away at the last second. There were many reasons he did, but none of them mattered anymore. She recalled some stories she'd read where people die and still miraculously survive. This wasn't that story. When people die in the real world, they stay dead. It was a fact Audra never stopped bargaining with.

Kathleen remained rapt, her eyes wide at the revelation that Audra had kept this hidden for so long. If Audra admitted she'd loved before, she might as well admit why she couldn't love again. Perhaps the closest she'd come was with her feelings for Kolbe, but she felt certain he didn't return her affections.

Audra ran her hand over the velvet of her maroon skirt. "He was nineteen when his mother died. He always said that once she passed, he'd leave to train as a knight. So, the morning she passed, I knew his departure was imminent. My mother left me alone with him to summon the mortician, telling me to stay behind and comfort him. But, truthfully, I was the one needing comfort. Losing Garrick was a greater loss for me, and he didn't realize the tears in my eyes were as much for him as for her."

Pressing her finger to her temples, Audra sighed. "After that, I went to check on him every day, anticipating the day he would tell me he was leaving. He never said it, but I could tell he was distant and distracted. I would ask how to help, and he would say he needed none, and he would walk me home. Sometimes he would talk about things on the way. Some nights, the walk was in silence. It broke my heart every time.

"Weeks, months, another winter passed, and I neared my eighteenth birthday, but nothing happened. Each day was the same: a quick visit followed by a twenty-minute walk home."

Audra closed her eyes, envisioning the way his short black hair rested on his head, or how his deep teal eyes used to make her heart beat. Why did the world give her someone to love so much just to take him away? No matter how many times she toiled over it, it was how she discovered how unfair life could be. There aren't always answers, and it was unfair that she didn't get to choose who stayed in her life and who left. Death never got easier. She just had to find a way to live without the ones she loved.

"Did he ever leave?" Kathleen asked, shifting so she rested her head on Audra's stomach.

"No... " Audra said. "He confessed that he loved me, and we kissed." Her eyes closed, trying to recall every intimate detail as the memory of that one spring night burned in her mind. Her mother was away at Hillsfield to discuss the shop's lease with Lord Byron, leaving Audra on her own that night.

Mystine had told her it was normal for Garrick to go silent while he grieved. Mystine urged Audra to allow him time and assured her he would talk to her like he used to when he was ready. Audra tried to be patient, but grew weary as each day passed. Then, one day, after learning some information while in town, she had suffered enough.

When she entered his home that evening, he was eating at the table with a bottle of whisky, as usual. He faced her and nodded, as usual. He resumed what he was doing without another word, as usual. She'd been angry that day, hurt, and unable to contain herself.

Audra had waited enough. She'd marched to his cupboard, grabbed herself a glass, and went over to the table with him. She'd poured a glass of whiskey for herself. He'd observed her, as if amused. Then, she'd sat across from him and swallowed the entire glassful, poured another, and stared at him, more serious than ever. "When are you leaving, Garrick?" she'd asked him, direct and bold because she couldn't live with the torture anymore. "Why won't you tell me?"

She remembered that his expression changed from amusement to something she couldn't interpret. He'd shaken his head. "I'm not ready to have this discussion today. Finish your drink, and I will walk you home once you're sober. Have you had anything to eat?" he'd asked.

"No," Audra had replied.

"Are you hungry?" he'd tried.

Maybe there was more, but they weren't the parts Audra remembered or dreamed about. The next words she said to him changed everything. "No. I meant, no, you're not walking me home until I know why you've been avoiding me. I get this feeling like you were going to leave and you weren't going to tell me." She'd looked at him to see how he would react, and his face had changed to something of guilt. She'd realized she'd guessed it. "That's it then? You weren't going to tell me? You were going to leave and hope I didn't notice, or care?"

She remembered how he pounded his fist on the table, startling her. "It was better this way, Audra," he'd said, and it hurt even more to have him confirm that he was, indeed, leaving. Worse, he wasn't going to tell her. "Being a knight means years of training, starting with no pay, having to do things on my own. I need to start being on my own."

She'd swallowed her tears and asked him, "When? When are you leaving?" She wasn't sure she'd wanted to hear the answer.

"Six months ago," he'd said. "That was the first time I planned to leave. Six months ago, because I vowed that I would leave the same day she died." Audra recalled her confusion. She knew he'd made a vow he would leave the same day his mother died, but months had passed since that day.

Garrick had looked at her, approaching her, the first time he had truly *looked* at her in months. He'd said, "The second time I tried to leave was the next day. Then the day after. Then the days faded together, and I had to re-resolve to go. So, I did. I promised myself I would leave when it got warmer again. It's been warm for two weeks now, and I'm still here, promising myself each morning that this day will be my last one here, and each night I find myself sleeping in the same bed again."

So, Audra had asked him, biting back tears, "What is keeping you from leaving?"

Without hesitation, he'd answered, "You are."

Kathleen squealed into a pillow, bringing Audra back to the present. Yellow walls, sunflower motifs, and the faint smell of citrus surrounded them. Kathleen hugged the pillow as if it were Garrick himself. "How did he say it?" she asked. "Give me every detail!"

Audra let herself get lost back into the memory, chuckling at her enthusiasm. "He said something like, 'I want one thing more than knighthood, and even though I know what's best for us, I can't leave because I want to see you just one more time every day. Then we walk home, and I want another walk. Even though I know I shouldn't be selfish and marry you because you deserve more, I still want you with every piece of my shredded heart, and it writhes me to my very bones.'"

Kathleen squealed again, burying her head in a pillow.

Audra recalled they'd got swept up in a moment of passion, sharing the whole evening, the whole night, and still lay awake as the sun rose the next morning. They'd learned of the deeper, more intimate desires of one another's souls. They'd connected deeply over their shared passion for desire. The darkest secrets that Audra held inside for so long, discovered deep between their every kiss that night.

She stopped before mentioning any of this, or Eva, the child she'd conceived from that single night. Kathleen flipped onto her stomach, frowning. "Wait. You said he died?" she asked, her tone subdued.

Audra nodded. "We planned to marry. My mother said she'd bless our union if he proposed. She loved him like her own son. The next morning, Garrick went to the kitchen, and I went to his room... collecting a few things," she said, cheeks burning at the memory as she changed a few details. "I heard a crash, and I predicted from the sounds it was a fight. Another man's voice echoed something I couldn't understand. I hid in the closet. Then everything went silent. Someone left, and I never saw who it was."

She described huddling in the closet for minutes that felt like hours until she had emerged to find Garrick lying in the kitchen, clutching his chest. She had cradled his head and begged him to survive. He'd died in her arms, turning cold and stiff in her lap.

A new detail surfaced in Audra's memories, one she often tried not to question. Larkspur was scattered around the room, shredded on the kitchen table and floor. The official cause of Garrick's death had been poisoning, though in her memories, she recalled pot after pot knocked to the floor, as if the poison had been part of the struggle.

Audra sat up. Did this connect? It might be a clue. It aligned with what Elijah had said: the murders all targeted those deemed "unchaste" in some way, like Margaret, Isabelle, and the lovers found in the street.

Had the same killer targeted Garrick?

Audra rose from Kathleen's bed, her heart pounding. An idea surfaced about where to search next. "Sorry, Kathleen, I'm feeling a little faint. I think I need to lie down," she said. In truth, she had no intention of sleeping. She couldn't save Garrick that day, a fact that tormented her endlessly. But a piece of him remained in this world, and she would do anything to protect that piece. Whatever befell Audra, Eva's safety must remain guaranteed.

9

Hillsfield's library boasted the richest collection in all of Althenia. Though it wasn't the largest, it was known for possessing the rarest books. Lord Byron allowed Audra to read any of them, as long as they remained in the library. In his free time, Lord Byron did little else but read, so surprised her not to find him there as Audra thumbed through the books on the second floor. Her fingers traced the bindings of old tomes while she searched for any clue she could find.

Ornate emerald carpets adorned the two-story room. On the second floor, a balcony overlooked the first, where a lounge area with brown leather sofas sat to the right of a spiral staircase. To the left stood the rare book collection, housed in dark mahogany shelves. Above her, a domed skylight provided the library's only illumination, and the smell of old pages filled the air—one of Audra's favorite scents.

"What are you looking for?" Eva's voice asked from beside her, making Audra jump. She turned to see Eva, her blonde hair arranged in several intricate braids around her childlike features. She wore a simple teal dress that matched the bright teal of her eyes.

"Oh. Hello, dear. I'm searching for a book about flowers. How was your tutoring session with Jed today?" Audra asked, steering the conversation away before Eva pried further.

"Boring, as usual. I wish I could go outside more, but Lord Byron says it's best to stay in until they catch the murderer. It's so dull indoors." Eva sighed and flopped into a blue armchair near the rare book section, staring up at the dome overhead.

Audra understood the desire to escape all too well. Inside the estate walls, time seemed to slow, and she'd felt like she was waiting for something—*anything*—to happen. Hillsfield often felt like a prison, where rules of propriety and social expectations caged them as much as the physical walls did. Her mother might thrive in a quiet routine, but Audra and Eva found it tedious.

"Why do you want a book about flowers?" Eva asked. Audra should have known better than to think she could stop Eva's questions. Her keen curiosity was unquenchable.

"I spotted a flower by the stables that piqued my interest," Audra said. "Speaking of which, it's been a while since we've ridden horses together. If you like, I can ask Kolbe if he wants to join us for a ride in the fields later?"

Eva perked up at once, leaning forward in the chair with her hands on the armrests. "Kolbe's back from Doth?"

Audra paused, her brows knitting together. That was interesting. "Kolbe's in Doth?" she asked, pulling a book from the shelf to skim its pages, hoping it contained the information she wanted.

"Yes, he left yesterday. He promised me a ride but broke his promise, like a big liar." Eva pouted. "Mother said he'll be back in a few days and that I need to forgive him."

Audra's mind whirled as she sat in the chair beside Eva, having found a page about delphiniums but found herself unable to concentrate on the text. Why would Kolbe have gone to Doth? That was where the masked man was. It seemed too coincidental.

Before they discussed it further, Lady Mystine appeared at the top of the spiral staircase. Holding up the plum-colored skirts of her dress, she called to them. "Pardon the interruption, my dearest daughters. We have company in the foyer, and I think we should

.. find something else to wear," Mystine said, eyeing Audra's maroon dress and somewhat rumpled hair. Pressing her lips together, she shook her head. "Eva, please go to the foyer and let Lord Byron know we'll join everyone once we've freshened up."

"Who is it?" Eva asked. Audra appreciated that Eva's youth allowed her to ask such blunt questions. Mystine was less patient when time was pressing, but she was gentler with Eva.

"It's Prince Elijah and a few members of the royal court," Mystine replied. "Now, off you go." Eva left the library like a fluttering butterfly, leaving Mystine to turn an all-too-knowing gaze on Audra.

Audra's heart sank and fluttered at the same time. The masked man had told her the prince would arrive soon, but between her sleepless nights and anxiety, she'd forgotten.

After Lady Mystine and Audra hurried to Audra's chambers, Mystine selected a navy dress from the closet and spread it on the bed. Audra spotted fresh lilies on the nightstand, replacing the tulips from that morning. She moved to her canopy bed with its ivory duvet, tracing the outline of the dress. She'd made it herself back when she ran the dress shop, complete with a large black bow on the bustle and delicate black lace trimming around the sweetheart neckline and three-quarter sleeves. Mystine pointed to the ivory-colored vanity, prompting Audra to sit. She undid the braid Kathleen had worked into Audra's hair the night before, letting the blonde waves fall free. Brushing them smooth, she pulled part of the hair back and tied it with a simple ribbon—an elegant, quick style suitable on short notice.

Once Audra donned the dress, Mystine sprayed vanilla-scented perfume over her hair and bodice, then surveyed her with approval. She took Audra's arm and tipped her chin, forcing their matching blue eyes to meet.

"Remember what I told you," Mystine said. "You must be the object of his every desire if this is going to work. Make him love you." Audra nodded. She understood that her survival depended on captivating Prince Elijah's heart. She might have given up on love herself, but perhaps it wasn't dead to him.

Mystine rushed with Audra in tow down to the foyer. There, Prince Elijah stood, handsome as ever in white garments trimmed with gold, his black hair brushed neatly aside. His smile brightened when Audra entered.

"Speak of your lovely wife and stepdaughter," the prince said to Lord Byron, "and here they are." Lord Byron stood alongside Kathleen and Eva. Next to Prince Elijah was an advisor, an older, formidable-looking man, and Pildrex, whom Audra recognized from the ball. Several palace guards lingered behind them. She noticed Kolbe was nowhere to be seen, further deepening Audra's suspicions about his trip to Doth. She also noted a large scar on the advisor's cheek and on Pildrex's forehead, a detail she hadn't observed at the ball.

Prince Elijah took Audra's hand and kissed it as she curtsied. "Audra," he greeted. "Shall we take a walk? You could bring a lady-in-waiting if you like, and we can chat in the garden. I've heard Hillsfield's gardens are breathtaking."

Her palms went clammy. She needed to enchant him, without fail. Mustering a smile, she said, "Yes, the gardens are a sight to behold. I would be delighted to walk with you, Your Highness." Her speech felt practiced, and she hoped he didn't notice.

"Please, call me Elijah," he corrected with a playful wink, giving her a half-smile that made her blush.

Looking around, Audra caught Kathleen's eye. Kathleen stood a few paces back, wearing an expression that all but begged Audra to choose her. "I'll take Kathleen with us," Audra announced.

"Excellent," Elijah said, extending his arms to escort them both. Audra and Kathleen each looped an arm through his as they led the way to the courtyard. They passed behind the grand staircase in the entrance hall, turning down a corridor that opened onto the estate's gardens. Audra couldn't help wondering if this visit signaled the end of her days at Hillsfield.

Outside, they descended several stone steps lined with matching vases, entering the hedged gardens. The shrubs were arranged in a maze-like design that formed the shape of a giant rose from above. Statues and flowers in full spring bloom hid behind twists of greenery. Soft shade fell over them as they strolled deeper into the garden, stopping by a central fountain. Elijah gestured for Kathleen to hang back, leaving him and Audra in a more private conversation. She noticed he hadn't spoken much yet and braced herself.

He spoke at last. "My father is in Doth with Kolbe Byron. He sends his regrets that he couldn't accompany me today. You'll meet him again another time, assuming I haven't bored you by then." He flashed her another wink, then leaned against the fountain's ledge. It was drained for the winter, still unfilled this early in spring.

"What business does he have in Doth?" Audra asked, trying to sound casual though her mind buzzed with questions. The king, Kolbe, and the masked man were all in Doth. It couldn't be a coincidence.

Elijah chuckled and patted the fountain ledge for her to sit beside him. "I'm told you're curious about politics, which I admire in a woman. Doth's ruling family has tried to marry me to one of their granddaughters, but I refused. Doth is in financial distress. It's not a good match. My father visits them to smooth things over so they don't take offense at our refusal. We accepted Lord Byron's generous dowry for you, which fosters better goodwill. Doth and Althenia rarely see eye to eye, so this marriage is helpful for us. My father and

Lord Byron don't much like each other, but they've found common ground here."

Elijah folded his hands into his lap, his feet facing toward her. His gaze lingered over her dress for a moment before returning to meet her eyes, a sheepish grin crossing his face.

Audra recalled Lord Byron's distaste for the king's well-known affairs, but she didn't realize the feeling was mutual. She was also startled to learn there was a dowry in place for her. Being "exchanged" made her feel more like an object than a person. In the countryside, she'd been free. In the confines of high society, she was a slave.

She fluttered her lashes, hoping to appear both curious and charming. "Is that why you're here, then? Official business?"

The gesture seemed to work. Elijah held out his hand, resting his arm on his knee. After a brief hesitation, Audra placed her hand in his, her heart pounding as she remarked the warmth of his touch. His gaze drifted to their joined hands while he spoke. "In part, yes. Mostly, I came to see you. The way we met at the ball wasn't what I had envisioned, and I want to know you better. I hoped we could spend time together before we wed."

He lifted his eyes to hers, and she noted the deep teal color they held, close to the hue of Garrick's eyes, a memory that made her chest tighten. She wondered if that was why he seemed so familiar the first night they met. She wondered if every time she looked at him if she'd always see the ghost of the person he would never be.

She drew in a slow breath, trying to push aside old attachments. "How long have you known about our betrothal? I only learned of it weeks ago, and I'm still in shock."

Elijah arched his brows. "I've known since it was arranged. When I heard you were a foreigner, the rumors worried me. Some claimed you were a witch. I admit I was superstitious. I don't think I came around to liking the idea until I met you that night at the ball. While I'm sure men say this to you all the time, I promise I mean it: you are the most beautiful woman I've ever seen." Audra blushed at the sincerity in his voice.

"I thought you already learned about our engagement," he continued. "How much were you told?"

Audra gazed at him, suspecting he was holding back more. "Not much. Only that it was arranged some time ago."

He nodded, giving her hand a gentle squeeze. "Yes, quite a while ago. My father set it up six years back after meeting your mother at her wedding to Lord Byron. He envied Byron for his blonde bride. They loathe each other's good fortune. My father wanted his own 'blonde beauty.' He had the nerve to ask Lord Byron about making you his mistress, but Byron refused. Since my father wouldn't give up, he arranged to have you as my bride instead. He even offered to waive your dowry. Lord Byron still refused to hand you over as a mistress and instead offered a much higher dowry than anyone else could match, on the condition that I wed you instead of the king." Elijah frowned, looking apologetic. "I'm sure you feel like a racehorse, being bartered for. That's the world of royalty, though. The bets are placed, but no one knows who wins until the end."

Audra felt her pulse quicken under his unwavering stare. She must capture his devotion, not just his passing interest. Her heart hammered as she realized how handsome he was. He was kinder than she predicted, too. The monstrous rumors she'd heard didn't match the man standing before her. She flushed, embarrassed as she caught herself staring at his jaw and his lips.

"Were you upset when you learned about this engagement?" Elijah asked, brushing his thumb along the back of her hand. The small motion sent tingling sensations along her skin.

"No," she said, smiling while trying to hide her nerves. "You're easy to speak with. I'm already growing fond of you," she added, ensuring she met his eyes and smiled in what she hoped was the most entrancing way possible.

A pleased grin crossed his face. "I'm happy to hear that, because I'm fond of you as well. There's another reason I asked you to walk with me. Beyond enjoying your company, of course. I wanted to invite you to the castle while we plan our wedding. You can help with any details you like, and I want you to feel at home there. After all, the future Queen of Althenia deserves to be pampered, and, well, Hillsfield is a bit... gray." He offered a playful smirk, and she couldn't disagree with that assessment.

"If you stay with me at the castle," he went on, "you can bring your own lady-in-waiting, and I'll see you have more ladies to dote on you, too. I want you to be comfortable in your new home."

Releasing her hand, Elijah dropped to one knee. Audra inhaled, surprised. He added, "I had another purpose in coming here. I wish to give you a proper proposal. I'd like to ask for your hand in marriage, my dear, so you may become the next Queen of Althenia. In return, I promise you'll never want for anything."

Though she realized she had no real choice, the gesture still charmed her as he pulled out a ring. At the castle, she might find more allies and more ways to keep herself and Eva safe. A tremor of doubt infiltrated: what if he discovered she wasn't a virgin? Could he love her if he discovered all her secrets?

She understood refusing him was unthinkable. Besides, the castle would have extra guards to protect her if the murderer was still at large, right? And if there was ever a chance to shield Eva, she had to take it. Even if that meant living apart.

"Yes, of course I'll marry you," Audra replied. Elijah grinned, sliding a large, gold-set diamond ring onto her finger. He lifted her hand to kiss her fingertips, then rose, guiding her to her feet.

He studied her, a shy pride in his smile. "May I... embrace you?" he asked. Audra nodded, allowing him to wrap his arms around her waist while she draped hers around his neck.

Over Elijah's shoulder, she spotted a statue of a gorgon by the hedge. Her heart thumped against his chest, as if it had just awakened after a long slumber. She would have to trust her instincts from here on out. If she enticed the prince to fall in love with her, maybe he would forgive any transgression he might ever find out about.

10

With one more day left before her meeting with the masked man, and still no success in the library's books, Audra realized her entire day would be spent pacing in front of the grandfather clock, waiting for sleep to come. Of course, she wouldn't be able to sleep that night, either.

The prince had left on the same evening of his proposal, an emergency arising that he said required his immediate attention at the castle. His absence made the days feel long and lonely. Before he departed, Elijah promised to send someone to escort her to the castle once she had time to pack, reminding her to bring along her chosen lady-in-waiting.

Kathleen squealed with delight when Audra asked her. They discussed the arrangement over dinner, as Audra wanted to help Kathleen find a suitable husband if she wished to remarry. Notably, Kolbe was absent during the meal. He had returned from Doth a few days earlier, but he'd been too busy with Lord Byron's affairs for Audra to confront him about it.

After dinner, Audra walked through the corridors back to the library, only to find Kolbe waiting outside with folded arms and a stern expression.

"You shouldn't have asked Kathleen to be your lady-in-waiting," he said, his tone matching his stance. "You could have chosen anyone, so why her? You and I both know that indulging Kathleen with courtly male attention will harm her. She'll become the castle's most notorious flirt and end up in trouble she can't escape."

Audra's cheeks heated, and she huffed. Who was he to tell her what she could or couldn't do? Realizing this was her first chance to speak to him since his trip to Doth, she ignored his admonition and went straight to her own questions. "Why were you in Doth for almost a week?"

Kolbe raised an eyebrow before scowling again. "None of your business. Who told you I was there?"

"How is it not my business? Elijah told me himself, citing it was about our engagement. Sounds like my concern," Audra said, crossing her arms.

Kolbe glanced around and exhaled in defeat. Then, looking at a nearby service closet, he said, "Come here." Before she knew it, he tugged her inside, shutting the door. The cramped space had no windows, just a single broom. It was barely large enough for both of them, and the darkness magnified the musky warmth coming off his body, which stood only inches from her.

He spoke in a whisper as soon as the door clicked shut. "It's my job to know what happens in the estate I'll inherit, which includes the affairs of those who live here. Yes, I went with King Henri to discuss your engagement. Now, about Kathleen..."

Suspicious of his sudden secrecy, Audra narrowed her eyes in the dark even though she doubted he could see it. "Eva told me you were in Doth, too. Interesting that she knew before Elijah said anything." Her eyes adjusted to the darkness, making out Kolbe's features. Over the years, he had avoided her company, yet here he was, inches away in a closet. His guarded expression gave nothing away.

For a split second, Audra wondered if Kolbe could be the masked man. That man had also gone to Doth and claimed to make it his business to know everyone else's secrets.

Kolbe sighed, appearing to give in to her questions first. "As I said, Lord Byron sent me to Doth. He wanted Hillsfield represented and asked me to purchase some larkspur—"

"Larkspur?" Audra almost screeched, but Kolbe cut her off.

"Yes, *shh*. Why are you acting so strange?"

"Me?" Audra repeated, lowering her voice. "You're the one acting strangely. Why are we in a closet?" She wasn't sure if the heat she felt was from their cramped surroundings or from being so close to him.

"Because I don't want anyone overhearing what they shouldn't," he replied. "Your father used to sell exotic plants, didn't he? Lord Byron said he wants to surprise your mother. He said larkspur was her favorite flower, and she hasn't seen it since your father died."

Audra blinked, looking away, thoughts racing as she tried to fit the pieces of the puzzle together. She had searched for that flower herself once. Was Kolbe lying? If he were the masked man, she doubted he'd admit it.

Despite this, she decided to probe him further. "When you told me you know more about me than I realize, what did you mean? What do you know?" She waited for a sign on his face to indicate he was hiding something.

Kolbe shook his head, dismissing her question. "I know enough," he said.

Rummaging through her memories, Audra recalled how the masked man also evaded direct questions with cryptic answers. She pursed her lips, choosing another angle. "How long have you known about my betrothal?"

Kolbe paused. "A while."

Her suspicions heightened. The masked man had known about her betrothal, too. It made her heart clench, anguished that he'd kept so many secrets from her. For years, Kolbe had avoided her, withholding truths that might have changed things. He claimed he was her friend, yet never let her in. She could admire him afar, but he'd never let her closer than sight.

Audra remembered the first time they met. It was ten years ago, when she was fifteen and her mother wasn't yet married to Lord Byron. She found Kolbe in Hillsfield's library, hiding from his uncle. That evening, they read poetry and teased one another. She believed he was interested in her. Afterward, he never contacted her despite his promises. Later, when she saw him collecting rent at her mother's shop, he arrived with another woman and acted as if Audra were invisible.

In the last few years, Kolbe hadn't been seen with any women. She once hoped it was because he harbored feelings for her. That, or he despised her. She also remembered the night he helped her after she found Margaret. He'd carried her back to Hillsfield and said he was her friend.

Feeling cramped in the closet now, Audra shifted. "If we were friends, why not tell me about my own betrothal?" she asked in a melancholy whisper.

"This isn't the right place for this conversation," Kolbe said, but Audra refused to back down.

"No, now," she insisted. "How could you claim to be my friend but hide things from me for years? Then you helped lock me away at Hillsfield with extra guards on my door? And now you have the *nerve* to order me not to choose Kathleen? She's my only friend. Meanwhile, you kept me at arm's length all this time. How dare you say I'm the one being selfish?" Her fury built inside, and she clenched her fists, glaring up at him in the dark. For a moment, she wished she could punch him.

Kolbe grabbed her arm, rougher than he should have, pulling her closer to whisper in her ear. The movement made her heart race as his firm grasp held her. She thought her entire body turned up at least one hundred degrees. "Your mother didn't want you to know your time with Eva was limited," he said, his voice low and urgent.

Audra yanked her arm away. Her eyes widened, and her heart pounded. How could he know about that?

She chose her next words with care. "So? Every woman's time with her sister is limited."

"If you say so," Kolbe replied curtly, his gaze locking on hers in the darkness. His eyes told her everything she needed to know, and she understood the implication: he discovered Eva wasn't her sister.

Audra pressed her lips together, a thousand thoughts churning. "How do you know?" she whispered. Her mother insisted that no one could ever find out. No one. How could Kolbe be aware of the truth?

The only person Audra ever told was Margaret. It was a night after Margaret confessed some of her own secrets about a lover she had in town, confessing stories of times she'd snuck away with him. Audra wouldn't have told Margaret if she thought there was any chance Margaret would betray her. It would hurt her if she had.

"No one told me, if that's what you're wondering," he said, shifting. Audra couldn't tell if it was the cramped setting, the conversation, or both that made him uncomfortable.

"How, then?" she insisted.

"I found out the week you moved here, when Eva was a newborn. My uncle told me to fetch your mother, but when I got to her room, I heard the baby crying. Nobody answered when I knocked, and after a few minutes, I assumed she might not have heard me. I worried Eva was alone. So I opened the door... and saw you breast-feeding her. I shut it right away."

Heat rushed to Audra's face, mortified. *Oh, lord.* "And then?" she asked.

"I asked my uncle about it, and he confronted your mother, who confessed. Lord Byron decided we'd keep it a secret at her request. She insisted you didn't know we knew. I gave my word, and I've kept it." He paused, then added, "I never meant to hurt you."

Audra let the silence linger. Why had her mother never told her that Kolbe and Lord Byron also knew? The way Kolbe spoke gave no indication of his personal feelings on the matter or if he thought any less of her for it. Is that why he avoided her all those years? "If you didn't want to hurt me," she said, "why tell Lord Byron in the first place? You knew it would be dangerous."

Kolbe swallowed, and at such close range, she could almost feel it. "I believed him to be already aware. I had no idea I'd discovered something he didn't know. That was my mistake, and for that I apologize."

Questions buzzed in her mind. Did Kolbe think she was immoral or unworthy? Was that why he avoided her? "Why are you telling me all of this now?" Audra asked.

"Because... *fuck.*" Kolbe backed against the wall with a frustrated grunt, then stepped toward her again. "Because," he said again, "I wanted to protect you."

"Lying to me was 'protecting' me?" Audra asked, her frustration unmistakable.

He sighed. "When I realized Lord Byron didn't know Eva was yours, I told him I'd marry you to safeguard your honor. That way, no one would ever discover the truth."

Audra froze, her entire body coursing with heat. At this rate, she thought she'd be cooked medium-well by the time she left the closet.

Kolbe had offered to marry her? Did he do it purely out of duty, or was there more to it?

"That same day," Kolbe continued, "I found out you were already promised to the prince. They asked me to keep it secret so you could spend more time with Eva at Hillsfield before you had to leave. None of us meant for it to be a prison. Your mother just wanted to delay your marriage so you could remain with Eva as long as possible. I'm telling you now because you're leaving. I'm trying to make amends for following orders instead of being the friend you needed. I reflected, and you're right. I wasn't always a friend to you."

Audra's heart pounded. A small, desperate part of her wondered if there was more. Had he ever desired her? Her mind screamed at her to stop, but her mouth moved on its own. "Did you love me?" she whispered, her voice shaking.

Kolbe's face tensed in the darkness. Her heart squeezed inside her chest. "What?" he asked.

Her pulse hammered in her ears, but she knew it was too late to back down. "I think I was clear, and my question was reasonable. You avoid me at every turn. You race out of every room the moment I enter. You never look at me. You ignore me whenever possible. I can't help but wonder why you would do all that if you don't have feelings for me?"

He seemed to regard her fiercely now, the intensity of his stare almost knocking the breath from her. "We can't discuss this. You're engaged to the prince, it would be treason for me to say otherwise. I could never love you. I did not, and I would not. I only wanted to protect your secret. That's all."

The words stung like daggers. As painful as it was, a part of her already knew he never felt the same. Yet, hearing it aloud still made her heart twist. At least now she confirmed it. He would never love her.

Trying to push aside her pain, she told herself it was for the best. If she were to marry Prince Elijah, she would let Kolbe go, once and for all. Perhaps now she would have the strength to do so.

Her hands trembled, so she clasped them together. Her voice quavered as she spoke. "I think I'll go to my room now. Please don't seek me out again unless it's a matter of business. I believe I outrank you these days, so if I want to speak, I'll summon you. I'm the future Queen of Althenia, and I choose my own lady-in-waiting."

Kolbe exhaled an exasperated huff. "I've never treated you as my inferior. I made damn sure of it. I've overlooked your sneaking out. I never used my authority over you." He stepped closer to her, pressing his chest against hers, and she made out the derisive look on his face. "If the 'friendship' you want is one where you control me, then yes, '*Your Majesty*,' I'll do as you ask. But don't confuse love with caring. Love is fickle. Caring is genuine."

"Please go," Audra murmured, tears threatening to break free if she said another word. Thankfully, he understood, giving a single nod before leaving her alone. With the closet empty, her heart grew heavier. The moment he disappeared, she sank to the floor as if held down by shackles she could no longer carry the weight of.

So that was it. A masked man he was to her, indeed.

11

Audra entered the library again the next morning. Dark brown mahogany contrasted against emerald green damask wallpaper adorning the room. Just as she arrived, she discovered company, startling her for a moment before she realized it was Jed. The smell of lavender wafted through the air as he approached her.

Lavender... The way he smiled at her made her think he'd found just the thing he was searching for. Audra raised an eyebrow, her heart thumping against her will.

She had always thought Jed was handsome, though not in the same way as Kolbe or the prince. Audra used to attend Jed's tutoring sessions with Eva as her escort, but Lady Mystine forbade it after catching Audra and Jed alone one night. Nothing shocking had happened that night, but Lady Mystine didn't believe it. Audra and Jed had exchanged books they'd discovered and enjoyed from the library, and through this, they'd developed a friendship over their love of literature.

One night, after Audra had finished a book she loved more than others, she couldn't wait to discuss it. In the dark hours, she'd gone to Jed's small, private chamber in the west wing of Hillsfield. Jed, as excited about the book as Audra, didn't think twice about letting her in.

After that, Mystine demanded that Audra never speak to him again, unless politeness required it while others were present. Otherwise, she was to avoid him at all times. It felt like one more rule to ensure she never enjoyed anything at Hillsfield.

Some days, Jed made it impossible to avoid him. At first, when she kept her distance, he wanted to know if she was upset with him. Then, he wanted to know if he could help her. He'd received flat responses each time, so he'd take the cue and leave. The sadness in his eyes each time made it harder to follow her mother's command.

This time, Jed had a different look in his eyes, one she wasn't used to seeing on his face. Was it excitement she sensed?

He confirmed it when he spoke. "Audra. I hoped I'd find you here. I saw some books you left open earlier, and I couldn't help but wonder if this was the book you might be looking for." He handed one over to her, and she saw the title. *Poisons and Posies.* An alchemist's book. She wondered if these books existed in Hillsfield or if Lord Byron banned them all.

Audra paused, trying to recall the titles of the books she'd left open. As she remembered, she flushed. One book about poisons, the lone one she'd found. Several books about flowers. She had placed them next to each other as she thought she had found some connected passages, to no avail. Audra looked at Jed with horror, and he replied with a wink as he handed it over.

"You're welcome," he said. "Also, I have a request. One day, there will be an open position as a tutor for the prince's future children. I heard about your engagement today, and congratulations are due. I hope you'll consider me to tutor your future children after all is done. If not, then I suppose this shall be my parting gift to you, Your Highness. My motive is not to use you for political gain. The choice is yours. I intend to make sure you understand you have one loyal friend, should you ever need it." He bowed, a sly smile on his face, then stood up and walked away before she could reply.

How did Jed know about this book, *Poisons and Posies*, and why did he have it? Why would someone read something like this without a reason? She recalled the lavender scent when she walked in. His grin hinted he held knowledge of something she did not. Where was he the last few days? He'd canceled all tutoring sessions with Eva, and she hadn't seen him once that week. He claimed he was sick. She hadn't thought to check before.

Was Jed the masked man?

Audra remembered she still had the evening to wait. It would be a sleepless night, so she told herself to think of it later and to read the book. Audra sat down on the nearest navy blue chaise, her eyes swallowing the words whole as she opened to the first page.

One chapter turned into five, then ten, then she fell asleep. It was the first time she'd slept in the last two days, the kind of sleep that pulled a person into complete unconsciousness. Nothing except brute force could wake her. The person who found her sleeping there made it easier to stay asleep by giving her a blanket and pillow sometime in the night... or morning... or afternoon. She slept through them all, including her anticipated appointment with the masked man.

Audra awoke, her eyes drawn to the sunset outside. Her equilibrium fought with her brain, making her believe it was sunrise instead of sunset, and that she woke up in time. She looked down to see that she was wearing the same dress from yesterday, but she didn't think she had time to change. To be safe, she rushed down to the balcony outside the library, then headed down the stairs and out of sight before anyone caught her.

She hurried toward town, trying to make it before sunrise, and she didn't notice it was getting darker instead of lighter until she neared the market. The market bustled with people, and she found it strange to find so many people out before sunrise. Then she realized the sun was not rising; it was ending its day.

Frozen with horror as she realized she'd slept through the meeting, Audra stopped. She'd missed it. Was it possible he still waited for her? Could she return the next day? She'd forgotten her cloak in her room, but in the dim light, she thought she could wind through the shadows to the apothecary's alley unseen. She waited half an hour until the sun left half a moon to guide her to the alleyway where she'd met the masked man before, stopping to wait for passersby until she reached their meeting spot from a week ago. At once, she spotted something on the ground. The shadows obscured it until she got near, finding bundled larkspur atop a folded note.

"*In case you find this letter, I found what you wanted to learn. I sent your friend a book that I thought you might be interested in. He should deliver it to you if he hasn't already. For whatever it's worth, I wish I could tell you everything. Believe me, it's best you don't know because what you could learn would get you killed. Your new home is dangerous, so be careful what you do there. I held up my end of the bargain, and we won't be able to meet again, so I bid you farewell.*

Your Friend"

She couldn't explain it, but the letter made her heart seep with melancholy. That was the end of him, then. She missed the appointment. He left her a note. Given the circumstances, she supposed it was kind of him to leave this note instead of nothing. She'd be on her own again.

Nothing she wasn't used to by now.

12

The next morning, Elijah sent a messenger from the palace along with several guards and attendants to prepare for her departure. He provided his royal carriage to fetch her and a lady-in-waiting of her choice: Kathleen. Kathleen spent most of the day assisting Audra in packing her belongings.

Kathleen, of course, had been ready ever since she was asked to accompany Audra. In truth, there wasn't much Audra cared to bring. Elijah had told her not to pack much, promising to replenish her wardrobe tenfold. Thrilled by the idea of a new royal wardrobe, Audra packed a few sentimental pieces and nothing more. Some dresses were handed down from her mother. Another reminded her of the matching one she had with Eva, which they had specially created for a family portrait once.

Audra smiled, recalling her mother that day. They had rescheduled the portrait seven times because one person couldn't be present due to illness or work. Her mother was sick that day, but insisted they proceed because she refused to reschedule again.

Lastly, she packed the dress she'd worn to the funeral of the only man she ever loved.

Her last night in the manor felt surreal, like waiting in Purgatory before moving on to a new life. Hillsfield always felt like a cage, and she'd feared she would spend her life there. She never imagined what might come next, and now that she knew, it excited her. This could be the adventure she had always wanted.

Audra walked out onto her private balcony, which provided the perfect view of Eva's window. Though she couldn't see inside, as Eva's room was higher and her candle had burned out an hour earlier, the sight brought a pang of sadness. She would see her in the morning, but it was hard to accept that their days together were ending. Eva had been in Audra's life since Audra gave birth to her, and now she had to learn to live without her.

She wished things were different. Heartache didn't begin to describe it. In some ways, it was like losing Garrick all over again.

Before Audra turned to go back into her room to attempt to sleep, her eyes caught a black-haired man with a black cape walking into view, his head down. For a moment, her heart pounded in fear, but on a second glance...

The man looked up at her, his face disguised by a familiar black mask. It still covered most of his face except for his lower jaw and mouth. Audra tried to recall those lips, comparing them to men she knew, but they all began to look alike after a while. Watching Kolbe's lips in the closet had made her think of kissing them. In her twenty-five years, she had only kissed one man. Though she didn't think she would ever love like that again, she still craved those feelings. She wondered if the prince would be a good lover.

Her eyes darted up to Lord Byron's room, but his candle was out, and she seemed the only one awake. The masked man walked alongside the gray walls in the courtyard. In the courtyard's center, a fountain sprang to life, and vines lined Hillsfield's gray-stone fortress walls. He walked the cobblestone path below her balcony, slipped into a shadow, and put a finger to his lips.

Audra bit her lip, unable to contain her smile. She thought she'd never see him again. His appearance was a surprise, sparking her curiosity to a new level. "I got your letter," she said in a hushed voice, hoping he heard her. He sat on the ground, back against the wall, his black cloak merging with the shadows.

"If it wasn't you, someone found it. Glad it was you," he replied, his voice low.

Audra sank to sit on the balcony's edge nearest to him, resting her head against a pillar. "You wrote it was too dangerous to meet again," she said, probing his intentions.

He ran a hand through his hair. "It is. I shouldn't be here, but despite every trinket of common sense urging me to stay away, here I suppose I am. I was disappointed when you didn't come. It felt like I was robbed of my tenth birthday, forced to stay nine for another year."

Audra leaned closer, straining to hear him. His words required careful listening in their whispered tones.

"I was never meant to greet you in the ballroom that night," he continued. "That wasn't the plan, but I saw Pildrex and sensed it had to be the most miserable conversation. Every logical thought told me not to approach, but still I went. Now I can't stay away, though I must. What do you suggest to ensure we never meet like this again, hmm?"

Audra smiled, clicking the tip of her tongue. "Quite the dilemma. I'm not afraid of you."

"Maybe you should be," he replied without missing a beat.

She paused. "If you want me to think of you as dangerous, tell me what it is that I should be so afraid of," Audra said, wishing for a closer look at him. She could only see the top of his head, his shoulders, and legs sprawled out as he sat.

"Damn, you're clever. You've always been clever," he complimented with a chuckle. This confirmed she knew him somehow. Was it Kolbe, then, or... could it be Jed?

What if it was someone who admired her from afar, which was why she couldn't quite identify those lips? She needed a closer look.

"I don't suppose you've come to tell me who you are?" Audra asked, smirking. She figured it wasn't probable, but she could still ask.

He humphed, raising a knee. "Only two people are privy to that information, and you're not one of them, I'm afraid."

She frowned, disappointed but not surprised. "It wouldn't break any rules if I guessed, right?" she prodded, attempting to sway him.

The masked man laughed, a deep, short laugh. He tilted his head up to look at her, and even from there, she saw the half-smirk. "Alright, wise-ass. Tell me your guess."

Doubt filled her, wondering if she dared say. If he was dangerous, what kind of danger? What should she fear? When she thought about Kolbe as the masked man, nothing seemed to jump out as a reason. What secrets might he hold?

What if she was wrong?

Audra considered, then pursed her lips. "Hmm. I need a closer look."

The masked man snorted, dismissing her suggestion. "Ha," he said, but it had no mirth. "That won't happen. If I come closer, you'll try to unmask me. I sense mischief."

Audra smiled, enjoying the teasing. She liked a challenge, and she felt mischievous around him. Not knowing his identity made her feel free to say anything, as if he were a mirage, beyond reality. She changed her tone, using a more flirtatious voice. "I thought you forgot something and came to visit."

He shook his head. "No. I said all I needed in the letter. What's your next theory? Maybe I'm figuring it out too." He laughed again, his voice deep. "Perhaps I wanted to see you one last time before everything changes. At the castle, it's different. As I said, be cautious, keep your secrets. You can't trust everyone, so don't trust anyone."

Audra eyed him, studying the only part of his face visible—his chin and lips. An idea crossed her mind. "Maybe you won't tell me anything, but maybe you'll do me a favor," she proposed.

He turned his head up. "What favor?"

A rueful smile played on her lips. She wanted to entice him, and it seemed to be working. His reaction might give her clues about his identity. "Leave me with one unforgettable memory of Hillsfield. Climb up here and kiss me."

Once spoken, she blushed, surprised by her boldness. On one hand, the banter and his allure fascinated her beyond explanation. Even not knowing him, his charisma and mysterious allure excited her in ways she couldn't describe. However, a man adept with words might recognize the power of his lips.

On the other hand, it was the most daring request she'd made in eight years since her last kiss. This man could be anyone, which was why indulging her curiosity before leaving her old life behind seemed harmless.

The masked man grunted, standing, dusting himself off. "You're the devil, woman. I won't climb up to commit what some would call treason. Damn you, siren," he said, pacing a few steps before placing a hand on his forehead. *Siren* seemed harsh. Before deciding how else to feel, he returned to her, looking up from beneath the balcony. "Audra, don't be foolish. The only man you should kiss is your betrothed. You said you don't know me, I could be anyone, so—" He stopped, releasing air through his nose, annoyed. Though correct about the impropriety, his refusal seemed excessive.

He could just say no.

The masked man shook his head. "I must go. Coming here was a mistake. Remember, you're to be the future queen, Audra. *The queen*. Your duty is to marry Elijah and stay safe. No kissing strangers. You're a servant to the prince, and your life depends on it. Queens don't kiss unknown men."

She didn't need a lecture from him. Rolling her eyes, grimacing, she shook her head. As he began leaving, she raised her voice to have the last word.

"Don't play the guilt card. I've had enough judgment from those who had no right to an opinion regarding the matter of myself. I've kissed one man in my life. *One*, eight years ago. My life choices were always made by others. For once, I wanted control. This—a kiss from someone already sworn to secrets. You've shown you can keep them. At this rate, my grave may be the palace itself, if you speak the truth. 'No' would have sufficed." Audra stood, feeling defeated. Everything was decided for her, and that was that.

The masked man looked down, pocketing his hands. "I'm going. Goodnight, Audra." He disappeared into the shadows along the courtyard walls.

Audra strained to catch another glimpse but saw nothing. What was she thinking? How could a stranger have such an irrational hold on her emotions? Had her solitude made her unable to wait a few more days to be with her future husband?

Inside, she closed the doors, returned to her bed, and lay atop the ivory satin sheets. Her thoughts scrambled. Kolbe. It had to be Kolbe—practical and righteous, admirable and irritating. She held back tears, knowing she'd inflicted this misery upon herself.

A tap sounded at the balcony doors. Her heart raced as she jolted back up on her bed. It was the masked man. She stood, straightened her nightgown, and opened the doors, standing back.

He sighed, checking around him to assure that no one else saw. Shoulders slumped, he returned his gaze to her. "Here's the problem. I'll regret it if I don't kiss you now, assuming you weren't toying with me," he said.

Audra flushed, surprised, shaking her head. "Good," he replied. His grin was unmistakable as he entered her room and shut the double doors. Her heart beat in a mix of fear and excitement, and she froze, unable to move. His eyes took all of her in for a brief moment before he continued, "One thing to take care of, first."

In a swift movement, he reached forward to touch her, placing his hands on her arms to spin her around. He grabbed her wrists, holding them behind her back as he pulled the sash from around his waist, commanding her to hold still. She didn't resist as he tied her wrists together with the sash, his lips near her ear as he whispered, "So you don't get any ideas."

Once the knot was secured, he wasted no time. The masked man spun her around, using his body to push her backward a couple of inches. Audra found her back against the wall as the mysterious man in her room pressed his chest against her breasts, closing the distance between them. She whimpered in surprise. His hot breath warmed her neck as he inhaled her scent. Her vanilla perfume mingled with his musky scent. Her heart pounded, amused... intrigued... *aroused*.

The masked man placed a hand on her cheek, using the back of one finger to caress it, while his other hand braced the wall, trapping her. The mask shadowed his eyes, yet she recognized the glint of familiar desire. He leaned close, his hand cradling her head, lips nearing her ear. "If you want me to stop, say so. I won't harm you."

She nodded, her breath shallow. Certain she wouldn't object, he pressed closer, lifting her chin. His lips met hers, his movements starting out passionate and slow. The last time she kissed a man was years ago, and she didn't remember it being anything like this. Those kisses had been uncontrolled by passion and inexperienced. These kisses were smooth, deliberate, and intent. It was unlike any kiss in her memory—practiced, controlled, full of longing. As he kissed her voraciously, her body responded with a burning intensity, drawing a soft moan that deepened their connection.

The minutes stretched, but when he pulled away, she felt it was too soon. His eyes lingered downward toward her breasts, glistening with sweat, and she tried to catch her breath. His fingers traced down her neck, pausing at her collarbone. A part of her wished he'd continued, but knowing her engagement, she recognized it had gone too far. Not knowing him didn't help. Audra bit her lip, hoping to entice him back for more. He grunted, then pressed his lips to her neck for a moment, making her gasp. His hands gripped her waist, pulling his lips away from her neck. When he stepped back, his hands clenched into fists at his side.

"Your prince is a lucky bastard," he sighed. "Not to state the obvious, but tell no one. Not a soul. Understood? I was never here." He studied her, her hands still bound behind her, and she thought she detected a smirk. "I'll arrange for someone to untie you... goodbye, Audra. For good, this time. You must marry the prince and be a loyal wife to him. For the love of everything, do not kiss anyone else, lest you hasten your end. Be wise."

Before she could protest his equal role in their kiss, he turned and exited through the balcony door, closing it behind him.

Left alone, Audra stood flushed, kissed, and bound. She needed a story for whoever might untie her, praying it wasn't her mother, or she'd face dire consequences before even leaving Hillsfield.

13

S tanding before the readied carriages loaded with her belongings, Audra held back tears as she stood with Eva. She contemplated if this moment marked the last time she'd see her. A decorative net swept back Eva's hair, fully visible to Audra as she towered over her. Eva stood between Audra and the carriages, frowning.

"Audra, why didn't you choose me as your lady-in-waiting? I'm your sister, and Kathleen is just your friend," Eva said, her big teal eyes gazing up at her.

"You're too young. You need to finish your schooling before you can live at the palace," Audra replied, though she spoke more to convince herself. "When you've learned all Jed can teach you, I'll invite you to court to be with me. I promise." Audra intended to keep her promise as soon as possible.

"I want to come with you," Eva said, sniffing. A tear fell from her eyes, puffy from crying, much like her own. The two of them always shared a close bond, even stronger than the bond between Mystine and Eva. Audra wished Eva could come, too.

Seeing Eva cry broke Audra's heart. "I'll send for you as soon as I'm able. Besides, you'll see me in a month or so for the wedding. There's plenty to prepare... maybe you could be my flower girl."

Eva brightened at the idea, her lips curving into a smile. "Lavender. I could throw lavender petals. Wouldn't it be beautiful, with purple petals all around?"

Audra raised an eyebrow. Too many books on flowers lately made any mention seem noteworthy. Hearing "lavender" reminded her that Jed and Kolbe both smelled of it the last time she saw them. The masked man had hinted at it, too. It wasn't uncommon. In Althenia, lavender was blooming, with fields on every wealthy estate. Even Lord Byron owned a large field, sold to merchants traveling worldwide.

"Why lavender?" Audra asked, curious if Eva knew anything relevant.

"Because," Eva said, "Lavender looks like larkspur, Mother's favorite. Lord Byron gave her an arrangement this morning, including larkspur flowers. He said he fetched them from Doth to surprise her, to cheer her when you had to leave." Eva kicked her feet, staring at the ground. "I wish he'd gotten me something."

Larkspur. The poison that was used on Isabelle. Now, the flower was in Hillsfield. The masked man went to Doth. So did Kolbe. Jed disappeared for several days without explanation... And he'd delivered her a book from the masked man.

Was Jed the masked man? Could he be the man who kissed her last night?

Audra pushed the thoughts aside. She'd mull it over in the carriage. "We'll discuss flowers later, but I love the idea. Now, hug me because I'll miss you." Audra embraced Eva, trying to savor the moment as much as Eva did. Two palace guards approached to inform Audra that the carriages were ready.

Though only a four-hour ride from the estate to the castle, the upcoming journey felt ages away. Audra smoothed the fabric of her lilac dress to calm her nerves. It was the same one she wore moving to Hillsfield, the nicest she had then. Today, she wore it as a symbol of her new life ahead.

This time, she had to accept whatever came her way. Despite the hardships of castle life, she needed to embrace it. It would be her final life, whether she saw it through or faced execution for treason when the wedding night revealed she was not a virgin. She entered the carriage with Kathleen, watching her mother comforted Eva's tears as it pulled away from Hillsfield.

The cobblestone streets made for a bumpy ride through town and the market. Kathleen and Audra traveled as lone companions in her new carriage, the first gift from the prince. Inside, lavender velvet seats adorned an ivory carriage exterior with golden accents.

The interior also showcased gold leaf trimmed with artistic beauty. A table folded from the door for playing cards, but they decided to wait until they left the cobblestone streets. During their ride, they watched the market through windows, people waving as they passed. People recognized a royal carriage on sight.

During a bumpier stretch, the carriage door flung open, closing just as soon as a person entered. The masked man, poised to cover Kathleen's mouth, locked eyes with Audra. Her heart raced, recalling their kiss the night before, wondering why he was here again.

"Could you tell her not to scream?" the masked man said, eyes on Audra.

Still in shock, Audra nodded, then complied. "Kathleen, he's a friend. I'll explain later. Please, don't scream."

Kathleen nodded, and the masked man released her mouth, instructing Audra to sit beside Kathleen. He sat across from them. "It'd be more proper," he said.

"As proper as forcing entry into a royal carriage," Audra replied with a playful smirk. She found his sense of propriety amusing after their improper meetings, including the previous night's kiss.

Remembering Kathleen's presence, Audra turned to her. "I realize you're confused, Kathleen. I'll explain after we see what he wants." Audra faced the masked man, trying to stare into his eyes to discern their color, but the mask's shadows obscured them even in daytime. She wondered if he'd stop her if she tried to remove it. Nonetheless, she wanted information about why he appeared, and curiosity took precedence.

"Who are you?" Kathleen asked, squinting at him.

"The less you know, the safer you are. I'm here to warn you. Castle life is changing. No slip-ups or indiscretions. You must always be on your best behavior, even when unobserved."

The masked man's words were aimed at Audra as he continued. "Nothing scandalous must thrive. Hillsfield comfort won't exist at the palace. I'm disclosing more than advised, but a war with Doth looms, and Dothian spies may infiltrate. Trust no one until resolved. As Althenia's future queen, you're a target. And you," he said, addressing Kathleen, "must be the queen's loyal friend. Your lives are at risk. No gossiping about the queen among other ladies-in-waiting. Protect her, even at your life's cost. Betrayal won't be rewarded. If the queen dies, you'll die with her. Trust each other, and you'll have one ally at the palace, which you 'll need."

Kathleen and Audra exchanged glances. Audra knew Kathleen to gossip, yet never about her. To a friend, Kathleen was loyal; to acquaintances, less so. Audra trusted her.

"I wasn't here. This didn't happen," the masked man said. "Palace life is different. Be cautious."

Confused and weary, Kathleen asked Audra, "Do you know his real identity?"

Audra smirked. "Afraid not."

"How do you know you can trust him?" Kathleen wondered.

"We can agree that we must be cautious at the castle. All of Althenia will watch us," Audra said, then addressed the masked man. "Anything else? Perhaps share the murderers' identities so we recognize whom to watch?"

The masked man chuckled. "Please, the murders are no mystery. It's the killer's knowledge that's perilous. Whom they know about," he replied, scrutinizing Audra. His hand clenched into a fist on his knee. She understood his implication. She was a target, and he came to warn her, but...

"You know the murderer?" Audra asked. Why hadn't she inquired sooner? Had he always known?

"No, if anyone asks. The less you know, the safer you are." It figured. Another secret withheld.

"Am I next?" Audra probed, seeking solace for recent torment. Maybe peace would come if she weren't weary of every shadow in her room.

Silence answered first as he examined her. Words weren't needed to understand his hesitance. Instead, he shook his head. "Follow my advice, and you won't be endangered."

The carriage transitioned from cobblestone to smoother dirt roads. Before Audra dug deeper, a whistle sounded. She recognized the same tune she heard at the masquerade, interrupting and triggering commotion outside.

"Don't worry, ladies, just a distraction. No danger today," he assured, then sighed, hands clasped. His eyes locked onto Audra's as if he longed for her again, and although the mask concealed his face, he visibly swallowed hard. "Time to go." He slipped out of the carriage as it stopped amid the outside chaos. Yelling ensued, inexplicable words reaching her ears, yet window views offered no clarity. Yelling ceased, and the journey resumed. His sudden exits no longer fazed her, though she longed to understand his motives.

She braced for palace life vigilance. To guarantee safety, discovering the murderer before being discovered herself was imperative.

14

After the masked man's departure, Kathleen returned to her side of the carriage. She pressed her fingers to her lip, staring through the window as they moved along the dirt path. Audra studied her, puzzled by her silence.

"He's a friend," Audra said after ten minutes, breaking the silence.

"But you don't know who he is?" Kathleen asked, her eyes avoiding her gaze. "How can you trust him?"

In truth, Audra wasn't certain she could. She drew in a breath, twisting her hair. "He had a chance to kill me once, and didn't. He wants to protect those at the castle."

Kathleen frowned. "Even me?" she asked, meeting Audra's eyes for the first time since his exit. Horse hooves and wheels on the dirt path muffled their words. Outside, palace escorts conversed, including their driver.

Audra pressed her lips together, unsure of her meaning. What danger could Kathleen face? "I don't think you're at risk," Audra said. "I believe the murderer seeks me."

Kathleen tilted her head, fingers still at her lips. "I don't know," Kathleen said. "There's something you should hear." She shifted, drawing and releasing a deep breath. "My husband's death wasn't a heart attack. I killed him."

The words came so softly, Audra strained to hear. She remembered Sir Bartholomew Barton, Kathleen's late husband. A plain man in his forties. At their wedding, Kathleen seemed captivated. Audra's visit to the newlyweds revealed nothing unusual back then. He died within a year, and Kathleen returned to Hillsfield after Lord Byron discovered Sir Barton's gambling had left him destitute at death.

"He was cruel," Kathleen whispered, tears welling as she gazed out the window. "Not at first, and not always. When he'd drink, he'd gamble. When he gambled, he'd lose. When he lost, he needed someone to blame."

A thick wall seemed to separate them. Kathleen had never revealed this much before. She shook her head. "After losing a fortune one night, he dragged me down a hall by my hair. He wanted relations, but his drunkenness scared me. I refused. Servants witnessed, but did nothing." Kathleen revealed a section of her scalp by pushing aside some hair, showing a coin-sized bald patch, uneven and round. A scar marked the spot, hidden beneath black waves. Audra g asped.

Kathleen covered it, her hands folding in her lap. "That wasn't all he did that night. I try not to remember. I spent my entire life believing love was something magical and kind. My marriage to Sir Barton shattered all my notions of what I thought love should be. One evening, Kolbe visited. Sir Barton invited him to dine. After, they went to drink and gamble in the parlor. I stayed with my brother. Sir Barton asked for wine, and I spilled some while pouring.

"Like a madman, he threw his chair back and grabbed my throat. He called me clumsy, irresponsible, and stupid. Kolbe protested, but Sir Barton claimed me as his property and said I was his to do as he pleased. Kolbe used the chair to knock him unconscious."

Kathleen fixed her eyes on the carriage wall behind Audra. She wiped a tear, her hands trembling. Audra felt ill, wishing she could have helped. She'd known of his gambling, but not his brutality.

"Kolbe told me to leave with him, but fear held me. That day, Kolbe had carried arsenic for a rat issue at one of Lord Byron's bakeries. He poured it in Sir Barton's glass, and..."

Kathleen sought Audra's reaction. Audra swallowed hard, stunned. "You poisoned him," Audra whispered.

Kathleen nodded, catching another tear. "Kolbe held his mouth open while I poured it in. We called the servants in and said he'd had a heart attack. Lord Byron prevented an autopsy with a bribe. No one discovered the truth." She covered her trembling mouth. "Audra, I fear someone knows and wants revenge. These poisonings seem meant for me."

Audra moved beside Kathleen, embracing her as she broke into sobs. Thoughts raced through Audra's mind. She'd considered Kolbe as the masked man, though something felt different about him. The masked man had admitted to killing. Thinking, Audra recalled her last fight with Kolbe where she'd demanded his silence. He'd saved Kathleen from her marriage... by killing her tormentor.

Audra felt tears threatening, hurt for what her friend had experienced. "Kathleen. Your abuser deserved punishment. Your secret is safe with me, and I don't think you're the target. At the ball, Kolbe and I met Prince Elijah. He said the murderer hunts unchaste women. Those who didn't wait for marriage."

Kathleen raised her eyebrows, pondering. "Yes," she said. "That does make sense. But... then..." Kathleen paused, her brow furrowed deeper. "Why would you be in danger?"

Audra swallowed. She hadn't meant to reveal so much with so little. The masked man advised keeping secrets close, yet also urged trust between them. However, murder was a greater sin, and Kathleen had confessed a secret much darker than Audra's. If they were to trust and protect each other, Kathleen needed to understand what secrets were being hidden.

"Garrick," Audra whispered, leaning to Kathleen's ear. "Eva is our daughter. She's not my sister." It was the second time Audra entrusted this to someone herself, squeezing Kathleen's hand as she withdrew.

Kathleen's eyes widened, her eyebrows shooting up. She seemed to process it before placing a hand over her mouth. "My god," she murmured. "You must be heartbroken leaving her at Hillsfield. I thought you were just close." Indeed, she was devastated. Only her mother knew, comforting her mid-night cries last night when Audra couldn't sleep and had finally escaped her binds herself.

"I told you everything," Audra said. "I learned your secret, now you hold mine. We must protect one another." Audra recalled the masked man's assurance she wasn't in danger, making her wonder if he knew of Eva. He never mentioned Eva, and she'd never disclose it. Something about him remained perilous, despite their shared kiss. She resolved to keep that secret private for now.

Audra reflected on Kathleen's admission of poisoning her husband, contemplating if Kolbe's role wasn't the masked man but rather...

She dismissed the thought. It seemed illogical that he was the murderer.

Kathleen shook her head. "I won't tell anyone either. I understand your fear, but it makes me wonder who that masked man was and what secrets he knows. Any guesses?"

Audra held back, suspecting Kathleen's brother the most. Especially now, knowing he'd poisoned someone. Instead, she shrugged and shook her head. "I don't think he's the murderer. He knows us, so maybe he's a spy for the prince."

Kathleen nodded. "I believe you. But... what if... it's the prince?"

Audra had considered this already. However, if the masked man was the prince, why conceal his identity at the ball? Did he want to meet her first without her knowing who he was? If it were the prince, would he mind her asking the masked man for a kiss? Why the secrecy?

This was the reason she must identify the murderer before being found. With Kathleen sharing her secret, the trust between them felt secure. No one would hear of what was shared, and their secrets exchanged in the carriage would remain concealed.

Hours later, as the horses halted before the castle, the sun towered over the Trobex mountains bordering Althenia on the south, east, and west. Doth lie east, where thick trees marked the countryside's end. She was glad she wasn't alone in her journey, though the masked man's abrupt appearance cut into her book-reading time.

The carriage doors opened upon stopping, unveiling the Althenian castle's daytime grandeur. Marble walls made the palace dazzle, sun rays reflecting off gold trims like lightning. Guards escorted Audra and Kathleen to Audra's chambers to acquaint her with her new ladies-in-waiting. They traversed vast hallways into a corridor reserved for the queen's quarters.

The chambers surpassed her expectations in splendor. Marble walls framed three interconnected rooms. One hosted ivory chairs, sofas, and a fireplace for entertaining. Another displayed a large canopy bed with a gold-leaf frame—the largest she'd seen. Soft rosewater satin sheets matched intricate floral room art. Unlike Hillsfield's gray stone walls, the palace boasted ivory splendor. The third room featured a grand bathroom with a golden vanity, a cast iron tub, and mirrors all around. Inside the bathroom lay a vast closet, already stocked with dresses, jewels, and shoes.

A servant instructed Audra to dress for the evening's dinner and dance, celebrating her arrival. Alongside her discoveries, she fielded what felt like a thousand questions about her bed linens' preferred fabric, colors, room decor, and flower arrangements for each weekday.

It was more than she'd imagined.

To her surprise, she felt more excitement than she'd known since leaving the countryside. Before her lay a life of extravagance. Every servant heeded her commands, anticipating her needs. They listened; an oddity after seldom feeling heard. At Lord Byron's estate, she felt akin to dusty wall photos or trampled grass. Here, she felt like the reddest rose people stopped to admire.

As new faces entered her chambers, she memorized each. One might be the kind to pluck the rose and kill it when seen.

Playing through faces as a seamstress measured her for a dress, Audra mused at the seamstress's unprofessionalism as she poked her with needles, recalling her dress shop days. An array of six guards was assigned for her walks. Two stayed outside her door to ensure safety. Audra committed their names and faces to memory.

Among them were her three ladies-in-waiting: Marianne, Alynne, and Tessai, each around her age. All bore the Althenian dark hair, Alynne's with a touch more brown. It didn't escape her notice that Alynne seemed to avoid Audra's gaze during introductions.

The king's advisor was particularly interesting. Julin, the king's trusted confidante and captain of the guards. Looking in his fifties, his black hair yet to gray, his presence commanded respect from all those around him. His brooding stature appeared similar to the masked man's, Audra noted. Though older, he wasn't unpleasant to look at. His lively, witty manner could convince her of anything.

She realized that meant danger.

Another to watch was the stable boy, Marke. Perhaps it was his clothes reminiscent of countryside boys, or how his gaze bore into hers, half-smirking when entering her chambers. Introducing himself, Marke mentioned the prince requested he visit her on the first day, adding horses would arrive the next day for her choosing. She remarked his lingering stare upon leaving, thinking of the masked man's warning not to trust anyone. Audra realized her disadvantage in uncovering the murderer. Castle residents knew far more about their future queen than she did about them.

She'd change that. Her new ladies-in-waiting provided insight on some suspects as they gossiped about their attractiveness, including Kathleen's favorites. About Julin, they noted his omnipresence around the castle and how nothing happened that he didn't find out about. Not unlike the masked man. She hoped, however, that Julin wasn't the man she'd kissed.

Last, she learned the stable keeper, Marke, possessed a reputation as a flirt, luring girls into stable kisses. Among young palace servants, he reigned desirable.

This was the new beginning. The real investigations started, and the hunt for answers would prove the ultimate challenge to determine if she could preserve her life... or perish trying.

15

Audra admired the white marbled walls of the palace corridors, her fingers brushing the smooth surface whenever she passed near them, still in awe of walking through such beauty. Every inch of the palace was as grand as the night of the masquerade. Flowers, chosen by the king and refreshed daily, adorned every hall. In vases on the walls, on every console table, and in large floor vases: flowers were everywhere. The marble gleamed beneath the glass windows, reflecting light across walls and ceiling in a glamorous display.

Who wouldn't love to live this life every day?

Audra longed to show it to Eva.

She, her ladies, and two guards made their way to the banquet hall, marveling at the art around them. The castle seemed to have twenty rooms for the sole purpose of entertaining. Audra expected to meet Prince Elijah there. As she entered, silence fell over the room. Tables lined the walls, leaving a central dance area. Much like the ballroom, windows dominated the walls, and a crystal chandelier hung from above. To her surprise, silence turned to applause, and nobles craned for a glimpse of her.

Adjusting to being the future Queen of Althenia wouldn't be easy. She still wasn't sure she understood what it entailed.

Despite searching the room, her betrothed was unfound. Instead, King Henri approached with a wide, welcoming smile. Sometime in the last two weeks, he'd acquired a new mistress. She bore black hair, long lashes, and eyes dark and deep. She winked at Audra as they made eye contact, making her flush and return her attention to the king.

Kissing Audra's hand, the king offered a boisterous grin. "*Ah*, my future daughter. We're thrilled to have you here to help prepare the most resplendent wedding this kingdom has seen. Meet my dear, Mistress June Lollifer. A true gem hiding away in those brothels, no?" he said, winking at June. Audra's face grew bright red, not escaping the notice of the king.

"Ah," the king said again, "I forgot you're from Lord Byron's estate, where lust is sinful. My dear, in the palace, we embrace our most sensual parts of ourselves. Desire makes life worth living." He locked eyes with June, their exchange smoldering and uncomfortable to watch. Audra pressed her lips together, unsure whether to stare or avert her gaze.

Audra swallowed. "I hope to discover everything the castle offers in time. Might you tell me where the prince is, Your Majesty?" she asked, looking for an escape.

The king's gaze lingered on Audra, making her shift as his eyes dwelt too long on her breasts. "My dear, it's rarer than your hair color for my son to attend banquets. He's always off on midnight rides and adventures. I tell you, if your beauty brings him round more often, I'll owe you my finest horse."

"Then you owe my future wife your finest horse," Elijah said, stepping out from behind the king, who jumped, then grinned. The king stumbled back, laughing, revealing he'd been drinking. In contrast, Elijah looked composed, sporting a silver tunic and black pants. His tousled black hair framed a face more handsome than she recalled. Elijah's eyes met Audra's, and he winked before turning to his father.

As the king steadied himself on a chair, he laughed at his clumsiness. "*A-ha*, we've found your weakness. A beautiful woman brings you to parties, eh?"

Elijah turned to Audra, smirking as if sharing a secret. "The most beautiful woman alive. Excuse us, Father. I'd like to steal her for a dance."

The king nodded, and Elijah led Audra to the center. He placed one hand on her waist and intertwined the other with her fingers, pausing to take in her appearance, noting her silver dress matched his tunic.

"Excellent taste in clothing. You look ravishing," Elijah said. "I'm delighted to see you again. How was your journey?"

His presence calmed her as they began. "It was fine, thank you." As they danced, she couldn't help picturing him masked, seeking familiarity in his proximity. Her heart raced, recalling the masked man's words about knowing the prince's affairs. He'd told her many times that the less she knew, the safer she was. Who knew the prince better than...

The prince?

Before either of them said more, Julin approached, interrupting their dance as he cleared his throat. Elijah halted, frowning. Julin nodded at Elijah, then Audra.

"Your Highness, a delicate matter needs immediate addressing," Julin said, his eyes flicking to Audra, then back.

Elijah sighed. "I was afraid of this. Does this concern the guards we sent to scout the forest?" His contorted expression suggested he foresaw the answer before Julin replied.

"Yes. It's best discussed privately."

Audra's heart sank. Curiosity stirred, knowing political details might expose details about the threats that surrounded her. Elijah turned to her, offering a half-hearted smile that was difficult to decipher until he spoke. "If you'd like to join, my secrets are yours."

The way Elijah looked at her with such sincerity made her heart leap in her chest. She spent days preparing her mind for the possibility that she would have to endure her life at the palace as another pawn in a game of chess. She didn't expect an invitation.

Surprised, she leaped at the opportunity. "I'd like to come."

"Your Highness," Julin protested. "It isn't safe for Her Grace's involvement in these matters."

"The queen decides her own safety. She'll come," Elijah insisted, offering his arm. Defeated, Julin grunted, leading the way out of the banquet hall. They followed, not venturing far before entering another room. Two guards stood outside, but the inside appeared empty. Resembling a study, the room had red carpets, furniture displayed all around, but no windows. The smell of dark bourbon and salt filled her lungs as she inhaled.

Once the doors closed, Julin turned his attention to Elijah, wasting no time. "There was a surprise attack with the guards you sent." He paused, glancing at Audra again, displeased. His unease with her presence was apparent. She wondered what he seemed to dislike so much about her, and the way he tensed up when she neared him made him more peculiar. Why did he dislike her being there so much?

Julin cleared his throat. "How frank shall I be, Your Highness?" he asked, gesturing by nodding to Audra. Whatever he needed to say, it was clear he didn't want her to hear it.

Elijah sighed. "As I said, she's privy to any information you need to share. Tell me," he said, offering Audra a reassuring smile.

Julin swallowed, shifting his weight. "Yes, Your Majesties." He cleared his throat once more before reluctantly adding, "The guards sent to spy were captured. Over half died, the rest returned, the bodies of the dead held ransom."

Prince Elijah's mouth twitched. He moved a hand to cover his face, shaking his head. Releasing Audra's arm, he moved away. To their left, a small table sat beside a maroon-colored armchair. Prince Elijah pressed his hand onto the table, leaning against it with his back turned away from both of them. "But we sent guards this time, not soldiers. One hundred."

When silence stretched, Julin sighed, stepping between them. Audra backed near the wall, listening as she tried to blend in with the decorations. She knew better than to ask any questions, lest the prince change his mind about her presence. Julin finished for Elijah. "Thirty-four remain, Your Highness. The attack was swift, and we were out-manned."

Elijah stood taller, turning around, his expression sullen. He shared no clues about his thoughts, and it bothered her that she couldn't read them. Glancing at Julin, he turned to Audra with a sigh. "Some object to my betrothal to another Althenian. Many say marrying the Dothian princess ensures peace. My father prefers your dowry to fund the upcoming war, believing the surplus afterward will introduce Althenia's next golden age."

Audra's mind spun. How large *was* her dowry? She thought about how she indeed was a sheep, sold away for a sum. It put her in a difficult position. Marriage to the prince funded a war. However, war could be prevented if he married another. Without ever meaning to, she was the woman standing between peace and war between the two largest kingdoms on the continent.

Frowning at the realization, she stepped toward him. "What do you want?" she asked. She wondered if he shared her reluctance. Could she be worth so much? Now, she understood why she was in danger. Thousands could die because of her, so thousands would want her dead.

Elijah's eyes met hers, a smirk tracing his lips. "I thought that was obvious."

Audra's lips parted. His eyes lingered, studying her, making her shiver. If asked a week ago what she wanted, her answer would have been different. Now, she wondered if the man she kissed was this one standing before her.

She flushed. If it was him... would the prince know more about her than she realized? Would he be angry that she had asked a stranger to kiss her? The masked man had warned her not to tell anyone about their encounters. Did that exclusion apply to him if she confirmed he was the masked man?

Julin interrupted. "Prince Elijah, we don't have time for this," he said, casting a look at Audra. "Our defenses are weakened because of this situation. If they choose to attack, we might not withstand it. I urge replacing our guards first thing in the morning as a priority. Our lives could be at risk."

Prince Elijah paced, moving toward Audra, stroking his chin.

Letting out a long sigh, he shook his head. "Sending palace guards was foolish, I told you we should send soldiers. Sixty-six of our loyal defenders, ambushed. How do you recommend we replace them on short notice?"

Julin nodded, prepared with a plan. "I've written to General Gerod for seventy of his most trustworthy soldiers by morning. Althenian protocol dictates that guards must train in the military for ten years before securing a position at the palace. Given the circumstances, I've indicated we'll take any soldiers who prove themselves dedicated to your cause. I trust him to ensure their loyalty."

Elijah frowned, shaking his head. "It's a large group to train on short notice. It's risky. Have our guards assigned to mentor the new ones. You must also vet each new guard yourself, and see to it that the new ones are reliable. Our current guards must take responsibility for their trainees. Any hint of rebellion, we'll imprison them for questioning, and you will handle their discipline. You're right—we can't afford weaknesses now."

Elijah moved to Audra, sighing as he took her hand. "I intend to know you before the wedding. I had hoped to share more tonight, to show you our world." His thumb traced the back of her hand, his expression somber. "I must attend to business, and I hope you understand. Please accept my deepest apologies. I don't wish to leave you, but our safety depends on my diligence."

In truth, she felt relieved at his seriousness. The castle is dangerous, the masked man had warned her. Elijah kissed her hand, his eyes sweeping upward to meet hers. Then he exited, swift like a bird diving for prey. The way he moved, his lips up close...

What was the possibility that Elijah was the masked man after all? Seeing him made her curious, attentive to details matching up. Were those the eyes? The lips she kissed? Did he already know everything about her?

Her mind swirled until two fingers tapped her shoulder, pulling her from a trance. Sir Julin stared at her, his brown eyes dull. He smiled, though his insincerity remained evident. "Come, Your Highness. Let's take your closest lady-in-waiting for a walk. If Prince Elijah insists on your awareness surrounding Althenia's politics, then it's time I explain a few things."

Julin guided them back to the ballroom where they weaved through dancing courtiers in search of one of her ladies. Audra found Kathleen, who looked uncomfortable conversing with June, the king's mistress. Grateful for the intrusion, Kathleen joined them. They exited the hall in another direction, where Julin led them further into the corridors, ensuring no prying ears followed.

Audra wondered whose ears shouldn't hear this.

After several rounded corners, Julin stopped, as if deliberating his next words. She held her breath, anxious for his revelation and hopeful he didn't change his mind to inform her of things. Sir Julin spoke, "Er, Your Highness, may I speak?"

Audra, eager, replied at once. "Of course. Forgive me. I forgot I must speak first now. Please, Sir Julin, tell me anything." Relieved he hadn't reconsidered, she waited, hoping for answers. She welcomed any clues that might keep her safe.

"There are matters you should gain awareness of concerning Althenia. We're under attack after twenty-six years of seeking peace with Doth. Spies have infiltrated, and we believe they entered during the masquerade where Mistress Isabelle died. These spies threaten to kill the king, leaving markings and threats around town, and they're offering to spare Prince Elijah if he marries their princess. More recently, they've targeted the king's mistresses."

The king's mistresses? Margaret, Isabelle... they were mistresses. The brothel women found in the streets, all former mistresses? Audra thought of June, eyes widening at the king continuing this pattern despite the consequences.

Julin shook his head, hands behind him. "Before your birth, King Henri was betrothed to Doth's Princess Mayla in an effort made to restore peace to our kingdoms. At seventeen, the princess was nine, which meant the wedding wouldn't take place for several years. He was a young man, known for his flirtatious ways with the noblewomen of the court. One drunken night, the king took a wife in secret, legally binding. King Ryou of Doth was displeased that the prince married another. As a result, Prince Henri's first wife was killed in her sleep, her body never found. The only evidence of her murder was the blood-stained sheets. Some blame Doth, others suspect King Rupert arranged her death to end the marriage."

Audra spotted a guard rounding the corner, catching Julin's attention. Julin signaled him with two fingers on his heart. The guard mirrored the gesture and left.

Julin continued as if nothing had happened. "Prince Henri wed Princess Mayla. The priest who married Prince Henri to his first wife declared the second marriage invalid without the first wife's body to prove her death. Princess Mayla ordered the priest to be imprisoned and executed as he riled up multiple conflicts. Some said this was the reason Princess Mayla experienced many miscarriages before birthing Prince Elijah after two years of marriage."

Audra remembered sitting with Eva once during Jed's tutoring on Althenia's past. Rebellion had erupted over Henri's marriage to Mayla. As a result, King Rupert was slain, and King Henri ascended, and months later Queen Mayla suffered a horrible doom. The story went that she'd attempted to save the horses from a barn fire and was burned to death during her rescue. Doth suspects foul play.

Now, Doth pressured Elijah to wed another princess to restore peace once more.

"Betrothal to you secures Lord Byron's financial support. Ending it risks his wrath. The king cannot afford to make an enemy of the richest lord in Althenia. Marriage to another Doth princess appears unfavorable with the Althenian council while their spies continue to threaten and endanger us."

Audra pondered Julin's tale. The murderer was Dothian, then. It made sense, she supposed. Knowing history's truth pieced it together.

Hazard within the castle loomed larger than she'd realized. She'd been mistaken to believe only one person wanted her dead. It was not one single person. There were many. Caution was even more crucial than she'd anticipated.

The masked man was right—ignorance *was* safer. Now that she learned, she wished she hadn't. Sleep would evade her as long as she remained conscious of the castle's threat.

"Sir Julin," a guard's urgent voice panted from around the corner leading to the hall. "She's poisoned. They found a way."

Julin huffed as he expelled an exasperated gasp. He turned to Audra and excused himself, cursing, "We warned him, we all warned him that she would die. Why take another mistress?" Audra realized Mistress June, seen minutes before, was now the latest victim of this grand scheme.

That meant... at least one of the killers was already inside the castle.

16

It would take time for Audra to uncover all the palace secrets, but her morning began with her ladies-in-waiting. Her black hair pulled back into a net, Alynne led the other ladies and Audra to her favorite place in the royal gardens. Their morning passed by quickly, admiring the fresh beauties of spring as they bantered. By noon, Audra called for lunch beneath a large willow at the gardens' edge. She suggested they lay blankets for a picnic. A fresh breeze passed as the women entered the willow's shelter, and Audra glanced at her ladies for their thoughts.

"Blankets?" Marianne asked. "You're not aware of your power, Your Highness. Call an attendant and request tables and lunch served here." Marianne and Tessai seemed intent on showing Audra her influence. Audra tried it by summoning two nearby garden servants, as Marianne instructed, and they set to work. The white metal tables and garden chairs preceded fresh sandwiches and charcuterie. As they dined, Audra marveled at the palace food's extravagant taste.

Though amused by her influence, she longed for attention from her future husband. Who was she to marry? He was the only man she should devote her gaze to now. Despite Kolbe's frustrating views, she knew he was right: loving anyone but Elijah was treason.

However, her future husband was elusive. Always gone, always busy. Perhaps in hiding, solving the murder mysteries, knowing they were by Dothian men who wished her gone. She understood his absence, but it didn't ease the solitude.

Alynne and Tessai gossiped about the guards, their chatter dull to Audra's ears. She found their conversations always about people, never ideas or anything that mattered. As the ladies finished lunch, an unexpected visitor arrived.

In the sunlight, more handsome than ever, he approached. Elijah wore a gold-trimmed ivory coat over a gold tunic, with white pants to match. She smiled, glimpsing him beneath the willow tree. Perhaps all her wishes could command reality, after all.

"Audra," Elijah greeted her, a smile playing on his lips. "I owe an apology again for leaving last night. I know I must do better and be more present as you become queen. I hope you will forgive me?" Elijah's contrite expression seemed sincere.

How long had it been since the last time anyone apologized to her? She couldn't recall. An apology from him was unexpected, and more valid than the reasons of others in her life who never would.

"There's nothing to forgive," Audra replied, standing to face him. His smile made her heart flutter with nerves and excitement. The intrigue appeared mutual, giving her moments of hope for their future life together.

Audra turned to her ladies, who curtsied to the prince. Kathleen passed Audra a rueful grin as Elijah extended a hand. "Ladies, I'll walk with my future wife alone, if you'll excuse us. I promise to return her in perfect condition."

Kathleen's and Audra's eyes widened. A walk? Without an escort? Alone?

After living years within the confines of Lord Byron's conservative household, the idea seemed foreign, even incredulous.

Taking his cue, she advanced and Elijah offered his arm. Both eager and calm, she accepted. Elijah led her toward the hedges into another area of the gardens. Unlike Hillsfield, palace gardens were more open, shaded by trees, and blossoming with spring flowers. She preferred the shade they provided over the grassy walkways.

At first, their stroll started slowly and quietly. Audra sensed hesitation in Elijah, as if his mind wandered. Maybe he needed her companionship to think. At Hillsfield, she'd use her walks with Eva to do the same.

Enjoying the peaceful silence, she mused how the palace felt like paradise. Servants catered to her needs, ladies-in-waiting might become friends. Alynne preferred to speak to the other ladies and never met her gaze, but Audra attributed it to shyness. Tessai, the youngest, loved to chat, growing close to Kathleen since their arrival. Marianne, her favorite other than Kathleen, held a more mature demeanor than the others.

Since it was the first time living away from her mother, it was also the first time that she noticed all the attention on her. Without her mother and Eva close, Audra stood out more than usual. At Hillsfield, her mother insisted she not attract attention and never to stare at others. Here, everyone stared at Audra without hesitation. At the palace, the whole world saw her, watched her, and admired her.

A thought crossed her mind, realizing that if anything happened to Elijah, she'd return to Hillsfield with Lord Byron: a life she'd detested without realizing it until the palace.

However, her yearning to reunite with some of the people there tugged at her heart. Eva never left her mind. Her heart ached during her first day at the palace. The pain reminded her of stones being laid on a building, with each stone representing one day she'd have to spend without her as the walls grew taller between them.

Elijah escorted Audra to a marble bench beside a round fountain at the garden center. In the fountain, two sculpted naked women danced with one another, using cloth to titillate and sway one another. Though the statue never moved, she observed that their seductive smiles appeared more intimate than any other statue she'd seen.

Out of sight from all the wandering eyes, she admired how to sun reflected warm blue hues on the fountain's waters. Elijah motioned for Audra to sit, joining him. To her surprise, he took her hands in his, looking into her eyes with a guilty grin. "How horrible you must think I am. This wasn't how I planned our meetings. I need to remind myself that we have our entire lives ahead of us, and it won't be this way forever. Disappearing as I have, I fear I've left a wrong impression." His eyes drew to their hands, then back to hers. Her heart thumped as she studied his hair, messier than usual.

"No apology necessary," she assured, blushing. "I understand. I'm your loyal servant, and I'll always follow your lead. I trust your wisdom in palace affairs far exceeds mine, so I realize you've done what's best for the kingdom."

Elijah eyed her, sighing, releasing her hands to rest on his knees.

"I feared you'd say that," he said, shaking his head, his eyes staring off into the distance. "I feared you'd see yourself as my subject, not as my equal." He paused, his hand touching her cheek for a brief moment before tucking a strand of hair behind her ear with a gentle gesture. Her heart pittered, though not the way it had that night in her room with the masked man. She couldn't help but wonder again if the man before her was the same she'd kissed.

Elijah continued, "When I first learned of our betrothal, I grew angry. Nobody consulted me, and I didn't seek a wife. I gathered information about you from nobles who had frequented your dress shop. I learned you have a spark in you, and that intrigued me. You don't follow all the rules like they're written in stone. I also overheard you were friends with one of my father's mistresses... Margaret."

At this confession, Audra flushed. *He knew.* Her heart raced. It didn't mean Margaret told him anything, right? Perhaps he only knew of their friendship. It wasn't uncommon. She'd met Margaret at finishing school, and she met many of the noble ladies her age.

Could the prince be the masked man she kissed? Audra studied his face, trying to find clues. He laughed, a gesture meant to be kind, but it made her more anxious.

"Don't worry, I'm not criticizing. She mentioned once you'd sneak out of Hillsfield to visit her. It's something I admired about you, in truth. I didn't want you thinking, my dear, I sought something you didn't possess. I meant to indicate I recognize you aren't the sort of woman to obey my every whim. I understand you value freedom."

He was right. Of all her desires, none ran deeper than her yearning for freedom. He added, "You seemed reserved when we met. I want to share everything I know so you can have the same knowledge."

Elijah smirked as his thumb drifted near her engagement ring, his demeanor both sheepish and devilish. Relaxing her shoulders, she considered letting her guard down around him. He wasn't so bad. He continued, "I should disclose... I have a secret. There's something you should learn." Elijah leaned in, his breath warm on her neck, making Audra shiver. Was it arousal or fear igniting within her? What did he know?

His musk lingered, making her flush. In a low voice, he said, "You are the most fascinating woman I've ever met. That's the secret." His breath heated her neck, and she felt herself melting as her limbs weakened. "I want a woman who loves freedom, craves pleasure." Her neck's hair stood on end, her heart thumping. What did he mean? He leaned in, pressing a light brush of his lips against her neck, whispering, "We want the same things. Luxury. And, desire."

Elijah ran his firm, muscled hand across her shoulder, down her back, and landed at her waist, breathing cold air down her neck. His other hand traced her neck, gauging her reaction. She didn't protest despite her nervousness.

"You're tense," he whispered, pulling his head back to examine her. "I'm sorry, I didn't mean to frighten you." He withdrew, placing his hands in his lap, sighing. Audra hadn't objected, but she acknowledged her heart felt distant. Though Elijah's appeal was apparent, he could also ignite her undoing if he learned of her past. She wanted to confide in him, but reasoned that no queen was forgiven for bearing a child pre-marriage to a king.

Torn between deceit and truth, she couldn't tell him. How can she love someone she can't trust? Now wasn't the time, if such a time existed.

Elijah cleared his throat. "I shouldn't have done that. I'm sorry. I saw something in you that I saw in myself. Women like you are rare." He stood, pacing nearby. "I got ahead of myself."

Audra stood too, gathering her navy skirt, seeking to comfort him. Perfection remained vital, and she had to find a way to amend this. Perhaps he sensed her fear. "You intrigue me too," she said, o-ffering what she hoped was a seductive smile.

Elijah shrugged. "I feel like we know each other better than we do. In my life, I dreamed of a wife like you. I recognize I need patience... it's not easy. What matters is your genuine desire. I'm not entitled to everything because I'm your future king and husband. It's the reverse. You're what I want. Therefore, the kingdom, including me, is at your command."

Audra's heart pounded as Elijah's words washed over her. So long she'd lived in the shadows that it felt foreign to be told such things. For the first time since leaving her home in the countryside, she thought she believed freedom might be in reach.

But only if he loved all of her.

She swallowed, nodding before speaking. "I'm overwhelmed by change. Please don't think I find you undesirable. I'm drawn to you more than you realize." Remembering older girls' flirting, Audra mimicked a practiced eyelash batting.

How much did Elijah know? Was he aware of the man whose shadow he may never stop living in?

His teal eyes recalled the man who once shattered her heart and left her in agony for years. Could she love her future husband as she once loved before? Could Elijah replace Garrick? Would she ever long for him the way she once did for Kolbe? Moving from a simple countryside life to Hillsfield's prison, she never envisioned a life of happiness. Never did she anticipate anyone so reminiscent of love lost.

She wished she could open her heart as Elijah had opened his.

She stepped closer. "What do you know about my life?"

Elijah smirked. "You grew up in the countryside with your parents. Your father, a traveling merchant, sold flowers from Doth. He died when you were fifteen. You opened a dress shop. Your mother remarried in the countryside and had your sister. When she married Lord Byron, you moved to Hillsfield."

To Audra's relief, Elijah seemed unaware of Eva's true parentage. Still, she hoped one day to share the truth and hold no secrets. Though she wanted to believe his promise to marry her, she feared Doth planned otherwise. The last one who promised such things to her died. She trembled at the thought of loving another just to lose him again.

Elijah offered his arm. "Let's return to the castle. I wanted to give you a grand tour. I'm hopeful your presence will convince my father to behave. I admit, I'm feeling a bit hostile with him today. Three murdered mistresses in a month, yet I predict there will be another in a few days. Julin said he explained this to you. Understand, I will find these killers before they strike again. My father fails to grasp the gravity, using mistresses as test subjects in an experiment. June's death didn't need to happen. He could have spared her by staying away."

Audra sensed Elijah's resentment toward his father. His voice seeped with frustration and anger. Except for Lord Byron, she'd not heard such criticism toward the king.

His statements were true. All the recent murders were of mistresses. From the sound of it, the king had no intention of putting an end to his ways.

A thought struck her. In some ways, Dothian spies weren't responsible. If the king recognized the consequences of having mistresses, he had the power to stop himself. He simply *chose* not to.

While Audra knew this truth deep down, she also realized the thought was treason.

17

Audra and Elijah spent the afternoon together, sharing stories of their pasts, though she withheld particular details. He gave her a castle tour and introduced her to the stables. In the evening, they joined the king and his guests for a sumptuous dinner featuring roast lamb, blueberry confits, assorted salads, and trays of fruits with creamy dips. She doubted she'd ever grow tired of the food.

After dining, Elijah introduced her to new card games in the drawing room. He refrained from further touch, but as the evening progressed, her desire for him grew. Near midnight, he escorted her to her chambers.

"I hope this makes up for my early departure yesterday. I'll be busy in the morning, but I'll send for you when available," Elijah said.

Audra smiled, blushing. "I enjoyed our time together. Thank you." After a moment of hesitation, he kissed her cheek and departed. Her chamber soon filled with eager ladies-in-waiting, desperate for details about her evening. Exhausted, she sent them away, needing time to herself. Kathleen looked the most disappointed but followed the others out.

The following morning, Elijah missed breakfast but invited Audra to join him for lunch in the library. Marianne and Tessai accompanied her, while Alynne and Kathleen stayed to watch a game of croquet between the king and his advisors. In her private study, Audra read about larkspur, a plant deadly enough to kill someone with twenty-five milligrams. Few details existed compared to other poisonous flowers like nightbane and wolfsbane. She studied their effects, forearming herself with knowledge in case she ever needed it.

After noon, Audra joined the prince in the library. Marianne and Tessai accompanied her at his request.

As she entered, Audra marveled at the library in daylight. Unlike Hillsfield's, this library was a vast circle. Cedar shelves painted white lined the walls, towering to a twenty-foot ceiling. Curved shelves formed rings within, creating stories like the earth's layers. Ladders attached to sliding hinges gave access to high shelves. A large glass spire overhead bathed the library in sunlight.

A path split the shelves, leading to a central space with sofas and tables. As Audra entered, she found Elijah with familiar company she hadn't expected to see so soon.

"Jed?" Audra inquired, interrupting an intellectual debate between Jed and Elijah. Elijah smiled, causing her to blush, and her redness grew deeper when Jed smiled, too.

Jed rose to bow, a formality she found ridiculous after years of knowing him. "Hello, Your Highness," Jed said, more rigid than usual.

While living at Hillsfield, Jed visited the castle on weekends when not tutoring Eva. Even though Audra recalled this, she'd never imagined seeing him here herself. He liked borrowing books from the castle and enjoyed debating politics with courtiers for intellectual stimulation. She recalled a conversation from years ago where he'd said she was one of the few who could keep up with him.

"What have I walked into?" Audra asked, glancing between the two.

Elijah gestured for Audra to sit with him at a large round table. The room was becoming a favorite, akin to the Hillsfield library.

Her two ladies took seats, flanking either side of Jed and the prince, leaving Audra a spot to sit between the two men.

"Prince Elijah and I were discussing the Althenian-Doth war from fifty years ago. But that discussion can wait," Jed said, smirking. "It's good to see you."

"Likewise," Audra replied. Her mother had forbidden their talks, a habit that still felt lawful at the castle. She addressed the prince, "This room is magnificent."

"I thought you'd appreciate it," Elijah replied with a pleased look on his face. "Jed tells me you love reading."

Jed told him, hmm? Could Jed be a prince's spy? He worked at both the castle and the estate, frequenting each. He'd know plenty about Hillsfield and the palace, making him the perfect candidate for spying.

Of course, he also worked for the prince, which made him the ideal person to know the prince's affairs. Audra pondered this as a servant poured her wine.

The masked man claimed it was his duty to know the prince's affairs and seemed well-versed about her. Who better to watch her than someone familiar with both places? The masked man also knew when she left Hillsfield, so he had to be familiar with both locales.

Could it be a coincidence? Was Jed the masked man? Or the prince?

And, if it was Jed, why did he kiss her? When he first began tutoring Eva, they'd flirted a time or two. Audra's mother caught them once, and that ended it. While she found him amusing, she never considered anything serious.

Audra swallowed, not wanting to linger on the answers to her questions. "I do love reading," she said, then posed a forced smile.

"I hear our library can't compete with Lord Byron's," Elijah remarked, glancing at the shelves. "However, we have more foreign volumes. Like Hillsfield, we treat our books with utmost care."

Audra recalled *Poisons and Posies*. Jed borrowed it from the castle, but now it resonated with her. The masked man said he gave it to Jed for her. Its origin was Milia, a western kingdom. Who better to locate a book in the palace than someone with access? She'd read most of it, learning Dothian men would be quite familiar with how to make poison from posies.

Before she responded, a guard entered and approached the prince. He whispered to Elijah, too faint for Audra to hear. Elijah nodded, and the guard left in the same abrupt manner.

Elijah smiled at her, but his eyes hinted at regret. "A small matter needs my attention—a servant issue. I apologize again. I'll return in a moment. Meanwhile, catch up with Jed."

Elijah exited, and Audra noticed Tessai's eyes admiring Jed's large, masculine frame. Tessai's glances bordered on flirtation as she tried to capture his attention, though Jed was oblivious, focused on Audra.

"Did you finish the book I lent you?" Jed asked.

Audra lied, wanting more time to finish it. "I think I left it at Hillsfield. Maybe Eva has it." She hoped mentioning Eva would ease tension. Two days away felt eternal. "How is she?"

"You left the book?" Jed asked, flustered by her answer. "That would be a problem, Audra, one we should focus on fixing at once. Where might you have left it? I'll fetch it today." Panic tinged his voice, revealing its importance.

Surprised by his urgency, Audra glanced at Marianne, who gave Jed longing looks, and Tessai's gaze never wavered from him. Neither reacted to his concern.

"What if it's lost?" Audra probed. The book had more value than he'd let on before, and she was determined to find out why.

"You lost it?" Jed's voice rose before he composed himself. He ran a hand through his hair before clearing his throat. "Finding it is crucial. You must understand its significance." He glanced at the ladies, acknowledging them for the first time. Their eyes lit up, resembling two eager dogs seeking praise. Undistracted by them, he regained focus on Audra.

"I'll claim responsibility if needed," Audra said, hoping for time to jot notes. She smirked at her captivated ladies, knowing their silence would be easy. She reassured Jed. "It's my fault, I'll handle it."

Jed relaxed with a sigh, nodding. "I'll send someone to check your room. We must find it. Your carelessness surprises me. It's unlike you." He shook his head. "Never mind that for now. You asked about Eva. Truth be told, Eva's struggling to focus without you. She tried sneaking out two nights ago."

Audra gasped, her heart pounding. Why? The streets were unsafe at night, no place for a seven-year-old. How could she think of doing such a thing? With grim dissatisfaction, Audra realized the hypocrisy of her annoyance, but her protective instinct flared anyway.

"She wanted to live with you at the castle, so she ran away. Guards caught her after leaving Hillsfield. She used the front entrance."

Audra smothered a smile, despite her worry. Well, that was her mistake. Sneaking out of HIllsfield required using the windows.

A horrible realization dawned that Eva was turning out to be just like her. Worse, Audra could not be there to discourage it. Her heart clenched at the mere thought of what could happen to her, and all the things that Audra would not be able to protect her from while living so far away.

"Tessai," Audra decided.

"Yes, Princess?" Tessai replied, tearing her gaze from Jed.

"Fetch a pen and paper. I'll send a letter back with my friend for my sister. I know what to say."

"I didn't know you had a sister," Marianne commented. "Mine is older, married to a townsman."

Audra smiled, pleased that her ladies wanted to know her, despite their romantic distractions. "Mine is seven, and it appears she's struggling without me." Tessai left, returning soon with paper, ink, and a quill.

Jed, Tessai, and Marianne attempted small talk while Audra wrote her letter. One day, Eva could be her lady-in-waiting, but not yet. Perhaps a message would encourage good behavior.

Sneaking out... Audra stiffened at the thought. She hated that her daughter transformed into a spitting image of herself, another consequence of her own actions.

Dear Eva,

I want you to remember I miss you just as you miss me, perhaps more than you realize. I think about you always and wish I could have you here with me. You would love everything about the castle. When you're old enough, I'll bring you here to live with me. For now, I need to do what's best for us.

Eva, my dear, you must do what's best for us, too. Jed told me you were caught sneaking away. This will only lead to trouble. Though it will be hard, you must wait until you are old enough before I can bring you to the castle. Mother will take care of you and help as I did. I recall you say she's stricter than I, but everything she does is out of love.

Remember what I used to tell you as a baby? One day, I will share everything I know. One day, I'll even tell you more about your father. Though he died too soon, he would wish for your safety.

Wait to see me, and you'll have the world at your disposal one day. There are rewards in patience. I will see you soon, and I promise to write more often. Every day, if that's what you need.

Love,

Your sister, and future princess, Audra

Writing those last words pained her. How often she longed to raise Eva as a daughter, not a sister. How could she guide her daughter away from her missteps if she couldn't watch her grow?

Audra finished the letter before Tessai sealed it with wax. Tessai handed it to Jed, who agreed to deliver it to Eva, tucking it into his pocket just as Elijah returned. Behind the prince, platters arrived, and their lunch was served.

"Writing letters?" he asked, seeing the ink and quill on the table.

"To my sister. She's struggling in my absence. We were best friends, and I miss her," Audra sighed. If unable to disclose the truth about their relationship, she could still express her love.

"That's good, writing to her. However... I'm sorry, my love," Elijah said, taking her hand to cup it between his. "I have business away from the castle, and I'm afraid I must again leave you. I'll return in a couple of days. This isn't our normal future. I promise." Elijah turned to Jed after releasing her hand. "Jed, will you accompany me?"

Jed rose as Elijah touched her shoulder, offering an apologetic look. Her thoughts spun as they left, wondering if Jed could be the masked man all along. She never should have asked the masked man for a kiss.

18

For the sixth night in a row, Audra watched from her window as the stable boy, Marke, approached the castle at midnight. Each time, he looked directly at her through her window. Standing inside her bedroom nook, she gazed toward the west side of the palace. Her view encompassed the castle's animal fields and a stable resting by Whisper Forest's edge, a quarter mile away from the palace. Night after night, she noted Marke turned back to the stable once he saw her watching. He'd toss his hair and bow to acknowledge her presence.

Tonight was no different. As Marke neared the castle, he glanced at her window, stopped, bowed, and smiled before turning away. Audra wondered if it warranted investigation. Feeling he wanted her attention, she decided this night to follow him.

Years ago, Garrick had given her a dagger after saving her from drowning. Since then, the dagger stayed strapped to her right calf, harnessed for quick access.

Holding the dagger in her hand, she thought of the man who'd gifted it. Its small blade and ivory handle symbolized a protectiveness she longed to see in Elijah. For now, she'd protect herself. She strapped the dagger back to her leg, preparing for whatever this night would bring.

Draping the black cloak she brought from Hillsfield over a plain gray dress, she aimed to pass as a servant. Audra rummaged through her closets for every bed linen she could find, tied the sheets together, and fashioned a rope for an escape route. Two guards outside her door thwarted conventional exits, so this would have to suffice. She tied the makeshift rope around the sofa by the window, preparing to descend.

Once on the ground, she took care not to crush the bushes that lay beneath her window, landing on mulch. As she situated herself, she examined her surroundings. The lack of moonlight behind clouds gave her complete darkness, and the absence of guards after midnight cleared the way. She headed for an old wall across the field, aiming to hide in the shadows as she crossed to the stables.

Glimpsing the stables once she found cover, a dim light glowed within. Nervous about being caught, Audra swallowed. If Marke attempted to lure her, she would remain hidden until she spotted him first. A trap wouldn't surprise her.

Reaching the decayed wall, she used it for cover to cross the field. Unlike Marke, she avoided the main road, sticking to shadows, and looked back once in a while to check for followers. After ten minutes of stealth, she reached the barn. Lurking in the darkness, she searched for a back entrance, eyes peeled for signs of entrapment. The rear door stood wide open, light spilling outward.

Using caution, she peered inside. As she peeked in, the masked man stood in full view, his arms folded, waiting.

The masked man, in his usual black attire, smirked as he saw her. Feeling curious and secure, she entered and shut the door. Inside, troughs held animal feed, hay stacked in a corner, and barrels full of alcohol occupied the majority of the space. A single candle illuminated the area, sitting atop one of the barrels near the masked m an.

He stood in the room's center, an appealing aura surrounding him in the dim candlelight. The mask served its purpose well, concealing his identity, despite her hopes to see through it. Her heart leaped, but guilt mingled with thoughts of kissing him, knowing she was engaged. Could he be the prince? If so, why these clandestine meetings? The way he stood with his arms folded reminded her of someone, but she couldn't quite place who.

"Good. You came," he said in a quiet voice, almost like a whisper. He leaned against a barrel. "I hoped the signal would bring you." His certainty unnerved her, as if expecting her arrival.

"The signal? Or trap?" Audra asked, raising her eyebrows, glancing around to confirm their solitude.

He chuckled. "The signal. Marke. I hoped you'd follow him. I predicted you well," he admitted, a sly grin playing on his lips. "If it were a trap, it'd be disguised as a weakness."

Audra flushed, wishing her heart wouldn't react near him. She hadn't expected to see him again, at least not like this. "Can you reveal yourself? Or am I wasting my breath?" Audra asked, though she anticipated his response.

"The less you know—"

"The better," Audra completed, sighing in frustration. It figured. She had a million guesses, but until she was certain, she wouldn't make an accusation. She shifted focus. "What are we doing in the stables?"

His grin faded, changing to something more somber. "I found something. Well, Marke did."

Her curiosity piqued. She stepped closer to hear him better, but knew he'd retreat if she got too close. "How do I know you're not Marke?" she asked, testing for information. She wondered if she could gain anything from arbitrary guessing.

The masked man remained serious. "You don't know I'm not Marke."

Audra stepped closer, stopping three steps away from him. It reminded her of approaching a feral cat she didn't want to spook.

He didn't budge from his position against the barrel. What was it about him she felt so drawn to? Their past banters echoed a touchless dance, both resisting their truths. She realized she didn't understand a single thing more about him than she did on the first day she met him.

But she wanted to.

Audra bit her lip, cracking a smile of her own. "Alright, mystery man. You won't reveal who you are, but you have no qualms about kissing me. Understood."

He laughed, adjusting his weight against the barrel. "Wait one moment, there," he said with a playful grin. "You asked for the kiss. I complied with my queen's wishes." He made a bowing motion, meant to mock her. "Besides, I'll remind you that you weren't one bit timid in returning it."

Her smile grew, her entire body heating up at the memory. It had been quite the kiss, even if it was wrong. Standing near him reminded her why she'd asked. "Well, you tied me up. If I wanted to object—"

"Did you want to object?" he interrupted. Though she couldn't see his entire face, she detected the sincerity in his voice.

Audra swallowed. "If I did, only one of us committed treason."

The masked man covered his mouth, hiding the visible part of his face, and dug his toe into the dirt. "At least I knew who I kissed. I could have been anyone to you. That bothers me sometimes."

She pondered why that mattered, of all things. He'd been the one concealing all the secrets. When she thought of her suspects, she could guess motives for any of them. She wondered if she could use that for more information. "Then why did you?"

He dropped his hand, looking down, toeing the dirt with his boot. "Opportunities don't always repeat."

It revealed nothing. His answers eluded her questions, frustrating her. "So you have a habit of kissing women who give you opportunities?" Jealousy tinged her voice, though she had no right to feel it.

The masked man met her gaze. "I didn't say I kiss every woman. I kissed you." Her heart raced. Straightening from the barrel, he unfolded his arms, fists clenched. "We need to change the subject before you get ideas again. Let's get to the point. I came for this letter," he said, handing her a twice-folded paper pulled from his jacket.

Audra approached with caution, taking it as he stepped back. Unfolding it, she saw her letter intended for Eva that she'd sent with Jed.

She flushed. "You read my letter?" she asked. If it was Jed, why read a letter she trusted him to deliver to her sister? It wasn't private, but she trusted Jed with it nonetheless. How could he betray her?

"I make it my business to know the royal court's affairs, and I must admit, this was intriguing," the masked man said. Anger flared inside her, tempting her to leap at him to unmask him. Remembering Jed left the library with the prince, she paused. If this man were the prince, she hesitated to act rashly. Kissing was impulsive enough. But why so cryptic?

"You mentioned her father," the masked man continued. "I pondered the curiosity of that sentence. I wondered why you couldn't tell her everything about her father already. I understand Douglas Freeman was a straightforward fellow, with no peculiar interests or hobbies." The masked man wiped a barrel's surface, as if checking for dust. "Naturally, I wondered what secret your mother kept about him. There had to be something about Eva's father she couldn't know. I do, indeed, wonder what that might be."

He turned from the barrel, a pointed look aimed at Audra. She stayed silent, refusing to reveal more information than necessary.

The silence lingered. He sighed. "I'll ensure the letter reaches Eva without further inspection." Audra doubted it. "In exchange, perhaps you'll share what Eva can't be informed about regarding her father."

Audra rocked, her heart racing. "Nothing she can't know. She asks about her father all the time. He died before she was born," she said, smashing her lips together. She took care to stick to partial truths, lest her lies would betray her.

The masked man scoffed, turning to pace a few steps, hands in his pockets. "Odd, isn't it? Lady Mystine rushed to marry a dying man, knowing he couldn't raise any heirs he'd father. As I learned the story, she almost died birthing her first child, you, yet you mean to tell me after eighteen years she still risked having another? Why risk it with a man who wouldn't be there?" He paced again the other way.

Her palms sweat. "It wasn't planned," she said, heart pounding. Not knowing his identity made confessing dangerous. But he persisted.

"Her third husband, Lord Byron, never had children. As a result, his bastard nephew became the heir to the wealthiest estate in Althenia. Byron's first wife was kicked by a horse while pregnant, leaving her barren and childless as a result. If Mystine's second child was uncomplicated with your help, and if both Lady and Lord Byron were fertile, why no more children?" He drew nearer, eyes never leaving hers.

The masked man stood close, his body inches from her, smirking. "Eva doesn't know the truth about her father because she doesn't know her real mother, does she?"

Audra's heart raced. He knew. Somehow, from one letter, he'd unveiled that Eva was hers. She didn't realize she'd given away so much with so little. Would this be her undoing?

Did this also confirm the masked man wasn't Kolbe? Kolbe knew about Eva, but the masked man didn't... unless it was a ruse.

She tensed, averting her gaze. He stepped forward, tilting her chin up with a finger, causing her heart to race with excitement and fear. Their eyes locked. If only she could see their color...

Making a quick decision, she acted fast, reaching for his mask. In a swift motion, he caught her wrist and twirled her around, arms crossed, her wrists held firmly in his hands. Her back warmed against his chest, his breath dancing across her neck.

"I told you not to try that," he growled. "My reflexes are faster, I'm trained to prevent that. I warned you." A faint lavender mixed with a woodsy scent wafted from him. The closeness reminded her of their kiss. She stifled a whimper.

He held her longer than necessary, a proximity she didn't dislike. It made her miss being touched. Whispering, he said, "The future queen has secrets."

"Secrets that could kill me," she whispered. If he were the prince, he should perceive why she stayed silent.

Still near her ear, he breathed, "Don't try that again."

His hands released her wrists, and her arms relaxed as he stepped away. She turned, seeing him watching her.

Breathing steadily, her lips parted. She pondered this man who somehow possessed power to melt her every resolve. Though she wished she knew his identity, the mystery also made him more alluring.

"I was right. Your reaction confirms it." He shifted, hesitating. "What was his name?"

"Whose name?" she asked, though she knew whose name he wanted.

"Eva's father, *Your Highness*." His gaze never left hers. There in the barn, barely lit by a single candle, she detected a certain coldness in his tone for the first time. His voice was mocking, almost, perhaps even... *jealous*.

Audra shook her head. "Just because you make it your business to pry into my life, doesn't mean I make it my business to tell you everything you want to learn. Are you asking me because it's your job to know everything about the future queen, or because you're jealous?"

"Who said it can't be both?" he said, a grunt escaping from the back of his throat. He shook his head and his lips curled into a scowl. "I have to be brief, we don't have all night. I will find out whether you tell me or not, but it will be much easier if you do."

Who did this man think he was to pry into her personal life like that? If it was Jed, then he didn't know her well enough to have such opinions. If he were the prince, why couldn't he ask as himself, like Kolbe had? Audra scoffed, folding her arms across her chest. "Like I said. He's dead. Mighty bold of you to demand such confessions when you won't tell me anything."

"For your safety," he said with a groan. His voice sounded forlorn, no longer riddled with spite. He sank his shoulders, and his jaw loosened. He sighed. "For whatever it's worth, I wish I could."

Silence followed, thick as tar. She steadied her heart, realizing whoever he was didn't appear to hate her for this. "Why did you come find me?" she asked, her voice quiet.

"I find it impossible to stay away," he responded. Audra's heart pounded. "But I must."

She scrutinized him, trying to put her thoughts into words. He was charismatic, haunting, and mysterious. He may be dangerous, but instead of frightening her, it excited her. She wondered if the secret of his identity would remain a secret forever.

At the confession, she blushed. She didn't understand why she felt shy about this man knowing her past. She felt naked. For the first time since meeting him, she never considered the possibility that the masked man, whoever he was, had genuine feelings for her.

The way candlelight reflected on his jaw reminded her of the prince, but she knew shadows to play tricks.

Perhaps Elijah could be the masked man. Much of the masked man's confidence echoed that of Elijah's, and their mannerisms often bore similarities. Would the prince use a disguise to talk to her? Would he conceal his knowledge about her kiss with the masked man? Would he be angry if he found out she was not a virgin, after all? Would he see less value in her, no longer wish to marry her, or feel like she lied to him all along?

Who better to know about the affairs of the prince than the prince himself? It would also explain how he held no concern about being caught at the moment. Where was Elijah during the masquerade?

"Does the truth disappoint you?" Audra asked, watching him. She despised herself for caring about his answer.

The masked man shook his head, exhaling a small huff. "I'm upset I didn't realize sooner. I'm afraid it complicates things, having evidence out there that the future queen of Althenia is not a virgin. Who else knows?"

Audra deliberated for a moment whether or not to be honest, her stomach churning at his questions. He wouldn't share his secrets, yet demanded hers.

If he were the prince, lying would gain her nothing.

"You. My mother. Lord Byron. Kolbe Byron. Kathleen. Others are dead."

"Such as?" he asked.

She hesitated. "Margaret Bristwood."

At the sound of her name, he stiffened. "The king's murdered mistress, Margaret?"

She nodded, his discomfort visible.

"Great," he muttered, but how he said it indicated it wasn't great. "I have to go. Return to the castle and don't tell anyone. Too many know already."

Panic rose as he headed for the door. "No, wait. Don't leave me without answers. It tortures me. If you won't tell me your identity or mission, then explain the emergency?"

He stopped near the door. After several moments of hesitation, he faced her. "Margaret gained favor by knowing secrets, spreading them, and manipulating men and women alike. Some secrets held more truth than others. The king sent her away because she caused chaos. I suspect she did this with you. Why would you tell her? I didn't take you for a fool. What I need to find out is whether or not she shared yours."

Audra gasped at his words, more upset by his accusation. Margaret shared everything with her, including how to kiss, and lovers she'd had. Her secret was mundane compared to some of Margaret's. Her friend wouldn't betray her.

"No. Margaret wouldn't have—"

"She would have, and trust me, she did." His voice was as stiff as his body. "The question isn't if, it's when? With whom? Your position as queen isn't finalized, and this could ruin everything. If Doth knows, things will worsen."

Audra and Margaret had shared many nights, confiding in each other and unmasking their truest selves. She trusted Margaret, even knowing her dubious morals. Now, a man who told her nothing tried to tarnish her memories. It seemed like he was punishing those tiny moments of happiness she stole while living in Hillsfield by minimizing the person who helped her most during all those years of mourning Garrick's death.

"She may have shared secrets, but she wouldn't have shared mine," Audra said, her voice stern.

The masked man frowned. "I must go," he repeated, moving for the door, but she brushed his hand as he grabbed the knob. He paused, looking at her one last time. "Stay safe. Stop prying for answers. It isn't your war to fight."

He disappeared, leaving her alone in the dark stable. Angered, she vowed his secrets would end next meeting. If she saw him again, she'd reveal his identity.

He was wrong. She felt certain Margaret hadn't betrayed her. If she was indeed a fool, it was for trusting a man who trusted her little. People don't hoard secrets from those they trust. They keep them from those who cannot be trusted. Therefore, it was clear that the masked man didn't trust her.

The masked man hadn't just restrained her. He'd *predicted her instinct* and matched it with his own. Reflection of that moment both haunted her and consumed her entirely. It rose like a memory with a heartbeat, threatening to restore a part of her she'd been certain had drowned.

But not for a name she could speak aloud. It was for a phantom, a shadow, a pulse in the darkness. The echo of yes in the chambers of forgotten no. A flame that consumed the forest and offered nothing in return.

The worst realization was that deep down, she realized he might be right. Her emotions, thoughts, and desires *were* all untrustworthy. She feared the mask, not because it concealed a stranger—*but because it might not.*

19

Morning arrived early. Audra awoke to her ladies-in-waiting bustling in her bedchamber. Groaning, she lamented their giddy excitement. She felt the exact opposite. Notably, for the seventh consecutive morning, Kathleen was absent. During their first week, Kathleen was involved in everything, but this week, she appeared only by noon, claiming illness or sleeping late.

"Why so early?" Audra grumbled, trying to understand their excitement.

"The prince invited you to breakfast. Now, up," Tessai chirped, stripping the sheets away with a grin. Audra scowled, wondering who made Tessai the future queen.

Sitting up, she surveyed the room for someone missing, despite her previous promises of timeliness. "Where's Kathleen?" Audra asked, accepting the robe Alynne draped over her shoulders, its luxurious fabric feeling exotic against her skin. She pulled it closer to her body, soaking in the extravagance.

"Haven't seen her," Tessai shrugged, showing Audra a claret dress with black beads adorning the corset. Black tulle overlaying the claret chiffon skirt looked more alluring than her own creations. "Madam Guiller sent the first three dresses. She wishes to discuss future designs later this afternoon... including your wedding gown."

Audra admired the fabric while slipping from her nightgown into a slip, corset, and the claret dress, accentuating her breasts in ways Hillsfield would never have permitted. Marianne twisted Audra's hair into a satin black ribbon that tied at her neck, the ends matching the length of her blonde locks. Red coloring painted her lips, her eyes darkened with Althenian luxuries banned at Lord Byron's estate. Though no stranger to her beauty, with Marianne's gifted talents, vanity swelled within. She hoped the prince would be pleased... or aroused.

She dismissed the thought. Her experience with one man happened after years of friendship before they became more intimate. The prince was a stranger, one who could alter her future forever... assuming he didn't already know her deepest secret. Still, she remembered enough about that night in the barrel room to recall how much she missed a lover's touch.

Her ladies and two guards accompanied her to the dining hall until Julin intercepted midway.

Julin's face bore its customary sullen expression. He bowed, and Audra allowed him to speak. "Your Grace, the prince needs a few more minutes. He asks for you in the king's study instead of the dining hall, without your ladies or guards. Ladies, dismissed. Your Grace, I'll escort you."

The plan change seemed minor, yet adapting to being alone with the prince was daunting, evoking memories of her latest masked man encounter. If the masked man wasn't the prince, her relationship with the stranger was another secret she couldn't tell him.

"How do you find your time here at the palace?" Julin inquired, guiding her toward another wing.

"Comfortable, thank you."

Julin glanced sideways. "I'm curious about those you've met. Anything noteworthy for me to investigate?"

Recollecting the masked man's warning not to trust anyone or share anything, she chose discretion. "Nothing of note."

Traversing the castle, a guard signaled Julin aside for privacy. Excusing himself, Julin bowed, leaving Audra nearby. She lingered, but within moments she eavesdropped on one word: "Kathleen."

Intrigued, Audra intervened. "Excuse me, gentlemen. As future Queen of Althenia, I insist on knowing what you are discussing?"

Panic flickered in Julin's eyes, giving way to a grim, annoyed smile. Though clear he didn't want her to know, she didn't care. "Yes, Your Highness. Polin informed me that the king's study is occupied. We need to move to another location."

Audra nodded, but she suspected more. "I see. I heard him mention Kathleen, my lady-in-waiting. Is she in the king's—" Audra paused as both men's expressions fell, confirming who occupied the room. Why was Kathleen in the king's study? The reasons she imagined were unsavory, but the men's faces signaled her intuition's validity.

Her heart sank, recalling conversations with Kathleen. She'd found it odd that Kathleen admired the king, but not surprising. Her late husband had been older, and age never bothered Kathleen. Seeing their muted reactions, Audra understood that where Kathleen was, so was the king. "No, no, no," Audra murmured, striding toward the king's study, Polin and Julin trailing.

"Your Highness, the king asked not to be disturbed—" Polin started, but Audra silenced him with a raised hand as she approached the study at the end of the corridor.

Audra paused at the door, her mind swirling with possibilities. Closing her eyes, she took a deep breath, steadying her emotions. This wasn't happening. "Is the king fucking my lady-in-waiting inside? Is that why he can't be disturbed?" Her tone was harsh, demanding answers.

Julin and Polin exchanged glances again. Julin stepped forward, swallowing. "They've taken mutual interest in one another."

Audra's skin prickled, every hair on her arm standing tall. The king made Kathleen his newest mistress, explaining her absence last week. She recalled swearing to Kolbe that Kathleen would remain safe at court. How could Kathleen be so reckless? Everyone knows what happens to those who lie with the king.

Audra's hands balled into fists, seething. "How could anyone allow this to happen? Kathleen is my sister, niece to Lord Byron—"

"Keep your voice down," Julin urged, moving closer. "The king rules without contest. Nobody has a say over the king. We regret that his choices involve someone close to you, but the king's will supersedes all."

Audra ignored him. She cared little that it involved the king's will. Kathleen's involvement made her a target, now Audra's responsibility to protect. The arrow of death now pointed directly at her head.

Disbelief and anger boiled inside her as she wondered how one man could be so selfish. What could Audra do about it? It hurt knowing Kathleen kept it a secret, but Audra should have detected Kathleen's chipper moods and restrained gossip behaviors. Kathleen's secrecy wouldn't void Audra's knowledge of recent events.

Kathleen didn't want Audra to know. The realization seeped of betrayal, a deep stab to her heart. How could Kathleen do this, knowing the consequences?

Audra's skin crawled, grappling with what to do. Who could she consult? "I need time alone. Tell the prince I'm unwell and will join him for dinner instead. Send my apologies." Meeting the prince now would betray her emotions. She needed time to compose herself, and as panic raged inside of her, all she wanted was to hide.

Julin pressed his lips thin, striding to her side, leaning close without touching. "Your Highness must understand not to speak of this," he said, motioning the guards to escort her back. Outside her chamber, she commanded the guards to remain in the hallway and entered alone. Sinking against the door, she buried her head in her knees. Slow breaths calmed her nerves, though helplessness smothered all hopes of clarity.

Why was Kathleen so foolish? Audra had told her the king's mistresses were murder targets. Why endanger herself? Did she have a choice?

Steadying herself, Audra moved toward her bedchamber. When she turned the corner, she halted. Jed stood at her bed's foot, nearly startling a scream from her. He raised a finger to hush her.

"Jed?" she asked, confused. Why was he at the castle, in her bedroom, alone?

"I know I shouldn't be here. I was going to return a book to the king's study and witnessed your discovery..." Jed hesitated, looking down. "It would be better if you hadn't known."

Audra flushed, shock turning to surprise. "You knew about K—"

"Whisper," Jed urged in a hushed tone. She studied him, wondering how much he knew. Though she didn't fear his presence, seeing him so soon after the letter felt suspicious.

Was it a coincidence, or a breadcrumb trail she'd missed all along? The masked man had found her letter through Jed, who was acquainted with palace affairs more than expected, splitting his time between Hillsfield and the castle.

She wondered, now, how she missed it. She found her eyes drifting to his lips, remembering the way it felt when the masked man kissed her. Her mind raced back to the times she used to read with him in his chambers at Hillsfield. Recalling the discussions they used to have, she remembered how he would tell her about science, philosophy, and astronomy. His cleverness was one of the reasons she felt initially drawn to him.

He was the masked man. He had to be. She straightened, her heart pounding as she considered ways to have him confess.

Audra moved from him, sitting at the bed's edge. "How long has it been happening?" she asked, deliberating which approach to use and wondering how much he'd disclose.

He entered her view, casual demeanor foiling her emotions. He rubbed his chin. "Since the masquerade, we suspect. First in letters, now like this."

Letters? It stretched further than she knew. "Why didn't you tell me?" Audra's lips tightened. "What are you doing in my room?"

Jed plopped himself into an armchair, signaling he meant to stay a while. "Protecting you from your own curiosity. Here, knowledge is perilous. The more important you are, the greater the risk."

She resisted eye-rolling, weary of warnings against knowing details of her own life. "If I'm in danger, I should know what to avoid."

"You avoid better without knowing." He smirked, as if he predicted this would irritate her. It had.

Audra huffed, turning toward her vanity, where she spotted a pitcher of wine she'd requested that morning sitting on a tray with an empty glass next to it. She walked over to pour herself a full glass before taking a sip, tasting it. Why, if she was in danger, did no one enlighten her? How did her own safety involve Kathleen and the king?

Audra collected her thoughts before replying, the tart taste of her wine clinging to her tongue. "The king's mistresses perish. Now, the mistress is my lady-in-waiting and closest confidante. We both understand this fact. Tell me, how does my sister's tutor end up more privy to palace affairs than I, the future queen?"

Jed chuckled. "I thought you figured that out by now. I spy for the future king, tasked with knowing Hillsfield's happenings."

Like the masked man had said. She lifted her chin. "Is it also your job to know royal court affairs? Is that why you misplaced my letter to Eva?" Her tone was sharp. She guessed but needed confirmation. Was Jed the masked man, a prince's spy for her protection?

Jed narrowed his eyes, silent. He scratched at the chair arm. "The prince's affairs, as future king, remain confidential. I wouldn't betray that. Now, I will enlighten you about what you witnessed. Or didn't." Standing, he cautioned, "Should you acknowledge it, Kathleen risks befalling prior victims' fates. Limiting this knowledge keeps her safer. The king is more discreet with this affair than others."

Some relief settled. As long as it stayed quiet, Kathleen might be safe. They agreed, at least, not to speak a word of it. However, Audra noted his evasion regarding the letter. She suspected something purposeful occurred.

Maybe Audra didn't know him as well as she thought. "What if the murderer already knows?" she asked.

Jed shook his head. "You know what happens."

His eyes lingered on hers. She took another drink, pacing, thoughts circling back. Yes, she did realize what would happen. Kathleen would die. How long could secrets last? The murderer was within the castle already. Was he already aware?

"Secrets stay secret in this case," Audra vowed, her voice solemn. "I wouldn't harm her. But silence doesn't guarantee safety." She recalled Kolbe's caution about Kathleen's flirtatiousness. The sting of culpability captured her, wishing she'd listened.

Jed stepped closer, and Audra tensed. Noticing, he stopped. "I'll do what I can. Lord Byron is aware of the rumors. Don't tell anyone else."

Audra nodded, staring at her hands. The way Jed spoke in cryptic messages convinced her she'd unveiled the masked man's identity.

"The less I know, the better. Right?" she quoted the masked man, watching his response. If he had one, the emotion was unreadable.

"Exactly. Go find Prince Elijah. He expects you, and if you don't go, you'll draw attention. Wedding preparations can distract you if you need something to think about. I'll leave after you. And by the way," he said, then reached behind her to grab a book off her fireplace. *Poisons and Posies.* "Since I see you found it, I'll return this. A lot of misunderstandings and time are saved when we're honest. Dishonesty wastes time that could have been preserved."

She wondered how he'd entered, though it was clear he wanted secrecy. Audra nodded, sighing. The hypocrisy annoyed her. Attempting once more for truth, she asked, "Will you ever tell me everything, Jed? Or is only my honesty required?"

Jed swallowed, shaking his head. "Some secrets are gifts, wrapped in silence and preserved for when the time is right. Others are weapons, designed to blind their victims. Most don't belong to me, so I won't be the hand that breaks them open. Go find the prince."

20

The walk to the prince's chambers dragged, the clicking of her heels announcing her presence down every hallway.

Arriving at Prince Elijah's chambers, she found Julin waiting outside, speaking to the guards. He gave a curt nod to acknowledge her before turning back to them.

"We will leave the future queen to Prince Elijah, and should you need us, we will be just outside," Julin said. He and the guard opened the doors, revealing the prince's room, lush with lavender flowers adorning every vase and setting. The smell wafted through the air as she entered, almost overwhelming her senses.

As Audra stepped in, Julin grasped her arm. "Make sure nobody gets hurt from this," he advised before closing the door, leaving her alone with the prince.

Elijah appeared seated on a golden tufted chair, engrossed in a book. Upon her entrance, he rose to greet her with a bow, which she returned with a curtsy. The sight of him, handsome and brooding, made her heart race. Hair-raising replaced the fleeting thoughts of attraction as she observed his serious expression, making her realize something was amiss.

Though Elijah greeted her with a smile, his demeanor reflected cold distance, unlike their last meeting. The guards closed them inside, and Audra turned as he spoke. "My father's mistress, Margaret Bristwood, wasn't like the others. She enjoyed exchanging information for secrets. She also loved the sound of her own voice and the power she had with words. We've established I know you two were friends, but... How close of friends were you, exactly?"

Surprised by his greeting, Audra flushed, frozen. How much did he know? What had Margaret divulged?

Furthermore, it confirmed the validity behind the masked man's accusation. Perhaps Margaret *had* betrayed her. Audra's heart split in two. What Margaret had said or how much she'd relayed, Audra couldn't be certain. She'd trusted Margaret. She'd been so certain of it that she'd pushed the masked man away in anger. Now, the connection she shared with Margaret was tarnished.

"Close, Your Highness. We met in school when I was fourteen," Audra admitted. Lying seemed futile, but she wouldn't volunteer more without first the accusation.

Had someone overheard her barn conversation? Was the prince the masked man?

Elijah's face registered surprise, then his notorious half-smile splayed across his lips. "Well, that settles it. The plan was simple. I planned to ask and discover who you are. If you lied, it confirmed that trust between us was impossible. If honest—" he approached, placing a hand on her hip, drawing her close. "Let's just say I hoped you'd tell the truth. I need reassurance that even when you're afraid to answer a question, you will give me the honest one. Not the one you think will save you. That's what I need in order to trust my future wife."

Her body warmed under his touch, her heart fluttering between fear and excitement. Was that all he heard? He wanted to confirm the depth of her friendship with Margaret?

As her heart calmed, his lips approached hers. She inspected his features, weighing them against the masked man. So much was similar: the sound of his voice, the curve of his lips, the length of his hair. Audra swallowed, hands trembling as she cleared her throat. "Elijah... do you remember our first meeting?" she asked.

His eyebrows rose, interest piquing. "I do. Outside the ballroom. Why?"

Audra hesitated, pulling back, unsure if she wanted to know the answer. Still, she couldn't help wondering about Eva's safety. If the masked man knew and he was Elijah, what did it mean for her?

He had to be. Lavender in the room, his mannerisms, all so evocative of the masked man.

"Were you the masked man I danced with at the ball?" she inquired. Her eyes flicked to his face. Elijah's chin tilted, and he tightened his lips, hands twitching.

"Everyone was masked at the ball. I didn't dance with you before our meeting, if that's what you want to know."

Was he truthful? If the masked man, would he avoid specifics? Audra considered her next question.

"You look disappointed," Elijah noted, his mouth twitching. He walked to a console table, where wine and glasses awaited. He poured both glasses, handing one to Audra.

He didn't drink first, watching her instead. She wondered if he was testing her trust. Audra examined the glass of wine, the merlot liquid rippling from her trembling hand. Audra raised the glass to her lips, taking a sip. Elijah smiled, then drank from his glass.

"At the masquerade, Dothian spies infiltrated, using masks to hide. My father thought it would be an interesting way to introduce you, as if your hair wouldn't give you away first. During Isabelle's death, guards warned about a mysterious man they found lurking in the hallway. It was a ruse to distract me. Isabelle wasn't the target that night," Elijah stated, eyes fixing on her. "The poisoned cup was meant for you."

She almost dropped the glass of wine. The poisoned cup was meant for her? She thought of the masked man and the whistle that pulled him away. Her heart skipped a beat.

"Why me?" she asked, unable to meet his gaze. She recalled Elijah telling her in the carriage after the death that unchaste victims were targeted. Elijah sipped, watching her response.

He waited for her answer instead of replying.

Audra inhaled, unable to move. He must have brought up Margaret because she'd spoken, revealing truths Audra had wanted hidden. Which truth, and how many? Did Elijah know everything, even about Eva? As she stood, he circled her, sipping more wine. He stopped at the window without looking out of it, leaning against the sill. Watching her. Waiting.

She looked at the wine, crimson akin to blood. She shut her eyes, shaking her head. "I understand," she whispered. "I wanted to tell you but I feared death if you knew. I realize my secrets wouldn't save me, but..."

He drank again, finishing his glass. Her heart beat so fiercely she feared it might burst. Setting the empty glass down on the windowsill, he didn't move. "The truth, Audra, is that I didn't know what was true. Margaret's secrets varied in predictability. Some were true, some were conspired fantasies. When a rumor claimed my betrothed lacked virginity, I wished it were false. Investigations followed so I could prove she was wrong."

Audra held her skirts, moving to set her glass on the table next to the pitcher. "I'm not a virgin," she whispered, watching the glass. "I shouldn't have kept it from you. I was frightened."

Silence lingered between them post-confession. She imagined guards seizing her to have her beheaded on the spot, but Elijah didn't move. She dared glance back, his gaze unwavering.

"No," he said, "You shouldn't have kept silent. Omission is quite a thief, stealing truth with sealed lips." Elijah approached, towering over her as she tried not to sink. After a moment, he reached around her, grabbing the pitcher from the table before returning to the windowsill to refill his glass. She waited for his verdict. Would he kill, imprison, or hang her for treason?

Seated again on the sill, he continued, "I doubted until the masquerade. You told me you thought you were a target. Your target status needed explaining. Reports tell me the night of Margaret's death, you were seen with Kolbe Byron, carried inside Hillsfield."

Someone had seen them. Elijah observed as Audra shut her eyes.

"Kolbe Byron never laid a hand on me that way. That's the truth," Audra asserted, flicking her eyes to meet Elijah's gaze and straightening her posture. "I injured myself going to see Margaret. Kolbe caught me sneaking out and insisted on accompanying me. I saw her dead, fell off a ladder, and he carried me back to Hillsfield. That's the end of it. He's loyal to you and never touched me that way"

Audra breathed to calm herself. "The man who took my virginity was someone I loved before my mother married Lord Byron. Before our betrothal, before any of this. I thought he'd be my husband."

Her cheeks flushed, her heart beating louder and faster with each new confession. She wished to flee, but everything else led to this moment of truth, and whether Elijah would have her killed for it. Her mind wandered to Eva, wondering if he knew about her.

Elijah sipped, swirling his glass. "Why didn't you wed?"

She swallowed, wishing she could perish on the spot, the uncertainty of the conversation's end unbearable. The dream life slipped further away with each truth she spilled. "He died," she said. "The next morning, he was murdered."

Elijah's gaze intensified, signaling something between amusement and distrust. "What was his name?"

The masked man had asked the same question the night before, and she didn't tell him. She had only ever said he was dead.

The prince, however, required honesty. Whether she liked it or not, she belonged to him. She was his property to do with as he pleased, like prized cattle purchased at market. As the owner, he could choose if he wanted to display, milk, or cherish.

"His name was Garrick Lorent."

Elijah tensed, but she couldn't determine his thoughts from his expression. Rubbing his chin, he turned to a painting depicting a past war between Doth and Althenia.

"Lorent," he echoed, tone seeped with hostility. Was it jealousy or something more? What now? "I've never heard the name. When was the last time you spoke?"

Audra frowned, a lump forming in the back of her throat. "Eight years ago, Your Highness. The day he was killed."

Elijah scrutinized her, chin raised. Audra shielded a tear with her hand, embarrassed about discussing Garrick with her future husband.

"Hmm," he murmured, sighing. "He must have been something rare to capture your attention. Tell me about him."

Her body tensed, discomfort seated deep. Must she? "We were childhood friends. His father abandoned him before birth, so his mother raised him alone. He helped on our farm, and we cared for his mother during her illness."

Elijah nodded, stepping away from the painting to gaze out the window. Audra remained still, uncertain of her fate and where this left her.

"Unfortunate, men not knowing their fathers. How did he die?" Elijah inquired.

The haunting memory returned. "Poison." She remembered the larkspur strewn about, the poison that also killed Isabelle and June.

"Larkspur?" Elijah asked.

Audra nodded, pondering the coincidence, but a puzzle piece was missing. The flower came from Doth, and his death had never made sense until she learned that Dothians murdered those who hadn't waited until marriage. Was that why Garrick was killed?

Elijah's tongue clicked, frowning as he drained his wine and set the glass down. Approaching, he loomed large beside her. "I'm sorry for your loss. I recognize this wasn't easy to share with me. A decade ago, Dothian forces assaulted Althenian serfs. The countryside was where they started. They raided homes, violated women, and killed innocent men. It took years to capture them and hang them for these crimes. Murders stopped for a while when we did."

Audra bit her lip, fighting tears. How could such maliciousness force innocents to suffer so?

In some ways, Audra felt as if she were grieving his death all over again. Having answers didn't make it easier, it made it worse. She supposed she always knew he'd been killed in cold blood. What she hadn't known was that he wasn't the only one. Living in the countryside, they never got news of much, and after his death, she couldn't get out of bed.

As Elijah towered, she remained uncertain of her place with him. What next?

She flinched when the back of his fingertips brushed her cheek. His eyes reflected hurt and something else she couldn't place. "I'm sorry for your loss. I still intend to marry you," Elijah said, softer than before. For the first time since arriving in his chamber, she relaxed. "Your secret remains safe if you promise not to withhold any more from me. I sense your reluctance with me, and I'll try to be patient. I don't want our wedding night to be forced, so I've delayed for you. But my father won't let it wait forever." He smirked, this time looking into her eyes, "And I don't want to."

Her heart twisted. He still wanted to marry her?

However, one secret remained. If he were the masked man, he had already uncovered it. She couldn't be sure he *was* the masked man, though. Revealing her daughter risked more than revealing lost innocence.

She couldn't risk it. Not yet.

"I can't marry you if I can't trust you," Elijah whispered. "Today, telling me was courageous. I predicted that you feared I might kill you. Harm isn't my intention," he said, fingertips tracing her hair, tangling a lock between gentle fingers.

She chose her next words carefully, longing for his secrets too. "You should know everything, now. My mask is off," she said, seeking his teal eyes, reminiscent of the dead man who stole her heart and had it buried with him. "Is yours?"

If he were the masked man, he'd understand her meaning. He released her hair, grasping her waist instead, face inches away from hers. "Some truths wait until marriage. Some secrets would be too dangerous to reveal now, but I promise to tell you soon."

Elijah leaned closer and drew her nearer, her heart racing. "There is one secret I can reveal. I'm glad you're not a virgin. This will make our wedding night more interesting for both of us, I imagine," he murmured. Audra shook as his hand traced up her back, stopping on her neck, his lips close to her ear. Audra closed her eyes, his whisper stirring her. His hand slid over her collarbone, resting his finger and thumb like a necklace around her throat. He didn't squeeze or attempt to choke her, but a shiver ran through her. "First, I need to know where your loyalties lie."

Audra swallowed, uncertain of her feelings. Was this hold on her possession or protectiveness? The kiss with the masked man resonated along with the way he'd held her after she tried to remove his mask. The feelings with the stranger had been charged by her desire, electrifying bolts of temptation throughout her entire body. This touch felt different, but she couldn't place how. The masked man had been annoyed by her participation in their kiss, and she wondered if that's what Elijah meant about her loyalty.

"I'll only kiss you henceforth, Your Highness. I'm loyal to you. Anything that happened before you was fleeting moments of weakness," she said, hoping it would assure him.

Elijah chuckled, pulling away from her ear to meet her eyes. "Your past entices, not disqualifies. I'm fascinated by a woman who enjoys her pleasures." His hand moved from throat to shoulder, gaze tracing her figure, unashamed. "Loyalty sometimes changes when facts do. Facts are mere whispers to ignorant minds and a clarion call for the wise." He kissed her jaw, a soft peck. Audra gasped.

Inhaling, he savored her vanilla perfume, fingers gripping the bare skin of her shoulder. "I wonder if you'll be loyal, knowing what's required for Althenia's sake. I wonder if you'll forgive me when you learn how many had to perish to save it." His hand settled on her hip, and her heart raced.

What did he mean?

He proceeded. "Whatever you've done before arriving at the castle is forgiven, as I hope you'll forgive my prior deeds. The scope of my protection extends as far as the truth. I cannot protect you from things you hide."

Elijah kissed her. Audra's hands grasped her skirts, caught between excitement and fear. Even with his lips on hers, her heart wandered, pondering Eva's safety and whether Elijah might help protect her if he knew.

Though their lips touched, her heart disconnected from it. Revealing the truth about Eva felt insurmountable, but as long as he didn't know, he couldn't love her. One cannot love someone they don't truly know.

If aware, because he was the masked man, would he wait for her confession? How long would he wait? She wondered if his secrets would be anything like hers.

Elijah pulled back from the kiss, sighing, examining her face as her body relaxed.

"Whatever shadows darken your mind, I hope one day you'll share with me," he said. "I sense there's something. Perhaps grief from the love you lost. I've burdened you enough today. Promise to consider it." As Elijah withdrew, she tasted the remnants of wine on her lips.

That kiss, loveless, recalled the masked man's passionate one. This one had been missing fire, harmony, and emotion. Distance remained, secrets concealed. Elijah's kiss, unlike the one shared with the masked man, fell short.

Another secret she hid: kissing a stranger while engaged. Elijah, frowning and displeased, returned to the pitcher and poured another glass of wine.

Why couldn't she let him learn everything? He'd been kind, passionate, and forgiving. Rich, charming, handsome. Yet, reckoning awaited. She still felt like a noose hung around her neck, waiting for the floor to drop beneath her. Just as he couldn't trust her until she revealed all her truths, neither could she let him in. They'd continue to dance, and she wondered if life in the palace would always be this way.

"I have a meeting about castle politics with my father. Clarifying rumors about various engagements," Elijah said, back turned. Was it about Kathleen? Audra's mind drifted back to her discovery of Kathleen and the king. Did Elijah know? He didn't glance her way, watching out the window. "You may go. I'll see you this evening."

Audra turned, walking past him toward the door. She paused when she grabbed the handle of the knob, realizing she remained alive, unharmed, free to roam the halls. She pondered if danger lurked about her or if the focus was on Kathleen.

Audra hesitated as she clutched the doorknob, turning back to him. Though silent on Eva, she sought to gain his trust another way. "Your Highness... I would like to request a favor."

He looked over his shoulder. "Oh?"

She gathered her skirts, nervous. "I want to send my lady-in-waiting back to Hillsfield. I fear Kathleen Byron ill-suited for castle life."

Elijah faced her, expression tight. "I wondered if you knew," he said, shaking his head. "I discovered it this morning, and intend to discuss it with my father," he sighed. "I can't send her back. Lord Byron is on his way to the castle as we speak. They planned in secret to marry tomorrow."

21

Kathleen's shift from lady-in-waiting to potential queen of Althenia gnawed at Audra all afternoon. Her stomach churned, wishing she'd known about it sooner. Something felt off, and Kathleen was in more danger than ever. It wasn't merely the king taking a mistress this time. He intended to take an entire wife.

Hurrying down the hallway with guards trailing, Audra reached her chambers. The doors were wide open, and inside, a swarm of servants packed her belongings. They were... her things.

"What's happening?" Audra inquired.

The servants paused, some glancing away as they curtsied. A young man in a plain gray tunic answered. "The king ordered your things to be moved from the Queen's Quarters to the tower room, where you'll reside henceforth."

Some servants continued packing, others leaving with arms stocked full of her belongings. "The tower room?" Audra questioned.

"Yes," he nodded. "Princesses traditionally stay there until they become queens. Since you were next to be queen, you were moved here. Now, Queen Kathleen will reside here until King Henri's passing, when Prince Elijah ascends as king with you as queen."

As another servant passed with a box, Kathleen emerged from the bathroom, speaking with Alynne. When her eyes spotted Audra, Kathleen flushed a deep shade of burgundy.

"Audra," Kathleen said, surprised in her tone. "I thought you were with the prince."

It felt surreal, like living in another world. Kathleen stood, shoulders slumped, eyeing Audra. Audra's stomach twisted, unable to explain why this betrayal resembled salt brining an open wound. Moving rooms wasn't the issue bothering her so much as Kathleen behaving as if nothing had changed. Overnight, and without warning, everything had.

"I returned," Audra replied, deliberating her words. She cared for Kathleen, but her actions had consequences. "Could we talk? In private?"

Kathleen swallowed, instructing servants to leave. Alynne and others shuffled out, guards closing the doors. Kathleen moved by the fireplace, which Audra couldn't help but realize belonged to her hours before.

"What have you done?" Audra asked, her voice barely above a whisper.

"I did what I had to," Kathleen replied, her voice calm as she folded her hands, sitting on an ivory settee with gold trim. She gestured for Audra to sit in another settee adjacent to her.

Audra sat, though she found herself unable to stop squirming. "You witnessed what happens to the king's mistresses. You've put yourself in danger, Kathleen. I told you everything I learned, but you didn't consult me once about this."

"I'm not his mistress," Kathleen retorted, a frown forming. "You wanted me to find a husband, and that's what I did. I chose to marry the king."

"Why?" Audra blurted, trying to make sense of Kathleen's decision.

Kathleen averted her eyes, appearing on the verge of tears. She didn't intend to shame her, but Audra hungered for understanding.

"You were protected. I wasn't," Kathleen whispered. "It was clear you were Lord Byron's favorite."

Audra released an involuntary laugh before covering her mouth, realizing the reaction might seem cruel. "Me? His favorite? Lord Byron hates me," Audra countered, finding the notion absurd. Lord Byron only communicated with Audra through her mother. Constant criticism of Audra's behavior foiled any claims of favoritism. "I didn't choose this, Kathleen. I had no choice, and no knowledge of the engagement until I told you."

"I understand that. I never chose Sir Barton, Audra. I won't be a pawn anymore, and you of all people should understand that. Out there, I'm regarded as used goods; a worn widow of a wicked man. I was avoided like the plague, so like you, I sought protection amid danger."

Audra's mouth fell agape. How was this protection? Being a target meant always watching her back, fearing someone might stab her at any moment. "I'd have been content living the remainder of my life in the countryside, raising children with the man I loved. I didn't ask for this life. You have a choice, Kathleen, and you can acquire safety by returning to Hillsfield."

Kathleen folded her arms, lips tightening into a thin line. Audra pushed her thoughts of betrayal aside, questioning Kathleen's perspective. She'd never judged Kathleen for what had happened to Sir Barton, so why didn't Kathleen tell her? With a long sigh, Kathleen retrieved a piece of cloth from the fireplace—the masked man's sash from the night they'd kissed—setting it on the coffee table. "You should take this to your new chambers. I didn't intend to harm you, Audra. I'm just... afraid."

Audra rolled her eyes. "Marrying him won't save you," she said, attempting once again to reason with her. "The last queen, Elijah's mother, died in a barn fire. Being queen puts a target on your back. What ensures you won't befall the same fate?"

Kathleen swallowed, shaking her head as if she refused to understand. "I'll be careful," she said. "Living in fear isn't an option anymore. As a servant to the future queen, nobody cared about my safety. You wouldn't understand what it's like blending in. Guards shadow your every step, you're surrounded by protection. But what about me?"

Audra's heart sank. Kathleen had a point about being overlooked, yet constant attention also invited danger. A guard, a lady-in-waiting... *Anyone* could be a threat.

Rubbing her temples, Audra sought the words to dissuade Kathleen. Not because she opposed her happiness... she wanted Kathleen safe, and this choice doomed her. "I could have sent you back to Hillsfield or arranged a guard for you."

"Stop trying to exile me to Hillsfield," Kathleen snapped, face flushing. "I refuse to live the rest of my life like my mother, alone and branded. I'd rather die. The king's interest is genuine, he treated me better than Sir Barton ever did. He cares for me, Audra. Otherwise, he wouldn't have proposed. I thought you'd be happy. If marrying the prince was your goal, you wouldn't entertain that masked man of yours. Now, you needn't marry him. The Hillsfield-Althenia alliance stands, freeing you to return if the prince weds the Dothian princess."

In truth, Audra hadn't considered all the ramifications of Kathleen's marriage to the king. With Kathleen as queen, where did she stand? Would her betrothal dissolve? Would Elijah wed the Doth princess? The thought made her ill. She understood Kathleen's reluctance to return to Hillsfield.

On the one hand, returning meant she could watch over Eva again. Daydreaming of their reunion, she envisioned fleeing to another kingdom with Eva to start a new life. The idea had always been a fantasy, but she'd never gathered the bravery. Her mother had done it, so why couldn't she? She could teach Eva farming, sewing, and dressmaking. It could be a simple yet fulfilling life.

Thoughts of Elijah stopped her fantasies. He still desired to marry her, despite her past. He'd said so. Would this change anything?

Audra rose, facing Kathleen, who avoided her gaze.

"Please, don't mistake my concern for jealousy. I want you to have everything you desire. If King Henri brings you happiness, I'm happy for you. But my concern stems from fear for you," Audra explained, seeking examples. "As a lady-in-waiting, you were invisible. As queen, eyes will be on you, scrutinizing your every breath. I don't think Elijah plans to marry the Dothian princess despite your marriage. I believe he likes me. I fear you've marked yourself for Dothian spies who eliminate threats."

Kathleen remained seated as she trembled, wiping a tear. "Please leave. Time will reveal my fate, and I made my decision last night. Your belongings will arrive in your new chambers by evening. I hope we're still friends, no matter what happens next."

Audra's heart ached. It was as if Kathleen had a death wish. Kathleen, once the joy of Hillsfield, would wed the king. Filled with melancholy, Audra turned to leave.

Two guards awaited her outside, and the cluster of servants surged in as Audra exited. She paused, glancing back one last time. The new room wasn't the issue. The hurt came from her final friend's determination to expedite her demise, and that nothing Audra said would stop her.

22

The evening's banquet differed from the banquets before. Silverware clattered against plates as nobles spoke in whispers. Kathleen sat across from Audra, eyes cast down, while King Henri presided at the head. Even he fell silent. Beside Audra, Elijah fixed his gaze on the king, unwavering.

Servants brought forth roasted goose, pickled eggs, salads, fire-roasted pig, and mountains of various breads. As food arrived amid silence, Audra observed nobles whispering to each other. Sometimes she'd catch their eyes on her before looking away, pretending they hadn't.

After several minutes that stretched like hours, Elijah threw his gold napkin onto the table, turning to Audra. His eyes held concern. "Forgive me for what's about to happen," he said, turning to face his father. The clattering silverware stilled, a hush falling upon the room. "We need to speak in private."

"We're eating. Share your thoughts here," King Henri said, dabbing his lips, blind to the room's tension.

Elijah's lips tightened. "Alright, if you insist. You cannot do this. Are you provoking the enemy on purpose? Marrying her won't ensure her safety," he snapped, then turned to Kathleen. "I apologize for my directness, Queen Kathleen, but since my father won't tell you the truth, I will. Our enemy intends to murder every royal in their path." Audra's neck prickled as Elijah voiced her fears. Kathleen faced real danger, and Elijah's warning confirmed it wasn't in her head.

The king smirked, shoving food in his mouth before replying. "Mind your words, my boy. You have no idea what you speak of."

Elijah stood, fist striking the table. Audra startled. "Don't patronize me," his voice rose as he grew more impassioned. "All your mistresses were murdered, one by one. I've been running the kingdom while you get drunk on wine and women. Your selfishness angers me."

King Henri's face maintained composure, tearing meat from a goose leg as if his mouth wasn't already bursting with food. "Don't speak of things beyond your knowledge."

Elijah's bitter laugh rang out. Audra had never seen such anger from him, and she wondered what their meeting before was about if not this conversation. "Then educate me, *Your Majesty*."

King Henri scanned the room as nobles averted their eyes, the way rats scatter when confronted by new threats. His gaze settled on Kathleen, who nodded in silent communication.

"Fine. Let's talk outside," the king said. Kathleen rose to join him, and Elijah turned to Audra, his face grim.

"Come with us," Elijah said, offering his hand. She took it, following the king and Kathleen to the hall. Once at a safe distance, the king turned to Elijah.

King Henri spoke low, guards hovering near. "She's pregnant. We learned yesterday. Lord Byron would wage war over this."

Audra's mouth fell open, eyes finding Kathleen, who stared at the floor. Pregnant meant their affair began upon arrival. Recalling Kathleen's flirtation with the king at the masquerade, Audra realized she'd missed the signs during her other preoccupations.

Audra studied Elijah. His eyes fixed on Kathleen's form, though signs of pregnancy were invisible, impossible to detect by sight. Realizing this, Elijah exhaled a frustrated groan. "You should never have placed her in this position. Marriage won't shield her from Doth's response to this offense."

"What response?" the king asked, his arrogant chuckle betraying ignorance. "You claimed you'd handle the enemy. If you'd acted as a king should, they'd be gone. You could have chosen their princess, and nobody would have died. I already did my part, I married one Dothian witch before. Wicked woman, your mother. Let Doth be Byron's problem and worry about your duty to find the murderers."

Before Audra considered what he meant about making it Byron's problem, King Henri clasped Kathleen's hand, smiling. "I've hired her a poison tester, and appointed four extra guards to her watch until then. If you can't secure the palace, I'll manage myself."

Elijah's face twisted into an expression between a grimace and a sneer. He turned to Audra, features softening for a brief moment. "Excuse me. I need to clear my head. I'll find you after supper." He kissed her hand before departing, leaving her with Kathleen and the king.

Audra stood stunned, appraising Kathleen's figure with disbelief. A child with the king?

Though Elijah's words were harsh, they echoed what she'd said to Kathleen earlier. She was not safe. Unless... Audra could help by finding the murderers first.

Kathleen's eyes brightened at something behind Audra. She turned to find Kolbe approaching, her heart racing at his handsome presence. Lord Byron strode behind him, guards in tow.

"Ah," the king's face shifted from contempt to cheer. "Lord Byron and his nephew. You've arrived at the perfect time. Join our feast."

Kolbe's gaze moved between the king and Audra, offering a slight bow. Their last exchange ended poorly, and his expression revealed none of his thoughts about seeing her again. Lord Byron's face held obvious displeasure. Kolbe's eyes never left Audra as Lord Byron held his focus on the king.

He couldn't love her. She knew this. At least, she wanted to know it, but her heart questioned and wondered, *"What if?"*

Kathleen broke the uncomfortable silence by embracing her brother, telling him she was happy to see him.

Lord Byron exhaled a long, slow breath through his nose. "Well, here we are," Byron said. "We'll discuss arrangements after supper. A fallen tree delayed our journey, so we're famished."

She wondered about Lord Byron's thoughts on the new engagement. He despised the king's affairs. Why hadn't he matched Elijah's outburst? Did he know of lurking dangers?

Did Kolbe?

Following the king and Kathleen, she felt Lord Byron and Kolbe watching as they strode behind her, perhaps wondering about her role in this affair. In the back of her mind, she heard Kolbe's unspoken reproach. *He told her so.* She never should have brought Kathleen to court.

After supper, the king, Kathleen, and Lord Byron left the banquet hall to discuss matters in private. Audra's eyes located Kolbe at the table's end, watching nobles dance. The king insisted on a celebration upon his return, commanding the court to welcome their new guests. Audra fixed her gaze as a young noblewoman approached Kolbe, fanning herself and fluttering her eyelashes like a ridiculous ninny.

She remembered Kolbe's patterns, yet through dinner, disappointment still prospered when he hadn't looked her way. Perhaps he kept his distance, following her last command to wait for her to approach him first. Now, the order seemed absurd.

The noblewoman departed with a wink. Then came a change: Kolbe looked at Audra, breaking eye contact when he caught her watching.

She reasoned he looked because she was his sole acquaintance there. Audra finished her wine, drawing courage from the glass. She stood and proceeded toward him, her heart pounding.

"Care to dance?" she asked. His eyes traced her dress, the claret shade bold in contrast to Hillsfield's muted tones. Lord Byron never allowed such colors. The pinkish-purple fabric clung to her form and accentuated her breasts, making her feel promiscuous and underdressed. His gaze traveled to her face as he swallowed.

"Alright," he said, rising to offer his hand. He led her to the floor as the music slowed, the tune changing from jovial to dramatic. His hand found her waist, causing waves of heat to spread through her entire body.

They moved in silence to the slow melody. She eyed his black hair sweeping over his brow, his brown eyes meeting hers.

"I owe you an apology for our last meeting," she said. His face remained still as she continued. "I rejected your words and didn't want to accept your answers, so I pushed you away. I want you to believe I'm always your friend, so you needn't treat me as your superior. I lashed out like a wounded animal, and my treatment was unacceptable. Please forgive me."

Kolbe's smirk set her heart aflutter. "No need to apologize. I was wrong about Kathleen."

Audra frowned at his response, surprised by his answer. She pressed her lips together before releasing a breath. The wedding didn't trouble him? "Truth is, I'm not certain you were wrong."

His brows drew together as he pulled her a smidge closer. "What do you mean?"

She realized his assumption about her anger. He thought Kathleen was the reason she reacted the way she had at their last meeting? "Wait," Audra said, "you think I was upset because you warned me about bringing Kathleen?"

Kolbe's eyes narrowed, one brow lifting as the melody surrounded them. "What else?"

What else? Audra shook her head. Their fight sparked because it hurt to discover that he never considered loving her. He'd told her he could never. She shouldn't care, given her engagement, yet his continued indifference stung. He hadn't thought of her that way, and he hadn't lost any sleep over their argument. Not once.

"Nothing," Audra said, her cheeks flushing. She returned to their conversation about Kathleen. "I believe the king's marriage puts her at risk. I think she might be the murderer's next target. I desire to find him first to stop it. I've kept silent here about this because I don't know whom I can trust here. Who would believe me over the assumption of jealousy?"

Kolbe's eyes calculated as he processed her words. "You think she's in danger? If my sister faces danger, I'll handle it."

Her eyes narrowed. How could he miss this? He was with her in the carriage the night the prince discussed the murders. "What do you know?" She recalled Jed's hidden knowledge, shivering at her past suspicion of him as the masked man. That kiss haunted her. If Jed were him, he would have used Eva for information about Hillsfield. The thought made her ill.

However, a tutor had the perfect cover. Her heart clenched in pain at the thought of Eva, wishing she could run to her now.

Kolbe's brows furrowed in response to her question. "Be more specific. Know about what?"

Either he played his part well, or truth showed in his confusion. This conversation demanded more time than a dance allowed.

"We need privacy," she said, "but my guards shadow me." Her tower room, designed to prevent escape from arranged marriages, offered no solution to sneak away from the palace with its barred windows.

Kolbe drew her closer. "Then tell me here." His face remained near hers for a moment longer, his eyes searching her face as if trying to discover a secret. "If you weren't upset about my telling you not to choose Kathleen, why were you upset?"

Surprised by his question, Audra deliberated her answer for a moment. Could she change the subject back? After considering for a moment, she relented. "I was hurt because you never loved me," she whispered, eyes dropping. Better to end this fancy. "It doesn't matter anymore. I'm happy with the prince," she lied. His face remained unchanged as the music ended.

Scanning the room, finding no nearby observers, she swallowed. "Let's move there," she said, pointing to an empty corner behind a column. "I need to share information." They passed various drunken nobles, catching snippets of their wine-loose talk focused on the subject of the king and Kathleen.

Once in the corner, Audra steadied herself. "Remember the masquerade, when we went to the carriage to discuss the murder with Prince Elijah?"

"I recall," Kolbe nodded. "Has the murderer been identified?"

Audra shook her head. "All I know is that Doth's responsible." She met his curious gaze. "They meant to kill me that night, not Isabelle."

Kolbe's brows drew together, head tilting. "Who told you that?"

"The prince," Audra said with an exasperated sigh. She wished he could keep pace, though his confusion confirmed he wasn't aware of this information. It confirmed he wasn't the masked man either.

Kolbe's expression stayed fixed as his eyes narrowed. "Doth isn't responsible for the murders," he said.

Audra closed her eyes, fighting frustration at his lack of knowledge. Weeks ago, she'd known little too.

"The king's advisor shared with me our history with Doth. He said that because Elijah refused their princess, they prepare for war. They send spies to murder anyone associated with the king as a warning of their rage." Audra's mind spun as she recalled Julin's tale. In truth, peace would come more easily if Elijah married their princess. Though she cared for him, being the cause of Althenia's unrest weighted her shoulders.

Kolbe's confusion remained, his head shaking. "That's wrong. I visited Doth with the king last month. King Ryou denied involvement in the murders."

"Of course he would deny it," Audra said, heat rising. His simplicity baffled her.

Kolbe swallowed, shaking his head at her perceived misunderstanding. "Audra, when King Henri and I were in Doth, we settled our conflicts. No Dothians attack Althenia, I assure you. Once your marriage links Hillsfield to the crown, they'll cease war threats. I sealed this by agreeing to marry their princess."

A burning lump formed in her throat, as if she'd swallowed glass. He was engaged? She had no right to care; she was betrothed herself, after all. A future where they were together was never meant to be, and she understood it now more than ever.

She recalled Julin's story. Doth threatened war, believing Althenia killed their daughter in the barn fire. The castle needed Hillsfield's wealth to fund defense.

She pushed aside her pain, swallowing the glass whole. Self-pity could wait. The pieces didn't fit. Kolbe visited Doth before she arrived at court. If war wasn't coming, why did Isabelle and June die? She remembered both Elijah and Julin's displeasure at the king's new mistress. Julin warned that discovery of the engagement meant danger for Kathleen. How could the king's closest advisor miss Doth's peaceful stance?

Audra pressed her fingers to her temples, closing her eyes. If Dothian spies weren't killing these women, then... who was? Her eyes swept the room for Julin, finding no trace. The prince trusted him above all, yet as she considered his twisted tales and rumors, clarity struck. His motive remained unclear, but his lies divulged the truth.

Julin had known about every move. Hers, Elijah's, even Kathleen's. Of course he had. He wasn't watching to protect. He was cataloguing his next move.

Julin was the murderer.

23

Another sleepless night tormented Audra as she tossed in her smaller, less comfortable bed in her new room. From her bedroom tower, she viewed every side of the castle. The Whisper Forest encircled the palace in each direction, as well as the other spires, balconies, and rooftops. A nearby balcony spire lay twenty feet below, but window bars thwarted any potential escape plans.

After speaking with Kolbe, Audra had left the ballroom to find Kathleen. Guards stopped her halfway to inform her that the security was on increased alert and that it would be safest to wait inside her room until the royal wedding.

From her window, she eyed the smaller spire with a balcony lookout meant to spot possible intruders. Two guards stood posted on it, watching every direction.

Twenty minutes after midnight, as the night reached its darkest hour, Audra heard shouts from the smaller tower. She crouched low to remain unseen, straining to hear words that repeated throughout the castle.

"Lock down the castle, nobody leaves. Guards post at every exit." The commotion inside and outside confirmed that something was amiss. Her heart pounded and her palms sweated. *Kathleen.*

Audra dashed to her door, opening it wide. Her guards barred her exit, crossing their swords to halt her. "Nobody exits or enters rooms. Security order."

Heart pounding, she clutched her nightgown. "What happened?" she asked, attempting to deny her fears. It could be nothing.

"The king, his bride, and the prince are missing."

If her heartbeat strolled before, now it sprinted. Two royal family members and Kathleen were missing? Did that mean... she would be next? Trapped to await her fate with no escape?

"Take me somewhere safe," Audra pleaded, her voice tightening. "Away from here."

"Protocol, Your Highness. You must stay."

From the bottom of the spiral stairs leading to her room, she heard a door crash open. A voice barked from the doorway, echoing up the spiral. "Grab her, kill anyone in the way, and bring her to me."

Time seemed to freeze. Guards turned toward the sound, blades prepared for battle. Someone was coming for her. Her hope lay with two guards at her doorway. One turned back, his widened eyes indicating his fear. Through gritted teeth, he hissed, "The rafters. The other tower when clear. Inside, now."

No need for further warning or instruction, she slammed her door, locking it as she looked around for a hiding place. In her circular room filled with plum-colored furniture, options were scarce. The wardrobe or under the bed was too obvious. Behind the curtains? Perhaps.

She darted to the curtains, hiding behind their velvety folds before the warning of the guard echoed inside her mind: *Rafters.*

Audra glanced up. Thick wooden beams crisscrossed the ceiling, strong enough to support her. From her bed to the wardrobe, she could reach them. Her days of scaling waterfalls would be useful now. Climbing swiftly, she heard clamoring at the door as metal clanged with metal.

With her dagger strapped to her leg, she ripped a hole in her nightgown pocket for quick access if necessary. She needed to be ready for anything.

As her chamber door flew open, she lay flat against the thick wooden beam, holding her breath. A gap in the beams allowed a limited view below. Her guards were missing as six men entered, donned in royal guard attire with helmets.

"She's not here," one said.

"Check everywhere. Look in the wardrobe, under the bed, behind the curtains. Find her." The leader's voice was raspy, and their helmets obscured identities. She swallowed, praying they wouldn't check above.

She observed as they ransacked her room, stripping sheets and searching every nook, as if she could be hidden in even the smallest recesses.

"What's the delay?" a new voice demanded upon entry.

She recognized this one. Elijah, in a bloodstained white shirt. She held still, heart pounding, witnessing the scene below.

"Dammit!" Elijah roared, swatting a vase of foxglove flowers against the marble wall. "He took her. I knew we couldn't trust that Byron bastard. He's working with them, I can feel it. Find him. Wherever he is, my lying whore of a bride is with him. Send our best dogs to search the grounds, they can't have gone far."

A gasp threatened to escape, but she stopped it. Using all the courage she could muster, she willed herself calm as the prince and guards left, their steps fading down the stairs. In silence, she waited, wondering if more would come.

What role did Kolbe Byron play? The blood on Elijah's shirt had her repeating the same question in her mind: *whose blood was it?*

Earlier, Audra had struggled to find Julin's motive for murdering the mistresses. Nothing made sense. As she hid from a bloodstained prince atop the rafters, clarity emerged like the ocean stilling after a storm. For the first time, she imagined a prince's reasons for killing mistresses.

The truth of Julin's story struck her. His tale of Doth wasn't to spark fear of the Dothians. His story had hinted at the murderers' true purpose. Althenia's people never favored Elijah because of his mother's lineage. Tales rumored him as cruel, wicked, and psychotic. She'd witnessed none of it, so she'd disbelieved such rumors. He'd shown her only kindness.

A half-Dothian prince wasn't a well-liked prince, she realized. Some called for another queen to bear another son. The murderer's hatred wasn't for premarital relations, like she'd thought. The murderer despised threats.

In this case, threats to his future crown. A pregnant woman carrying the king's child posed a problem to a despised prince. Potential heirs. Margaret's mangled body flashed in her mind, insides torn and displayed. Audra pressed her lips tight.

Oh, lord. She was betrothed to the killer.

Audra covered her face, stifling sobs as she continued to lie still. What had she done? She'd told him so much about herself. Her mind drifted to Eva. Whom had she told in the barn that night?

Could it be Kolbe?

Minutes passed in silence as she formed a plan and steadied her tears. She remembered the guard's second instruction: the other tower when clear. On the other tower, she remarked those guards had left. Between her tower and theirs stretched the palace roof, with a courtyard on the far side of the other one. If she reached the other tower, perhaps the wall might offer escape.

Or, it offered a quick way to die. Better than her betrothed's blade, she reasoned.

Grabbing her black cape, she ran barefoot down the marble steps as quietly as possible. At the bottom, the door stood open. She peered around the corner in both directions.

The hallway was clear of guards or witnesses. Without over-thinking, Audra darted across the hall toward the door leading up to the other tower. She didn't dare look back, pulling herself into the stairwell winding up to the lookout spire.

She quieted her breaths, listening to ensure no one had seen her. No use climbing to the top if someone would push her off. Silence reaffirmed her safety, so she ascended the stairs, emerging onto the lookout balcony.

Under the stars, the night seemed still. For a moment, she forgot her peril as she gazed at the constellations. The lookout tower's wall varied in height; some places stood taller than her, others she could climb over. The walls twisted inward on the bottom half, complicating any descent. As she moved to the balcony's edge to view the courtyard, her eyes caught a rope tied to one of the tower's large forkheads, leading down to the courtyard.

Was this a trap?

Castle dangers were familiar, but this felt different. Kathleen and the king were missing. Her betrothed wore a bloodied shirt and searched for her and Kolbe. She recalled more of Julin's story as she looked around for signs of someone beneath her. What had Julin said? The king had married another before the Dothian princess. Had he said the first wife was murdered? Or was the marriage an-nulled?

What became of the king's first wife?

Audra pulled her cloak tighter, looking down at the rope de-scending twenty feet. She wasn't a stranger to heights or rope escapes. As she stared at the courtyard, thoughts of Kathleen and Kolbe inside the castle gave her pause. She was certain Kolbe could defend himself, but he didn't know the castle's secrets as she did. Could she abandon Kathleen?

Since she'd arrived at the castle, she'd sworn to find the murderer before he found her. He'd found her first, but did he realize she'd found him? Even if she escaped with Eva to another kingdom, who was to say he wouldn't find them?

Sitting against the spire wall, she pondered again. Why was the rope there?

"I know you're not afraid of heights."

She jumped at the voice above her and sprang to her feet. Looking up, she saw the masked man perched on the spire's roof edge, dangling his feet. Her heart pounded, a mix of excitement and fear. How long had he been watching?

"How did you get here?" Audra asked, keeping her voice steady.

He gestured to the rope as if it were obvious. She supposed it was. Another question remained: who had placed the rope?

"I intended to find you inside, but saw you leaving the rafters in your room. I hoped you'd come this way. You've always been quick-witted, you know that?" The masked man grinned.

Ignoring his chipper tone, not feeling in the mood for banter, she calmed with his presence. Perhaps he could help her. "I need to find Kathleen. She's in there somewhere."

For a moment, he stared at her. "You don't mean you intend to go back inside?" he asked. "It's too late for her. The king is already confirmed dead."

Audra swallowed, his words taking time to sink in. The king. Dead. Could the blood on Elijah be his father's? Had he killed him?

If he had... he would never need to worry about another potential heir again.

But where was Kathleen? Or Kolbe, for that matter? Unless he stood before her now, supporting the prince's claim that Kolbe had escaped. But if this man was Kolbe, why wasn't he worried about his sister's absence? Perhaps he realized she was safe.

Audra crossed her arms, pressing her lips together. "I understand now why you didn't want me to discover anything. Learning my fiancé kills women for sport certainly complicates things. The question wasn't who. It was why. The part I couldn't make sense of regarded your involvement in this, unless... King Henri's first wife had a son." The theory might be a stretch, but she needed to understand. Women were dying. Her betrothed was killing them.

So, who was the man behind the mask?

He propped a foot up against the wall, hand on his chin, then looked at her. "Yes," he whispered. "I'm the firstborn heir."

Audra sucked in a breath, her mind reeling at the discovery. No wonder Elijah wanted to eliminate all threats. An older brother threatened his position as future king. Julin hadn't told her about Doth to imply they were the threat, he'd wanted her to see how Elijah pinned his evil deeds on them.

"And I know you?" she asked.

"You thought you did," he replied. "I told you to stop seeking information, but you found it anyway, endangering yourself. You did what I told you not to. If we leave now, I can get you to safety. I can protect you if you come with me. But if you return inside, I cannot. I fear if you do, you'll never step foot outside again."

Audra swallowed, hearing his words, but her mind wandered. Kathleen might still be alive inside. She knew the castle by heart. Maybe she could convince Elijah she'd gotten lost. "Are you certain it's too late for her?" she asked, her voice meek.

He paused before answering. "No. I'm not certain she's dead. People are searching for her. *You* need to run."

"The wrong people are looking," she snapped, shaking her head. "People who want her dead. She carries another heir—"

"I know."

"How?" she demanded. If not for the circumstances, she would have screamed the question.

He remained silent, eyes fixed on her, allowing the question to linger in the air far longer than she would have liked. "Audra, the wedding was a catalyst for catastrophe. We weren't prepared for this outcome, we lack the current advantage. Nothing went as predicted. Believe me, I've done everything to keep your loved ones safe."

Frustration boiled over her. His constant secrecy felt like a deliberate torment, blindfolding her while others controlled her fate without answers.

Even from below, she saw him swallow before he spoke. "Come on, Audra. It's time to go. You'll know everything soon enough. It isn't safe here."

Tears threatened as Audra hesitated, unsure about leaving before confirming the fate of Kathleen. What if she could save her? What if it wasn't too late?

"I need to go back," Audra whispered, glancing at the door. "I have to try."

A stomp sounded, and she turned to find the masked man had leapt from the roof to stand before her. "No. Climb down the damn rope, or I'll carry you down."

Audra scowled, cheeks flushing with heat. "If you won't show your face, you don't get a say in who I protect. You have no right to tell me I can't look for my family." Her nostrils flared, weary of the men in her life always giving her directions. She longed to forge her own path, without the influence of riddles and secrets telling her which way to go.

"The one you need to protect is you," he argued. "Do you want to marry that man? A prince who killed Margaret and perhaps Kathleen? If so, then waltz back in and take your crown, *Your Majesty*," he mocked, the same way he had in the barn. "That's your alternative to being murdered. That's why it's better to wear a mask when hiding one's true intentions."

His words struck a chord. She'd have to feign adoration for Elijah if she wanted to claim innocence. Yet without assurance of Kathleen's safety, the risk felt necessary.

"Dammit," the masked man whispered. "You're going back in there, aren't you?" He growled as he paced away from her, igniting her body's heat despite her anxiety.

"Why do you care?" Her voice felt small against his growl.

The masked man closed the distance between them again. Her heart leapt, drawn to his musky scent. "I thought *that* was obvious," he replied, his dark eyes piercing hers.

Audra hesitated. Then she went for it. She reached her hand up to grab his mask, but as in the barn, he caught her wrist, spinning her, pinning her arms to her chest. Her back pressed against his large, muscled frame.

His breath warmed her neck, mouth near her ear. "You knew what would happen if you tried," he said. "Not here. Are you mad, woman? Behave yourself."

Audra smirked, feeling devilish as the adrenaline surged. She didn't know him, but she trusted him, and around him lust enveloped every fiber of her being. The attraction was unexplainable. She didn't know his name, but he knew much about her. "I knew," she said, turning her head to meet his eyes. Their faces close, she spotted those eyes drifting to her lips and back. He swallowed, not pulling away.

"Do you know who I am?" he asked. Her heart thumped. She wished she did, but the mystery also intrigued her. Was he an admirer or an acquaintance? Sometimes she was convinced he was Kolbe. Other times, Jed made more sense. Most times, neither fit.

"I know I trust you," she replied. "And I daydream about your lips on mine all the time. I wonder how often you regret that." She blushed at the confession, realizing this might be the last time she could uncover his identity. If she returned inside the castle, she might never leave. The least she could do would be to unmask him.

The masked man didn't loosen his grip on her wrists as he held her. He answered instead, "I never once regretted that kiss." He leaned in, lips brushing hers for a moment. He pecked her, a brief touch before he pulled back and sighed.

He shook his head. "Not now. We need to get you to safety. Please, don't return, Audra. If you do, I can't promise rescue again."

Audra gazed at him, his presence an irresistible allure. "I'll manage," she said. He frowned. "What if you told me who you are?"

He sighed, still holding onto her wrists. His grip loosened, but only a bit. She still wouldn't have been able to break free, even if she wanted. "The real man behind the mask might not be the one you see in those daydreams. I don't think I can live with the look on your face if you discover I'm not the man you thought I was."

Audra scoured her memories, trying to figure out who it was that she daydreamed about. In truth, he might not be wrong. If it wasn't who she suspected most, then maybe it was best she didn't know at all.

She recalled Kolbe was a bastard, but what she remembered of his father was that he was a baron who left his mother with two children when they were young. She wondered at the possibility of the king being his father. It wasn't impossible. But if Kolbe were the real heir to the throne, who would be the heir to Hillsfield? Could that be the reason he kept his secret identity? Would Lord Byron know the man behind the mask?

She didn't remember much about Jed's parentage, but she remembered the way he behaved as if he knew something when he was around. He'd outright admitted he was a spy.

As the man behind her held her wrists, she realized whoever was behind the mask was a fantasy of her imagination. Someone she wanted to exist, a hero to distract her from reality. The reality at that time was that her betrothed was a murderer, and she now had a duty to do what she said she would. She promised she would kill the murderer before he could harm anyone else she loved. That included Kathleen. If even the smallest possibility remained that she was alive, Audra had to save her.

"I'm going in. Are you coming or not?" Audra asked.

The masked man released her wrists, stepping back from her. He put his forehead against the back of his hand on the wall. His head rolled from one side to the other. "I can't," he said.

Audra's hands folded together as she watched him, her heart sinking. "You said you were going to come find me. Why not Kathleen?"

He swallowed, not removing his head from the wall. "Because I fear it's too late for Kathleen. You're out here, safe. Your freedom rests twenty feet below, and you want to go on a suicide mission to find someone who's already dead. I find myself torn inside my mind. The part of me that wants to protect you, and the part of me that must protect Althenia from that monster. Don't make me choose."

She watched the masked man, and she thought she sensed a drop in his voice. In all this time, she never considered that the man behind the mask had real feelings for her. Her usual suspects never displayed that in real life. As she tightened her lips, she understood the choice she had to make: the real Kathleen or the fantasy of a man in hiding.

Audra turned toward the door. As the masked man saw her decide, he moved forward to take hold of her wrists again, this time pushing her back against the wall of the tower. He pinned her hands above her head with one of his, his other hand caging her against the marble wall behind her. She looked right at his eyes, fierce and determined, but black beneath the disguise of the mask. Her heart thumped as he pressed his entire body against hers, not unlike the way he'd done in her room at Hillsfield.

"If you're going to make this decision, then let me be selfish one more time." His breath danced against her cheeks as he spoke, and her entire body burned as he leaned in and pressed his lips to hers. Her heart burned an entire fire, raging with sparks and heat as he held her there, unable to move her hands above her head even if she wanted to.

Unlike their last kiss, the desperation behind his kisses was more evident this time. He used his lips to pry hers open, his tongue tracing her top lip. Her body submitted to him, utter desire controlling her thoughts as their tongues danced, and she moaned, sending him into a frenzy like it had that night in her room. His hand on the wall moved to her shoulder.

The masked man traced the bare skin of Audra's shoulder, his hand moving down her chest. His palm pressed firmly against her skin as he neared her right breast. She couldn't believe how much she wanted him. It was irrational to desire someone that she didn't know, but the memories of what it felt like to have a man's hands on her consumed her above all else. She heaved her chest against his lingering hand as he moved his palm to rest against the top of her breasts that stuck out from her nightgown. Audra whimpered.

His hand slid beneath the neckline of her nightgown. The masked man cupped her bare breast, groaning as he grabbed it. She gasped, her body squirming against him as his large hand squeezed over her sensitive nipples. As he pressed himself even more against her, she noticed his erection through his trousers. Audra didn't want to stop. Heat radiated between their bodies, and Audra found herself pressing back against him, her mind losing all control of her senses.

Her body hadn't indulged such passion for years. Not knowing the man behind the mask should make her wary, instead, it excited her. This man desired her, and it made her flush as her fantasies got away from her. His lips connected to hers over and over, his hand squeezing her breast and playing with her nipple between his pointer and middle finger. Every noise she made turned him into a rabid animal, and every touch made her kiss him harder to keep herself from getting louder.

She wanted him in more ways than she would ever admit aloud. This heir to Althenia who kept so many secrets she wasn't certain she'd ever learn them all. Still, he was no doubt as attracted to her as she was to him, made clear by either one's inability to stop.

He humped his body against hers, just once, causing another pant to escape from her lips between kisses. He paused, his lips lingering inches from hers. When he didn't return for another, she opened her eyes, squirming her body against his. His lips, the only part visible, parted open as he studied her. As she observed him, at first, she could only wonder why he stopped. After focusing on his face, she realized what it was she'd done. She'd allowed a man she didn't know to touch her.

Yet, she didn't regret it. If she was going to die, she might as well take a few of the good pleasures from life before she couldn't. She knew they needed to stop, though. Her friend needed her, and time spent with the masked stranger wasn't supposed to be part of her evening. More pressing matters waited.

The masked man sighed. "Promise me, you'll do whatever's necessary to make it back out of there. I'll stay close until sunrise. That's all I can wait," he said, nodding to the door. "Exit this door, and head to the treeline in the east. Find the Whisper Tree with a pink ribbon. Wait there, and I'll find you."

His expression unreadable behind the mask, he held her wrists still above her head to prevent unmasking. "In the library, there's a bookshelf of lighter wood that hides a latch on the third shelf from the bottom. Behind it, there's a secret entrance leading to a private room. The royal family had it built for protection from invasions. Search there for Kathleen, but do not do it alone."

He kissed her once more before releasing her wrists. They crashed to her sides, blood rushing back into them. Moving to the rope, he turned to see her one final time before shaking his head. As he scaled down the wall of the tower, she felt in her heart that it could be her final sight of her strange ally. If they met again, he'd be the last surviving heir of Althenia. If she saved Kathleen and lived through this, he'd no longer be the masked man.

24

Peering around every corner, Audra slunk through the dark palace, heading for the library. Several times she paused, waiting for guards to pass, shouts echoing throughout. They called for room checks and announced clear halls.

After almost an hour of sleuthing, she reached the library, finding the door ajar. The moonlight from the glass dome ceiling made shadows scarce, so it would be difficult to hide in their darkness. Instead, she intended to move with efficiency, darting through the bookcases. Audra stopped at one of a different color, exactly as the masked man had described.

"Audra?" She jumped at the whisper, stifling a scream. Her heart raced until Kolbe emerged in the moonlight.

To her surprise, he embraced her, the familiar musky smell enveloping her senses. One question lingered: had the masked man removed the mask to assist her?

"I heard them say you were missing," he said, sighing into her hair. "I hoped you escaped."

She'd hoped the same for him. "I'm trying to find Kathleen," Audra replied, swallowing.

"As am I," he said, fists clenched at his sides. "I fear it may be too late."

She nodded, understanding. She'd been warned her efforts were futile. Still, she had to try.

Kolbe eyed the bookshelf. "A secret room should be here, but moving books didn't work. I tried every single one on this shelf. I hid upon hearing someone enter."

She wondered if his confusion was genuine or feigning ignorance. The masked man had mentioned the latch. Audra crouched, spotting the black latch on the third shelf, and she unhooked it. The bookshelf swung inward. She gasped, glancing at Kolbe.

For the first time, she noticed her friend's normal stalwart character appeared wrought with panic and exhaustion, his tousled hair and weary expression evident. She'd never seen him this way. Inside, fear and adrenaline consumed her soul. What did Kolbe know? The masked man knew Elijah was the murderer. Did the man in front of her know, too?

If he did, he didn't show it. She felt her dagger strapped to her leg, ready for whatever waited inside. "Let's go."

Kolbe sighed, looking at Audra. "I suppose you won't wait outside if I ask?"

Audra shook her head, pulling up her skirt to reveal the dagger strapped to her leg. "I'm coming."

"Of course you carry a dagger," he grumbled, a mix of disapproval and anxiety in his voice. When their eyes met, his expression softened to one she didn't recognize. "Fine. If you must come, stay behind me." He collected an unlit candle from a library table, lighting it with flint and steel he found nearby. Kolbe led the way to descend the spiral stairs, closing the bookshelf behind them. With the dim light guiding them down the staircase to a hallway, she followed behind him toward a lit room at the end of the hallway.

Kolbe gestured for silence, holding a hand up as he peered into the room. Her heart pounded with anticipation, and she rubbed her hand on her dress to dry the sweat. He gasped. Next, he rushed forward, crying, "Kathleen!"

Her heart sank all the way to her stomach. By the inflection of his tone, she anticipated his findings foreshadowed tragedy. Elijah had struck again, another person close to her this time. Pain gripped her chest, her throat tightening from the imminent tears threatening her eyes as she prepared for what she'd find ahead.

She entered a small, round room with potion-lined cabinets. The smell of damp stone and blood filled the air. The room reminded her more of Hillsfield than the palace, and no furniture decorated the room aside from the cabinets and potions. Against the back wall, Kolbe knelt, cradling Kathleen's lifeless, bloodied form. Despair broke him. The cry would move even the most devious siren to tears.

Audra rushed to his side, horror-struck by the scene as it came into view. Blood pooled around Kathleen's waist, her stomach cut open, her lifeless body on the ground as Kolbe picked up her corpse and pulled her to his chest.

She couldn't believe it despite seeing it herself. Only hours ago, Kathleen had been filled with joy. Kathleen had thought she was finally receiving the life she deserved. The sight of her friend's mangled body was nauseating, her world shattering further. Anger turned to sorrow, and sorrow turned to tears.

Kolbe's sobs were deep as he held his sister's body close, repeating, "No, no, no." Tears spilled from Audra's eyes as well, grabbing Kathleen's cold, stiff hand.

But... where was the prince? Why leave her like this, a single candle left behind? Audra tried to process, trying not to think of the horror Kathleen had endured moments before her demise. Her death, alone in a hidden cellar. This wasn't the fate Kathleen deserved. Her friend, who used to rescue kittens and left a smile on everyone's face: gone. She'd endured much in her life, and Audra sobbed at the memories as they snippets surfaced, dating back to when they met.

Kolbe's expression shifted from grief to fury. His eyes hardened as he used his sleeve to wipe his tears. "I'll kill him, I fucking swear. It's a hidden royal passageway, which means—"

His realization hit them at the same moment he paused.

"The prince," he whispered under his breath. "The mistresses. It never mattered if Kathleen married the king. Heirs were always the motive for the murders."

"I just discovered it myself," Audra said, uncertain if Kolbe's reaction to this news was genuine or feigned. Would he keep up with pretenses at a time like this?

Kolbe studied Kathleen, and Audra debated her next move. Before he replied, another voice interrupted, coming from the doorway.

"You know, it would be treason to accuse the prince of murdering her in cold blood." Both turned, standing up. Kolbe unsheathed his sword, and Audra wielded her dagger. She'd seen this man before, but her memories took a moment to catch up. The man's grin revealed yellowed, rotting teeth, unbothered by their weapons pointing toward him.

Pildrex. He'd danced with her at the ball before the masked man's interruption. The masked man had told her about his rottenness, though she'd already discovered his foul character before his warning.

Pildrex tucked a lock of black hair behind his ear, chuckling. "I'm afraid this complicates things for you both, you see. Nobody was supposed to find this place."

Audra sneered, piecing it together. The masked man said the prince was responsible for the murders, but was he? What motive could the prince's university friend have to commit these acts?

The prince had insisted Pildrex wasn't a great friend. She'd been stupid enough to believe him.

"Did you do this? Did you murder my sister?" Kolbe's voice was direct and demanding, unhindered by Pildrex's presence.

"Ah, your sister. Now it makes sense who you are. Yes, I'm afraid I did."

Audra's heart pounded. Kolbe's breaths resembled winds of anger, a vein of his neck popping out as he gripped his sword tighter. "Why?" he demanded through gritted teeth.

"Your sister complicated matters. Many dislike Elijah inheriting the throne amidst Doth tension. Some even suspect the prince of siding with Doth. We can't entertain ideas of another heir replacing the prince, can we?" Pildrex bared his teeth, like a predator viewing his next meal.

Kolbe lunged at him with his sword, but Pildrex anticipated the move, dodging the blow with a quick side-step maneuver. Drawing a smaller sword, Pildrex advanced on Audra, who had no time to react to his speed. Pildrex wrenched her dagger arm by seizing her wrist and twisting it behind her, bringing the blade of his sword to her neck. She squealed in pain from the twisting. Kolbe halted mid-swing. Heart thumping, she held still to avoid getting cut by the blade against her throat.

"Three royals dead in one night would be quite the scandal, wouldn't it?" Pildrex jeered. "One more step, and I'll slice her throat. I sent guards on a hunt outside to find a friend of ours, and time runs short for me to remove the body. Alas, I can't escort you both from this place, and I can't kill King Elijah's bride without permission. So, let's put our minds together and think about how we are to get out of the situation with everyone alive, hmm? I will kill her to defend myself and use her as a shield if you try anything, understand?"

Kolbe dropped his sword. "I'm Hillsfield's heir. Killing me without your prince's nod would also be unwise. I've dropped my weapon. Now, drop yours."

Ignoring him, Pildrex straightened, relaxing. "Hmm. I know. I'll lock you in with the former whore queen's rotting corpse while I fetch guards to assist me. Step back from your sword."

Kolbe obeyed. Pildrex sniffed Audra's hair, sending shivers down her spine. "Drop your dagger, love. Don't do anything foolish. We wouldn't want to waste such a pretty blonde cunt for His Majesty now, would we?"

Audra released the dagger, hearing it clang against the stone floor. Pildrex faced Kolbe. "Kick your sword here." Kolbe used his foot to nudge the sword across the floor toward Pildrex. In swift moves, Pildrex released Audra, shoving her on the ground towards Kolbe. He stole their weapons and exited with them, locking them in

The moment the lock clicked, Kolbe rushed to her. "Are you hurt? Did he harm you?" He kneeled, his hand touching the small of her back as he examined her.

Audra touched her throat with a brush of her hand, checking for blood. She felt the blade's memory but no cut. Heart racing, she swallowed the truth of their situation. They were caught, and escape looked unlikely.

Meeting his gaze, she questioned what lay beneath his surface. Did the prince capture the masked man too? Who was Kolbe in truth? And what, exactly, did he know?

25

Audra sat up, pulling up her skirt to reveal a rock lodged in her knee from the crumbling stone floor. Distracted by the blood, she didn't notice Kolbe's gaze fixed on her bare leg as she exposed the injury for examination.

Kolbe swallowed, brought to attention by the sight of blood. "You're hurt. Can you pull it out?"

Audra nodded, trying to grasp the stone, but yelped in pain at the first tug. It was deeper than she thought. "I can't. It's too painful. Kolbe, can you—" Before she finished, he yanked the stone out, causing another yelp, followed by relief. "Thank you."

Kolbe untucked his black shirt, tearing a strip of fabric from the bottom and eyeing the room's potions. "Think anything here might help?"

Audra shook her head. "Best not to try. We need to find a way to escape."

Kolbe sighed. "There's no escaping. I'm Hillsfield's heir, you're the prince's betrothed. If we run, they'll find us. The prince has no limits to his lack of morals and who he'll murder. You and I are no exceptions. I helped Lord Byron escape to return to Hillsfield for your mother and Eva. We should have run. Now, we play his game."

Audra recalled the masked man's warning not to return inside, stating it was too late for Kathleen. He was right. "He'll kill us both, won't he? We'll both die unless we fight."

After ripping more of his shirt to receive one long cloth, his tattered garment revealed his chest as he tended her wound. "I understand the temptation to fight, believe me. I wish nothing more than to avenge the death of my sister this instant. However, if I intend to survive, I must beg for my life and plead unconditional loyalty. If you want to live, you'll do the same. If he banishes you, you'll go. If he still wants marriage, you'll accept."

Audra pressed her lips together, irritated by his words as he used the cloth to bandage her leg. *Ugh*. What a stupid, stupid man. Before she could stop herself, the words flew out of her mouth as well. "You stupid man." She regretted the words as soon as they exited.

Kolbe looked surprised, his expression shocked. Covering her legs with her nightgown, his brows furrowed. "What?"

"Nothing," she said, her heart beating faster.

Kolbe scoffed. "No, please, enlighten me. I find my sister dead in Althenia's most powerful home, committed by the most powerful man, and you called me stupid?"

"I'm sorry," Audra apologized, pulling her legs to her chest, unable to look at Kathleen's lifeless body again. Now wasn't the time. She should have held her tongue. "I didn't mean it."

Kolbe persisted, unwilling to let it go. "You did mean it. Why say it? Everything I've done was to protect Hillsfield, my family. You're part of my family. So tell me, why am I so stupid?"

Shifting her body to face away from him and Kathleen, she faced the wall of potions, pondering their purpose. Why were they hidden down here? Hidden things often hold secrets. Was this Elijah's poison room?

Rolling her eyes, Audra bit her lip before responding. "How fortunate I was to be in Hillsfield's care. You treated me like a sister, and I recognize I should be grateful."

Kolbe sat beside her, hands on knees. "Why criticize my suggestions on how to keep you alive, then?"

"Because," Audra said, releasing a long huff, eyes darting everywhere to avoid meeting his. "The life you suggested for me requires marrying the man who killed people I love, and that is no life. I'm angered by you."

Kolbe didn't respond for a long moment. From the corner of her eye, she saw him look down, tousled black hair falling over his forehead. At last, he whispered, "But it is living."

While she knew he intended to keep her alive, no matter the cost, the one he suggested wasn't one she could accept. If she married him, she'd live in fear that he'd slice her throat at any given moment. Could someone so evil even be capable of love? "Life without love isn't living, it's just existing," she said. "My mother tells me that. I don't want mere existence in this world anymore, that's all I've done for eight years. You, however, seem content to simply exist until the day you die."

Her words lingered in the cold room. She wrapped herself in her cloak, the damp stone floor chilling her toes.

Sensing Kolbe's gaze on her, she couldn't bear to look back. All those years she pined, searching for something she once had and lost. Every time, he never failed to disappoint her with his lack of reciprocated feelings. Not once. Never did he consider her that way. Her mind drifted to the masked man. Lust fueled his movements tonight, the exact opposite of control. Maybe what she sought in the masked man was something she longed for in Kolbe that didn't exist.

Maybe that was enough reason to believe Kolbe wasn't the masked man. He wouldn't have acted the way the masked man had.

Kolbe moved, sitting across from her, right knee next to hers. Then, he did something unexpected. He placed a hand on her covered knee, meeting her eyes. They didn't blink or waver, holding steady.

"You always had it wrong, Audra," he said. "I wasn't a glacier stuck in the frozen oceans to the south. I was burning, alive with fire. Not the slow burn of a candle. I was the raging roar of a wildfire. It takes a great deal of effort to bridle my most ravenous desires. Every time you express annoyance with me, you put my resolve to the edge of its limits."

Audra watched his tear-marked eyes, his stare intent. Her heart thudded. "Kolbe," she said in a low whisper. "This is not the time to ask this, but if we die tonight, I must know. Please, give me an honest answer this once, tell me it wasn't in my head. Did you ever love me?" Her heart clenched, unsure if she wanted to hear the answer, but hoped with every fiber of her being that this time he told the tr uth.

"Did I? No," Kolbe swallowed. "That implies I stopped." Her eyes darted up to meet his, a sincerity in them she'd seldom seen. He continued, "I still love you. Since that night in the library when we met when we were young, you found me hiding from Lord Byron. You might as well know before whatever happens next."

Her heart twisted, sadness and wonder exhausting her mind. She clung to each word as he continued. "I may never be able to have you, but I'll love you every day. Every part of me knows I won't be the man you marry, but that doesn't mean I didn't spend every waking moment abhorring that knowledge. You once told me that I never met your eyes, and this was the reason you doubted our friendship. But, I couldn't," Kolbe stopped, exhaling as he regarded her. "I couldn't because every time I looked at you, I longed for something I knew I'd never have."

Audra fell speechless, unsure how to respond. She'd thought he avoided her out of distaste, tolerating her like a bothersome younger sister. "Well," he said, "I suppose I've already said too much, so I might as well finish. I couldn't look at you because when I did, each glimpse made me wish for another path. You were meant for the future king, and anything else... was treason to even consider."

Audra memorized him, her heart pounding as he brushed her cheek with the back of his fingertips. He continued as she sat in silence, feeling his fingers against her skin, her heart fluttering. This confession of love differed from her last. Both times, she'd waited years. Last time, she'd expected to marry the man who'd said it. Now, the man confessing swore that the idea of marriage was impossible.

"Not once," Audra said, "did you ever consider the irrational choice?" She recognized her question was bold, but men's iron control over their emotions baffled her.

Kolbe watched her, face close, eyes fixed on hers. "Not if it risked your safety."

Audra released an ironic laugh, empty of amusement. "Look how that worked out."

His hand shifted from her cheek to her shoulder, expression grim. "I know. I regret not fleeing with you and Eva. My duty bound me to Hillsfield, to learn the businesses and to run the estate. If I didn't do it, Lord Byron had no other heir to inherit the fortune. My passion for you wasn't meant to be. Now I'm trapped in a room with my murdered sister, regretting my loyalty to her killer. Such loyalty that I couldn't stay in the same room as you without wanting to justify why it should be me who marries you, and not him. Every reason was selfish. Now, look. He's taken my sister. Soon, our lives may follow."

Audra nodded at this truth. She didn't know if she would see the sunrise ever again. The masked man promised to wait, but their situation made that reunion impossible.

She drew breath as Kolbe cupped her chin in one hand. "If I die without kissing you once, I'll never forgive myself. This is my most selfish act, but I'll treasure the memory until death."

Kolbe pressed his lips to hers. Her heart fluttered, lips tingling with each passionate kiss his soft lips demanded from hers. She draped her arms around him, sighing into the embrace. The kiss continued, every sensation filling her to her core. Breaking for air, his hand rested on her shoulder, eyes locked on hers with sad longing. His fingers traced small circles along her arm, and his sigh sounded forlorn.

"Could you have loved me as much as you loved him?" he asked. The question caught her mid-reverie.

She frowned. "As who? The prince? I never loved him."

"No," he shook his head. "As much as Eva's father."

Her face warmed at Garrick's mention. Her first love embodied everything she yearned for, possessing many traits Kolbe shared. Kolbe was the first man who ever held a candle in comparison...

Except the masked man who'd sparked that same flame.

Studying his lips, she tried to match their shapes, but with how many lips she'd studied the past two months, she doubted her memory's accuracy.

Audra choked down her fear. She needed to hear the truth, once and for all. "I know I'd have found happiness with you, wanting nothing more. We could have been unstoppable. When we kissed... I hoped you were the masked man," she searched his eyes for reaction. "Are you?"

26

K olbe's intent gaze met Audra's, about to speak when the door burst open. Guards entered, swords drawn. She recognized Julin following Pildrex. Pildrex spoke first. "Get up. The new king demands your presence in his chambers."

They stood, guards nudging Audra forward, a sword pointed at her back. Three surrounded Kolbe as they ascended to the library and down the halls toward Elijah's chambers. Each step quickened Audra's pulse. When she glanced back, Kolbe's eyes were downcast.

So, this was how it ended. The murderer had found her first, after all. On top of that, he held the highest power in all of Althenia. She'd been foolish to think she could have stopped him.

At the prince's chambers, guards halted them.

"These guards aren't all permitted entry," one observed.

"I'll take their place and supervise," Julin declared. With King Henri dead, Audra wondered about Julin's role in the palace. She never quite figured out where his allegiance lay.

"Yes, Captain. Let them pass," the guard allowed. Entering, Pildrex pressed Audra's dagger to her throat. He motioned Kolbe in first. Keeping the blade at her throat, he guided her inside. When they entered, they found Elijah at a table with Alynne, half-dressed in provocative attire.

So that was why Alynne always avoided her gaze. She'd been sleeping with her future husband. Elijah's eyes held amusement, loathing in every expression he made. How could he kill so many innocent women? Compared to her feelings of despair, his calm demeanor despite his father's death left no doubt of his guilt. If there were doubts before, they vanquished now.

Elijah clicked his tongue. "Well, I suppose we have much to discuss, don't we, my love?" he said to Audra before turning to Alynne. "I'll send for you tomorrow. Best scurry to bed for now, sweets." Alynne nodded, exiting with a look of defiance toward Audra. Her betrayal was a passing sting amid larger concerns. Elijah turned back to Audra, gasping in mockery. "My god, losing such a prize would be tragic. Pildrex, remove the knife before you hurt her."

Pildrex obeyed, allowing Audra to breathe for the first time since they'd entered. He sheathed the dagger in a holster meant for a knife.

The next moments blurred. The instant Pildrex secured the dagger in the holster, Kolbe lunged, reclaiming the dagger and thrusting it into Pildrex's back, piercing his heart. Audra gasped. Kolbe shielded her by pushing her behind him to stand between her body and Elijah's, aiming the dagger at Julin, the closest foe.

The prince summoned guards, and they rushed inside to stand between Kolbe and the prince, swords drawn. Kolbe pulled Audra closer, retreating to the room's edge.

Once shielded by guards, Elijah stood, releasing a laugh. "My, my, who knew Hillsfield's heir would defend the future queen with such fierceness? I'm not sure what to do with you, her lovesick friend." Uncertainty plagued her mind as the odds of escaping grew slimmer, and fear consumed her soul.

Kolbe gritted his teeth. "The engagement is off. As Hillsfield's heir, with more land than the palace and as a key supplier for Althenia, I demand she return with me."

Elijah smiled, amused, folding his arms. "I'm king now, haven't you heard? I need her to eradicate Althenian royal blood in our future heirs. As it turns out, only one eligible maiden with that golden hair exists in Althenia. Importing a new bride from another land risks another uprising. The nobles love her. Therefore, you cannot have her. What would I be left with?"

Elijah paced the floor, considering his options. "Here's a counteroffer. Give me half your land and I'll spare your life."

Kolbe snarled. "No. Go ahead and kill me. Start a civil war with Hillsfield, if that's what you think is best."

Audra glanced at Kolbe, horrified. Elijah was a known murderer, and Kolbe's defiance wouldn't save him. Elijah would do it

Elijah stared, the look on his face indicating he deliberated making good on his threat. "You fascinate me, young Byron. Enlighten me on something, would you? My spies peered into your history and found no details on your father. How does a bastard inherit Hillsfield, hmm?"

Kolbe remained silent, dagger steady.

Elijah prodded. "Perhaps we share a father. Mine sowed seeds across Althenia, intent on reproducing like Charles, the King of a Thousand Wives, it seemed. He loved everyone except his lawful wife. Did you know my father trapped her in a barn and burned her alive? That truth eludes history. When they write my story, I'll be seen as the hero who halted Henri's harlotry."

Settling one arm across his chair as he sat, Elijah's calmness taunted them. "Lord Byron never had a son of his own, did he now? I gave you an offer to preserve your life, and you refused. I should have warned you that it will be mine either way. I'll seize the land then, withholding such unless an heir appears. The law shall state that only sons may inherit lands henceforth, not nephews. Once Lord Byron dies, the kingdom claims it. I see no downsides, do you?" Elijah licked his lips, a curt smile on his face.

"Lord Byron has his own army. If you kill me, you won't have them for your cause any longer," Kolbe spat. "I know you cannot afford that at a time like this."

Elijah chuckled, shaking his head. "My, such bravery for a bastard. I don't need the heir to Hillsfield to defeat my enemy. I need her. She's what he'll come for. You? A nobody standing in my way. Guards, let us show my bride what happens when she betrays me. Pierce Kolbe Byron's heart."

"No!" Audra cried, panic consuming her, but the word fell into nothingness. Kolbe shoved her backward to the ground, and the following scene burned into her mind.

In chilling harmony, as if choreographed, guards threw their swords like spears. Audra cowered, Kolbe unmoving, shielding her and receiving the full impact of their javelined swords. One sword cut his right thigh, another pierced his left shoulder. A sword grazed his stomach and fell to the ground, and another lodged deep into his rib cage.

Audra's throat seized as she peered through her hands. Time blurred as she screamed, watching Kolbe sink to his knees, then fall to his side, limp as the body of his sister.

Her breath caught, tears streaming as she witnessed it. The prince had murdered at least two friends before and now added a third for her personal viewing. The pain that followed resembled agony she'd sworn never to endure again. For the second time in her life, she watched as a man she loved lost his life. Through tear-filled eyes, she fought unknown hands gripping her arms, thrashing with all her strength and screaming loud enough the entire palace would hear.

"That's the cost of betrayal. Take her to her tower. Lock her in. I'll deal with her later," Elijah said, his voice tinged with false remorse. "She'd never have loved me while he lived." Audra fought as two men pulled her from the prince's chambers, but her screams and struggles proved futile. Her two strongest allies in the castle lay dead. She wished her heart would stop rather than continue beating. She thrashed, yelled, and cried out for help. She faced marriage to the man who destroyed everyone she loved.

Once guards threw her into her room, the door locked her inside. She wailed against the door, her head pressed against it as the scene of Kolbe's death replayed in her mind. Speared with swords. Fallen because he'd dared protect her.

Audra envisioned that this wasn't the end of Elijah's wrath. Eva was still out there, vulnerable. She had no way to warn Eva or her mother to flee. As long as they were alive, they remained tools for his manipulation against her.

Nothing would ever be the same again.

27

Audra languished in her marble prison for days, seeing only meal bearers. In these darkest hours before more miserable ones to come, she managed mere bites. Endless worries plagued her thoughts.

In the end, she'd lost. The brutal murders of Kolbe and Kathleen left Lord Byron heirless, plunging his lineage into uncertainty and shadow. If he desired, Elijah could weaponize anything, even Eva, and Audra felt helpless to stop him. Guards posted outside her door at all hours, never permitting exit. For days, she grieved. Tears puddled on her pillows as she sank deeper into despair. Seven days passed without news. She realized she could be there for a long time before she'd see freedom again.

By the third week, she stopped bothering to change clothes. Not even her ladies-in-waiting appeared, so nobody noticed anyway. Through her windows, she saw nothing. Without distractions, she waited, yearned, begging her window for magical aid. She had to escape somehow, if only to ensure Eva's safety.

After forty-seven days, different visitors arrived. Her hair unbrushed, and wearing the same dress for six days, two guards entered. She recognized the ones who'd killed Kolbe. Behind them, Marianne and Tessai appeared. She felt relief at Alynne's absence. Any change welcomed her after weeks of loneliness. If the time for her death ever came, she thought she'd feel fear. Instead, she welcomed the possibility that her misery might end soon.

One guard spoke. "King Elijah commands you to prepare for your royal wedding. It will take place in two hours. These ladies will assist."

Seeing Marianne and Tessai brought unexpected joy after spending so much time in solitude. At least Elijah showed sense by not sending his mistress. Though he ruled without mercy, he at least maintained the decency not to flaunt his indiscretions.

Fighting would be pointless. The king had demonstrated her powerlessness. With Eva's safety uncertain, she'd comply. If it meant serving the king of wickedness, she wouldn't resist her fate again.

Her ladies worked, brushing her hair, bathing her, and dressing her in her Althenian wedding gown. Though she'd chosen it herself, now she loathed every detail. The tulle layers, the sweetheart neckline, the puffy sleeves. Everything felt wrong, knowing the man who'd see her wear it had destroyed her life.

They worked through hair and makeup in silence, transforming her into a bride. Their questions about her imprisonment went unasked, exchanging glances of pity when they thought she wasn't looking.

Though she appeared like a queen on the outside, inside, she felt like a sewer rat, rotting away where nobody could see her. Not long after they finished, the guards returned, leading her out of her room for the first time since Kolbe's death.

They escorted her toward her doom, leading her to her fate of misery. After turning a corner into the hallway outside the throne room, Julin appeared, dressed in light blue attire fit for a royal wedding.

"King Elijah sends me to escort the queen down the aisle. Guards, report to the palace entrance. Six are posted, but we need twenty guards there. Gather twelve more for the main entrance for protection against a potential siege."

The guards departed as Julin offered his arm to Audra. She took it, hopeless. Her former opinion of his wisdom now seemed hollow. How could someone wise have permitted such beastly behavior that night? She stood friendless and alone, accepting she had no one on her side.

"Come, my queen. The king awaits."

Marianne and Tessai followed as Julin led the way toward the throne room. Before entering, Julin directed them down a skinny corridor. "Ladies, down this hallway. Take that door to the throne room and wait inside the foyer. Someone will signal your entrance in five minutes."

They curtsied, complying with his order. Once out of sight, Julin led Audra in the direction of the throne room. He also led her past the throne room, quickening pace as he commanded her to keep up. Her heart raced in confusion. Where was he taking her?

Around a corner, he pushed her into a servant's closet, following.

"Audra, I've cleared your escape route. Here," Julin said, presenting a dagger—her dagger. Kolbe's last weapon he'd used to defend her that night. "I believe this belongs to you. Take it. Kill anyone who attempts to stop you, but your path should be clear. The west wing entrance stands unguarded. I relocated them to the front entrance five minutes ago. Run to the stables, go as fast as you can."

Was this... Freedom? He was letting her go?

For the first time since that terrible night, hope flickered. Before handing it to her, Julin gripped the blade in his hand, slicing as he withdrew it. Not even a wince crossed his lips as he handed it to her, bloodied. "I'll claim you took it when I grabbed the wrong end. Two dead guards lie outside the west wing doors, they were the ones assigned to escort you down the aisle. They were Elijah's men. Step over them."

Her heart pounded, trying to understand. Who was Julin, if not a foe? "Are you the masked man?" she asked, her voice weak. What if it had been him all along?

Julin smirked, shaking his head. "No, but he awaits you and arranged this escape. We need him well, and without you, he isn't. I see that now. When you reach the stables, go right. Take the first stall's black horse, already saddled. Marke assured me she's the tamest. Ride south through the Whisper Trees. Follow pink markers for a mile, then you'll see one orange one. There won't be any more markers after the orange one, so trust your instincts and head northwest until dusk. Around that time, if you kept on course, you'll find a meadow with an abandoned barn and a burnt-down home. Wait in the barn, he'll come find you before dawn. Hurry. I'll delay them."

Audra nodded, realizing her misjudgment. Julin protected her from the beginning, somehow allied with the masked man. "Thank you. When I get the chance, I'll repay this."

He smirked. "Escape first. Repayments can wait. Now, go."

Audra crept through corridors, sleuthing through the west wing and out the exit, finding the dead guards. She dashed toward the stables, keeping low in daylight, never looking back.

Inside the stable, she found the black mare in the front right stall, mounting with ease. The horse responded to her commands, eager for both rider and journey.

A line of pink Althenian whisper trees marked the forest's edge. The woods earned their name from travelers getting lost, following rumors of mystical whispers of creatures that filled the forests at night. She galloped across the field, spotting the first pink marker as she approached the treeline and entered. Following the line of markers, she grasped their direction. At the orange marker, she pressed on, using the sun's position above the mountains as her guide. When certain she could, she halted, looking behind her. Quiet trees assured no pursuit.

Freedom smelled of sweet whisper leaves, or the breeze on her skin, welcoming her to a world she thought was lost forever. Knowing her pursuit remained possible, she turned the horse forward again and rode on.

Every sound made her check for followers. During the journey, a stag bolted at their approach, startling her. Once in a while, cliffs appeared, requiring detours. Julin hadn't mentioned these obstacles, making her question her path. One cliff took her thirty minutes to navigate her way to the bottom. Looking up, she struggled to recognize her starting point. The trees all blended after hours of riding.

Trusting her instincts, she continued, praying she'd stayed on course. They crossed rivers, the horse protesting those parts but pressing through. Audra stroked its neck, memories of her farm horses in the countryside surfacing. "Good girl," she soothed.

As sunset neared hours later, her hope wavered. No signs of the meadow appeared, and the thought of the night in the woods unnerved her. While the sun hung low in the sky, they found a cluster of wild asparagus sticking out of the ground. The horse grazed while Audra managed a few stringy bites of raw, uncooked spears. Her stomach growled, reminding her how long she'd starved in the castle.

The prince's vileness struck her. How had he expected her to love him one day? The memory of his past kiss repulsed her. The setting sun and her decreased appetite moved her to continue, hoping the meadow was near.

All sounds made her jump, bringing her mind to wonder if he would capture her and thrust her back into that world. As darkness approached, she pressed on. She couldn't be sure she'd stayed on track, but she clung to hope. Her blonde hair and wedding dress would betray her to any observers, so if she didn't find it soon, she feared what might happen.

Dusk painted deep purple skies, wind replacing breeze. Rain clouds gathered above, threatening a long night if she didn't find shelter.

Another hour passed. Weaving through trees, she wondered how much farther. The horse stopped at a stream to drink. Every direction mirrored the last in the hilly landscape, and she considered she might be lost. Her stomach growled. She urged the horse forward through moonlit darkness. Leaves crunched, trees rustled, raising her hackles.

Then, as she almost lost hope, a meadow opened between two large trees. The meadow stretched half a mile, full of long-bladed grass. Relief flooded her. A lake gleamed at the edge of the meadow, and at the treeline's edge stood a barn. The horse, whom she decided to name Annette, approached the shelter gladly, pausing to drink from the lake fifty meters away. Moonlight danced on rippling water as it lapped the muddy shore.

Inside the old, creaking barn, aged hay filled one corner. Finding it empty, she studied her surroundings while awaiting the masked man. The smell of rain enveloped her nose, indicating it drew near. As she relaxed in silence, she pondered how different life would be if her mother hadn't wed Lord Byron. She wished she'd stayed with Eva in the countryside, running the dress shop in town, even if she had to do it alone.

Part of her always sought something more. Once upon a time, she'd known unrequited love.

But not all stories could end happily ever after.

28

Hours passed. Rain came and went in rotations. Sometimes, Audra watched the trees for pursuers, her fear gnawing at thoughts of capture. Freedom felt precious after weeks of confinement. She worried for Eva's safety, whether Lord Byron reached Hillsfield, and if he knew Elijah's murderous intent. Did Lord Byron survive? If so, where was he? Would a civil war be waged over Kolbe's death?

The stable fell silent as rain ceased a third time. Sometimes Annette's whinnies and silent whispers of wind broke the quiet. Hunger struck after weeks of lost appetite. She found a raspberry bush and devoured most of the ripened ones. Moonlight through the barn window illuminated her surroundings, and her eyes adjusted to the night's hue. Complete solitude felt strange after constant company in the palace, always surrounded by guards, servants, and nobles. Even forbidden to speak to any of them for the last forty-seven days, even trapped, this felt different. What would Elijah do if he found her before the masked man?

Memories of friends haunted her. Kathleen welcomed her to Hillsfield with gossip, making her belong like she'd always lived there. Only Kathleen knew of the masked man's kiss, a secret taken with her to her death. All along, she suspected the masked man was Kolbe. Doubt now plagued her. Could it be Jed? Why conceal his identity? What secrets lay in his past?

Kolbe. Before his death, he'd confessed his love had spanned years. Her heart ached with memories of his protective gaze whenever she thought of him. All those years, he'd avoided her eyes, resisting the urge to want her, keeping her safe. In the end, his protectiveness sealed his death.

Despite her attempts at denial, she recognized Kolbe was gone. After her first love's death, she didn't want to live anymore. She'd considered taking her own life before discovering she was pregnant with his child. Eva's existence kept her from despair. Now, nothing prevented her from spiraling into darkness, especially if Elijah had found Eva.

Time crawled through her panic, the worry for her daughter consuming her emotions. With each passing second, her nerves sank deeper into quicksand, her mind spinning in infinite circles. She longed for Kolbe and Kathleen. Their murderer wore the crown. She'd committed treason.

No happy ending seemed possible.

After her fifth bout of tears that night, she left the barn and approached the lake. Her dark reflection stared back as she placed her hand into the lake to test the water's warmth. Unlike the river she grew up near, this lake felt tepid.

Seeking reprieve from her fears, she untied her cumbersome wedding dress. Yanking on the strings, she stripped to her undergarments, leaving the muddy dress on the shore. She waded into the cool waters of the meadow lake, sinking her toes into soft mud, taking time to breathe the aroma of fresh water.

Once waist-deep, she dove, feeling the water brush against her skin. Surfacing, she stood, gazing at the moon hanging high in the sky, dark clouds looming. She hadn't been allowed to do this since leaving the countryside.

Floating on her back, she remarked the clouds as they danced with the stars. She found a place of calmness, the water's weight supporting her. In the distance, she thought she heard her name through water-filled ears.

She stood, spotting the silhouette of a dark figure by the barn. The figure was close enough to hear water splash when she stood, and close enough that she glimpsed traces of the outline of his mask. Her heart leaped as he approached, stopping at the edge of the shore.

Many times, she thought of what she might say to him, and it all wanted to come out at once. The last time she'd seen him, he'd kissed her. She'd spent the last forty-seven days trapped in her room, unknowing whether or not this man was still alive. It felt surreal to have him there after all this time. All those days she spent on her bed drawing shapes with her mind made her recant him, the way he grabbed her breast and kissed her like he'd never see her again. Back then, she didn't have the self-control to stop herself from reciprocating. Now that the man she first suspected was dead, she didn't know if she had the same feelings of attraction toward him. All that time, she supposed she thought it was Kolbe. Now, she wasn't sure, and any other options dulled in comparison.

Audra spoke first, rushing her words. "I need to find Eva."

The masked man released a slow exhale, his relief evident. "Thank god you're safe. Eva, your mother, and Lord Byron are protected. I'll take you to them when you're ready."

Audra blinked, relief mixed with curiosity about his involvement. Why would he protect her family?

"You know everything?" she asked.

"Yes, my spies—"

Audra interrupted, anger flaring now that she heard her daughter wasn't in Elijah's control. "Were you aware that I spent forty-seven days without talking to anyone, or leaving my chambers, fearing that at any moment I could be killed? If you were alive, and you knew I was alive, why didn't you help me?"

Moonlight revealed his frown. He crossed his arms, shaking his head. "I wanted to. I freed you at the first moment possible. The wedding was our chance with the prince distracted. It wasn't an easy task. If I'm being honest, I wasn't certain you were alive. He wanted you hidden, and he succeeded."

He remained still outside the water, watching her inside it.

"Also," he added, "I hope you'll consider not drowning yourself. Your mother and Eva wait for you. Clothes from your mother are in the barn with the horses. I'll wait there while you finish your... swim." His eyes traced her form. "But not long, it's best to travel at night."

Audra submerged herself in the water up to her neck. She felt coy. "I'm not leaving until you reveal yourself."

At this threat, his tone changed. "You'll need food," he replied without missing a beat, a small chuckle escaping his lips.

She shrugged. "I can fish."

"With your bare hands?" he asked, smiling.

Audra stood her ground. "If I'm hungry, I'll find a way."

"I can swim too, you know," the masked man said, releasing a full laugh. "You're impossible. I'll be in the barn when you come to your senses."

Exhaling disbelief, she asked, "Wait, you won't tell me? Before, you wouldn't tell me because you said it was dangerous. Am I, therefore, meant to assume risks remain in knowing your identity?"

He turned back, arms still crossed. "Just believe you're safe now, and that needs to be enough."

She splashed at him, her annoyance evident in her scoff. She stood too far from shore to wet him, but she wished to bother him as much as he bothered her.

His lips curled into a smirk. "Did you just try to splash me?" he asked, amusement coloring his voice.

"It was a warning," Audra said. Inside her mind, conflicting emotions swirled. Fury and annoyance at his constant secrecy washed over her. She remembered their kisses, his hands on her, the way his breath felt against her neck. Despite not knowing his identity, her desire prevailed. Guilt knotted her thoughts as Kolbe's memory haunted her. She felt fickle for feeling this way so soon after his loss.

Or, was she fickle? Was there any chance Kolbe somehow survived?

He snickered, compelling further irritation from her. "A warning implies impending danger if I don't change my ways," he said. "What a tongue you have. Your tongue's always held sway, I suppose."

Audra found herself smiling for the first time in ages. Whenever she attempted to picture a man behind the mask, nobody made sense. It couldn't be Kolbe, and though she acknowledged it, hope clung like a shadow. However, her past confirmed that dead men don't return to life.

If she went with him, she wondered if her freedom waned. After days confined, the water's embrace felt like breathing air. In a swift moment of courage, Audra blurted her next question without overthinking. "Join me for a midnight swim?" Audra asked, her heart pounding. Would this man bear scars where she'd seen swords pierce Kolbe? Or would he be untouched?

The masked man tensed on the lake's edge. His lips tightened to a thin line before he spoke. "The siren sings, and I ebb and I flow. Why do you like to taunt me? No, I can't swim with you. It's improper."

"It's also improper to kiss the future Queen of Althenia if you're not the future King of Althenia," Audra teased, biting her lip to hide her smile as she toyed with him.

Without pause, he answered, "Then it's a good thing I'm the true King of Althenia."

Though he once confessed he was the firstborn heir, Audra hadn't grasped the full implications of this knowledge. Before, it seemed like an elaborate game of pretend. Now, hearing him call himself the king, she paused to consider it. If Julin's story about the king's first marriage was true, then the child from that union would be the rightful heir. She'd spent so much time trying to determine who he was to her that she hadn't considered who he might be to Althenia.

This wasn't just some ordinary, star-struck madman. She hadn't kissed an obsessed servant. The masked man was intelligent, studious, and clever. He was someone with access to knowledge, privy to multitudes of information, even if he didn't yet sit on the throne. Could Jed be the secret heir all along? Or...

Was Kolbe somehow alive, standing before her?

The masked man tugged off his black shirt. Clouds obscured the moon, making scars hard to see, but his silhouette displayed a toned frame that made her blush.

Whoever this king was, thoughts returned to how he'd kissed her in her bedroom and on the tower balcony. She recalled being tied up, a memory she replayed more often than she'd admit.

She watched as he untied his sash, her mind returning to their first kiss. He unbuttoned his trousers. As he stripped down to his undergarments, he spoke. "The siren's call fetches another sailor. The sailor wishes it mattered to the siren that he was more than just another man she'd consume."

Audra furrowed her eyebrows as he entered the lake, maintaining distance as he waded into the same depth as her.

"What do you mean by that?" she asked.

He stayed close, yet far enough that she couldn't attempt another unmasking. Splashing water away from her, he replied, "I wish it mattered more to you who's behind the mask. That's what I mean by that."

Audra paused, a scowl plastering her face. "Of course it matters, or I wouldn't insist you tell me," Audra said with defensiveness. "You said this is improper. Why is this improper if you're the king? A king can claim what he wants. Perhaps you're the one who is already engaged, and that's why these meetings are forbidden. If you're the true heir, my engagement to Elijah means nothing. So, answer, why is this improper?"

The masked man smirked, enjoying the exchange. She was beginning to resent his casual approach to the conversation, taking pleasure in teasing her. "Because, king or not, we're unmarried young people and attracted to one another. Therefore, as a member of the house of Hillsfield, headed by Lord Byron, who strongly opposes premarital relations, this offends your family. Wouldn't you agree?"

Audra flushed. The reasoning was innocent enough, and he was right about Lord Byron's disapproval. However, that hadn't stopped him from grabbing her breast the last time she saw him.

She raised an eyebrow. "It didn't stop you from sneaking into my room to kiss me," Audra quipped. "It didn't stop you on the tower balcony."

"It's not stopping me very well right now either, is it?" he asked.

The masked man floated closer, over an arm's length away. The water reached her neck and his chest, exposing his shoulders. Her heart sank, a frown pulling on her lips. His unmarked shoulders meant Kolbe wasn't him.

If not Kolbe, did that leave Jed? He was her last suspect.

It wasn't like she'd never thought of him that way. She'd considered him handsome, clever, and mysterious. There had been fleeting moments he made her heart flutter, but he wasn't the man haunting her dreams each night.

If she were honest, only one man ever visited her in dreams.

She sighed in defeat, aching again as she accepted he wasn't Kolbe. Now, it didn't matter who he was.

"You're right about one thing, I confess," she said, attempting to hide her disappointment. "It doesn't matter who you are. Perhaps I'm a bit of a flirt and suspicious of true love. I already discovered what happens when you put all your eggs in one basket. Someone can steal the basket. It's better to divide the eggs."

The masked man inched closer. "Yes, well, that's just it. I want to know whether or not I was that basket?"

Audra hesitated. But, in truth, she already knew. "No," she said in a dull tone. She frowned. "You couldn't be."

"How impossible could it be?" he asked. His voice laced with passion, even desperation.

Audra stalled. Her lips parted. Then, in a moment of complete clarity, she knew who the man was behind the mask. Not one bit of it made a single penny of sense, but the more she studied him, the more certain she grew.

It was *Him*.

29

Audra studied the only part of His face she could see: His lips. The skin under His nose, His chin, the sharp curve of His jaw. It always looked familiar, yet there had remained a disconnect. The disconnect being that she witnessed his death.

The disconnect being that he'd been dead for eight years.

He wore his hair differently from the way he used to. It used to be short. His hair was longer now, styled in the fashion many Althenian men wore their hair. He seemed taller than her memory recalled. His voice sounded different, deeper than she remembered it. His frame was larger, older, stronger. As she let herself consider the real possibility, she felt certain it was him.

Audra swallowed, taking in the man before her. She stepped closer, placing him within reach. He didn't move. His eyes watched hers, and hers watched his, a familiar stare between them. Tears threatened as her breath hitched. She didn't realize she'd held it until she released it.

She said his name aloud, disbelief choking her voice. How? How could this be true?

"Garrick," Audra said, voice faltering.

"Audra," Garrick whispered.

Her breath caught again, rendering her unable to gasp or swallow. Her heart felt like it stopped as she pondered the impossibility of it. Their last night together, eight years prior, they'd made love all night, young lovers lost in each other's passion. He'd promised to marry her, then... the morning after, she remembered the clamoring, the horror she felt when she found his body lying on the floor. She'd cradled his head in her lap as he died. She watched them bury the casket. She cried and mourned and yearned for him. She almost took her own life, unable to live with the despair until...

Until she discovered she was pregnant with Eva. Eva resurrected that lost love and gave her hope for something good in the world. She was the living proof of his existence, and her life was enough to keep her going.

Yet, he was not dead. He stood before her now, alive.

Her heart felt like seedlings sprouting after a fire. When fires turn forests into dust, rebirth hatches after a time in the ashes. Her childhood friend stood before her. The man she spent eight years trying to forget materialized like a hallucination in front of her eyes. How could she have known he lived? Furthermore, how was the man she grew up with the firstborn son of King Henri?

It didn't matter. In that moment, she understood the love of her life stood in front of her. For that moment, why or how didn't matter. He was alive. After all that time, the man she'd mourned every day of her life was alive.

Rain poured, thunder rumbling overhead. Already soaked, she noticed neither as her tears mingled with rain. She leapt, using the water to buoy herself, wrapping her legs around his chest. He gripped her hips, holding her close, reciprocating her passion and desire. Arms encircling his neck, she sobbed, burying her forehead on his shoulder.

"I thought you were dead, you asshole," she cried, hands grasping his shoulders, making sure he was real. "Eight years, and now you're here."

She pulled back, seeing the mask still on. He remained silent, watching her reactions. After studying him a moment, Audra's fingers traced a line from his shoulder to his face, pausing at the base of the mask, seeking permission. Since he didn't protest or move her hands away, she removed the mask, revealing every chiseled feature he possessed. She tossed the mask to shore, studying him, her heart pounding.

He was exactly as she remembered, yet nothing like the man she remembered at all. Garrick's teal eyes bore into hers. His dark eyebrows offered his face a handsome, enigmatic appearance. An aged scar ran from his scalp to his eyebrow, and she wondered if it was part of why he hid. It didn't diminish his allure in the least.

Garrick. She sobbed, afraid it was another cruel dream she'd wake up from at any moment. The rain grounded her as her arm wrapped around his neck, her hand gripping his head as she kissed him. He drew her flush, eager for her kiss, consuming her lips the moment their lips touched.

She never thought she'd do this again. She'd pictured many possibilities of the identity of the masked man, ranging from Lord Byron to the countryside boys who used to tease her for her blonde hair. She never imagined this resurrection. How was any of this possible?

Audra hummed with pleasure as Garrick's kisses continued, their lips synchronized in perfect harmony. Neither felt bothered by the pittering rain, and the occasional cracks of thunder remained unnoticed. Even though he held her as tightly as she held him, she wanted more.

After several minutes, Audra broke the kiss, breathless and bemused. Garrick exhaled, and Audra eyed his mask on the shore before meeting his gaze, clinging to him.

"I thought you were dead," she repeated, rain pouring between their faces as she clung to him. "I watched you die. I attended your funeral."

Garrick nodded, frowning. "I know. I owe you every explanation. We can go to the barn, and I'll explain. You're the third to discover my true identity. I broke my oath not to tell you yet."

Audra released her legs from his body, finding footing in the muddy lake. "Why?" she asked, searching his face for answers. How had he gone so many years without telling her he was alive? "Do you have any idea how long I toiled over tears for you?"

Garrick's frown deepened, eyes darting away. "Let's go to the barn. I'll explain everything."

Tears threatened again, hoping he had a plethora of good reasons. Despite herself, she placed her hands on his neck, kissing him again. He reciprocated with equal fervor.

She withdrew again. "I have so many questions," she said, choking on her words. Caught between hurt, shock, joy, and desire, she couldn't decide which one needed the most attention.

"I know."

She kissed him again, pulling back moments later.

"You better have a good reason," she warned. It was all of the emotions. She wanted to keep him close as he explained himself, and to push him away all at once.

"I'll tell you all of them," he promised, unmoving, awaiting to see if she'd give him more.

Questions burned inside, conflicting with desires to never leave his side or to barrage him with questions.

After several stalled moments of staring at one another in the lake, Garrick sighed in defeat. "Let's get shelter in the barn," he urged. Audra nodded this time, and they waded out.

Viewing their clothes onshore, the sight of her wedding dress beside his tunic stirred emotions, mirroring a memory from long ago. Closing the gap between them, she tugged his face into another kiss, unable to control herself. His lips remained ever willing, ever ready, ever anxious for any ounce of physical affection she gave him. His kisses juxtaposed with the hesitancy in hers. His resembled a starving animal, hers remained cautious and uncertain.

Audra pulled back, as she had times before, her thoughts gathering. "No, no more kissing. You need to explain yourself. Why did you leave me? I thought I beheld your death."

He nodded, head cocking toward the barn. They gathered their soaked clothes, and he followed as she ran the short distance to the barn. Once at the entrance of the creaky, wooden shed, she turned around to assure he was still there. A part of her feared his disappearance if she didn't keep him close.

He hadn't vanished. Seizing the moment, he pressed her body against the barn, cold raindrops falling between them. He took her dress, flinging it inside with his clothes. Swirls of fog danced between them when their lips locked again, this time with more passion than the times before.

He hummed a noise of satisfaction and mumbled against her lips, "Damn, it's indescribable how much I missed you." Maybe this wasn't a dream. It was him, alive, urging her to let go.

After minutes of kissing in the rain, Garrick pulled her into the barn, where it was drier despite rain leaking through the old boards. They remained by the entrance, locking lips with all the fervor either could muster. One of Garrick's hands moved beneath her undergarment top, smoothing over the soft skin of her belly.

Audra gasped as his thumb grazed under her breast, her heart fluttering. His touch ignited long-buried feelings she'd forgotten. Even as the masked man, he'd roused these emotions. Before, she couldn't explain it, but now it made perfect sense. Her body remembered him, and she'd compared the masked man to him several times before. Perhaps her subconscious recognized him as the same man. She wondered if her body recalled that night's caresses, and that explained her intense and immediate attraction to him. The familiar stranger was her first love all along.

To Audra's surprise, Garrick pulled his lips away this time. Fog swirled between their faces as rain outside tapped around them. "Do you realize how long I've waited for this? We have to stop before I lose my mind. I promised not to compromise your honor... er, again." He chuckled, pecking her lips once more, hand steady beneath her breast. "You aren't making it easy to keep my promises."

Audra's eyes drifted over his chest, his muscles appearing more defined than she remembered. Meeting his gaze, she offered a devious smile.

"I made no such promises," she said. Garrick's body tensed, his rigid muscles hardening. His lips twitched, and his fingers tightened their grip on her, as if involuntarily. She'd once given everything to this man. Though eight years had passed, her lust for him remained completely unhindered.

Tracing one of her hands over his bare chest, Garrick sighed at her touch as she moved her hand lower and lower. His breath shallowed until her hand pressed against his fully erect shaft through his trousers. He groaned, head tilting as she stroked him.

"We can't," he murmured, but the look in his eyes indicated his true desire. "I promised Lord Byron I wouldn't touch you."

Lord Byron's name snapped her from her lust, shifting her mind to reality. "Lord Byron?"

"He's one of the others who knows my identity. Well, one who can prove I'm Althenia's firstborn heir."

Fresh betrayal stung, though she tried to understand. She wondered how long Garrick had known his lineage, and what role Lord Byron played. Did he always know?

"What happened that morning?" Audra asked, dropping her arms to her sides. Garrick's hand lowered to her hip. "I cradled your head in my lap. I watched you stop breathing."

"Alright," he said, eyeing the horses. "I'm not supposed to tell you this. If that vile half-brother of mine captures you, I fear what he'd do to get information from you."

Audra remembered telling Elijah about Garrick's death. He'd tensed at the name and asked her when she last saw him. She swallowed. "Margaret told Elijah I wasn't a virgin. You were right about her. When he asked who, I named you."

Garrick's body tensed at her confession, touching his jaw. "I guess it's good that I didn't reveal myself while you lived there, then. How much does he know?"

"He didn't ask much. I told him the truth: I saw you die. He asked nothing more after that."

"I imagine that's why he imprisoned you. My spies couldn't verify your survival, and Elijah allowed no one near your room. He posted guards at the bottom of the steps but refused to let anyone go up except a girl he sent to set meals outside your door. I believe her name was Alynne. My spies told me plates of food would return untouched, so they couldn't be certain. He used you to bait me to him. I couldn't risk coming sooner."

Audra recalled those tower days. Hours dragged like torture, mealtimes were unpredictable. She hadn't known Elijah kept her hidden, but in fairness, she didn't know anything when she was held captive.

"I'll do everything in my power to assure he can't harm you again," Garrick continued, interrupting her thoughts. "We spent eight years apart because of that man. One more day would've broken me. It was pure agony waiting for this. That first time I saw you in the alleyway the night of Margaret's death, I lost all control to stay away."

"Start from the beginning," Audra said, urging him to tell her all the reasons he never told her he was alive.

Garrick ran his hands through his black hair, releasing moisture trapped in it from the rain. "That morning, eight years ago, after our incredible night we shared, everything changed. The details are blurry, but while fetching us tea before telling your mother of our marriage plans, a seven-foot man restrained me. Some sort of concoction was forced down my throat. The next thing I remember, I woke in darkness, stones on my eyes, and lying on a stone pillar with a cloth near my head. A stranger stood there, capping a bottle, saying he was pleased I woke easily."

Garrick paused, watching her reaction. Audra moved to sit on a bundle of aged, brown hay in the corner. He followed, but instead of sitting, he paced before her.

"You met him. Julin, the king's advisor. On a drunken night, young King Henri married my mother, Cynthia Lorent. He knew her through his childhood friend, whom you also know, Lord Daniel Byron himself. My mother was Lord Byron's cousin, a secret she took to her grave. They struck up a forbidden affair, and the king and she eloped one night when they were seventeen."

Garrick checked her reaction again as he paced. Audra hugged her knees, resting her chin on them, listening and trying to picture it. Cynthia had never told Garrick the identity of his father, one of the reasons he took so long to confess his love back then. He thought Audra deserved better than the unwanted bastard of an unnamed nobleman.

"Their marriage angered Doth because Prince Henri was already betrothed to their princess. They threatened war unless he annulled it. My mother was banished, sent to return to her family, and given empty promises of lifelong care."

Garrick's anger showed when he shook his head. Audra remembered their poverty when she met them; locusts destroyed their crops the year they met, putting them on the brink of starvation. King Henri didn't keep that promise.

"Her parents rejected her and turned her away. When she was homeless, she discovered she was pregnant with me, and she feared for my life. She foresaw I'd be hunted if anyone found out. She asked Lord Byron to marry her, but his traditional values led him to deny her, banishing her to the countryside. As you know, Lord Byron tends to be self-righteous. My mother was the first to disappoint him, so she received the full extent of his wrathful judgment. Though he bought our land, he demanded she never seek his aid again. Julin told me this the day I woke from the sleeping concoction."

Audra connected Julin's story about Doth's tensions and the king's first wife to Garrick's mother. She hadn't connected the story to Garrick's mother then. Questions multiplied, but before she formulated any into coherence, he continued.

"After my mother died, Elijah got wind that my mother had a living son. Born a year after me, and my existence unknown to King Henri, Elijah was named heir. As King Henri's affairs increased, the murders of pregnant women in brothels began. Elijah hid bodies at first, concealing his deeds. When that failed to stop the king, the murders became public."

Garrick stopped, watching Audra process. Deep in thought, she pieced the information together.

"That morning, Julin had drugged me while his giant man he hired held me down. The sleep mimicked death. I don't remember you finding me or falling asleep. He was assigned to murder me when Elijah found out about my existence. Instead, he faked my death and saved me, refusing to serve a king who murdered women and children. Elijah had discovered me the day before. Julin said everyone must think me dead for me to live."

Pausing to consider his story, Audra averted her eyes. "You didn't know you were the firstborn heir before then?" Audra asked, clarifying this wasn't a secret he kept all along.

Garrick sat beside her, grabbing a piece of hay to play with between his fingers. "No, not until Julin told me after I woke."

Audra recognized a small pain in her chest, shoving it down to contemplate the chances. Her childhood friend had been the true heir to Althenia all along. Still, he might not have known then, but he'd known for eight years.

"You didn't tell me you were alive," she said, unable to meet his gaze. Though relieved he hadn't always known his heritage, the betrayal lingered. He'd abandoned her with their child, ruining the rest of her life. Why had he never attempted to inform her?

"It was dangerous. Julin said to stay hidden. I had no army, no allies, nothing but him. He warned that returning to you meant risking discovery, endangering our lives. He promised that if I waited, practiced patience, I could tell you after claiming my throne."

Audra's heart sank deeper. "You promised that night to marry me, then left me with a child—"

"I didn't realize Eva was our child," Garrick cut in, throwing his hay aside. He offered his hand, but Audra turned away. He sighed. "Your mother married Douglas Freeman. Then, after he died, she wed Lord Byron. I believed the story that Eva was your half-sister. I considered no other alternative. The letter Jed gave me revealed she was ours. I never meant to abandon you."

"But you did." Audra faced him, tears welling. "What were you doing that I couldn't have helped you?"

"It was dangerous, Audra. I had no defenses. I still don't have enough. Ever since dancing with you that night at the masquerade, despite Julin's and my advisors' protests, I desperately wanted you to figure it out. Back then, I stupidly thought it would be easy for you to figure out. I hoped, deep inside, you'd still be waiting for me
"

How was that fair? Audra scoffed. "I thought you were dead. How could I have known you weren't? What about the casket they buried?"

"Dirt," Garrick replied. "Nailed shut after they claimed poison defiled my body. After my body was sent to the mortuary, Julin paid the mortician to forge the autopsy." He covered his mouth, considering. "I understand what you thought, what everyone thought, but I hoped you, of all people, would recognize me."

Audra turned away, fighting tears. "You wore a mask. How was I supposed to know? You have no idea how hurt I feel. I spent years being used as a pawn in everyone else's game of chess. If you allied with Lord Byron, how could you allow that? Why let me live with a murderer?"

Garrick clenched the hay beneath his hands. "I had no control over any of that. Lord Byron wanted nothing to do with me at first. To him, I was another one of Henri's bastards. His alliance changed after learning about the death of his kin. While a tragedy for Byron, his alliance greatly aids our cause. We'll need his wealth to rebuild after the war."

"War?" Audra asked. She remembered once thinking Doth responsible. What of Kolbe's betrothal to their princess?

Garrick smirked. "The war for my birthright." Audra's face fell, realizing another heir meant the bloodshed wasn't finished. "Don't worry. Odds favor us, and bloodshed will be minimal. I'll first need to secure Lord Byron's help when I return. Though I'll owe him apologies first. Many urged me not to rescue you. I anticipate a severe scolding upon my return."

Audra closed her eyes, more questions multiplying with each answer. "You still have so many secrets. If you're the king, and you knew I was alive, why follow the commands of others? I could've stood beside you, but instead—"

"Instead, you were safe," Garrick said, his voice decisive, indicating this topic wouldn't be up for discussion.

Audra wouldn't have it. No more would she allow others to decide her path. She stood, brushing her skirt. "I will finish speaking when it's my turn, and not be interrupted. I spent six years imprisoned at Hillsfield, a slave to powerful men's rules. I had no choice in any manner of my life, rarely allowed to even see my own daughter. Propriety forced me into a life I didn't want, shaming me into silence. Everything was secret. I lived as an outsider with a rich lord who despised me, yet he had every control over me, even though he wasn't my father. You could've prevented it by keeping your promise. No matter what, we were supposed to be facing everything together."

Tears fell as she wiped them, no longer trying to hold them back. "Instead, I survived without voice or choice, enduring silence where I wasn't welcome or wanted. You stole the decision from me to let me choose if the danger was worth it. Was I really safer in a castle with a prince who'd kill me for the most damning secret you left me to bear alone?"

Garrick fell silent, considering her words for a moment before he stood, approaching. She wiped another tear.

"How alone you must have been," he said, his tone colder than before. "I told you my spies watched Hillsfield. I was certain, for a while, it was Jed you admired. I thought that was why you attended all of Eva's lessons. Now that I know she's ours, your attentiveness to

her education makes sense. Therefore, it was Kolbe Byron, wasn't it
?"

Audra pressed her lips together. At the mention of Kolbe, her
heart broke in two. She clenched her fists to contain herself from
shoving him. "Don't speak ill of the dead."

He scoffed. "I'm not speaking ill. I'm asking a question, or are
you the only one who gets to? I'd bet you thought the masked man
was Kolbe. He was the one you thought you kissed, even after all my
hints I tried giving you. You never considered me, you were too busy
loving him. So perhaps all those years you blame me for were not so
lonely, were they?"

Audra's lips parted, his words stinging. After considering multiple ways to respond, she settled on one and stepped closer. "The
thing is, if that's all true, you would have no right to know. For eight
years, you allowed me to believe you were dead. I owed nothing to
a deceptive dead man. I only had that night with you because you
promised you were going to marry me."

Her voice shook as she paused to steady herself before finishing. "You took liberties that were never yours to take. If anything you
said that night was true, you'd have told me you were alive. I planned
to end my life before I found out about my pregnancy with Eva. I
didn't want to live in a world without you, but you forced it upon
me. You had choices, I had none. You decided my fate for me."

Garrick growled, but Audra didn't flinch. "I kept you alive so
you could be angry at me now in the first place. I listened to the
counsel of my advisors, but with great agony. If you think knowing
you were out there alive made it easier for me, you're wrong. It made
it so much harder to stay away."

Audra shook her head, frustrated that she needed to repeat
herself. "It should've been my choice, too. Why can't *you* understand *that*?"

Rain and thunder still synchronized outside the barn. Leaks from the roof dripped small puddles around them. Their horses whinnied.

Garrick swallowed, inches from her. "The fate of the kingdom relied on my duty over my selfishness. Try to understand me."

Audra moved to the old, rotting fences of the stables where their horses stood as witnesses to the scene. They stood apart like shy, introverted strangers unwilling to meet.

"Was I right?" he asked. "Did you love Kolbe?"

Audra's lips tightened. "Do you have any right to know?" she snapped. She had loved him. Only because the man she truly wanted never told her he was alive.

He wasn't the man she remembered. Her best friend would've included her. He would have run to her and insisted they face it together. He would not have kept so many secrets.

Garrick remained still, standing in front of a creaky wooden roof leaking above. "I see," he said solemnly. He sounded hurt, but if so, it was caused by a situation he created. She faced the rain-filled doorway, ground muddying as rivers of water pooled inside.

Garrick eyed the ground, moments of silence drowned out by rain. After several minutes of paused conversation, he sighed. "This rain won't stop tonight, and it's best to travel in darkness. Your horse needs to stay here. One of my spies will collect it in the morning and remove the markers. We'll ride together on mine. It should take two nights to reach Eva and your mother if we leave at dusk tomorrow."

Walking to his horse, he retrieved a dress from his satchel. It was one of hers she'd left at Hillsfield. "From your mother. Better than the wedding dress, though getting wet is inevitable. We'll leave when you're ready. I'll wait outside."

Taking the dress, he left without another word. Her heart sank. She both desired him passionately and felt utterly betrayed by him.

Years of rules, boredom, and misery he could've prevented. Alone, she touched her lips, remembering the fire they shared in their kisses. How swiftly the embers dissolved to ashes as the inclemency of verity rained down.

30

Morning dew covered the leaves on the pink Althenian Whisper Trees. Fog hovered over the treeline as rain diminished to trinkles. Their soaked bodies stopped when they approached a brown rock ledge, providing cave-like shelter underneath. Garrick dismounted his black stallion, leaving her back feeling cold without his warm body behind her. Rain faded as he tied the horse's reins to a tree. Neither had spoken a word since leaving the barn.

Audra slid off the horse, wringing the fabric of her navy dress as Garrick retrieved items from his satchel. A thin pad, an even thinner blanket, and chains attached to animal traps. He tossed the bedroll under the ledge, followed by the blanket and satchel.

"I'm setting traps for food. Hopefully, we catch something while we sleep," Garrick said. He didn't wait for her response before disappearing behind the trees. Audra eyed the bedroll and blanket. Comfort never looked so inviting, though she noted there was only one.

She crept to them, drawn by the promise of rest. Cold rain had prevented sleep during their ride, so exhaustion consumed her. The bedding stayed dry, safe from the rain in the leather satchel. Untying the bedroll, she spread it beneath the ledge before checking the satchel for another roll. There wasn't one.

Guess he expected them to share.

Inside the satchel, her wedding dress's inside layers remained partly dry. She ripped the wet layers from the dry, examining the thick layers of cotton. As dawn neared, she eyeballed her soaked dress clinging to her form. Sleep would be impossible while wet.

Checking outside the ledge, she confirmed she was alone. With Garrick away, she yanked off her dress, then stripped the sleeves from her undergarment top. She fashioned makeshift clothing from the dry wedding dress pieces, tying them together. Not her usual craftsmanship, but better than sleeping in wet clothes.

Garrick returned five minutes later, carrying wood. "Sorry for the delay. Most of the wood was too wet." He dropped the pile, noting her spread clothes and torn dress. His mouth twitched, turning away as he stripped to his undergarments. Audra blushed, turning away to finish braiding her hair, securing it with another cloth of torn fabric.

He chuckled. "Nothing you haven't seen before." His eyes found her on the bedroll. "That's for you. I'll take the ground. I'm used to it."

As he built the fire, Audra watched him arrange kindling, noticing the firmness of his muscular frame. The image recalled their days in the countryside, when she'd watched him tend to the fire during their infamous night. At the time, she'd felt complete, as if she'd received everything she desired. Now, he was like a penumbra, neither here nor there. It was hard to believe he was real.

What would her life be like if he'd married her? She avoided getting lost in such daydreams before, as they'd served only to hurt her, but he pain of lost possibilities seeped in. Eva would know her true mother. Audra never would have been engaged to Elijah.

Kathleen and Kolbe would still be alive.

After he finished the fire, Garrick caught her staring. She flushed, turning away.

"You haven't said a word since the barn," he said. She knew.

"What do you want me to say?" she asked, feeling snarky. "Thank you for saving me from a situation your lies created?"

Garrick touched his temples, groaning. "Always such a brat. Once you realize the circumstances were bigger than you, maybe we can have a rational conversation. For now, I haven't slept in two days and I'm exhausted."

Garrick stood, moving from the fire. Rain returned beyond their ledge shelter. His horse whinnied, seeking cover under the tree, finding a new patch of grazing grass.

He sat beside her, resting wrists on raised knees, swallowing. "I did come for you once. That was the first and last time I defied Julin's orders."

Audra raised an eyebrow, waiting for more.

"When I woke from the sleeping concoction, Julin claimed Elijah killed you. For the first two years, I thought you dead. For those two years, my motivation to take the throne was to make the bastard suffer. Revenge drove me. Then, my spy reported your mother's marriage to Byron, sharing that you would move with her to Hillsfield. That was when I learned you were alive."

Garrick squinted, watching the rain create a waterfall outside of their ledge, creating a cascading wall. The water moved downhill when it reached the ground, away from their shelter.

That gave him two excusable years, Audra thought. What of the other six?

"When I learned this, I nearly killed Julin for the lie. I challenged him to a duel. He gave me this scar," he touched his brow, pointing to the one she noticed last night. "That was humbling. If the time came, I thought I could beat that old man in a sword fight. The original cut was more like an L-shape, but the bottom didn't scar. I left Julin, intent on finding you. He had mentioned your betrothal to Elijah and urged patience. I refused. Originally, I had this mask made to cover my healing wound. Afterward, it became a necessity. I hadn't returned to Althenia since the morning of my feigned death, so none except Julin knew I lived. I went to Hillsfield masked to hide my identity, hoping to find you."

Garrick twisted a grass blade between his thumb and forefinger. "The rain should last all day, so the sun won't disturb our sleep."

"Then what?" she pressed.

Garrick sighed. "I was foolish in my approach. Guards stopped me at the gates. I sought peace, so I didn't harm them. I demanded an audience with Lord Byron. He came to the gates when I told the guards to inform him I was the son of Cynthia Lorent. I told Lord Byron I was the true heir, thinking this mattered to him.

"Then, I demanded he marry you to me instead of Elijah. He called me the king's bastard, denying my claim to the throne. He was one of two who discovered my mother's secret marriage and pregnancy, and could even confirm it. He said my claim was weak, that I should remain in hiding, and start life anew. He threatened to hand me over to Elijah himself if I ever returned to Hillsfield."

Audra's lips pursed. "You stayed away because of Byron? He's not my father, or me."

"I know," Garrick muttered. "That wasn't what stopped me. That mistake nearly ruined everything. One of Byron's gate guards spied for Elijah. The spy informed Elijah that I lived. Before, he thought me dead. Julin was imprisoned for treason, sentenced to hang. He was my greatest asset in our plan to reclaim the throne. Without him, I had nothing. My attempt to claim you doubled Hillsfield's guards. Elijah set bounties, so I fled to the southern isles."

Audra swallowed. The southern isles were lawless lands, home to fleeing criminals and banished courtiers. "You said King Henri never learned you existed. Why didn't Julin say something?"

He studied the falling water. "He tried. My father was a drunken fool. Julin ran the castle affairs so King Henri could party, drink, and bed courtier women. Since Henri wouldn't hear politics, he was often uninformed. The day before Julin faked my death, someone unknowingly tipped off a castle spy that my mother had a son. When Elijah turned eighteen, he had taken over the castle affairs, so the news went to Elijah.

"He sent Julin to kill me to eliminate the threat. Julin approached my father first, informing him that he'd had a son with my mother. King Henri, in a drunken stupor, named me a bastard and approved Elijah's command to have me murdered. I suppose the threat of another Dothian war might have inconvenienced his lifestyle." Garrick's tone sounded bitter as he explained, shaking his head. "Julin chose to ally with me after the order. He said neither Henri nor Elijah possessed redeemable qualities fit for a king."

Her heart ached as she noticed his somber expression, his eyes fixated on the ground. "What about Julin's sentence to hang?"

Garrick readjusted. "Dumb luck saved him. The missing brothel ladies were noticed. Elijah poisoned them, hid their bodies, and after a few went missing, the town talked. To him, they were threats to his crown; to the town, they were daughters and friends.

"The owner of the apothecary supplying poison to the crown, a man named Pytr Bagish, switched the vials of poison to sleeping potions to help the women escape. He was caught. Two days before Julin's scheduled hanging, Pytr was arrested. At Pytr's trial, knowing death was inevitable, he saved Julin's life by falsely testifying that the vial for me was also swapped. His testament absolved Julin of guilt, and his titles were restored with a promotion to Captain of the Guards. The king and Elijah swore to never question his loyalty again."

Listening to his story, her chest tightened. So much had happened that she'd never heard about. She wondered if the potions in the room where Kathleen died held stored poison vials. She sighed. "And Jed?"

"Jed was my first spy. Jed's mother was a brothel victim seven years ago. Julin found Jed sneaking into the palace to assassinate the king, nearly succeeding. Julin swayed him to seek revenge by joining us instead, convincing him he'd be more useful gathering information.

"Jed's an expert sleuth, both observant and intelligent. Once recruited, I gave him a letter meant for you. He searched for you in your room, and finding it empty, he snooped. He found a journal by your bedside, tore out the last page, and returned my letter to me with the stolen page."

Audra tried remembering a journal from six or seven years ago. "I don't remember keeping a journal. What did it say?"

Garrick sighed. "I carried the page in my pockets for a while, throwing it in the ocean when I returned from the southern isles. It read something like: 'When I look at you, I remember I can love again. You fill my heart with joy. You're the reason I breathe, the reason I hope, you're the person I'd follow to the end of the world. You mean more to me than anyone I've ever known. I wish I could tell you how much I love you. I wish, I hope, I dream.'"

Weaving his fingers together, Garrick stared at his hands as if the letter were still in them. Audra recognized it by the words. It was from a journal she'd written for Eva in some misled hope that one day she might be able to reveal the truth to her daughter. After four years of writing in it, Mystine had found it and tossed it in the fire, fearing it might fall into the wrong hands. She didn't speak to her mother for months after that. If pages were missing, Audra never knew.

"That was a letter for Eva," she said.

He nodded. "I realize that now. I pieced that together once I discovered she was your... *our* daughter. I thought it was for someone else, and I clung to this ridiculous hope you were waiting for me. I thought the page meant you loved another more than me. So... I tried to forget you and kept my distance."

More miscommunication from a lack of conversation, more self-inflicted hurt. The situation was more complicated than she thought, but so much could have been different if she'd known. Exhausted, she pulled the blanket around herself, lying down. Temptations of sleep gnawed at her despite her swirling thoughts. Garrick grabbed leftover cotton fabric from her dress, wadding it before lifting her droopy head to place it under her.

As she faded, her heart pounded. What if she wasn't falling asleep? What if she were about to wake up? She jumped, panicked, and sat up to scan for him. Her heart calmed. Still there.

"Jump dream?" he asked, smirking.

Her heart raced, tears threatening again. Sore, tired eyes weakened her ability to fight her emotions. "I'm afraid when I wake up, I'll discover myself back in that tower. Like you were a dream."

Garrick knelt beside her, frowning. "I'm not going anywhere. Not unless you tell me you don't love me and never want to see me again." His fingers brushed her cheek. His touch grounded her, reminding her he was real. Relief washing over her, she closed her eyes.

"Garrick," she whispered. "Lie beside me, so I can be sure." Her thoughts steadied at the thought of his body near, warm, and with a beating heart. She lay down, scooting to allow him room on the bedroll.

"As you wish," he replied. Moving behind her on the bedroll, his warmth was reminiscent of walking indoors after spending hours frozen in snow. Taking the makeshift pillow from her, he slipped one arm beneath her head, the other wrapping around her waist. Pouring rain and the sound of the cackling fire lulled her into the deepest sleep she'd ever know until the day she died.

31

Audra woke with her head on Garrick's bare chest, one of his hands resting on her hair, the other on her hip. His scent resembled a mix of dirt and woodsy notes. Rain continued pouring outside, forming a wall of water that pooled into a pond beyond their ledge and drained downhill.

As she regained consciousness, she stirred, watching her hand on his chest rise and fall with his slow breaths. Gazing at his face, she marveled at his statuesque features, more mature and refined than eight years ago. He would be twenty-seven now, but some features gave him an older appearance.

Her eyes moved lower, blushing at the small tent pitched in his undergarments. Much time had passed since that night, but desire yearned to remember those feelings. She pondered how many more differences she'd discover in his stories. Could she still love someone she wasn't sure she trusted?

Outside the ledge, the horse whinnied a warning cry. Heart panicking, she peered through the water streams toward Garrick's stallion, which appeared spooked. She sat up, alerted.

"I see a horse," a male voice said. "This way."

Throat tightening, Audra lightly shoved Garrick, whispering his name. He jolted awake, instinctively grabbing his nearby sword and pointing it at her. Fear tinged her as she sucked in, but she motioned toward the noise.

Realizing his mistake, he lowered the blade, guilt flashing until he focused on the sounds of the threat.

The outside voices persisted. "If there's a horse, there's a rider. Scout the premises, and stay alert. If the princess is near, she won't be hard to find."

"Shit," Garrick muttered under his breath. Outside, she caught a brief glimpse of men in royal guard uniforms. Three were visible, each on horseback.

Garrick dressed fast, tugging on his trousers and donning his mask, then crouched before her. "Stay put," he warned, exiting the cave.

Did he plan on handling all of them alone? Audra grabbed her dagger, but he'd already vanished, his direction unknown. Observing her surroundings, she decided to stay. While the waterfall provided coverage, if the guards examined it long enough, they would see everything inside.

Panic set in, realizing Elijah had found her after all.

Not far from her hiding spot, sounds of clashing swords reached her, followed by one guard calling for help. Heart pounding, her hand covered her mouth.

Then, behind her, another voice rang out. "The princess! Under the ledge!" Startled, Audra jumped, turning to see a guard entering the cave with a drawn sword, rushing toward her. Clenching her dagger, she braced for defense, even if it would be useless to fight a sword with a dagger.

As she stood to her feet, holding her dagger in front of her, the guard stopped short. His lips curled into a mocking smile. "Don't tell me you think you can best me? Drop it, and I won't have to harm you. King Elijah will be pleased to have you returned in one piece."

Audra stood taller, refusing to allow fear to consume her. "You'll have to do more than harm me to bring me back. I won't return, except as a corpse."

The guard sneered, raising his sword. Her heart raced as she dodged his first blow, using a quick maneuver to slice his wrist. He gasped, anger flaring as his jaw fell open.

"You bitch," he snarled, gritting his teeth. Another guard entered from the other side of the cave. Clanging had ceased outside, signaling the battle's end. Bracing for doom against two skilled fighters, she backed against the wall. The first guard yielded his sword for another swing, but before the sword fell, the new guard swung too. In an unexpected turn of events, the second guard's swing aimed at the first guard, cutting him down.

Audra viewed the bloody scene before her, astonished. The first guard fell to his knees, and the new guard finished him with a throat slice. Heart refusing to settle, her eyes darted between the dead guard and the one who saved her, wondering what she witnessed.

To her left, Garrick reappeared, expression shifting from panic to relief. His bloody sword hung at his side, with more rain-washed blood dripping down his chest. A breath of relief released through his nostrils.

"Thank you, Duj," Garrick said. "You'll be rewarded for that."

Duj nodded. "Nearly a hundred guards and soldiers search for her, Your Majesty. The remaining soldiers prepare to march."

Garrick heaved his shoulders, exchanging a look between Audra and his bloodied sword. "Guards never ventured this close before. We must hide the bodies in case others come this far."

As clarity struck her, Audra realized Duj was one of Garrick's spies. News of hundreds searching felt like a short-lived escape, making it difficult to calm herself.

"Can you divert them?" Garrick asked.

Duj shook his head. "They found your markers, so they know to come this way. Elijah's men found the horse left in the barn."

Garrick tightened his lips. "Alright. There's a river a quarter mile east. We'll dispose of the bodies there. I'll take their horses with me. Report a rebel attack and claim you escaped. Point them east, and don't mention us."

"Of course, Your Majesty." The men hauled the body out. Once away, Audra collected her damp navy dress, changing from her makeshift one. Exiting, she saw the men loading the dead body onto a horse. Garrick returned, having shown Duj where to look for the second dead guard.

"Are you alright?" Garrick asked, his teal eyes searching hers. Rain had washed away blood from his chest. Audra hugged herself, clinging to her elbows, looking down. More were coming. They were heading the right way. Were they safe? Garrick continued. "You're in shock. I saw the guard's wrist cut. Was that your d oing?"

She nodded, unable to do more. This was what he'd meant when he said war was coming. As long as she was being hunted, she knew she wasn't free. Also, this was what he'd meant when he told her he was dangerous and had killed before. The man she once loved wasn't the same man he was then.

"I'm sorry," Garrick said. "They haven't come this close before. I thought we had a better lead, or we wouldn't have stopped to rest. I'll help Duj, then we should eat quick, and leave. Start the fire while I'm away."

Nodding again, Audra noted her skirt's hem drip, gathering mud from the ground. Garrick stepped closer, the remaining blood now washed away. He pulled her close, embracing her. His wet, warm chest comforted her in her daze. Closing her eyes, she relaxed into his arms, steadying her breaths.

He held her long, whispering reassurance before releasing her. Once he departed, she returned under the ledge. She made herself useful by rolling the bedroll, folding the blanket, and packing the dress pieces in the saddlebag. After securing the remainder of their things, she readied dried sticks for a fire, lighting it with the flint and steel Garrick had used that morning.

Minutes before, the specter of death had loomed large, and its presence continued to haunt her.

The rain relented, fog lifting from the forest's trap. Gray clouds parted for an orange sunset. Eyes darting toward every noise, she watched the forest trees and waited. At last, Garrick returned, hiking up the hill alone. In one hand, he carried traps; in the other, he held a small catch.

Reaching the ledge, he tossed empty traps into the saddlebag and approached the fire. Up close, she saw he'd caught a rabbit. After kindling a new fire, he skinned it in under a minute by the ledge's pond. Her stomach growled. She hadn't eaten since finding the raspberry bush by the meadow.

Garrick cooked the rabbit before stomping the fire out. The cooking finished as the sky turned purple and dusk surrounded them. Breaking the spit in two, he offered her both halves and let her choose. "Not palace fare, but it'll fuel us for tonight. We'll reach the canyons by morning."

Audra's mind drifted, considering Althenian canyons. She'd never seen them before, only heard. They twisted and turned into hundreds of different labyrinths, providing the perfect hideout if one could navigate them. Many were lost in the narrow canyons, turning in circles for days if they didn't know which way to go. "You said my mother and Eva are there?"

Garrick nodded. "When you didn't come to the treeline that night, I went to Hillsfield. Byron was there, his army preparing to attack Elijah. I stopped his rage and urged him to save his soldiers for war. His army could sway battles, we could use his aid. He agreed to examine our camps to determine if he'll join us. They await us there."

Eating another bite of tender meat, Audra thought of Eva. There'd been a time she feared never seeing her daughter again.

"Does Eva know?" she asked.

Garrick's puzzled expression met hers. "If I'm her father? No. I saw her once with your mother, arguing with her. She's a spitting image of you, it's jarring," he said with a chuckle. "Personality, too."

Audra smiled. Yes. She knew all about it.

"When I came to rescue you, your mother was the only one at camp that I informed of my mission. Julin helped arrange it, but Lord Byron thought a crew would be too visible. I went alone, alerting only your mother. Lord Byron is intimidating, but he listens to her. I suppose we're all fools in love for beautiful blonde women."

His eyes met hers, and she blushed. He wasn't wrong about Byron. Lord Byron had a soft spot for Mystine, willing to bend for her desires.

However, Garrick's use of the word "love" struck her. Once, Audra had convinced herself this man was the only one she'd give her heart to. But eight years had changed much, and her heart sank with the thought.

She closed her eyes. "I did love him," Audra whispered, turning to the fire. "Kolbe."

When her eyes flickered to Garrick, he swallowed. Her cheeks reddened, and he grunted. "I guess I knew. It was wishful thinking to believe otherwise. I heard he died protecting you. I'm sorry you witnessed it."

Audra's heart clenched at the memory of swords piercing Kolbe. It wasn't the first time she'd seen a man she loved die. His death had hit her differently, but still hard. Tears threatened again as she took a deep breath.

"I planned to end my life after you died," Audra said. "The day I planned it, my mother realized I hadn't had my courses in months. Eva saved me. Losing you was the hardest thing I've ever endured, Garrick. Losing Kolbe wasn't easy either, but his was different. I grew up with you, I loved you so much that I didn't think I'd recover. Sometimes, I wonder... what if I'd acted a day earlier?"

Garrick frowned. They finished eating, and though she was still hungry, it would suffice.

"I'm glad you didn't," he said. "I couldn't have stopped it. I thought you were already gone. My pain turned to vengeance. I realize you resent my secrecy during all those years. Maybe you seek an apology, but I can't offer one. I'm not sorry for keeping you safe, even if you hate me for it."

Audra met his gaze, firelight flickering in his stubborn eyes. She didn't hate him. But what else didn't she know? "I don't want to argue now," she said, standing, brushing her damp dress.

"We don't have to argue," Garrick said, standing too. "You're alive because of it. You're welcome."

Audra rolled her eyes. "Let's go."

He appeared annoyed, motioning surrender, pulling on his shirt. "Fine," he said, grabbing the saddlebag.

As Audra turned, Garrick caught her wrist, sending electricity through her. Annoyance turned to heat as her eyes found his.

He sighed, but didn't release her. "If I'd come... would you have chosen me?"

Her lips parted, considering. Would she have chosen him over Kolbe? The answer was obvious to her, and it bothered her that it wasn't obvious to him. Freeing her wrist, she backed away, her gaze still on him.

"I guess you'll never know," Audra said.

She turned, approaching the three horses, grateful for her own mount. Garrick's failure to acknowledge the pain he'd inflicted made forgiveness impossible. She wanted to release the past and focus on a new beginning. Withholding information indicated he thought he knew best for her, like a parent shading difficult truths from a child. If she forgave, could she trust he wouldn't withhold from her again if the war went awry? Or would his royal authority and protective instincts forever shield her from truth, eternally imprisoning her in a state of darkness?

32

Hidden deep in northern Althenia's reddish-gray canyon walls lay a rebel warcamp. Thousands of ivory tents sprawled across a grassy field inside the canyon walls.

In the coldness of dawn, few remained awake. Garrick led the way, masked, and Audra followed through the maze-like canyons with the third horse trailing behind the one she rode. Her tell-tale hair hid under a black sash as they traveled. Canyons narrowed and widened at various intervals, some spots requiring a tighter squeeze to pass.

Maps of the canyons had never been completed due to their complexity and multitude of secret passageways. She lost track after several turns, the sea of ivory tents appearing after a particularly narrow passageway, requiring extra squeezing for the horses.

At the end of the narrow pass that opened to the warcamp, a man awaited at the opening. His surprise was evident at Garrick's arrival.

"Your Highness, we awaited your return," the man said. He turned to Audra, frowning. "What is she doing here? You were given specific instructions. We needed you at camp. She can't be here. They'll have hundreds searching for her." The man's frazzled expression gave her pause. What instructions?

Garrick tensed, approaching the man. "Change of plans, Lord Sherritt. Julin reported her alive, imprisoned. An opportunity arose for rescue. Secrecy was required."

Sherritt's jaw dropped, incredulous. By the look on his face, it was as if he'd heard the most horrific news imaginable. Garrick loomed over him, and Sherritt sneered.

"Byron's settlements are unconfirmed, Your Highness," Sherritt said. "He won't like your disappearance for two nights. If she were imprisoned, that's where she should remain." Sherritt examined her, longer than she liked, frank with his animosity toward her.

"Let me handle Byron," Garrick replied, unswayed. "Don't forget to whom you speak, Lord Sherritt. I desired her rescue, so she may be returned to her family. Lady Byron is her mother, so your respect is required. Find her a tent. Get guards posted. We'll talk after resting."

Sherritt straightened, still upset. "No empty tents, Your Grace. Byron's army's unexpected arrival filled all vacancies. Tents remain overcrowded at present."

Garrick sighed, his demeanor calm despite the hostility. "She'll use my tent, then. I'll find room in a soldier's tent. If your allegiance is genuine, demonstrate your belief in me as king, Sherritt. I've decided."

Yes, that was the problem, Audra mused. *He* decided. Things were to be his way and only his. If she were his wife, would it mean eternal entrapment? Never an opinion, never a say. Not unless *he decided*.

Sherritt flushed, bowing in submission, his tone changing. "Yes, Your Highness. I'll post guards outside your tent."

Sherritt departed, and Garrick motioned Audra forward. "I'll remain with you until guards arrive." After delivering the horses to a guarded corral, Garrick led her through the maze of tents, the rising fog clearing as the sky grew orange over the canyon's walls.

Audra studied the grass as she followed Garrick to a tent lodged near the canyon's dead end. "Why doesn't Lord Sherritt want me here?" she asked, turning to Garrick. Feeling like an interloper, the first impression confirmed her status as an inferior in this new world.

"Inside," Garrick gestured her forward.

Audra entered, taking in the dawn-lit royal scene. The royal tent held woven rugs covering the grass, a fur-covered bed in one corner, and a locked chest at its foot. A table strewn with a red cloth held maps and books, and another table large enough for twelve diners dominated the entrance space.

Garrick gestured to the bed, unlocking the chest to retrieve a black duvet. Weapons and armor gleamed inside. "Sleep here. I'll return when you wake. Come and go as you please, you're not a prisoner. Guards will protect you, so bring them to see your mother and... erm... sister."

Audra sank onto the bed, watching him avoid her gaze. Questions and hurt remained, though sleep tempted her, too. "If you realized the castle was dangerous... why not stop me before I went to the palace?" In fact, she remembered him as the masked man, encouraging her to go. He'd said she had a duty to her husband.

"I didn't have the men to take on both Hillsfield and the crown. We'd have risked discovery. Your ignorance of my survival protected my location. With Byron's help, we'll have the power to take the throne. I believe Elijah's murder of Byron's kin ensures his alliance."

Audra pondered, realizing Lord Byron knew of Garrick's survival all along. Kolbe might have, too. All kept silent while she was punished for one night's sins.

Garrick moved before her, lifting a strand of her hair between his fingers. Her heart twisted, the image familiar. He used to love playing with her hair as a child. The memory used to haunt her some nights when she'd mourn him.

Meeting her eyes, he smirked. "I'll send your mother and Eva when you wake. Ask the guards. I have business to attend, but I can look for you after we both handle our affairs... If you wanted."

His fingers continued to twirl her hair for a moment, then he released her curl. He swallowed. "I understand you might want nothing more of me now that you're safe, and that slaughters me."

Her heart churned, torn between the hurt of his eight-year deception and wanting to believe he had no choice.

He had choices. He just didn't make the one that would have allowed her to have them, too.

Why must this villain feel so like the other half of her missing soul?

Removing his mask, he stepped closer to her on the bed, his thighs touching her knees. She resisted the urge to pull him closer, logic warring with desire.

"On your sixteenth birthday," Garrick said, "we snuck away to the waterfall. Your mother forbade us from being alone, so we left without telling anyone. Do you remember that night?"

Yes. Audra thought of that night often. She'd analyzed it, replayed it. It was the night she grew aware of her feelings for him.

"I asked you to kiss me." She blushed, heart fluttering at the memory. Pain followed. "You rejected me."

His mouth quirked. "I didn't reject you." His grin widened. "I told you it wasn't my kiss to steal. I said it belonged to your true love."

She rolled her eyes. "Sounds like a rejection to me."

He stepped closer, tilting her chin up. Her heart skipped an entire beat, wanting to give in. "It took willful restraint not to devour you every moment I was near you. Your scent tortures me now as it did then. You're still the most beautiful, clever, thoughtful, and funny woman. I never met another woman who compares. That night, I believed you deserved better."

Audra's heart raced at his confession, but the conflicted feelings rattled her. She removed his hand from her chin. "You can't intoxicate me this way," she whispered as his breath tickled her neck. "If I knew you were alive, I would have chosen you. That's what you want to know, isn't it? I loved you more than any other man. But you changed. The man I fell in love with would have told me."

He smiled, undeterred. "Such a brat." She withheld a smirk at his jab, folding her arms instead. "Everyone changes, Audra. My feelings never wavered. The circumstances did. You're replaying the past and failing to see I'm here now, telling you all the reasons I couldn't sooner. Yesterday, I feared you'd never love me again. This morning, it occurred to me that your first reaction to your discovery wasn't this stubborn version of you refusing to let go. First, you cried. Next, you kissed me. Then anger followed. My patience clings to the knowledge that your first reaction was to want me."

He paused, rolling his broad shoulders back, his teal eyes making her shudder. She turned away, confused by memories of his goodness against the uncertainty of his true self. How much of the masked man was really Garrick?

Taking her hand between his, he added, "That night of your birthday, I said your true love would be a lucky bastard."

"Yes," she whispered. "I recall it was the same problem then, too. Much of our lives, we could've been happier if you'd included me in your decisions. Your suffering then was as self-inflicted as today. You chose what was best for us both."

He sighed, releasing her captive hand. "I don't agree that I've self-inflicted this injury. I believe duty was the culprit, and I didn't self-inflict my duty as the true ruler of Althenia. You've seen what kind of man would rule if I ignored my place as king."

Audra inhaled, shaking her head. "I see you still don't understand, so I'll make it clear." She stood, making them chest to chest.

He didn't budge, unbothered by their closeness. "If we wanted each other, you should've shared your story. You decided for both of us. It was *our* decision to make, not yours alone."

Garrick nodded, stepping back, appearing defeated. She grabbed his hand this time, forcing him to face her, determined to be heard this time. "You wanted to know if I would have chosen you, Garrick. For me, the choice wasn't between choosing which man's rules I prefer to follow. The choice was about which life would give me the freedom to decide for myself."

Releasing his hand, she awaited a reaction. Instead, he turned, replacing his mask. "Ask guards to take you to your mother and Eva when you wake. Goodnight, Audra." He left without another word, leaving her heart more befuddled than ever.

33

A fternoon sun whispered through a tent's slit, waking Audra when it reached her eyes. Light revealed the contents inside with new colors. A map-covered table with wooden seats stood inside, bookshelves lining all edges of the tent walls, holding various scrolls. She stroked the unfamiliar soft fur beneath her, covered by a feather-stuffed silk duvet. Colorful, dirt-stained rugs covered the ground.

Outside, the voices of two men approached. She moved off the bed to draw closer, recognizing Garrick's voice first.

"What could we have done differently? We weren't positioned to proceed with the attack, and your personal relationship to the matter is familiar to me, I assure you."

"The reason that you had delayed was Audra. That damn girl is the very cause of every problem. You ran off for two days to risk your own life and crumble this entire kingdom for a silly girl."

She recognized the second voice, too. Lord Byron's words confirmed her suspicions of his disdain. The years of cold shoulders and harsh looks were as she'd predicted. He'd never liked her; he'd simply tolerated her for Mystine.

"I intend to make her your future queen, if she agrees. How she feels about you then will be the ramifications of your treatment," Garrick said. "Don't forget you turned away my mother all those years ago, your own cousin. You played your part in this, too, didn't you, Lord Byron? We share the same goal, to make amends for past mistakes. Allot your army and secure our finances, and our new alliance will wash away the footsteps in the sand."

Audra recalled that Garrick's mother, Cynthia, had sought Byron's help when cast away from the palace. Intrigued, she sat on a wooden log, listening.

Byron scoffed. "My money. That's the only thing all you kings want from me. Hillsfield: the convenient bank of whoever wants to reign. Elijah murdered my kin, my wife's daughter is hidden somewhere in this camp, and you vanished for two nights without a word. You told no one of your whereabouts. Now, you dare to demand funds?"

Despite Byron's unusual fury, Garrick remained calm, a trait she never possessed around Lord Byron. She'd be shirking. "If your goal is to avenge your niece and nephew, why hesitate to join forces? My mother died by his hand, too. We share an intense hatred for him. My forces rushed to save Kathleen the moment Julin told us of their engagement. You know as well as I do it was too late the moment King Henri laid a lustful hand on her."

Byron always followed the exact law, conservative in his views. However, she recalled Lord Byron's knowledge of Eva's true parentage. Though he never spoke a word, Audra reasoned that this explained his contempt toward her. While his knowledge didn't affect his love for Mystine, she remembered how Lord Byron used to make weekly visits to the dress shop to visit her mother. He was kinder to Audra back then.

His first wife died bearing a stillborn. Like every nobleman in town, beautiful blonde Mystine captured him. For reasons Audra never understood, Mystine reciprocated his love.

Lord Byron grunted, returning Audra's mind to the present. "Soldiers and money won't resurrect my family, I'm afraid. You desire a woman most. A king needs to defend his crown above all to be a proper ruler."

Audra's stomach sank, disagreeing with Lord Byron's claim. She thought Garrick already prioritized everything before her.

Garrick released a large exhale. "A Dothian madman sits upon the Althenian throne, and it's he who is responsible for their deaths, not me. I'm guilty of falling under the spell of a beautiful, blonde-haired, fiery woman. As it is, this supposed sin we both have in common. I urge you to consider what Althenia has to lose and decide whether or not that means anything to the wealthiest man in the kingdom."

Garrick wasn't wrong. Lord Byron fell for her mother, a woman with no prestige. His marriage to her caused a scandal in the beginning, with various noblewomen sneering at her mother every time she walked by. Byron sighed. "I'll consider and return when I have an answer. Meanwhile, I'm taking my wife and her daughters to Hillsfield's safety. People don't die under my protection. As her lawful guardian, I demand Audra's release."

Garrick laughed. Her chest tightened at the idea of returning to Hillsfield. "As if either of us have any say in that," Garrick said, chuckling. "You'll have to conduct that business directly with her. She doesn't listen to anyone."

Audra smirked.

"She obeyed me," Lord Byron said, "when under my care."

"Oh, certainly. I'm sure the only times she snuck away are the ones you heard about. If you say so," Garrick said, his voice dripping with sarcasm. Audra stifled a laugh, covering her mouth.

"You'll command it," Byron growled. He sounded upset, his tone growing more aggressive with each new sentence. For a moment, neither spoke. Then, Lord Byron's voice changed, as if intending to cut Garrick with words alone. "Your posterity was protected, and mine was the cost. Don't forget that."

Audra frowned. With the death of Byron's kin, he'd lost all potential heirs. In this instance, she agreed; Byron lost copious collateral because of her.

"I hope one day you'll see it differently, Lord Byron," Garrick replied. "They can't return to Hillsfield. Elijah will search there first for Audra. We would both do anything to protect our loved ones. When I asked for her hand, you rejected my suit, calling me a bastard. You'd said I had no right to ask. My parents' marriage was legal, but the annulment never finalized. The king committed bigamy. I obeyed your commands, left her alone, believing one day you'd see I'm best for Althenia. Giving her to me might have saved your heirs. Blame me if you must, but acknowledge your role in all of this."

Audra's lips parted. She'd never heard anyone speak to Lord Byron that way.

Lord Byron sighed. For a moment, Audra heard only silence, making her wonder if they had walked away. Then, Lord Byron spoke. "My pride is my conscience telling me when things are right or wrong. My intuition is seldom wrong, and it tells me an honorable man would not have deflowered the woman he said he loves without first marrying her."

Audra drew her eyebrows together. If that was a concern of his, why didn't Lord Byron allow the father of Audra's child to marry her when he came back for her? Irritation crept in as she pondered this.

Garrick answered, "It's in a storm that we live our bravest versions of ourselves. Passion is a storm, often unpredictable. Your hypocrisy astounds me. I understand the reason your marriage to Lady Mystine was so quick was because there was a passionate kiss shared in the shop. It must have been quite the kiss to rush a wedding."

Audra blushed. She had never heard that rumor before. Her mother had spoken about Lord Byron for years back then. When Lord Byron proposed, the news shocked no one. She wasn't aware that something had occurred between them before their wedding. "Don't worry. Few know," Garrick added after a moment of silence.

"Let Audra decide about Hillsfield, then," Lord Byron redirected. "Until that's decided, bridle your passions and focus on the kingdom. There will be time for women aplenty later."

Audra pressed her lips tight, emotions churning. As king, Garrick could take many women if he wanted. Byron's contradiction of his principles angered her. He'd opposed King Henri's ways but encouraged them for Garrick? Why such hatred for her?

She awaited Garrick's reply. "That's what I've been telling you. There's only one woman for this king. She's the same one I always wanted. All this was for her. You must understand if we're to ally. I couldn't let her marry him to become his plaything. How does your wife feel about your contempt for her daughter?"

Audra's heart pounded despite her attempts to still it. He defended her. Her mother often turned a blind eye to Lord Byron's treatment, claiming his kindness displayed in other ways. Perhaps guilt drove his dislike. He'd rejected his desperate cousin while sheltering his wife's daughter, who shared the same sin.

Their voices faded, too distant to hear. She paced the tent, mind whirling through memories, trying to assemble a puzzle without edges, pieces refusing to fit.

Turning back on her heel, Garrick entered, his shirt half-open and revealing part of his chest. He nodded to her, fists clenching and unclenching at his sides.

"I've secured you a cot with the medicine nurses. They'll teach you. You'll learn fast, and I thought you might like to feel useful here."

Audra considered this potential new life. Here, she could be something different. A nurse, a seamstress, someone useful. Though life with Elijah ended, being Queen of Althenia remained possible, dwindling on her consent. Garrick's words to Byron about wanting only her sent her heart racing with mixed fear and excitement. She'd loved palace life, despite its dangers. Would royal life differ with Garrick? Could he give her the life she wanted?

She moved to the twelve-chair table. Garrick stood opposite, masked. "What time is it?" she asked. The light outside dimmed toward night.

"I didn't want to wake you. I let you sleep through the morning and afternoon," he said, sticking his hands in his pockets. "Perhaps I shouldn't have."

Truthfully, she'd been uncertain he'd return after their argument that morning. His presence pleased her nonetheless. Gripping a chair for support, she said, "I heard you speaking with Lord Byron."

"I hoped you would," he replied, unreactive. Garrick circled the table toward her. "He hated me since learning I fathered your child. After thinking you dead for two years, finding out you were alive made me want to steal you away from Althenia. To win, we needed Byron's alliance. As I told you, he chose Elijah, threatening my life if I approached you. I wrestled between duty and desire. Julin promised patience would reward me."

He took the final steps toward her. Unable to help it, her eyes traced his exposed chest before remeeting his eyes. He grinned. "That wasn't all I wanted you to hear."

His nearness filled her with heat, her heart thundering.

"I was your only love?" she asked.

Their bodies pulled closer, near touching. "Even believing you dead, I wanted no other. Finding you engaged to Elijah, I wanted to flee with you. I refused Julin's attempt to speak for months after I discovered the truth. Everything was complicated."

His fingers traced her neck as he removed his mask, revealing every handsome detail about him. His teal eyes sought permission before doing anything more.

Her hand touched his chest, her eyes fluttering to meet his gaze. Why did she continue resisting this man who loved her so deeply?

His hand moved to her neck as he leaned down. A voice interrupted outside the tent. "King Laurent, your dinner. May I enter?"

Laurent? "Come in," Garrick said, dropping his hand and replacing his mask. His last name was Lorent. She wondered why they called him Laurent, not Garrick.

A man wearing a simple tunic entered with a silver tray, flushing at her presence. "Pardon, Your Highness. I didn't realize you had company. Shall I fetch more?"

"I've eaten. It's for her. Another wine glass, thank you," Garrick said, gesturing.

The man set the tray near the table's head. Garrick seated her before taking the head position, adjacent to her. They watched the servant portion bits of food onto a second plate. Roast beef, carrots, peas, potatoes, and desserts. Then he poured wine into a tiny cup. Her stomach growled at the aroma of her first full, warm meal in weeks.

"He tests for poison," Garrick explained, eyes never leaving the servant. "Elijah doesn't know this location, yet, but one can never be too careful. They volunteer, paid to protect their king."

The man sampled each item, one by one. "No poison I taste, Your Highness."

"Thank you, Frederick." Garrick slid him coins. Frederick departed with a final curious glance at Audra.

She devoured the meal without restraint. Every pea and slice of meat dissolved in her mouth, Garrick sipping wine beside her. When her ravenous stomach filled, she slowed.

"Eva and your mother are expecting you. I can bring them here, or escort you there. They don't know you're in my tent." He chuckled. "I thought it best to obscure your location for now. Absurd, hiding like children at our age. They're relieved you're safe. Your mother hounded me for hours this afternoon until Byron intervened."

Audra smiled, standing, her appetite fading at thoughts of reunion after three months. "Take me there?"

He nodded, standing. He finished the wine, gesturing to the exit of the tent.

Outside, white tents stretched like a labyrinth within the reddish-gray canyon walls. She followed beside Garrick as he navigated through them, stepping over ropes once in a while, his hands in his pockets. Audra clung to her skirts, examining his mask. "Why do you wear the mask?" she asked.

"I had it made to disguise the scar, and then it became a matter of ensuring your safety in particular. Its main purpose was to protect you. Leaving you in suspense for a few months was simply a bonus," he said, smirking. "About four years ago, while gathering recruits for the rebellion, we visited town. A countryside boy recognized me. You might remember Jack," he said.

Audra's face scrunched at the memory of Jack. "Yes, I remember him. He used to deliver the letters, and he would smear dirt onto my arm. He thought it was funny to chase me," she said, but then laughed. "I suppose he was a child."

Garrick grunted. "He caused a bit of trouble four years ago. The mask was off, and he recognized me. He said my real name. I went by Laurent back then to contain my identity. Julin cut out his tongue after he uttered my name that once. While horrifying and quick, I understand now it had to be done. Concealing my identity smothered any affiliation with you. Since you were engaged to the man hunting me, the mask kept you safe. If Elijah discovered ou r affiliation, I feared you'd never be safe a day in your life."

They passed identical tents, marked apart by small details. A fishing line by one, an empty crate outside another. At a large tent, he stopped. "The medicine tent, you'll sleep here. Your mother's nearby. When you're finished, ask soldiers for directions."

She memorized small landmarks along the way, pondering his eight years building this life. How many tents at first? How many battles had she never heard of? How many deaths to achieve his goals?

After rounding another tent, he turned to her. "Now you're here. I promise he can't harm you again."

"You've broken promises before," she said, the words exiting her mouth before she thought them through. He winced, turning away. The truth hurt them both. She'd made peace with the decisions he'd chosen, but what happened next if the war went awry? Would he hide for another eight years?

Ignoring the comment, he pointed to nearby tents. "Seventh on the right, marked by lavender vases. You'll know when you see it."

She didn't want him to leave. "Come with me," Audra said. "I can introduce you to Eva, if you like."

Garrick swallowed, shuffling his feet as he observed them. "Soon. I have to take care of something," he said. "I've reached the maximum limit of my capabilities today and must rest before I become irrational."

Her heart sank, disappointment setting in. He continued, "When you're done, you can escort yourself back to the medicine tent, and—" Garrick paused, a sort of longing in his eyes that mimicked her temptation to reach out and assure he was still real. "If you ask a soldier for me, I will come find you."

He stepped close, his breath on her neck made her shiver, despite nearby soldiers watching them. He lowered his voice to a low rumble. "I'll wait for your forgiveness. I acknowledge you wanted the truth years ago, but I wanted you alive. I'm sorry I didn't give you a choice. I never intended your suffering. Though I hate to admit this, the situation surpassed our love. Althenia's welfare depended on my life. My welfare depended on yours, and... *Eva* deserved more."

He pulled back, her body rising with heat. He was right. A life in hiding might have suited her, but Eva didn't deserve to live in fear. He winked, vanishing like the masked man behind velvet walls.

34

"Audra!" a voice called as she entered the tent.

Audra turned, her eyes finding Eva as she jumped up from a chair. Eva's blonde locks were tied back in a ribbon, and she wore a simple white dress. She looked older than Audra remembered, more mature yet still childlike. Eva ran to Audra, and the two of them enveloped each other in a tight hug. After all this time, relief set in at the sight of Eva's safety. Audra crouched, pulling Eva close, breathing in her flowery hair as her fingers wove through her golden locks.

"Mother said she didn't know if you would ever come back. I told everyone you were strong and you could fight, and I was right," Eva said, wiping tears from her small cheeks. As she pulled away, Audra observed the concern in Eva's eyes. "You came back. I missed you so much."

"I missed you so much more," Audra replied with a squeeze.

She moved over when her mother approached and fell to her knees, holding them both. "Oh, Audra. I was so worried. They didn't have the men to mount an attack to rescue you, so we brought the Hillsfield army to help. When King Laurent approached me and told me in secret that he was going to rescue you, I felt hope for the first time. This afternoon, when I received word that he rescued you, I wanted to find you. He told me to let you sleep. That so-called king walking around here wouldn't tell me where they kept you. I followed him for two hours, but he wouldn't budge. He's a stubborn mule."

Audra smiled at the thought of her mother trailing Garrick for two hours. He must have hated that. It was the first glimpse she had seen of her mother from their countryside days in a long time. Audra narrowed her eyes, tilting her head. "You didn't recognize the king?" Audra asked with a smirk. She watched her mother as she pulled away and furrowed her eyebrows.

"No. King Laurent remains masked. Lord Byron said he swore to never remove it until he claimed the throne."

Audra nodded. She couldn't blame her mother for missing it. If anything, it comforted Audra that she, too, overlooked it. Not only that, but it meant Lord Byron never told her mother about Garrick's proposal all those years ago. She didn't know he was alive, meaning Mystine hadn't kept this secret from her. This was a comforting relief after being lied to so often.

"Mother," Audra said in a hushed tone, unable to keep the secret. Her mother half-raised him. "You know him."

"Do I?" her mother asked, pulling back. Mystine appeared lost in thought, her lips pursing as her eyes narrowed, "Do you?" Her second question brimmed with excitement. Audra hesitated, unsure if she should share this.

"Who?" Mystine's third question was louder.

She opted to share, needing someone else to understand the complexity of her toiling emotions. "Garrick... he's alive."

Lady Mystine's lips parted, eyes wide, her body freezing. Her expression shifted from wide eyes to furrowed brows, then to raised brows and wider eyes.

"Lorent," Mystine mused, connecting Garrick's name with the king's supposed name. "No. That doesn't make sense. Cynthia told me his father was—" she stopped, realizing Cynthia might not have shared everything. "She said the nobleman who fathered him had a new wife and child and didn't want anyone to know his identity. Not even me."

Lady Mystine stared off, then shook her head.

"Of course," Mystine added in a whisper. "King Henri was the man. My god." Her mother puzzled over her memories, nodding occasionally as if verifying facts. Then, her eyes snapped to Audra's, and Eva watched, amused.

"Who's Garrick?" Eva asked, trying to decode their looks.

Audra swallowed, looking to her mother. Mystine eyed Audra.

"An old friend from the countryside where you were born," Audra told her. If she ever confessed that Garrick was Eva's father, he needed to be present. Now didn't seem the time to tell her, not before their future was certain.

"Audra fell in love with him," Mystine said with a smirk, her eyes twinkling playfully. Eva gasped, hand over her mouth. Audra's cheeks pinked as she turned away, folding her hands together.

Eva's curiosity piqued at Audra's embarrassment.

"I thought Audra was in love with Jed," Eva said. "Audra's in love with the true king *instead*?"

Audra snorted. Knowing Jed was Garrick's first spy made her wonder how she missed the signs those years. She mistook Jed's curiosity for flirtation. He was gathering information, and she unwittingly provided it. No wonder Garrick had such knowledge of her as the masked man.

Accepting defeat, Audra sighed. "I loved Garrick more than any other man," she whispered. "When I thought he died, a part of me did too. I never fully loved another man again because I couldn't give my whole heart to anyone. Now that he's back, I feel so broken and damaged. I don't know if I can love like that again."

Mystine reached forward, tilting Audra's chin up. "Love is terrifying, dear, but so is jousting. That makes it exciting. The risk of losing everything in one moment is the price you pay for joy. If you don't love with all your heart, you aren't living. You're just existing. As someone who just existed for years, I can tell you this: It's scary to love, and you must feel that fear if you want to live the life you always wanted. If what you wanted was something dull," she added with a chuckle, "you would have loved Hillsfield."

Smirking, Audra pondered her mother's words, repositioning to sit on the ground. Eva laid her head in Audra's lap. Audra wanted to tell her mother about Lord Byron's role, but she knew it wouldn't matter. Her mother would defend him, saying he was a traditional man who preferred traditional ways. Mystine wouldn't understand his responsibility in keeping Audra and Garrick apart.

She also didn't trust that he couldn't do it again if the war was lost.

Believing it best to keep quiet and not ruin whatever plan Garrick arranged, she decided to let it go. Mystine cocked her head.

"You seem unhappy knowing he's alive," Mystine observed, her motherly instincts reading every expression in Audra's worry-filled thoughts.

Audra played with Eva's hair, combing through strands with her fingers. "I'm afraid of finding happiness and losing it again."

Mystine frowned, placing a hand on Audra's shoulder. "You might as well cut your heart out now, then. If you're too afraid to love, you won't have a life worth living."

35

After spending three hours with Eva and her mother, Audra departed. Most of their conversations revolved around life at Hillsfield. She learned Eva enjoyed the piano and showed notable proficiency. Audra described life at the palace, with Eva absorbing every detail. As night fell, Eva drifted into sleep, sprawled across Audra's lap. Taking this as her cue, Audra embraced her mother again, exiting the tent.

Trusting her memory, she navigated through the maze of white velvet tents. At some points, she lost her way and asked guards for directions, an occurrence that repeated with each new turn. Once she found herself outside the tent she intended to enter, the darkness within invoked a sense of nervousness. Two guards stood outside, exchanging glances when she approached.

Though she knew she should be at the medicine tent, the yearning part of her heart that longed for Garrick overwhelmed her better judgment. Despite everything, the magnetic pull between them remained undeniable. Even when he was masked, that craving never dulled.

Though eight years had passed since that fateful night, the memory hung vividly. On sleepless nights, she often recalled the night they shared—how he touched her with reverence, how her own hands chased echoes of that sensation. The memory of his lips had never dulled.

Pausing outside the tent, she exhaled, observing her breath form clouds in the dense night's fog. Legend warned of people losing their minds while wandering in these mist-laden canyons, the fog so thick it obscured all visibility. This phenomenon was most common in the summer after a rainstorm. It was as though a curtain of smoke descended from the sky, a gentle, swirling waterfall of spiraling mist surrounding her. A pang of apprehension touched her heart as she noticed the guards before her beginning to disappear into gray mist. One cocked his head, permitting her entrance.

Tentatively, she gripped the tent's entrance, noting how the fog seeped in but did not pervade the interior. Understanding why the tents were made of velvet, their thick weave retaining moisture while blocking rain, she realized their function in keeping fog at bay. She slipped inside, securing the flaps behind her. Her eyes adjusted to the scant lighting within as she looked towards the bed, noticing a lump beneath the duvet. Assuming he slept, she moved around the table, shed her shoes, and crept toward him, eyes adapting to the tent's dim light.

Once beside him, Audra noticed his form lay concealed beneath the black duvet. Suddenly, a voice startled her from behind. "You're lucky your hair is so bright, or I would have needed to approach with this," Garrick remarked, holding a sword.

She jumped and saw him at the end of his bed, placing his sword atop the chest. Heat washed over her as she took in his form in its entirety. Besides the mask, he stood completely naked, his physique on full display. Audra felt sheepish at her intrusion's boldness.

"Why are you naked?" she stammered, averting her eyes. His muscled frame piqued her curiosity, tempting her to look again. Garrick stepped closer, his smirk evident, unconcerned by his current state of undress.

"You're the one who snuck into my tent. I thought you were an intruder, so I armed myself. I was asleep until I heard your approach outside," he explained, standing mere inches from her now as their gazes locked.

"Don't you have your guards to warn you?" she asked.

Garrick chuckled. "Guards are as good as their instincts, but even the best may falter, so I remain careful. I'm alert to every rustle around here. Usually, if someone needs my attention, the guards call from outside and give me a moment to dress. I didn't expect a trespasser," he said, the twinkle in his eye indicating more intrigue than annoyance. "Why did you come?"

Audra hesitated, trying to justify her presence. Willpower encouraged her eyes to remain on his face. Although she considered several explanations, the truth surfaced: she didn't want to be apart from him.

Despite the years of silence and the secrets they hadn't shared, she grasped that her own reluctance had kept them apart since their reunion. Everything she longed for over the past eight years stood right here, but she had been pushing him away. Deny as she might, she still loved him. She never wished to return to the reality where he ceased to exist.

Solidifying her resolve, she took a deep breath. Drawing her hand to her back, Audra tugged at a ribbon securing her dress's bodice, loosening the fabric. Keeping her eyes fixed on his, the sleeves slid off her shoulders, and the gown dropped to the floor. Naked, breasts bare, curves exposed, she bit her bottom lip.

Garrick's eyes weren't timid as they lingered over her form, his erection growing larger. She stepped toward him, pressing her breasts against his chest. Placing her hands on his chest, her fingertips traced his skin. One of his hands grabbed her waist, the other weaving into her hair. His hardness pressed against her stomach, throbbing against her.

"The days spent next to you were torture, smelling you," Garrick whispered, his nose meeting hers, warm breath against her lips. "God, you're intoxicating. I had to pretend I wasn't seeing your nipples cling to your undergarments that night in the lake. I couldn't tell you how my throbbing cock begged me to take care of it all night. I realized you needed time, but I wanted you so badly. I'd never had such animalistic urges as the ones I had that night. Whether or not you were aware, you tortured me that night. If I kiss you again, I can't promise to possess the willpower to stop this time."

Audra arched her breasts closer, anxious to have their lips meet. "Is that a threat or a promise?" Audra asked, smiling playfully.

He admired her as he grinned. "Mmm. A promise, if you're obedient."

"And if I'm not?" she teased, moving her lips closer, desperate for a taste.

"Then it's a threat," he said. Garrick let out a low pleasure noise from the back of his throat. He glided his arm around her waist and pulled her body as close to his as possible before kissing her neck once, breathing her in. "Does this mean you forgive me?"

Audra sighed with impatience, planting a single kiss on the groove between his neck and shoulder. "Promise there won't be any more secrets. Whatever happens next, we are equals. I go wherever you go, and I will learn everything you know."

His fingertips traced the spine of her bare back. "No more secrets," he agreed. "Never again."

Garrick weaved his hands through her hair as Audra's hands slid behind his back, up to his shoulders. He kissed her, firm, his lips molding to hers in eager familiarity. Audra's body shuddered, feeling sensations she thought had died long ago. He grasped onto her bare curves, his throbbing member against her lower stomach as they intensified their kiss.

As it turned out for Audra, these feelings hadn't died. They'd been sensations left dormant for eight years. Now, they were volcanic and eruptive, her body begging for his attention.

Garrick pried her lips open with his tongue, her heart sparking, excited, and ravenous. The truth was that she could never feel so overjoyed to see any other man behind the mask. Of all the possible surprises, his was the least suspected but the most welcomed.

Wrapped in his arms, she felt he had missed her just as much.

Lifting her, he placed her on the bed, her legs wrapping around his waist. He removed his lips from hers to study her face, ensuring she wanted this as much as he did. Audra whimpered, motivating him to continue, using his large frame to flatten her against the bed as he crawled atop her small physique. He kissed her neck, her shoulder, her clavicle, down to the top of her breasts. Audra gasped as humid air from his mouth fell over her nipples.

"I've died and gone to heaven," Garrick exhaled, leaning down to lick her right nipple. He remembered it was her favorite one, and the way she arched her back increased his appetite. Pleasure shot through her body as he licked and sucked her breasts, her gasps and wiggles encouraging more impassioned movements.

Memories seeped into her mind, her toes curling as she succumbed to her lust. He was everything to her. In childhood, she had resisted wanting him, terrified to love someone who didn't return her feelings. He had. She never imagined another chance to relive that night, but his touches reignited her flame.

Audra's fingers weaved through his hair as Garrick continued licking and sucking on her nipple. A hand slid toward the inside of her thighs, gently spreading them. She moaned as his middle finger pressed against her clit, bringing attention to how wet and sensitive she was. Smiling, he stopped.

"You have to be quiet," he laughed. "Others are sleeping, and I made promises not to touch you again unless wed. Clearly, I overestimated my ability to see you naked and not lose my fucking mind. You're so beautiful; I want to ravage every inch of you."

Leaving her breasts, he traced a line of kisses across her stomach toward her hips. Hand smoothing her thigh, his mouth hovered above her hips. "Open," he commanded, guiding her legs apart. His face replaced the opening, burrowing between her legs as his tongue saturated her spot. She released a gasp, his mouth sucking on her clit as she dug her fingers into his hair, her lips smashed together to repress a cry of pleasure.

This was new.

"Sometimes you switch from king to caveman, you know that?" Audra gasped with a strained voice. He responded by burrowing deeper between her legs, causing her to release another restrained gasp as he continued tracing her folds with his tongue, teasing her entrance. She squirmed beneath his firm grasp on her hips, feeling more and more sensitive with each lick, doing her best to stifle her moans.

When she felt an orgasm brimming, he pulled back, allowing her to catch her breath. He caged his body over hers again, reconnecting their lips with voracious kisses. The outside of his shaft rubbed against her sweet spot, drenching part of his member against her soaking wet pussy. She had never wanted anything so much in her entire life. She bucked her hips against him, ensnaring him with her legs, demanding more.

"The caveman is the side of me that's making you crave me as much as I crave you," he said between kisses. "It's the wild inside of me that made you tighten and fasten around my cock over and over that night. I never wanted to stop." His tongue demanded passage inside her mouth, playing with her tongue as she welcomed it. Her body steamed, impatience causing her to whimper.

Releasing his lips from hers, he kissed her neck tenderly. "I also wanted to make love to you, the king to his prized queen. I may be the ruler by birth, but you don't realize that *you* reign over *me*." He straddled her between his legs, placing his fingers on her clit. He rubbed her slowly with one hand and played with his cock in the other. Once in a while, he rubbed the tip of his member near her entrance, taunting her. She bucked her hips against him more than once, attempting to feel him inside of her, desperate to relive the memories of the best night of her life.

"Alright," Audra breathed, unable to wait any longer. "You win. I offer obedience. Keep your promises and carry through. If there's never action, then threats stay threats."

Garrick chuckled, leaning in to kiss her lips, this time tender, slow, and passionate. Slow enough to demonstrate he planned every movement he made with his lips against hers. He sighed into her as he moved to kiss her nipples again, cupping the other breast in his hand before moving his fingers down to rub her clit again in circular motions. He watched her arch her back as she drew nearer to begging.

He chuckled, enjoying his art of titillation. "You're the definition of perfection. I'm consumed by my desire to have you."

"Then stop being an asshole and have me," she whispered. "Have me, all of me."

This time, Garrick wasted no time to arrange his body, drawing his cock near her entrance, erect and throbbing with anticipation. She gasped at the sensation of his tip against her hole. She recalled how he'd worried about hurting her the first time. While she didn't have another man to compare him to, she was certain their bodies were made for one another. She couldn't wait to relive the memory, whimpering as she waited.

"Please," she begged. "We've waited long enough."

It was enough for him to ascertain she wanted him as much as he desired her. Sliding the tip of his cock into the entrance of her hole shot sensations from her hair to her toes. Impatient, desperate, Audra used her legs to push him deeper inside of her. She gasped as he stretched her walls, forcing his shaft deeper inside of her until his tip kissed her cervix. Her fingers dug into his back, unable to stop herself from moaning loudly enough that she was certain the entire camp would hear. He clasped a hand over her mouth as he slid back out again, grunting his own sounds of pleasure.

Stroking her walls again, this time with more precision and power, Audra squirmed with desire as he picked up speed. The only thing keeping her from crying out was his hand over her mouth as he shoved his entire shaft in and out of her again, again, and again. He was relentless.

Every time she moaned, his excitement grew. Within moments he was fucking her as deep and as fast as his cock allowed, groaning with each of her moans as he stuffed her over and over again. She came with his shaft penetrating her deep, her body losing all other sensations. Her toes curled as she gripped her legs tighter around his body. Her walls squeezed him, thirsty and intense, forcing him to orgasm in turn. This time, she covered his mouth as he released the contents of his balls inside her starving pussy.

Just like the first time, they spent the entire night together, but this was not enough to cause them to slow down or stop. Instead, they used the moments of exhaustion to kiss, stirring his erection awake again minutes after each release. Sometimes, she rode slowly on top of him, stroking his hard member inside of her until they were fucking again, like dogs in heat.

Audra wondered how, and if, they would ever find it in them to stop...

36

The dawn welcomed a cold, blue glow to the morning mist, where two lovers stirred awake to witness it. A thick fog welcomed the first appearance of the sun beneath the horizon, casting a gentle glow into the tent.

At some point, they'd both fallen asleep, exhausted from their evening. As cool air breathed into the tent, the lovers stirred awake and took shelter under the animal skins, warming their bodies next to one another. This stirred them to wake once more, and an hour passed before the blue dawn offered golden light.

All that time, Garrick thrust inside of her with long, slow strokes, feeling every sensation of her walls clamping around his shaft with each small orgasm. He kissed her during each thrust, his goal to award as much pleasure as he could muster. Audra remained eager to receive it. She liked the feeling of his erection all the way inside of her before he'd roll his hips, grinding against her clit. She basked in that feeling of pleasure, surprised she could take every inch of his hardness inside her.

He wasn't in a rush to get her to another big orgasm. He could do these movements as long as she wanted, and her want was unending. Neither was she in a hurry, so she enjoyed every thrust, every hip roll, and every grind. Sometimes, she clamped her legs around him to pull him closer, attempting to entice him to quicken his pace. Instead, he'd nibble on her neck and whisper, "Not so fast, you temptress." He'd push in a little harder, once, then resume his pace, distracting her in other ways.

He'd kiss her. He'd make a low noise, indicating his level of shared pleasure. He'd whisper in her ear that he wanted her more than anything. He promised to never make her go another night without making love to her, lest she refuse him. She knew, without a doubt, it would take something dire to get her to refuse this any night.

At last, he rearranged his position to bend his head to her breasts as he thrust in and out of her, his tongue stimulating her right nipple. Her nails dug into him, exploding into another orgasm. Her walls grasping around his cock caused him to get greedy, fucking her through the orgasm until he came inside her for the fourth time that night.

Satisfied for now, Garrick leaned down to kiss her neck as he pulled his member out of her.

"You are insatiable," he said with a huff, lying down beside her. Garrick pulled her closer to his chest, craving her body next to his.

"I believe it takes two people to do such a dance," Audra said in the same teasing tone. She traced her hand along his chest, chiseling the lines of his abdomen with her fingertips. Would her heart ever stop leaping when she looked at him? She placed her lips on his shoulder, kissing it.

"Hmm," he mumbled. "I can't feel that, there."

"Feel what?" she asked, kissing his shoulder again. "This?"

"That," he said. "No feeling there for six years." His eyes narrowed as he gazed at the top of the tent, sighing before he added, "A horse kicked me."

She sighed, moving to kiss his jaw instead. "I understand your decisions, I think," she said. "But I wonder what life may have been if things were simpler back then. If you were a countryside boy in love with a countryside girl, do you think we would have been happy?"

Garrick grabbed Audra's hand, kissing her knuckles. "I acknowledge the hell I put you through with the burden of raising our daughter as your sister. I imagine the torment burdened you because the father never married you. I promised to marry you, stole your virtue, and disappeared the next day. Allow me to spend the rest of our lives providing a grander one for you both. We would have been happy, but security and safety were less guaranteed."

She paused, stopping her hand as it traced the muscles on his chest. "You're right," Audra said, her tone soft. She wished she believed a new life awaited her, but the war remained an obstacle to hope. "It's forgiven now. Let's never think of it again."

Garrick nodded, sighing as he played with her hand, hair, anything to touch her. "Marry me, Audra. Today, tonight. I'll never leave you again if I have a say. You'll be by my side as the Queen of Althenia, and I promise to be more present for any future children. You always wanted to be a mother, and I wish to give you as many children as you desire."

He paused, smirking. He added, "Lord Byron told me to announce we eloped in Ingress before Eva was conceived. We met again last night. He agreed that once I claim the throne, we shall claim her as the heir."

Audra sucked in, heart fluttering with more excitement. "A female heir?"

Pushing a strand of hair behind her ear, he examined her. "You wanted to change things for the better. Soon, I will be the most powerful man in Althenia. We can make any changes we want. I desire you to rule it with me."

Audra grinned, kissing him once. A life where she didn't need to hide the truth of her daughter had never before felt tangible. She thought the secret would die when she did. "We better tell Mother, then... and figure out how to tell Eva she's a princess."

Garrick drew Audra's lips to his for a short moment again before sighing. "*The* princess. Yes, I agree. Those will both be top priority when we get out of bed. First, I thought of something fun we might try one more time before you're a married woman..."

"You said I'm the insatiable one," she laughed as Garrick kissed her neck. As if they hadn't been awake for the past hour and most of the night for that cause...

"I suppose, if I were a modern man, I might say I was projecting."

Audra snickered, shaking her head. "I'm afraid, sir, there's too much to do. I think you're avoiding confrontation. It's time to meet your daughter." Audra rolled out of bed, moving to dress so Garrick couldn't attempt luring her back. Excited, her heart beat. Though she also wished to lie in bed with him all day, the future queen carried responsibilities, too.

The first she owed to her daughter, who deserved to know the truth about her parentage at last.

After dressing and breakfast, Garrick and Audra made their way to her mother's tent. As they walked, she observed the usual bustling of the camp. Soldiers trained in a field to the right, and others spoke with tradesmen. Once they reached their destination, a guard informed them that Mystine and Eva were last seen with the horses. They pivoted toward the corrals near the entrance of the canyon.

Mystine and Eva stood outside the fences, offering the horses treats, petting their muzzles.

Garrick stopped, watching as Mystine handed Eva another slice of apple. She offered it to a brown mustang, giggling as the horse slurped it from her hand. Audra waited, knowing she shouldn't push him.

After another minute, she sighed. "You don't have to go at the same time as me. I can go first to introduce you."

Garrick shook his head. "No. I must be the one to do this. After all these years of absence, she deserves to hear this from me."

Audra grabbed his hand, squeezing it as he turned to her. Would Eva be upset to learn Audra was her mother and not her sister? Would she be angry about the deception?

Garrick squeezed Audra's hand in return before kissing it once. "Alright. Let's go."

Together, they walked toward the corrals, where Audra's mother noticed them first. Mystine's face lit up, meeting his approach halfway as she enveloped Garrick in a hug. "Oh, my son. How you've grown," Mystine said, pulling back a touch to look at his face. "I'm sorry I hounded you yesterday. You should have told me. I mourned you, too, you know."

Mystine pulled back from the embrace, examining him, her hands resting on his shoulders. Audra mentioned that she'd told her mother last night, which he agreed would be necessary to proceed.

Mystine continued, "It's forgiven. I suppose we both wanted her for ourselves, didn't we?" She smirked, offering a knowing glance toward Audra before they all turned to Eva. Her small body skipped toward them, joining their circle, eyes darting between Garrick and Audra. Garrick appeared as one might after seeing a ghost from their past. To Audra's surprise, Garrick removed the mask from his face. Eva studied him.

"Your eyes are teal. Like mine," Eva noted, her personality on full display. "I haven't seen anyone else with teal eyes before. Harlaina said you wore that mask because your eyes are scary and red. I see that wasn't true," Eva said. After a disappointed breath, her tone shifted. "Aren't you the one they say is the real king of Althenia? That Elijah is the second born, and you are the true firstborn?"

Garrick's lips curled into a smile. "That is what they say. I suppose it's true. Of course, nobody told me until I was nineteen. How old are you?" he asked. "Seven?"

Eva smirked, crossing her arms. Her head tilted to the side. "Seven and a *half*, actually. Why did everyone keep it a secret from you?"

Garrick chuckled, crouching to meet her eye level. Audra stood behind him. "Because," he said, "sometimes people keep secrets to protect us. My mother understood if Elijah discovered I was the king's first son, he'd kill me. She died without ever telling me. I was angry for a time, but I forgave her because I understand she wanted to protect me. Mothers worry about safety, you know."

Garrick changed positions, kneeling on one knee. Watching their introduction made Audra's heart melt. In all the time she'd spent angry about his silence, she hadn't yet considered how he'd reacted when the truth was revealed to *him*. It must have shattered him.

"You look like your mother when she was young. Identical," Garrick said, glancing at Audra. Eva followed his gaze.

Eva furrowed her eyebrows, confused. "You mean I look like Audra."

Audra held her breath, turning to Mystine. Mystine nodded. Garrick noticed the exchange, turning back to Eva. "Like I said," he replied with a wink. "Your real mother."

Eva stared, her eyebrows flickering. Audra held her breath.

"Wait," Eva said, turning to Audra and Mystine, searching for confirmation. Still holding her breath, Audra wondered how Eva felt about knowing her sister was her mother all along. Would this unravel their bond? Mystine nodded again, verifying the truth.

Garrick smirked as Eva turned back to him. "You're smart like her, too."

Eva's face twisted as her mind went to work, making the connections. She turned to Mystine again. "Is this the news you said I'd learn today? If Audra is my mother, who is my—" Eva paused, as if recalling Audra's stories last night about the countryside boy she fell in love with, and the king he became.

Would Eva be sad? Confused, betrayed, hurt? Eva gasped. "Then... that means you kissed Audra before you were married?"

Audra and Mystine covered their faces to stifle laughter. Garrick didn't bother to contain his. "Well, yes, we kissed," he confessed, "but we married first."

It was a lie, but Audra remembered Lord Byron's insistence on the tale. "Elijah tried to murder me after we wed, so I needed to hide until I had an army," Garrick said. Audra grinned, beaming as she observed their first meeting. Relief washed over as Audra watched Eva's mind illuminate at the news, noticing she didn't appear angry. She was curious. "We'll have a vow renewal ceremony tonight, so we can bring you to the castle after the war. You'll be our daughter when the danger is gone."

Eva considered the idea, her face beaming as she looked at Audra. Even though Eva thought Audra was her sister, the bond they shared had always been closer. Audra had tried to be present as often as possible without raising too much suspicion. Clearing her throat, Eva asked, "Does this mean I'm a princess?"

"Not just any princess. The heir to the throne. The next ruler of Althenia," Garrick said, then smiled. "That's a lot to learn about in one day. What do you think?"

"That's why we have the same color of eyes," she mused. "So... does vow renewing mean you're getting married again? Why do you need to get married twice?"

Before Garrick replied, there was noise behind them, causing Mystine, Audra, Garrick, and Eva to freeze. At the narrow entrance to the canyon, a small fire ignited in the grass before it. The guard posted by the entrance stomped it out, panic evident as he withdrew an arrow from the ground, looking up.

Audra's eyes followed, peering up at the top of the canyon walls, where thousands of archers stood, bows readied. Each of the arrows pointed down, right at them. "Is that..." she trailed off, uncertain she wanted the answer.

"Elijah," Garrick confirmed, his tone shifting to seriousness. "There were lookouts supposed to warn me of this."

Before she could respond, another man entered through the narrow canyon entrance to their hideout, waving his arms. "Siege!" he yelled. "Siege! We've been besieged!"

"There's one," Garrick sighed, annoyance seeping through his words. His jaw stiffened, and his gaze intensified.

As the scene unfolded, soldiers gathered around protecting their king, swords drawn. Audra and Mystine shielded Eva, watching as another man walked through the entrance of the canyon. Her heart pounded, her mind spun. The man spoke to the guard, words too distant to hear. As her eyes cast upon the archers, the full scope of their situation dawned on her. What once seemed an impenetrable hideout now showed the vastness of its weakness.

One exit. Surrounded by flammable cloth, wood, and grasses.

Death was inevitable. But she never predicted this ending. Her heart raced as the realization sank in.

The guard and the man by the entrance finished their conversation as other soldiers approached. After conversing, two stayed by the entrance, and two headed toward them.

"Your Highness," one said as he came near. "The enemy sent a messenger. They wait on the other side of the narrow. We are surrounded, and they've blocked our access to the gorge and the river. We are trapped. Elijah requests you."

Contrasting her fear, Garrick remained calm, commanding the soldiers around him. "Take my wife, Mystine, and Eva to Lord Byron. Notify the captains to prepare for war. Six of you will accompany me, the rest of you return to your captains."

Soldiers obeyed, moving to positions as they repeated commands. Some gathered around them, circling them as they raised their shields above them. Audra grabbed Eva's hand, turning to her. "Don't be scared," she said. "They will protect you, you won't be harmed."

Confused and innocent, Eva nodded. "I'll be brave," she promised. "Aren't you coming?"

Audra shook her head, pulling her daughter into a final hug, tears welling in her eyes. "No. If I hide, no one will ever believe a queen can rule." Audra turned to see Garrick watching them. He nodded, indicating his solemn agreement. Eva ran to Garrick, embracing her father for the first, and perhaps final, time.

"What will happen?" Eva asked.

"Nothing bad," he answered, but the way he held her showed he wasn't sure he believed it. "You'll be safe. We will be back in time for the ceremony. Alright?"

Guards escorted Mystine and Eva away, their bodies lost in the sea of armored soldiers. Garrick touched Audra's shoulder, his face grim and uncertain.

"Must you come?" he asked.

"Together. You promised," Audra replied.

He nodded, sighing. "Together," he echoed. He gestured toward the archers atop the canyon walls, shaking his head. "As long as you recognize this isn't a negotiation. For him, it's his final lap of victory."

37

Entering the narrow canyon leading toward her doom, Audra's clenched fist dug into her palm. Garrick appeared much calmer as six soldiers trailed behind them.

Halfway through, Garrick paused, turning to whisper in her ear. "Don't be frightened. Fear is the enemy. Whatever happens, know we all did everything we could."

He kissed her once, then offered his arm, and they walked the remainder of the narrow. Once the clearing to the main gorge appeared, so did Elijah and soldiers as far as her eyes saw, crammed between the gorge's canyon walls in every direction. She spotted another face she recognized: Lord Sherritt.

Garrick stopped outside the narrow path's opening, standing ten feet from Elijah, circled in by guards. They barricaded access to the river, and she analyzed that killing them wouldn't even be necessary. They could starve them out instead.

Elijah smirked, crossing his arms in front of his chest. Gloating.

"I see you've delivered my wife to me. You made this even easier for me, didn't you? First, you left markers to show us the way. Then, your smoke led us right where we needed to go. The tops of the canyons are left unguarded, and only one lookout before this? No wonder Lord Sherritt offered to join us. This is pathetic."

Audra's heart dropped at Elijah calling her his wife. What happened if he made her go back with him? What if she had to watch Garrick die all over again? The thought sickened her.

"She doesn't belong to you," Garrick said. He looked to Lord Sherritt, shaking his head. "I hoped you were wiser, Lord Sherritt. The punishment for treason is death."

"The only treasonous ones stand before me," Elijah answered, laughing. "Considering Audra is still betrothed to me, I'm afraid to inform you she *does* belong to me. She'll rot in that tower the remainder of her days." Elijah said, and dread consumed every part of her.

Elijah chuckled. "I must say, what poor planning you have around here. Only had to capture the one guard. It's laughable how poorly planned your rebellion was. And you call yourself the king? Please. My dead mother's grave is more guarded than this camp. Can't say the same for your mother's."

Audra examined the guards around them, her doom impending. One snap of his fingers, he'd light the whole camp aflame. One word, and a swarm of guards could pounce on them. Elijah offered a grim smile, making Audra's heart sink as she remembered everything he had done. He'd killed Margaret, Kathleen, and Kolbe. He'd tried to take away the love of her life. He imprisoned her for over a month.

All this time, she'd had nightmares about returning to that life. The worst possible scenario was, at that moment, transpiring. Audra felt helpless to stop it. Garrick didn't say a word, so Elijah continued. "You should have stayed scattered in your underground rebellion. You were much more difficult to find when you scattered like the rats you were. Much easier to find when you made this large encampment. Thank you for that. I don't believe we've officially met, *brother*," Elijah said, spitting out the word with complete disgust.

Garrick remained silent. Elijah continued as he strolled between some of the guards, "What I didn't discover until a moment ago was that Audra had a secret daughter who was also my niece. This complicates things but also makes everything clear. This was it. This was the answer to my problems."

Elijah's grin at Audra made her feel sick. She clenched her fists, ready to thrash anyone who came near her. "If I want the love of the people after this rebellion is squashed, I thought marrying a beautiful woman loved by all the noblewomen, therefore their husbands, might gain me sympathy. Then Margaret talked. What were the odds that the woman I chose was also the secret whore of my greatest enemy?"

Garrick's grip tightened on his sword, moving to stand between Elijah and Audra. "If you try to touch her, you'll be dead. That is your only warning."

Though Audra knew the odds were stacked against them, she smirked as she saw him being the man she fell in love with all those years ago. He'd always been brave, even when it was madness. It was clear they were outnumbered and surrounded, and the chances of his survival were slim. Garrick would never surrender without a fight.

Elijah snorted, stopping between some of the guards. "Well-played, brother. We've been doing this dance for many years, haven't we? Every time I thought I had you figured out, you were one step ahead. I knew one slip-up from you and I would be back on top. Now, here we are. The duration of this rebellion has come to an end," Elijah said, curling his lips into a malicious grin.

"You're correct," Garrick said, fearlessly unbothered. Audra's heart hammered, knowing what came next. "It's time to find out who won. Unless you are here to yield?"

Elijah snorted again, looking right at Garrick as he laughed. Audra didn't blame Elijah. The odds were unquestionably in his favor. Yet, she saw that Garrick still intended to fight. "Please," Elijah said, "if you'd like to embarrass yourself, then go ahead. Try and kill a few of the royal guards, you might win a fight or two. If that's how you wish to die, by all means, expedite the process."

Audra observed Garrick, who replied smoothly, "You've heard the tales, then. So you know it would be more than a fight or two. That's why you brought so many personal guards." Garrick gestured to them.

Elijah snickered once more, cracking his neck. "Alright, then. Play your cards. It will be amusing," Elijah said, crossing his arms.

Heart thumping, ready to fight, time slowed as she realized that the next few minutes would change their entire lives. She waited for Garrick to lurch forward. Instead, he whistled three familiar notes. Surprised by the unexpected response, Audra recognized the tune as the same one he whistled when Audra met the masked man for the first time on the ballroom floor.

His whistle echoed through the canyon walls, disappearing into the depths. Elijah furrowed his brows in confusion.

Then, the whistle was followed by the response of many whistles from almost every guard and soldier in the vicinity, who, in almost perfect unison, drew their swords and pointed them toward Elijah.

Audra's lips parted, astonished. This is what Garrick had told her. With Julin working on the inside, he had replaced the guards in the castle. He'd even turned Elijah's army against him. Judging by the looks of it, he succeeded in replacing almost all the guards and recruited most of the soldiers. She recalled the wars Elijah spoke of, the former guards captured in a battle she heard Julin tell Elijah about. In truth, they'd told her this solution all along.

This time, Garrick took the chance to grin, triumphant. "Those of you not yielding a sword toward this imposter appear to be outnumbered." He lowered his voice, turning to Elijah. "That's a relief. I wondered where most loyalties truly lied."

Garrick turned about the clearing, scanning the guards that surrounded them. Lord Sherritt attempted to leave, but guards stopped him, shoving Sherritt to his knees, binding his arms behind his back.

Garrick continued, his voice reverberating through the canyon walls. "For those who weren't informed, you've been serving the second-born son of Althenia, who has usurped my place as the rightful heir and tried to have the firstborn murdered. He did it while murdering every other heir and potential heir. He killed innocent mothers in cold blood. While our usual way of recruiting is more explanatory, we invite you to support the true king. Those who refuse will die," Garrick said.

The canyon walls echoed until the sound of his voice disappeared in them. He paced the small clearing, his eyes set upon Lord Sherritt, and his voice lowered to address him. "I told you the punishment for treason is death. I wish you trusted me. Now, you'll never get the chance to."

Garrick made a motion, holding a fist into the air. Seconds later, ten arrows pierced Lord Sherritt. Audra looked up, remembering the archers. They must belong to Garrick, too. She realized the danger never existed; the first fire arrow in the hideout was a warning.

Some of the other, more confused men looked around. Some moved to draw their swords to join the rebellion against Elijah, while others hesitated before succumbing. In the end, all turned on their former false king.

Garrick sneered at Elijah as he walked toward him, a few guards standing between them with their swords pointed away from Garrick now. "I should thank you for coming to me, Elijah. It saves me the trouble of having to come to you. You didn't wonder why nobody stopped you on your way in? Why we didn't have guards on top of the canyons? Why the smoke stacks drew you to us? You assumed ignorance. No. We were expecting you."

Garrick shook his head as if disappointed. "However, it's clear that the only rebellion was yours, trying to deprive me of my birthright. As I am the firstborn son of the first legitimate marriage, *I am* the true king. *You* are the son who murdered King Henri, so it will be you who faces trial for treason. Not me, and not the woman I love. As everyone in Althenia knows, the punishment for treason is death. As King and sovereign judge of this kingdom, I declare you guilty."

Garrick turned to look at Audra. His eyes looked sad, shaking his head as he sighed. "Your timing couldn't have been worse, Elijah. It angers me that you involved my family in your mess. Left me no time to make sure my daughter didn't have to witness the archers. Julin shall be released from imprisonment for aiding my wife's release from the palace. We are grateful for his war expertise, allowing this moment."

"I'm already here, Your Highness." Julin stepped out from behind soldiers, removing a metal helmet as he approached wearing soldier armor. "Everything went according to plan, except for the warning guard. Elijah succeeded in capturing him, so I apologize for the late notice."

Elijah looked around, defeated and confused, searching for an ally. Captured between pointed swords, he was helpless. Elijah attempted to command guards to lower their swords and to seize Garrick. His shouts were to no avail, and not a single guard heeded his commands. Instead, two guards grabbed his arms and shoved him forward toward Garrick, removing Elijah's sword from its sheath.

Garrick approached Elijah, standing a few paces in front of him. "I'm sorry it had to end this way, brother," Garrick said with a sigh. "I always wanted a brother. I just didn't think he would be an evil tyrant who murders women and children for sport."

Elijah glared, his voice coming out as a hiss. "I never killed any-one."

Rolling his eyes, Garrick folded his arms across his chest. "That's what makes you a coward. You paid someone else to kill them for you. A man of conviction will do his own dirty deeds." Turning, Garrick scoffed, rolling his shoulders as he ana-lyzed the guards, still pointing swords at Elijah. Audra scanned them also, the number of weapons nearby making her feel uneasy.

Elijah turned to Audra, snorting as he gestured to her. "You mean a man of conviction beds and impregnates a woman without marrying her? Is that the conviction to which you refer? Because in that case, we have that in common. I guess we will never know which one of us the baby inside of her belongs to in eight months or so. She'll tell you it's premature, I'm sure."

Audra straightened, angered by the lie. They never shared that sort of intimacy. Garrick didn't flinch, turning to Audra for clari-ty. "He lies," she said, shaking her head.

That was the only answer Garrick needed. He paced back to-ward Elijah and cocked his head to the side. "If the queen has any future children whatsoever, they will be mine. Let that be under-stood."

Elijah's laugh resonated with madness, unfazed that the tides had turned against him. He wouldn't go down without hurling more venomous words. "Spoken like a fool in love, blind to the de-ceitful nature of beautiful women." He turned, glaring at her before lifting his chin, baring his teeth. "What was his name, the other one? Kolbe? I'm certain he had a go himself a time or two."

Audra felt a surge of indignation, but Garrick spoke first. "Guards, lower your weapons," he ordered, gesturing to Audra to wait as he turned back to Elijah. "Enough. The time has come to end your reign."

Elijah attempted to step forward, but guards held him back. Demanding release, he found himself ignored until Garrick commanded them to let go. Elijah swatted at one guard as they stepped back. "What? No mercy for your brother? No exile, no negotiating?" For the first time, Elijah's voice sounded like a plea, accepting he was no longer in control. His reign of terror was over, and no guards would aid him.

"You don't even deserve the death I'm going to allow. It's too kind for you," Garrick retorted, his voice resolute.

Elijah lifted his chin. "And what death is that?" he asked, swallowing. For the first time, Audra sensed an unfamiliar emotion in Elijah: fear.

Garrick nodded toward Audra, standing nearby, motioning for her to come. She hesitated as she neared the man who had destroyed the last eight years of her life. "Your death will be whatever the queen chooses. Whatever she decides will be far kinder than what I've longed to do since the day you took everything from me." Garrick's fist clenched at his side, turning to Audra with approval.

Audra turned to Garrick, her brows knitting together. "Why me?" she asked. Both had ample reason to despise this man, and Garrick had as much right to decide his fate. While Elijah had murdered her friends, he hadn't directly tried to kill her. Garrick, on the other hand, had been his target for years.

Garrick offered a small smile, taking her hand. "Because we're equals, and I promised you an equal say in these matters. Let me prove it. Choose his death. The army is at your disposal."

Audra contemplated, watching Elijah's eyes flit between them. He was responsible for the deaths of Margaret, Kolbe, and Kathleen. Memories of them made her blood boil. He isolated her for forty-seven days, making her wish death had come. Worst of all, he'd stolen the love of her life for years. That time was lost forever. As rage brewed inside her, she imagined the perfect punishment for the man who killed all those innocent women.

"I'll do it," Audra decided, meeting Garrick's eyes for approval. His mouth twitched upward in response.

"That's a bold decision," Garrick acknowledged, laying a hand on her shoulder. "One that can't be undone. If you kill someone, their blood is always on your hands. Can you live with that?"

Audra didn't need time to decide. She was no stranger to the ghosts of dead men in her dreams. They were nothing compared to the monster that haunted her in her wake. "If I don't, he'll always possess me."

Garrick squeezed her shoulder, nodding in understanding. "Then... guards, hold him back," Garrick commanded. Moments later, guards restrained Elijah, his struggles futile. In desperation, Elijah begged for his life, but Audra wasn't swayed, and his pleas fell on deaf ears. With her dagger, she thrust it into his throat. The former king choked, faltered, and fell to the ground at her feet.

Unmistakably perished by the hand of a woman, and by his own accord, not one person remained in the world who'd grieve him.

38

The moonlight reflected off the Agrove River, a half-moon hanging in a cloudless sky. Pink Althenian whisper trees surrounded Garrick and Audra, his finger tracing the back of her hand. The river's sweet scent wafted under her nose, a slight warm breeze tickling her skin. Aside from chirping crickets, the night was silent. Sitting on furs they'd brought from Garrick's tent, Audra glanced behind them, toward the darkened entrance of the hideout canyon. The river wound through the broadest area outside the hideout, its cliffs obscured by trees and grass.

Lord Byron insisted on a wedding ceremony that evening. In attendance was Eva, her mother, Lord Byron, Julin, and the priest. Meanwhile, soldiers and guards celebrated their victory. After the brief ceremony, they joined the celebrations. Some soldiers returned to their families while others stayed behind to prolong their merriment. One man's death saved the lives of thousands.

As the breeze brushed Audra's skin, she felt pride in the man beside her who made it possible. Shadows danced on his face, and her gaze fastened on him as he brushed her skin. She felt comforted knowing the man she'd pined for had returned for good. As her husband. As the King of Althenia.

Audra wore a simple light blue dress brought by her mother from Hillsfield. A floral crown adorned her hair. Garrick played with her curls, kissing her shoulder as he admired her. She smiled, heart pounding with each touch, the sensations more effective each time. He was here. He was alive. He was hers forever.

After celebrating, they slipped past guards to find privacy. Eva slept soundly in Mystine's tent. Tomorrow, they would go to Hillsfield with Lord Byron and Mystine to gather Eva's things and move her into the palace. Eva eagerly awaited the adventure.

Audra smiled, recalling a conversation with her mother from earlier that evening. "My mother told me something tonight. She is pregnant, even at forty. She kept it secret from Lord Byron until last night to ensure it wasn't another miscarriage. They'd tried for years and had given up. She's known for four months." The news had brought Audra joy. After having Audra, her mother hadn't wanted more children, but her marriage to Lord Byron rekindled her consideration, despite previous failures.

Garrick raised his eyebrows, surprised. "Hmm. I suppose that means there will be an heir for Hillsfield, after all." He looked contemplatively toward the river, noting its dark, rapid fury.

He sighed. "Lord Byron blames me for Kathleen and Kolbe's deaths. It was a tragedy, no doubt. This news must be a relief for them, securing another heir. I'm relieved I won't have to rely on him for money now that the palace funds will be available to me. There's much to learn about the kingdom's affairs. This may be the end of the war, but another war always looms on the horizon. Doth won't be happy about Kolbe's and Elijah's death." He narrowed his eyes as if pondering potential outcomes with Doth.

Audra hadn't considered the future much. What seemed a simple murder became a large political battle. Two brothers at odds over a throne, Kolbe a pawn who'd lost. Her heart ached at the memory of his sacrifice for her. His life, tragic as it was, left her feeling culpable.

Garrick had mastered the game of Althenian politics. He shouldered the blame, regardless of who bore responsibility. She knew she'd be there to defend him, no matter what happened next.

"Do you want to be king?" Audra asked, verbalizing a recurring thought aloud. What was it like learning you were born with such a destiny? She wanted to learn everything she'd missed over the last eight years.

Garrick sighed, gazing across the river, deep in thought. He draped his arm around her, drawing her close. "Not at first. I refused when Julin first told me. I wanted to come back to you. That's why he lied about your death. He wanted to persuade me there was nothing to return to." Garrick frowned, shaking his head to dispel the memory. Despite disapproving of Julin's deceit, she understood his reasoning.

"He said I'd always be vulnerable to Elijah's wrath if I didn't fight. I could accept my destiny and live as a king, or live my days in hiding. Perhaps duty should have driven me, but the truth is that I was more motivated to avenge you." He offered a small smile, slumping his shoulders while closing his eyes.

"Then," he continued, "learning you were alive changed everything. I wanted to give you the life you deserved, not one of running and hiding. While becoming King bears a great responsibility, I'm calm when I remember you'll be beside me. I swear never to leave your side unless you demand it. You're not my prisoner. You're my desire."

Her heart fluttered at his words, unable to restrain the smile on her lips. Cupping her chin, he kissed her once on the lips. "We've overcome much together, and always will," she said, affirming her agreement.

Tucking a strand of hair behind her ear, he leaned in to kiss her forehead. Another breeze passed, and she shivered. He responded by wrapping them in the duvet, holding her close for warmth. "I remember everything with you," he said. "Our night in the barn before you went to school, your father's death, the cold winters and dry summers. I remember all the ways you and your mother helped us. I learned never to doubt your abilities after the time I was deathly ill that winter. You trudged through the snow on foot, venturing hours to town, fetching the medicine to cure me. Alone. For that, I believed I'd never deserve you."

"You were dying," Audra recalled, reminiscing on that night. "You would have done the same for me."

"You saved me," he said, tapping her nose once with his finger, then he combed his fingers through her hair. "You could have frozen to death fetching medicine that night."

"I didn't freeze," she replied softly. "I returned with the cure."

He squeezed her shoulders, chuckling. "You decided you weren't going to wait for the gods to save me. I always admired your ability to defy the offerings life gave you." He paused, caressing her cheek. "What about you, Your Highness? Do you wish to be Queen?"

Audra smirked. If she didn't, it would be too late to back out now. "I believe marriage already made that decision for me, hmm?"

"You still have a choice," Garrick said, his tone turning more serious. He searched her eyes. "You'll always have a choice. While I desire you above all else, this was never your burden to bear. Did marrying me stem from obligation, or is this your decision above all others?"

Reflecting on their recent exchanges, Audra resolved to end his doubts. She responded by hiking up her skirts, straddling his lap, and kissing him. His amusement was clear as he steadied his hands on her waist.

"I *chose* to marry you," she said. "I could've run. Even while I was angry, I still didn't want to break your heart. I realize you always believed you didn't deserve good things, but you did. I didn't love you for power. You were the kindest boy and an even greater man. That was why I loved you then. I love you now. I always will."

He wrapped his arms around her, pulling her closer with a sigh of relief. "You always know what to say to get me out of my head. I've also chosen you, Audra. Nothing you do could change that. While painful heartache remains possible, nothing would make me stop loving you. You're the only woman I'll lie with each night. When I'm lost and uncertain who I can trust, you're the one I'll know I can turn to."

A breeze ruffled his hair, his teal eyes watching her as if meeting her again for the first time. She encircled his neck with her arms.

"It doesn't matter if I'm a queen or a peasant, as long as I'm yours. We'll forge an empire to withstand any foe, Dothians or otherwise. I've already chosen. I've chosen to love you and stand by your side," she said.

Audra's promise moved Garrick, who breathed hot air onto her neck, causing her to gasp. His fingers entwined with her hair. "Under our reign, Althenia shall become the greatest kingdom history has ever known." He kissed her neck before pulling back, brushing back an unruly blonde lock.

"Where shall we begin?" Audra asked, grinning.

"Hmm," Garrick mused, a sly smile spreading as he kissed her for the hundredth time that night. After, his lips lingered near hers, his hand brushing her leg as it made its way under her skirt and up her thigh, eliciting another gasp. "Let's start where all good stories begin: 'Once upon a time...'" As his lips met hers, commencing the rest of the story, the background faded away. When he laid her back, each new kiss begged for two more. For the rest of the evening, two childhood friends made love under the moonlight: unmasked.

The End
... of a New Beginning.

Special Thanks

F irst, a big thank you to my children who are too young to read this book. I expect one day they'll come to me, embarrassed by the smut. Until then, thank you for sharing some of your time with my work so that I could create something amazing.

Next, my cat Simba, for sitting on the keyboard and forcing me to rewrite entire chapters. The rewrites were definitely better than the original.

Melissa, for encouraging me that the entire thing wasn't total garbage, and for giving me confidence to keep the spicy scenes in. You're the greatest always and I'm grateful for all your notes and insights.

My Girlfriend. Or, Amy. Thanks for the funny lines ("Are you suggesting I climb up naked?") and teaching me that "chesticles" is somehow a real word. I spared the other readers, but we know where that word belonged.

Rose, for creating a wonderful and most stunning cover. I couldn't have imagined anything better myself.

One editor in particular, Maryssa. Your edits rocked off my socks. Thank you for the depth you provided and enriched my story with.▢

Cheshiregrins. Twenty years ago you found a thirteen-year-old girl on a site called Harperteenfanlit. I was writing a rendition of a Cinderella story where Cinderella was blind. You gave me my first literary critiques and taught me the difference between writing and craft. I don't know your real name, but you taught me to be a better writer. Because of you, I never stopped learning. If you ever find my books, I hope you're proud of what I became. One day, please come find me and let me give you the proper thank you. You made me what I am.

Last, my husband, Patrick, for enduring my shenanigans while I spent hours writing this. Je t'aime plus.

ABOUT THE AUTHOR

H annah Rose Lewis is an English and Women's Studies graduate from Brigham Young University. She lives with her husband, three children, and five spoiled cats in Utah. In her free time, she likes to perform with her comedy groups, nerd out on games, and build blanket forts with her infinite collection of minky blankets. She enjoys conspiring new ways to make her readers cry.